A.J. SCUDIERE

NIGHTSHADE

FORENSIC FBI FILES ✦ BOOK 1

D1453068

UNDER
DARK SKIES

DEDICATION

This one is for an amazing group of women.

These remarkable ladies are my beta-readers and the best friends a girl could ask for.

Eli—who has been there in so many different capacities throughout my life. She is my sister and partner in these endeavors, there for every step, the ones that drive us to drink and the ones that lead us to celebrate.

Andrea—who is always on top of everything. She makes sure that we all "Do," that we walk the walk.

Victoria—who makes sure that we do it with style and warmth. She always has an open home, open kitchen and open heart.

Andrea and Victoria were my friends in college and both welcomed me right back into their lives when I showed up in their town years later. Thank you.

Julie—whom I was lucky enough to sit down next to last year. As we introduced ourselves, I had one of those moments of insight that this person was going to be a great friend. Every week she proves that insight to be right.

I am so amazingly grateful for each of you, every day.

Thank you so much to everyone who helped with this book . . .

From my beta-readers, who are always willing to point out what's good in a draft and what needs work. I particularly love when you contradict each other!

To my mom, who happily emailed me small-town Texas details.

To Dr. Jennifer Scudiere, who helped with fun pathology things and what Donovan might be able to smell. You are a good cousin!

To my Daddy and to Guy, both of whom are always there, always have my back. Their unending support is just that—unending. Thank you both so much.

Finally, to Wade, for being a great friend and for letting me borrow your likeness for this book. I didn't make you any more badass than you already are. It's physics, bitch!

PRAISE FOR A.J. SCUDIERE

"There are really just 2 types of readers—those who are fans of AJ Scudiere, and those who will be."
-Bill Salina, Reviewer, Amazon

For *The Shadow Constant*:
"The Shadow Constant by A.J. Scudiere was one of those novels I got wrapped up in quickly and had a hard time putting down."
-Thomas Duff, Reviewer, Amazon

For *Phoenix*:
"It's not a book you read and forget; this is a book you read and think about, again and again . . . everything that has happened in this book could be true. That's why it sticks in your mind and keeps coming back for rethought."
-Jo Ann Hakola, The Book Faerie

For *God's Eye*:
"I highly recommend it to anyone who enjoys reading - it's well-written and brilliantly characterized. I've read all of A.J.'s books and they just keep getting better."
-Katy Sozaeva, Reviewer, Amazon

For *Vengeance*:
"Vengeance is an attention-grabbing story that lovers of action-driven novels will fall hard for. I hightly recommend it."
-Melissa Levine, Professional Reviewer

For *Resonance*:

"Resonance is an action-packed thriller, highly recommended. 5 stars."

"For we are the granddaughters of the witches you could not burn."

--author unknown

"We stopped checking for monsters under the bed when we realized they are inside us."

--author unknown

Locard's Exchange Principle (1910)

Dr. Edmond Locard, a medical doctor and early forensic scientist, is credited with the idea that "every contact leaves a trace."

Though he had no solid evidence of it at the time, Locard believed every time two objects came in contact each left evidence of the touch on the other. He also believed that, one day, we would be able to scientifically prove this.

Forensics:

The study of evidence to discover how past events occurred.

Many divisions of forensics exist, from standard crime scene investigation to forensic archeology and even to forensic accounting.

All inquiry into scientific fact to re-create a crime scene is, thus, forensic investigation.

Witches:

Ergot

It is now believed that the Salem Witch Trials were not so much an issue of witchcraft as the result of town-wide ergot poisoning. The weather conditions in 1692 were perfect for the growth of this rye mold. The effects of ergot poisoning are surprisingly specific: hallucinations of people taking flight and the feeling of being pinched or pecked at.

Zombies:

Rabies

Rabies infection is one plausible—though not proven—probability for the origin of the Zombie myth. Rabies infection in humans dulls brain function, reduces sensitivity to pain and creates the overwhelming urge to bite others. Biting is necessary for disease transferal through the saliva.

Tetrodotoxin

Unlike the rabies theory, tetrodotoxin use is well recorded. This poison puts the victim in a death-like state, creating paralysis to the point of complete lack of response. It also reduces the heartbeat to a rate so low it cannot usually be detected by non-mechanical methods. Victims are often buried, exhumed, and then told they are the reanimated dead.

Vampires:

Porphyria

This is actually a blanket term for several diseases that alter heme—the oxygen carrying molecule in human blood. Porphyria eats away at the skin and gums, making the affected appear both corpse-like and fanged. The disease also gives the victim a strong aversion to foods high in sulfur content, such as garlic.

Werewolves:
?

INTRODUCTION

Eleri Eames stepped off the grounds of Lakewood Hospital and into her own recognizance for the first time in three months.

Quite certain she wasn't ready for release, she stood on the curb with her plastic bag in hand, her clothing and wallet clear to all who drove by while she waited for her friend Wade to show up. Unbeknownst to her, Agent Westerfield—her new boss at the FBI—called the hospital yesterday and demanded her early release. So today she stood on the curb, no longer being treated.

Intent on her healing, Eleri avoided most contact with the outside world for the past three months, but she'd spent the entire previous afternoon calling old partners and friends still in the Bureau. Only one had even heard of Agent Westerfield. All her friend offered was a vague recollection from more than ten years ago.

In a startling move, Westerfield called her yesterday in her room to inform her that he was her new boss. No sooner had she sputtered at the announcement, than she was catching her breath again to find out that she was on a case—starting immediately. The man gave very little information about the assignment.

At first Eleri tried to put her foot down, being very clear that she belonged in the hospital to finish her healing. When that didn't work, she argued that she couldn't continue doing the work she'd been doing before. It had landed her a hospital stint that lasted three months and should have been four. While Westerfield had agreed the work would be different, he stayed fuzzy about everything else.

So she stood on the curb, waiting for Wade. She held a clear baggie of her worldly goods and no more information than she'd had yesterday.

Apparently it didn't matter if a person's rehab was done, when the FBI called, the hospital signed the release papers and nearly shoved her out the door. She would head home, and though she didn't need it, she would immediately shower in her own bathroom, with her own shampoo and slide into her jeans. She would pull her suits out of the closet and check her wardrobe to see what needed dry-cleaning. She didn't know what the case was, but Westerfield assured her she'd be on it very soon. She had to be ready to travel.

Eleri wasn't quite sure why she'd agreed to become part of his unit. She honestly wasn't sure that she had agreed to it, but somewhere along the line it became official. She would be getting a new partner, though Westerfield had been vague about that, too.

For the next two days she contemplated the one piece of information she was given—the name of the unit that she wasn't allowed to ask around about. So she asked everyone. She asked everything she could. But she never said the name.

NightShade.

1

Donovan Heath could tell from the start that his first assignment was not going to go as planned. Senior Agent in Charge Westerfield was not what he expected. Donovan had talked to the man on the phone a handful of times and they'd exchanged more email than could be counted. The medium, stocky-but-strong build was as expected, though Donovan really would have thought the man would have that comic-book city commissioner look with the gray being smart enough to stick to the temples. Westerfield's was everywhere. Still the pictures Donovan looked up online didn't show the unbelievably blue eyes that looked at Donovan as though he were a piece of meat that had not yet passed inspection. The photos also failed to show just how shockingly white and overly perfect Westerfield's teeth were. Donovan didn't trust men with perfect teeth. There was also that quarter the lead agent walked back and forth across his knuckles, as though the meeting was not interesting enough and he had to fidget.

Donovan might have overlooked the see-through-you eyes and the too-white teeth, but he couldn't get past the scent that Westerfield wasn't right. Something about his smell . . .

His new partner sat beside him—also a shock, if Donovan was admitting things—sagely nodding at the list of dos and don'ts that Westerfield was reviewing with them. It was a formality, this first meeting, a chance for either of them to back out and he was considering doing just that.

Eleri Eames, his new senior partner, seemed to have no such desires. She didn't seem to sense anything was off about Agent Westerfield. Donovan managed to avoid outwardly flinching. As a child, he learned quickly that his sense of smell was stronger than everyone else's. He learned not to show when things smelled "off," not unless the stench was overpowering and everyone else around him was reacting.

So Donovan Heath, newly minted FBI Agent, sat quietly, nodding each time Agent Eames did and contemplating the wisdom of his decisions.

He was ambivalent about so many things. Sitting here, wearing non-sneaker shoes and a suit when he felt he should shed it all and go running free, was a decision he wasn't sure was in his own best interest. He would not have anywhere near the opportunities to run that he was used to and he wasn't sure how that would affect him—if at all. Aside from a stint in junior high when he'd been going through puberty, which was its own personal hell, he'd never tried to not run.

He wasn't sure about his partner. Her bio included only a headshot, so he knew she had pale green eyes, rounded cheeks, full lips, and a smattering of freckles that sweetened an already friendly face. But it didn't show that she barely passed five-foot-four and he could see she was wearing heels. She probably stood five-two if she stretched, making her an odd accompaniment to his six-foot-three.

Her emails had been all no-nonsense. Even the personal details—where she grew up, what led her to the FBI—didn't give him a clue at all to the fact that she spoke every word with a crisp accent. It was almost Southern. When he listened closely, he heard faint traces of something he couldn't place. What was easy to see and place now that he met her in person was money. Old money.

Eleri Eames probably did not need this job. Maybe she had been vacationing for the past three months. She sure hadn't been working for the FBI during that time. Donovan had been in training, working his ass off. Living in the new clime of Virginia, in and around all the FBI recruits, the vast majority of whom were years younger than him.

Yes, he was of two minds about his ability to run. He'd have new places to go and more opportunities to get caught. He was of two minds about this job. The old one had gotten monotonous and he needed something new, but Donovan was no longer so sure this was it. And he was of two minds about his new partner. She was his senior partner, but looked like she was fresh out of high school. She was younger, higher ranked, and oozed the scent of real wealth.

Donovan, always a loner, was wondering what the hell he'd gotten himself into.

ELERI HUNG BACK until SAC Westerfield noticed. Agent Heath clearly wasn't interested in heading out for a beer and some get-to-know-you conversation even though they were in his hometown. She'd had that before; her last partner had met her, grinned, stuck out his hand and given her his best good-ole-boy impression while suggesting a beer. This time she was the senior agent, and admittedly at a loss.

"Eames?" Westerfield finally acknowledged her over his shoulder.

"Sir, if you have a moment, please." Her shorter legs left her perpetually feeling like a small child struggling to catch up. From the back she could see that his gait was as perfect as his smile and she wondered if he'd been crafted as a fully formed adult from a kit of some kind.

He nodded as he walked, letting her introduce the topic. It showed he trusted her here in the hallway, where people could listen, where other agents could hear, not to discuss the case they'd been assigned as their first. Luckily, she'd gotten all her questions about that answered back in the room. Well, at least the ones she could think to ask. No, this was a different topic. "How much has Heath been told about my history?"

There was a clear shift as he realized what she was referring to. "Only what was in the docket. Anything else?"

"No, sir. Thank you." She always said thank you. Even when she didn't mean it. It was bred into her bones like so many other things she'd inherited. She was beginning to wonder what her genetics would say if someone could really read them.

Westerfield was already down the hall, leaving her in the dust the moment she paused. Agent Heath was far ahead; she caught sight of just his pants leg as he turned the corner. He was wearing Doc Martens—not unheard of, but not the usual dress shoes associated with a suit and tie. He was clearly uncomfortable in the clothing as well as the building.

Without her trying, her brain turned to what she did so well: she analyzed. He was mid-thirties, she knew that from the paperwork she'd been given. She knew he'd been a medical examiner until about six months ago when he left that position and began agent training. He was pretty ripe to hit the Academy, but he wasn't the only one. Each class had a small handful of older, more experienced trainees. But even then, ninety-eight percent of them were ambitious go-getters. Heath was not.

She automatically began pulling on threads. His emails had little to no tone in them; he likely wasn't one to place much stock in opinion or gut instinct. He had an MD in pathology. Another score in the science column. Eleri would bet her trust fund that the FBI had approached him, not the other way around. She would bet that he was growing bored doing autopsies—even though he was reportedly very good at finding even the most odd and obscure causes of death—and that he'd considered the FBI's offer as a new opportunity. He appeared undecided about his choices, even though he already invested more than six months in testing and training.

And she was standing in the hallway when she should be chasing after him. She should be extending a drink invitation as the senior agent. She should be making certain that their partnership worked well, but he was already a good distance ahead of her. So Eleri did what she always did when her legs weren't fast enough, she pulled out her phone and called.

He was frowning when he answered. "Doctor Heath."

She laughed. "I believe it's 'Agent Heath' now." No, he had not reached out to the FBI. "Look, I was curious if you were available later tonight or for lunch tomorrow, to go over the facts of the case. It sounds like we're going to ship out in the next few days to start the legwork."

There was a pause. He was quiet, this one. No good-ole-boy aw-shucks here. She was going to have to be the talker in this partnership. "Lunch tomorrow. I admit I'm not familiar with the area. Do you know a place nearby?"

When he declined, she looked up a burger joint she knew and picked a time when it would be emptier. They would want space to spread out files without people seeing and without dripping ketchup on them. Clearly he would want a place where he didn't have to wear his suit.

She wondered how many he even had.

"I'll see you tomorrow." The words sounded almost forced out of his mouth, as though pleasantries had not been part of his upbringing, and then the line went dead.

Eleri mentally added that she would also have to be the social one, but she was anxious to see what he brought to the unit.

She'd worked with agents with law degrees and psychology degrees but never a medical degree.

So she hitched her bag over her shoulder and headed home after the short meeting. She had paper, photos, and e-file backups of all of it. She'd come of age just prior to the e-revolution and still believed in laying things on a table top and looking at all of it. Her psychology classes had taught her that hand writing something stored it in the memory much better than typing it did. And her colleagues always laughed at her the first time she took notes by hand. But only the first time.

She and Heath had two days to get up to speed enough to start work. They had notes and phone numbers from agents and police departments who'd worked parts of the case or related crimes. It made for heavy reading.

Being behind the wheel of her own car was still an unusual feeling. She'd driven herself everywhere since she turned sixteen. But for the last three months she hadn't driven at all.

So the ability to pull over and get her favorite pizza had her stopping in and waiting while a small pie baked. She hadn't had good, greasy pizza in forever, and her mouth watered as she tried to sit patiently on the hard take-out bench and do nothing.

There was no one to call while she waited; she didn't really have friends. Like many agents, her work consumed her, much to her parents' dismay. They kept her busy with events, so she went out plenty, but she didn't meet anyone like-minded at these things. So she didn't rack up lovers or friends with ease. Plus, she was unusual looking, a byproduct of a heritage she wasn't supposed to mention.

She sniffed at the pizza as the oven was opened time and again and mentally reviewed the case.

Probable cult.

Possible guns. Likely militia of some kind. But it was currently unclear if they were protecting their legal or religious rights. Well, "rights"—Eleri mentally added the quotes—freedom of speech and all that, but you couldn't just declare yourself a sovereign nation in the middle of Texas, though many had tried.

There was no real case, just a watch, until one week ago when a woman named Ruth came forward from Joseph Hayden Baxter's City of God and said that she recognized one of the children there from an old missing child photo. An undercover agent, a telephoto lens, and a big risk had produced a picture that Eleri agreed was likely the missing Ashlyn Fisk, although Ruth said she knew the girl as Charity.

That was when the FBI had been called in.

Though they had a slim amount of medical information, the woman who had gotten out of City of God would give no last name. She refused to reveal any other identifying information. Then, of course, Ruth disappeared, leaving no last name, no social security number, no fingerprints.

There would have been nothing to do for it—you couldn't follow evidence that didn't exist to a city that no one knew where it was. There was the additional problem that "city" was a generous term by any standards. But Ruth was not the only one.

Before her, a woman was found on the side of the road, beaten within an inch of her life. She'd died having uttered only one phrase repeatedly: "City of God."

There had been rumors after that. The FBI had found an old online presence for City of God. Though it was long since taken down, and only a reference to an idea, several names were linked —most notably, Isaac Hamry and Joseph Hayden Baxter. Baxter was the worst; he got all three names, like any good suspect did. His writings were radical. He believed in the sparest interpretation of all laws. He believed that he was exempt from a handful of said laws, each for a different—but obviously logical—reason. He quoted the Constitution and the Founding Fathers, usually improperly.

Eleri usually disliked her subjects just because. If they hadn't done something wrong, they wouldn't be in her crosshairs in the first place. Maybe they only made the mistake of joining up or befriending the wrong person; she'd seen that plenty before. But still, good people who stayed out of trouble never got called by that middle name, except maybe by their mothers. But she disliked Joe Baxter for his misuse of her precious Constitution. His clear disregard for the actual facts he was citing got her hackles up. Using twisted logic ranked in Eleri's book up there with kicking puppies.

Everyone was accountable under the law.

You didn't like it, then be thankful you had a government that allowed you to say so, to petition, to write bills, and run for congress, and change your laws.

She knew people got away with all kinds of crap. And she hated it.

Just in case there wasn't enough pressure on her, the case itself was a minefield. The FBI responded, fast and with force, to all missing children claims, but this was more tangled. The missing Ashlyn Fisk was tied to several other missing children, all linked by an unknown set of fingerprints associated with their abductions. All the cases were over ten years old. One of the cases was that of Jennifer Leigh Cohn—daughter of FBI Special Agent John Cohn, missing eleven years, body never recovered, all leads gone cold. Also Cohn was an old partner of Westerfield's, which was how he'd caught the case in the first place.

No pressure there, Eleri thought to herself on a sigh. Find Ashlyn, find Jennifer? It was a longshot and Agent Cohn would not be happy if it didn't pan out. She was grateful she didn't know Agent Cohn personally, that the case wasn't more disturbing than it already was.

Now, Joseph Hayden Baxter was in her sights.

And Donovan Heath was her new partner to help take him down, find missing children, account for the dead girl, and handle the various other crap they would run into along the way. Heath was so newly minted that he was still shiny, even if his demeanor didn't match. Unfortunately, Eleri doubted her ability to be the partner to bring him into the fold. She didn't think she had enough in her these days to prop herself up, let alone someone else.

So she drove home, ate her pizza, and stared at the papers spread across her desk. Looking at the photos lined up on the small monitor and the documents in overlapping shots on her big monitor, she realized that she was not ready for this.

When she'd first joined, there had been a note in her file: "No Children." It wasn't hard and fast, clearly it would come up. Eleri had been pissed off when she learned it was there. But then she understood. Some agents just had things they shouldn't do. Hers was any case with children. But as she looked at the City of God file she realized she was really close. Some of the missing girls were young—not kids, really, but young.

While she stared she realized something else, she should never have been released this early.

2

The run had done Donovan good. Bare feet, long strides, no one to answer to. The loamy smells of the forest told a story. His sensitive nose said there were deer by the dozens back among the trees. Coyote by the hundreds. And a lone bear. Out of territory recently, but now gone.

The sunlight filtered down, warming him, and Donovan savored the smells of his home turf. It would be a while before he could run like this again. His property backed up onto the woods so he could head out, undisturbed, at any time. Three thousand acres of national park land. He would miss it.

Today he started with the sunrise and stayed as late as he could, judging the time by the angle of the late morning sun. The distance he covered had been paltry, but he had a meeting. If he was lucky, he'd get in an overnight before he had to fly out, but that was a mere two days away. The timing would be tight.

Showering was one of those activities that almost bothered him. The results were worth it, but he wasn't keen on getting wet. Still, he used scent-free soaps to wash away what he picked up on his run. The smell of sweat didn't bother him, but it bothered others so he scrubbed it away. He scrubbed a little harder, always wary that someone with as good a sense of smell as him would detect the forest on him.

Columbia, South Carolina, should have been his stomping grounds. He worked in Providence Hospital before Westerfield had pulled him out and offered him this. But Donovan didn't stomp. It seemed Agent Eames, with her rich traveler vibe, could easily find more about where to go and what to do around his hometown than he knew.

Familiar as the drive was, he let his motor memory do it for him while he worried what he'd gotten himself into. He wondered if one could just back out of the FBI at the last minute. After all, they had invested nine months testing then training him just for this position. How angry would they be if he dropped out two days into the assignment?

Sad when the only thing keeping him on the job was that he had no idea what he would do if he didn't do this. So in the end it was his lack of other ideas that kept him from copping out. Besides, he liked a good burger, and investigative work at least *sounded* interesting.

Large sun umbrellas dotted the front of the burger joint, and he found a parking spot nearby. He was two minutes early when he walked through the door, but he wasn't surprised to find Eames had already staked a table but hadn't ordered. He could almost feel the grease in the air from the burgers and the fries and suddenly he was ravenous.

Ignoring his stomach for a moment, he checked her out as she waved him over, clearly having been watching for him. She was in some odd kind of shiny pants that looked like a hybrid between work slacks and yoga pants. She had on a skinny T-shirt with something going on in the sleeves. Not in jeans like him but definitely dressed down. Today Donovan had conceded only to a shirt with buttons; he'd gone to work in sweatpants before. Then again, he worked in a morgue, in a basement with dead people who couldn't give a shit what he looked like. His lab assistants might have, but he was standoffish enough to make sure they didn't say so. He interacted as little as possible with police officers and physicians who worked on the living, always making sure he gave enough quality information that his lack of formal work attire would be ignored.

Eleri smiled as she held up a credit card and a paper menu with her order marked on it. "If you don't mind ordering for me, I'll expense the whole thing."

And a good day to you, too, he thought.

Maybe she would be okay. Or maybe she was just a good investigator and had already realized that platitudes and common niceties rolled off him unnoticed. "If it's expensed, what does it matter?"

Her head cocked a little to the side. "Fill out one expense form and you'll see it's a generous offer."

Color him convinced. Her order and notations were made in precise handwriting that fit neatly with the coddled upbringing and private school education obvious in her posture and speech. As he approached the counter, Donovan saw that the credit card was from a bank in Virginia that whispered of *History*. It was a color his own credit rating didn't even have hopes of aspiring to and likely something the little burger joint hadn't seen before.

The girl behind the counter didn't even look at him as he spoke. She was intent on punching in his order on the screen in front of her, a screen Donovan thought she should have already memorized as the way she slouched behind the counter reeked of long days doing exactly this. She didn't check the card—perhaps because the total was nothing that required a signature—and handed it back.

Thinking he could have easily robbed the place and no one would have an adequate description of him, he sighed and checked the card. He sure as hell hoped he couldn't be mistaken for Eleri Grace Eames.

Returning to the table, he balanced large slippery cups of

soda, straws, napkins and umpteen packets of god-knew-what sauces. Eleri stood to take the drinks and clearly had a plan for where they were to go on the already subdivided table.

Eleri Grace Eames was the living, breathing opposite of the girl behind the counter. Eleri buzzed with energy reined; the burger girl had exerted just less than enough to get the job done. Eleri was laser focused, alert, and clearly hyper-aware of everything around her—which Donovan found odd. Given the pampered existence she must have lived, how had she not ended up the lazy one? Why was she not married and getting facials and wondering what dress to wear to another charity event tonight?

"What?" Her voice startled him.

Crap. Now he was the one not paying attention.

"Just thinking that the order will likely be a surprise." He ad-libbed, even though it was the truth. At Eames's raised eyebrows he elaborated. "Girl at the counter was paying zero attention. Couldn't pick me out of a line-up of midgets."

The smile was a shock. The laugh heartier than he expected. "It's a good thing I'll eat just about anything, then. So you've now gotten away with credit-card fraud. Great way to start your career with the FBI."

"Career" was stretching it, but he didn't correct her. Instead, they dove into the file, Donovan pulling out his matching copies of documents, but with his own added notes. "Baxter was raised in a small town in a small church that kept its followers close—Zion's Gate. Sounds like he was raised cult-style."

He didn't need to look at the notes.

Eames frowned. "That's not in the record."

"I found his parents and called them." He didn't like small talk, but he could do it. Found it meant something if he had a purpose for it.

She nodded to him as if awarding a silent point. "I figured our job was to start on that tomorrow."

"I called yesterday afternoon, since there wasn't much in the file about his upbringing. Anyway, both parents have colorful arrest records. Lots of protests, mounting the Ten Commandments in front of the courthouse in a major city that considered it vandalism. That kind of thing."

"So he started from a strict religious upbringing. That's another point in favor of his leading some fanatical cult." She shuffled the papers looking for something, maybe.

Donovan kept going. "So I called the church, said I was moving my family there." That had been fun actually. Playing the strict husband for no one but the lady on the phone. "I was rude to my 'wife' in the background. I was rude to the lady on the phone. I asked if the church kept their women in line." As he spoke, Eames's auburn brows climbed higher and higher. "I asked if I would be turned in for abusing my children, but not in those words. I suggested that all medicine is a sin and asked if the church had property that a working man and his family could reside on if they joined."

He watched as she waited in anticipation of his answer. He counted the moments until she caved and asked, "And?"

"Never a twitch. In the end the only thing that surprised me is that she answered the phone and talked to a stranger. I'm new at this, but I'm pretty sure I got seriously shut down. They do not believe in child abuse, though they do believe the man is head-of-household by nature of his genitalia."

Eleri stifled a giggle as their burgers arrived. Well, the counter girl came out, scanned the room and called out the order, because she had no idea who Eleri Grace Eames was nor that a six-foot man had stood at the counter. She did not recognize his long angled face, short dark hair, dark skin, curt, non-localized accent. All in stark contrast to the owner of the card.

He stuck to Eames's established segregation of the table, keeping his tray on his left. A quick look and an inhale and he was shocked the burger order was actually correct. The girl was so slow she hadn't even yet made it back behind the counter.

Eames proved some of his earlier assumptions as she refused to speak with food in her mouth. Her dainty hand coming forward, covering her full lips, should she be forced to say something before she finished chewing. But she shattered others. She dug into the burger with the gusto of someone long denied good food. And while she was petite, she wasn't all that tiny. She was athletic rather than starving, and she wasn't hurting for food. She swallowed and smiled. "That's a good burger. My senior agent called a lunch here the one other time I've been in this town."

He watched as she dug back in, then made short work of his own food. For someone who looked like she was going to town on that sandwich, she sure didn't make any real progress on it. Stopping again, she set the burger down, wiping her hands on a paper napkin before leaning forward just a little. "I have to confess, I've never been the senior agent before. This is new to me."

Donovan shrugged. "I've never been an agent at all before. So you can screw it up seven ways to hell and I won't notice."

They catalogued what they could about the mysterious Ruth. Then she surprised Donovan by asking his assessment of the medical records of the woman who disappeared. "I really work best on dead people." The look on her face said she figured as much, but she didn't look like that was necessarily a bad thing. Eleri Eames smiled and waited. She knew the trick: first one to speak loses. But she smiled and acted as though her waiting was the most natural thing, as though she wanted to hear what he had to say about the medical records. So he caved and spoke.

He'd been thinking on this but wondered what she'd say. "Ruth apparently escaped the compound, afraid for her life. Sought out medical treatment at a hospital—not with a physician —and then returned to the compound. According to the nurses who treated her, all one of them the locals managed to get on record, she regretted her decision and went back to the City of God to beg forgiveness."

Eleri nodded. That was a matter of record. "You know it doesn't mean the local police bungled it."

"Doesn't it?"

"Of course not."

He looked at her in a new light. She was already a contradictory mass: driven but not as ambitious as he originally thought. Sheltered but open-minded. Privileged in a way only the American upper class could be. He was almost stunned to find she was nice. She seemed to veer to the best case scenario—not something he saw much of in the agents from the Academy. His teachers had thought the worst of everyone around them. One even stated he didn't care if your spouse died during the training, he would simply assume you were lying. But here was Eames, telling him the botched record was fine.

"The woman was clearly an adult. There were no signs of abuse. She wasn't carrying a contagious disease—the diagnosis was shingles, of all things. She didn't even dress oddly, not that anyone reported. She simply wanted to remain anonymous. There was nothing to suspect, except that she kept referring to a city they'd never heard of. As busy as local stations often are, it's surprising there's even a record." She leaned back and looked through him a little, and he felt the moment her inner senior agent reared its head. "I don't go into things assuming errors are the result of poor work or that they even are errors. Don't worry, I'll call bullshit if I see it, but the locals often hate us on principle. The problem is we need them and they need us."

He was getting the "play nice" lecture. Donovan wondered if he remembered what "nice" was. Instead of playing nice, he played his card. "I don't think the diagnosis was right."

"What?"

He wasn't certain and he said so, but she asked him to go on. "Shingles used to be rare in someone that young. But it's currently moving into a younger population as the varicella virus evolves." She didn't seem to need the explanation of the chicken pox virus, so he continued. "But it presents along the dermatomes." He gestured oddly at his sides and arms, there was no good way to explain it. "It makes specific patterns on the skin and rarely shows up on both sides of the body at once."

Eames was nodding, her eyes looking into the middle distance as she absorbed that. "Which doesn't match her record."

"Right. I think she might have had measles. Misdiagnosed." He leaned forward. "If the hospital maintained a blood sample, we can check it."

"Okay, but what does it mean if she had measles instead?"

"Measles is a universally vaccinated disease. Well, for anyone who attended public school, that is."

Once again, he could see the gears turn in Eames's head. "So she wouldn't have been vaccinated, no public school records. Thus looking in the missing persons records might be pointless if she was City of God born and bred."

"Right. And if we can identify the remains of the dead woman —" no one had yet tried, but now she was FBI property, "we might be able to find Baxter and his followers."

He had tonight to run, to sleep under the stars. Then Donovan Heath, lover of woods and foliage, was off to the middle of nowhere Texas, to find human remains and a cult leader. He had, at the same time, a bone-deep dread of what he was about to do and a gut-deep certainty that he would be good at it.

3

Planes were always a bitch. While many people didn't fit in them, Eleri did—and she still thought flying was a bitch.

She would have driven, but Columbia to Dallas was just too far to make it worthwhile in a rental car. There was the added problem that a case could take you anywhere and often speed was of the essence. So she was driving a different airport rental car through the backwaters of Texas with her new partner by her side, thinking that he finally fit into the seat allotted to him. He'd been practically folded into the airplane. Thank goodness he was fresh from the Academy, which meant he was in good shape. Anyone of his height carrying spare weight wouldn't have fit into the plane seat at all, and it wasn't that small.

She had worked during the flight, refusing to sleep in the company of strangers. Clearly not everyone had been taught this gem of etiquette, as many of her fellow passengers fluffed pillows and dropped off into oblivion. It had been ingrained into her, embedded during childhood, like not wetting your pants or always using a fork. To Eleri, the act of actually sleeping with someone was far more intimate even than sex.

Pulling the car into the lot the GPS led her to, Eleri sighed to her partner. "Tell me you brought jeans."

They stuck out like sore thumbs—or rather like FBI agents—here in Brownwood. They needed to blend into the crowd so they could do their job, so they could go as long as possible before the locals started wondering why the Feds had shown up in their little town. They now needed to get checked in and change clothes before they headed out, and they needed lunch first, too.

Finally, after they slogged through registration, they silently filed up the elevator. The hallway looked long, and Eleri worried that she was already tired of it. If not the case, then the trip.

Brownwood was nothing to shake a stick at. This hotel, all two stars of it, was the nicest guest spot in town. It was on the other side of town from the hospital, but that was a whopping eight-minute drive according to her map program. Hopefully it was enough distance that small-town word wouldn't travel faster than they did and beat them to their interview.

Her phone buzzed five minutes later. Donovan's text read "ready."

Damn him. She hated being the girl. But dammit, she was going to brush her hair. It was going into a ponytail given the heat she should have expected. She was still wearing her lightweight slacks even though the temperature was pushing eighty. These trips always required a super-size suitcase. There was no way to predict when she might get home. They might get sent to the next place from here, and the third place from there. It was also impossible to know what she would need when she got to a new location—case in point: Brownwood, Texas.

Looking the town up online was not enough. Maybe it was because she had compared Brownwood to the smaller nearby towns of Brookesmith and Zephyr. But she'd overshot on the clothing. They were nowhere near the point in a case when she would need to make anyone nervous, and the nurse they were looking for wasn't under investigation at all, so casual was the way to go. She texted Heath back and stepped into the hall, already feeling the push of the air on her skin again.

Her stomach growled in greeting as he stepped through the door. Relief that his attire was in the right range warred with embarrassment that her GI tract had decided to alert everyone in hearing distance that it had not been properly fed. She could feel the blood creeping up her cheeks. Luckily her skin didn't show it too much and the lighting in here wasn't the best.

Heath still grinned at her. "Tex Mex?"

She nodded. Two could play the minimalist word game, but it would only work for a little while, only for logistics. They had a cult leader to track and several missing kids to find. Her stomach turned; she wasn't supposed to be on cases like this.

Following their Internet search, they followed small streets to the restaurant, which Donovan rejected on some vague principle. He got out of the car, gracefully unfolding himself from the passenger's side, but before he was fully upright, he made a face. Looking as though he had already tasted bad food, he shook his head. "Let's try the next one."

She didn't question him. Eleri believed in gut instincts, she believed in the brain doing things the conscious user wasn't aware of. It didn't mean they weren't valid. She just hoped that Agent Heath's instincts extended beyond Tex-Mex and maybe into more valid investigative fields.

He grinned as he got back into the car and gave her the address of the second option. "Hey, nothing derails an investigation faster than bad Mexican food."

She shrugged. "Bad Chinese food."

"Bad sushi."

She shuddered, but he was right. At the second stop he gave his seal of approval and while they ate she asked him about Ruth's hospitalization. "I was wondering last night, wouldn't the hospital see that the treatment for shingles wasn't working and realize they misdiagnosed her?"

"Not necessarily. Shingles is viral and it's embedded in the nervous system. There's not much to fix; mostly they treat for the pain. So if she had measles, whatever they treated her with would have made her feel better while it passed." He shrugged.

So it could have been a missed diagnosis. Eleri understood shingles but apparently not the finer details. She was finding it interesting working with an MD. Normally, she was the agent with the biology background. Of course she also had psych and forensic science, but far more agents came up through the ranks with some kind of criminal justice degree: criminology, legal ethics or an actual J.D. It was odd to have someone pull out the biological minutia she missed. And it was probably good for her.

They found the nurse who spoke to the local police about Ruth. It had been two weeks since the mystery woman left the hospital against medical advice, but RN Elaine Coates's recall proved solid. When she was asked about other patients, she recalled details there, too. They'd struck gold finding someone with a sharp memory and a reason to pay attention to this particular patient. The nurses all simply found Ruth "odd." It wasn't normal for a conscious person to have no identification other than a first name. With Ms. Coates's help, they expanded the file to include that she had been taking Ruth's vitals one night and heard the young woman muttering to "take her north."

The nurse also reported hearing secondhand statements about Ruth having hitched a ride to the hospital, though Eleri and Agent Heath weren't able to find anyone who claimed to have heard that directly from Ruth. If they put those unconfirmed pieces of information together, Ruth could have come from the open area between Brookesmith, Zephyr, and Mullin. Satellite activity indicated that something was there; whether it was the City of God remained to be seen.

After setting the nurse up with a cup of coffee and a video link to a sketch artist, they checked out the security system. Not shockingly, that turned up a big goose egg. A place like this, small town, there was no such thing as three-week-old footage when nothing wrong had happened. Of course they didn't still have it. So there was no image of the mysterious Ruth, not even a grainy profile shot.

Hours later, they gave up in favor of a steak dinner. They were in Texas after all. In fact, if you looked at a picture of the state, they were practically under the X. As though Baxter had chosen a spot so obvious he could hide his cult in plain sight—already marked on the map.

Sitting in the back of the restaurant, under a chandelier made of antlers, on a seat upholstered in cowhide, Eleri wondered if the seat cushion was going to shed on her. Maybe they offered complimentary lint rollers after dinner with the hot towels? But she listened to what her partner hadn't said before.

"There's no blood sample. Small place, you know? They focus on those that are there, not those that left."

"Which means no diagnosis of measles and we could be chasing our own tails." Brilliant. Westerfield had warned them this case was going to be a bitch.

"But from what Nurse Ratched said when I interviewed her, the diagnosis was definitely not shingles and could have been measles."

Frowning, Eleri took another bite of her tiny steak surrounded by mounds of buttery mashed potatoes and tried not to feel her arteries hardening. Her brain turned. Confirmation bias could always be a problem; had he asked leading or limited questions? She should have been there. Though he was stamped with the Academy's seal of approval, it was her ass on the line. Not only was she the senior partner, she had a full-on newbie sitting beside her. Oh, and he was apparently recruited—as evidenced by his lackadaisical regard for regulations. He followed them but without the hyper-aggressiveness of those who fought to be there. She should have been given an eager new agent, one with a clipboard and heartfelt desire to help the American people, not a cynical cadaver cutter looking for a change. So she questioned Donovan closely. What did he see that made him think it was measles? What other diseases or symptoms did he ask the nurse about? Did the nurse believe the diagnosis?

While he answered everything calmly, she could feel tiny spots of resentment welling up on him like blood from pinpricks. So she threw in a last question. "Why did you call her Nurse Ratched?"

"Because I'm older than you. Because I wanted to see if you got the reference." He sighed. "Because I wanted to see if you have a sense of humor."

She'd sat straight-faced until then, but at that last one, Eleri lost it. Her head went back and she laughed loud enough to turn other patrons her way. She laughed loud enough that her mother could probably hear and disapprove from all the way in Virginia or Kentucky, whichever home she was holding court in this month. "Heath, I have a psychobiology degree with so much abnormal psych your head would spin. Of course I've seen One Flew Over the Cuckoo's Nest."

"You're not old enough to have seen it."

"Shut up." He almost looked surprised. Good. "Neither are you. It's a damn classic, Heath."

"Donovan. Please." His plate was empty. Moreover it was bone dry. The bread basket had been reduced to a pile of crumbs, which might explain the missing pool of butter on his plate. But she had to pay attention to what he was saying. "I was Dr. Heath until now. I was just 'Heath!' all through med school. I was Heath in high school and undergrad on the track team. I could stand to be Donovan for a while."

"You're still Agent Heath in public." She sat back, dinner no longer appealing. "I'm not surprised you were a runner."

"Good sport for poor kids. You only need shoes. No equipment, no court, no animal."

"Animal?" She envisioned hawking, dog training, or snake

charming. Something of his look whispered of the Far East. Maybe the long straight nose, the dark chocolate of his hair, or the ink of his eyes.

"Are you going to eat that?" He distracted her from her odd thoughts with his request.

She pushed the plate his way, wondering how much he ran and trying not to calculate the calories.

His smile was amused. "I was talking about horses. Tell me you didn't have horses growing up."

"I did." She had a USDF medal, a wall full of fluffy colored ribbons and more than one shiny gold sculpture from winning her level.

He nodded like he understood. He couldn't.

Little girls loved ponies. So her parents bought Eleri and her sister ponies. Then, later, she couldn't quit.

"English?"

"Of course." Out here, they rode western. They'd passed a man on a horse—just out on the side of the street—as they headed toward the hospital. It had been all she could do not to tell him to sit up straighter, use both hands on the reins, and for God's sake, get his horse's feet off the pavement! She'd held her tongue. Clearly, the animal was not being tortured. That was just her. "I swam in college."

"Still requires a pool. Pools are expensive."

"Your college didn't let you into the pool? Did they charge a fee?"

Her plate came back to her, clean as his was. He'd better run far.

"No. No fee. But by then, I hadn't learned to swim. Still can't do much in the water." He shrugged as though it was no big deal that he had no access to a pool. She'd had one in her backyard. She'd always been a fish.

He cut off her thoughts with a wry grin. "Thankfully, there's no swimming requirement for the Academy. It would have gotten me cut."

Suddenly the gulf between them yawed and she was ready to be alone. "We started our day early and now it's late. Let's head back to the hotel. Tomorrow we have a dead girl to identify."

No segue. Eleri lacked the energy for one. Heath—Donovan —didn't seem to require them. She told herself at least he talked during dinner and hadn't reverted to his usual two-syllable maximum. But with the way the conversation went, she wasn't so sure she was happy with the outcome.

They were almost back at the hotel when he broke the silence. "We call them simply 'bodies', or 'the deceased'."

She looked at him sideways, not understanding.

"You're not the first agent I've heard use the term 'dead girls' like it was a thing."

Oh. That. "Sadly, it *is* a thing. There aren't necessarily the greatest number of dead girls; there are definitely more dead men. But there's a gender bias, and 'dead girls' is definitely a bad thing. A 'dead girl' is always considered part of a bigger problem." Eleri thought for a moment. "It's a sad statement on society. Dead men are often dead for a particular reason—something they did or didn't do. Dead boys are often considered the same—well, once they are old enough to not be kids. But dead *girls*? Well, they're often dead because they're girls. Or at least we think of them that way. Ducklings at the shooting range. Easy prey. So a dead *man*? You figure out what his problem was, why he got himself dead. But a dead *girl*? You look for a predator."

On that depressing note, she parked the car and they headed up to their rooms, quiet once again.

Eleri didn't speak a word, utter a sound, listen to anything but ambient noise before climbing into bed and sacking out. Maybe that was why she dreamed of dead girls. Then she dreamed of Ruth. Dreamed of the woman in a plain red T-shirt, jeans, and sneakers, hitching a ride in a rig painted orange with big blue flames. The driver was white-haired, rheumy-eyed, and nearly fused into his seat. He looked at dream-Ruth oddly but reached out to help her into the cab. She needed it, sick as she was.

Then the image changed around her and she was still Ruth, but there were people all around. Plain T-shirts, jeans with dirt on the knees, a room full of smoke, singing, and voices lifted in anger. She feared for her life.

Then she was Eleri again. On her horse at the practice ring. She was ten years old and she was alone.

That's why she woke up already stifling the scream that tried to come.

She shouldn't have been released from the hospital. She wasn't ready.

4

Donovan looked at the remains of the "dead girl"—as Eames had so eloquently called her. He was used to fresh bodies; he used bruises, stomach contents, blood, vitreous fluid from the eye, basically anything he could see or touch, to make assessments. His standard practice involved running analyses of any of those fluids and tissues, checking for the presence of any compound he could guess should be tested for. That was something he was good at.

He'd been one of the best, hiding away in a small hospital, doing his work, quiet and solitary if not happy.

Here, he had a box of bones. It was all that was left of the actual girl. There were records, photos, statements, and clothing all in a file. But nothing he could examine further the way he was used to. The authorities couldn't identify her, couldn't return her home, and couldn't cremate her either. In the end, they cleaned the bones and put her in a box with a number.

It didn't seem to bother Eames; it seemed she was perfectly accepting of turning up somewhere and finding only half of what she needed. She shrugged at him. "Part of the job. You can get frustrated by it—"

Which he was.

"—or you can just look at it as part of the challenge."

While that was the better option, he didn't feel it. Donovan held the skull, his hands at home in the latex gloves provided by the small local office. The two of them had been left alone with the bones. They had flashed badges and been let in. Donovan didn't think the woman at the desk had ever seen an FBI badge at that proximity before, so she'd have no idea if they were forged. He and Eames could abscond with the evidence and no one would be the wiser. Trying to tamp down his thoughts of using his shiny new badge to perpetrate crime, he checked the teeth, taking photos on the camera he held.

He could do his part—match or discard dental records. Eames was the forensic specialist here. While she didn't have a PhD in forensic anthropology, she had multiple forensic majors and a lot of hands-on experience. He let her line up the ribs, spine and long bones, looking for cause of death.

The file was slim. To them this was just a single dead girl.

The local office was stretched thin. The small town didn't even have a police department, which meant the district was covered by the sheriff's office. The sheriff also acted as the coroner— declaring the girl dead on the scene. Passing motorists, a young couple, had spotted her crawling along the roadside and stopped to help. She died before the deputies could arrive on the scene. It had taken them thirty minutes to get there. The time and distance would have shocked him, but he lived the same way—at the very edge of a small town outside a bigger one. Living outside the city limits meant no police department had jurisdiction at his home.

Job one was determining if this was the missing Jennifer Leigh Cohn. His lungs contracted, though he'd never met the agent who was her father. He knew nothing of them except what he and Eleri had in the file they carried. But the ache in his chest, the thought that this wasn't just a dead girl, but somebody's missing daughter was more involvement than he wanted. It was why he liked to work his cases before he knew anything about them. It made it harder to invest. Instead, Westerfield had invested them, like it or not.

He had a stack of files on missing women from an extended search area. So he started comparing. The skull—he refused to think of her as "possibly Jennifer"—had reasonably healthy teeth. One tooth had a cavity that was getting bad but had not yet been filled. One filling in a back molar was silver and the compound identified it as having likely been done before 2005. That helped a lot. But lack of dental work left a lot of candidates in the pile.

Beside him, Eames examined the evidence before reading the file the locals had compiled on the girl. Eames didn't want to be influenced, she said. She was also talking quietly to herself and making notes. He didn't take her for a mutterer.

She must have caught that from his face, because she looked up. "Sorry. I hope it doesn't bother you."

"That you talk to yourself?"

"It's a technique." She sighed.

Since when was that a "technique"? Head tilted, he waited for an explanation on that one.

She didn't hesitate to set him straight. "Some psychologists consider four levels of thought. Input: I listened and understood the words and basic meaning. Consideration: I can think about these ideas. Verbalization: I can organize these thoughts enough to speak of them. Writing: I can organize these thoughts into complete and distinct pieces and understand them well enough to apply grammar and commit them to a lasting document. So by talking it through, I hit level three. The Consideration level is often nebulous and doesn't require complete or formed thoughts. Verbalization does."

Well, crap. She made a case. He really had not paid attention in psych. Then again, why should he? Cadavers didn't have thoughts. "Go right ahead and talk to yourself then."

She did, but this time he listened in.

"No damage or breaks to long bones. Though there is evidence that the radius was broken and healed in the past. Possible defensive wound." Looking scientific in her magnifying glasses, she picked up the bone and examined it, her expression intent. Reaching out, she turned on a small recorder and repeated a little. "There are no perimortem or recent breaks to the long bones of either arm. However, the right radius exhibits evidence of a past fracture. Several years old from healing evidence. Possibly a defensive wound. The healing pattern indicates the bone was not properly set. There is no evidence of modern medical techniques applied to the healing process."

Eames turned the recorder off and looked up at him.

"Not that many reasons for a group of people to not seek medical attention." If they were right about the measles, now this . . .

She went back to her mumblings and he continued through his stack of photos. Face after face of missing young women assaulted him. It was more bothersome that these were just the claimed ones. So many went missing and no one reported it. Abusive parents who didn't want anyone finding out what they'd done. Negligent parents who just didn't care that their kid had disappeared. Kids with no parents; foster kids, whose paid care-takers wanted to continue getting money from the state. Donovan shut up his inner monologue before he got depressed. People were not his favorite species.

He hit the last one and the air gushed out of him in relief that he had not found a definitive match to Jennifer Cohn. He was also disturbed that he hadn't found any salient match—had he matched these bones to some other girl, which would have ruled out Jennifer. But no. Unfortunately, he still had too big a stack of "maybes." The problem—well, one of the many *challenges*, to use

Eames's optimistic language—was that some of the missing reports were recent, but many more were old cases, cold cases. Like Jennifer. Any of them could have been this twenty-something woman up until about five weeks ago. A lot of them had been missing a long time. Donovan ignored the heartbreak their families would feel and sifted again.

This time he sorted for the break to the right radius, but none had that mentioned. "How old was that break? Can you give me a minimum number of years?"

"Three minimum. After that I can't tell."

He was able to pull two out of the stack. Each had been missing less than three years and neither had a break to the arm. Given the odd healing, there was no way it would have gone unnoticed by the parents.

Eames looked up at him. "She was muscular. Hardworking, physically. And had been for some time."

"What's 'some time'?"

"Probably several years. Maybe her whole life given the apparent bone density. I'd need tests to be sure." She didn't look up at him, just lifted the remaining pieces of a person and gleaned what she could. "I'm guessing they don't have the solutions for a density test here."

He didn't contradict her but pulled a handful out of his "maybe" pile, pushing them into the "definitely not."

Eames tossed out a real gem the next time. "She was left-handed."

Now his stack was winnowed to fifteen. All natural brunettes, or could have been given the age progression. Only a few recently gone missing, and each of those four had been athletes in school, thus matching to the musculature his senior agent saw evidence of. Most had disappeared when younger, elementary or junior high age. He stopped his stomach from rolling and distanced himself. He compared the last five against the photos taken before they'd interred her bones.

"There are none left. Except Jennifer."

ELERI LOOKED UP SHARPLY. Donovan held the stack all in one long-fingered grip. Previously he'd had two piles. "Jennifer?"

It was unusual to have the "maybe" pile down to one. Especially since they'd weeded the missing with a tendency to over-accept before they even got here. But he shook his head at her and thrust the pile out. "You check it."

She did.

A handful of the girls had records of previous dental fillings that weren't present in the skull. Since the teeth were still attached, there was no denying the rejection. Other dental anomalies or features weeded still more. Faster than his initial assessments, Eleri set aside each girl they knew had made it until three years ago without a break to her right radius. Then she pulled out the ones who'd gone missing recently—the ones she had info on that were clearly not this strong, physically fit girl now laying on the table as a bone puzzle.

The left-handedness ruled out more, the pictures completely discounting the last few stragglers in the maybe pile. "You're right."

He didn't take offense at her checking his work. They would be checking each other. Unlike the movies, there were no asides for a quick view into the bad guy's secret lair. Joseph Hayden Baxter was simply an unknown quantity, one they would uncover only with the evidence they gleaned and built. So they would always double check.

"There are still options." She told Donovan.

"Of course."

"Unreported among the missing. The file could be older and not registered into the national database. Or she was taken from another quadrant of the country." All valid reasons this might not be Jennifer. They hadn't checked outside a particular geographic radius. Secretive cults didn't tend to travel. Which was a shame; it might have made this guy easier to track.

Donovan's next words led her to believe she was on the right trail.

"His parents raised him on church property, here in Texas. Outside the little town of Nolan, which is outside of Sweetwater. It's about a two-hour drive from here." He added that last bit as though he could hear her thinking about taking a day trip to talk to the elder Baxters.

"It's not just them. I'd want to talk to anyone who knew this guy growing up." Kids raised in cults were notoriously hard to get a handle on. "I'm not sure I'd trust much those two have to say. Certainly can't take it at face value, but maybe we could get something."

"Tomorrow?" He didn't look at her. Once again, he held the dead girl's skull in his latex-covered hands, turning it one way then another before setting it down with a sigh. He opened the file, reading through it, before starting to rummage through the box the sheriff's office had maintained.

Eleri had no idea what he was looking for. Indeed, he was like a kid raking through a toy chest, checking and discarding toys as he went. But he'd been one of the top-rated MEs around the South. He was one that people sometimes shipped their bodies to when no one could figure out what happened. So while Eleri was unsure what he was doing, she trusted it was valuable and turned back to the bones.

This girl had been beaten to death. Her face swollen. Pictures had been taken before they cleaned the bones, but it wasn't easy to match the body to smiling photographs of missing girls. The only thing they had for certain was that this wasn't Ashlyn Fisk. Ruth's confirmation of seeing the girl at City of God was beyond the timeline with this death, and the dental work was a clear negative.

Lining up the ribs showed a series of bruises and breaks all occurring right around the time of death. Near her spinal column, radiating fractures indicated she'd been hit with something rounded and hard—maybe the tip of a work boot?

Her skull had a dent from something making impact there, too. If they could find the item that made the fracture, there might still be hair or at least blood on it. That would help determine if this girl fell onto the object or was struck by something swung at her.

Eleri pulled her thoughts back. Too much wishful thinking. What she needed to do was categorize the shapes and types of things she would be looking for, so she might recognize them later if she saw them. There were only minimal characteristics, but she was good at this. Too much time in the FBI had her looking at everyday objects and wondering what damage it could do to soft tissue and bone.

"Eames."

Pulled from her reverie, she lifted her magnifying glasses. Since she was never able to talk to someone looking at her intently with googly eyes, she tried not to do it to anyone else. She corrected him. "Eleri, please. Westerfield was right. This is a clusterfuck and we are in it. Might as well go first names, it's gonna be a while."

He nodded, but that wasn't why he'd spoken. Looking off to the side a little, he opened his mouth, and his next words startled her a bit. "There's something you should know about me."

Automatically, her brain went horrible places. She tracked killers, profiled masochists with no conscience, saw brutality that most people didn't know existed, and she managed to keep her breakfast down most mornings. But she was already reining in her thoughts as he spoke again.

"I have a really good sense of smell. Really good."

He was looking at her earnestly, so she floundered a moment before saying, "That's very nice for you."

A small laugh pushed out of him, one she didn't know existed, and it startled her.

"I can smell when someone has come in contact with someone else who has been smoking. Perfumes and dyes drive me crazy."

She nodded, and he seemed to take it as a sign to keep going. "Someone put a cat in our rental car before we had it—"

Eleri felt her mouth open. Her bad sense of smell had been legendary at the Academy. Her eyes were half again as good as most people's but by scent she often could only distinguish that something tasty was baking, not what it was. Wines were rated only by the bite of the alcohol on her tongue or the smoothness thereof. There was no such thing as a "bouquet" in her drinking world. She loved strong flavors in her food, maybe because she couldn't detect the subtle ones. So Donovan saying he could *smell* that a cat had been in their rental car was well beyond her.

"—I can smell some toxins and the occasional cancers on dead tissue. It's how I know what to test for in an autopsy."

Her grin was disbelieving. "What are you, a dog?"

His smile disappeared.

"I'm sorry. I didn't mean that as an insult. It's actually kind of amazing. I sure can't smell that well. You'll get no arguments from me if you say you smell something." She put her hands up, warding off his offense and only then did she notice he was holding the brown evidence bag that the girl's clothing had been placed into in one hand. In the other, he held the dirty, bloody, plain T-shirt she was wearing when she died.

"Holy shit. You found something, didn't you?"

He nodded.

5

He didn't usually tell people what he could smell. It was the first step down a slippery slope and it was foolish to believe he could stand on the slope and not slide. Unfortunately, it was just as foolish to take a job based on his ability to solve crimes and not use the skills that got him there.

He'd needed a change, but as he looked at the wide-eyed interest on Eleri Eames's face, he wondered again if this had been a bad choice. It had seemed so serendipitous when Agent Westerfield showed up at the morgue flashing his badge. Donovan had let the man in, thinking there was more to one of the bodies than the hospital or police had mentioned. The FBI had been in for cases before. The only trepidation he felt was concern that the Feds had come to take away one of his cooler cases.

But the body Westerfield was there for was Donovan's. He wanted Donovan working for the FBI. Greater chances to do more, bigger cases. The upside was that he would stay in an insular world again. NightShade was its own unit, with its own agents. They worked in pairs, and ideally stayed in those pairs for very long partnerships. Donovan had immediately thought of black-suited agents mating for life like the penguins they resembled.

So it would be Donovan and one other agent, both of them reporting to Westerfield. Much like the morgue where he worked in Columbia. Small, few people, everyone in his or her place, Donovan mostly left to do what he did. The travel was a downer, he wasn't really keen on that, but the rest sounded interesting to a man who had become jaded at his work. The work alone had sustained him in his life; he had few relationships and most of those were by circumstance. He had no true friends.

Somehow he hadn't predicted this.

Somehow he hadn't been ready for the upheaval.

Why he hadn't thought it would be so strange, why he thought he could slide right in and slowly adjust was a mystery even to him. It had been stupid.

In his morgue, he was one of only three MEs and the only permanent medical examiner on staff. While MEs in general were considered weird to the normal population, he was weird among even that odd group. They plugged their noses against the smells, while Donovan shrugged it away. Decaying flesh didn't smell bad to him, it just was. It seemed he reacted to a corpse the way other people reacted to raw steak or old flowers. Seasoned MEs barfed at some of the smells that came in, but not Donovan.

And why would he plug his nose? Why did they? There was so much there that they ignored. "How did you know he was poisoned?" they would ask him. He wanted to ask back, "How did you not? He stinks of arsenic."

Donovan would lift organs closer to his face. He could distinguish not only the smells but the layers of them. Like a chef could name ingredients with a sniff, he could name diets from a kidney. Some medications could be distinguished by inhaling near the liver. Accelerants hit him like a brick wall. That was what nearly made him lose his lunch.

With his new partner, would he be left alone to sniff at things?

If he didn't use what he had, what good was he? Though he was already considering leaving the Bureau, he was not going to wash out. All he had was his work, he couldn't be bad at it. Not when he could be good. So he reached his toes out onto that slippery slope and didn't know if Eleri's relatively positive reaction would turn out to be a good thing or a bad thing.

The shirt had reeked of blood and sweat. Fear sweat. Infection. Probably from her wounds. The pictures of the body showed that previous cuts she had sustained were not properly treated. She had breaks to her ribs and a crack in her femur that would have made it hard to breathe and to walk. Yet it seemed she made it a decent distance in the Texas heat.

He wished they'd sealed the shirt in a metal container. Though they should, no one really did that. It was reserved for things with fumes or items that were waterlogged—found rags soaked in volatile accelerants, guns covered in mud. The very fact that the Bureau didn't have a standardized method of preserving what he could detect put him way out on the scale and he knew it. So he was left with standard operating procedure. Brown bags for biological evidence meant the shirt wouldn't grow mold, but the scents would fade over time.

The dirt ground into the fabric was a red clay. It was hard to see against the color of the cotton, but he could smell it. He didn't tell his partner about the sweat or the infection, but he did tell her one other thing. "Oil. She lived near oil, probably a well, given what's around."

Eleri frowned. "That doesn't narrow it down much. You mean like very close? People do have the occasional backyard well."

She was thinking. He interrupted.

"And burning. It's natural gas. They burn it off the oil wells."

"They add that smell so people will know when there's gas in their home. It doesn't come out that way."

"I know, but when it burns off the wells, the burn has an odd scent of its own. And she was around it. A lot, I think."

"Like work over a gas stove?"

While she watched, he lifted the shirt and gave a subtle inhale again. "I think more than that. A lot of gas burning and untreated—unscented—gas. For a while. It's really in the fabric."

"You can smell that?" She was shaking her head. "One day I searched my purse for peppermint gum and didn't find it. When I scratched my face I smelled the mint on my fingers. That was a big deal to me."

He laughed. "You have mint gum in your purse right now."

"No. I have it in there a lot, but there's none now."

In spite of her initial odd reaction, she was taking him at face value—which was good. He couldn't afford for her to see any further. Instead, against all his past training where his oddity was concerned, he smiled and told her, "You have some in there."

Squinting sideways at him, she peeled her gloves and turned away from the dead girl. She was digging through her purse for only a moment before she held up the partially empty pack of gum. "Well, I'll be damned." But she laughed.

He didn't tell her the rest of it. He never told anyone. But step one was okay.

"Do we head to Zion's Gate or out looking for oil wells?"

Mr. and Mrs. Baxter sat looking at Eleri as if they had no idea why she was there. The pink couch where they perched was exactly what Eleri would have expected of them. The home was small, white with white trim, and very much like all the other houses around.

Zion's Gate seemed to have no issues opening their literal gates and letting the two agents in. Pastor Jim had smiled wide and offered them a tour, happily answering many of their general questions about the church, the grounds, and the occupants. In fact, the place was more of a commune than just a church, with all the members putting money and food in a central store and all getting what was doled out by Pastor Jim and "the committee."

"Any adult member can apply to be on the committee, but selfishness is not tolerated. Nor is laziness. We're here to do God's work and no other." He pointed to the buildings one by one, but to Eleri's mind only the church was distinctive. The spire reached up to God, the cross high in the air, easily the tallest structure on the land. All the other buildings were like the houses, white on white. Apparently their God was not fond of color.

Then again, when it came to the people, their God did seem to appreciate a diversity of color. Eleri was impressed. She expected to be confronted with white-bred middle-American church life, but Pastor Jim's skin was a deep ebony. Young children of at least three identifiable races and a variety of mixes played in a fenced playground area. No one seemed to notice skin color except for her; she filed the thought away and went back to cataloguing the activities she saw.

People moved from one end of the compound to another, always with a purpose. They functioned more like a village from the late 1800s but dressed in jeans and loose shirts. They looked like any modern group, minus those few women in too-tight jeans and those few men in grubby T-shirts with sexist comments on them. They all said hello as Eleri and Donovan followed the pastor around on the brief tour.

While he pointed out TVs in the common areas, there were no communication devices allowed in individual homes or possession. The school taught only the basics for state requirements but covered every aspect of the Bible. They looked in on a class in session, and all the students waved while the teacher seemed to not mind the interruption at all.

Everyone was friendly, but it was the children Eleri looked to. Children were smarter than adults about accepting the truth, and though they could lie, they didn't know enough to perform the task truly effectively. While she immediately assessed Pastor Jim as a possible child molester—he was in the best possible position if he wished it—none of the kids responded to him in any way other than as a beloved leader. Those not in class for whatever reason threw themselves at him, hugging his legs; one small boy came up and apologized for some minor infraction. Pastor Jim set the two FBI agents on hold for a moment to kneel down to the child's level to discuss what happened. Before he left, the kid nearly tumbled Pastor Jim with a big embrace.

It was hard to fake that—to get that many kids to lie that well, at least in Eleri's opinion.

In her admittedly simple inspection, Zion's Gate seemed legit. People worked diligently and stopped to pray at seemingly random intervals. No one complained.

This man was proud of his work here, proud of what they accomplished. He tempered it with the necessary, godly humility. The gardens were a thing of beauty. Pastor Jim invited them to stay for lunch, though Eleri refused, visions of poisoning dancing in her head. She imagined their bodies buried beneath the tomatoes, fertilizing the veggies. She was at least polite about it.

Their refusal to stay rolled off Pastor Jim's back. He answered every question, managed to convey the odd practices of the church without sounding legitimately crazy, and he didn't seem to have boundaries about what the Feds could see. When Eleri asked to be shown where the kids were, or pointed out a specific building, he easily led them around, showed them inside. No outward appearance of deception. She'd have to investigate him more, later.

After the general tour, he took them to sit with the elder Baxters. Though they seemed unclear about the reason for the visit, like the good pastor, the couple had no qualms answering questions. They had the smaller house because Joseph was their only child, though he no longer lived with him, and they no longer claimed him since he left the church.

That was when it got interesting.

Mark and Lilly Baxter believed their son was God's punishment on them.

Lilly's voice crackled from both old age and grief. "I always thought Joseph was our one chance—our first chance. Maybe because we did so poorly with him, we weren't granted a second chance, another child." Her head hung; clearly she deeply believed that her son was her fault.

Eleri was more of the mind that children came randomly. She only needed to point out loving couples who remained childless and mothers on the street doing crack and leaving their children unattended. She did not believe anyone was watching over the children of earth. Biting her tongue, Eleri reminded herself that this was not about her beliefs, even if she might have soothed the older couple.

Mr. Baxter beat her to the punch anyway. "I think maybe Joseph was punishment for past sins."

Next to her, Donovan tensed. She could feel it and hoped the Baxters couldn't see it. She wasn't ready to ask them what they thought their past sins were. Honestly, it wasn't important, so she focused on Joseph. "What did he do that made you think that?"

Mark Baxter looked to his wife, waited for a not-so-subtle nod, then looked Eleri right in the eye. "He was eight when I first saw the coincidences. He was a good kid. Great. When he was little, he tried our patience and tried to get away with things. But we talked to him about trust in God, about trust in his parents. He seemed to understand. We punished him when necessary. By age twelve he'd calmed down. Seemed everything was going to be fine. He was a good kid. Solid grades, did his chores mostly."

"But?" Eleri pushed and wasn't surprised when Mr. Baxter changed his focus to Donovan. Churches like these seemed to be male-centric. Never mind that she was the senior agent.

"When he was with his friends he was always the leader. At first it seemed like a good skill for him to have. Then I caught him getting the other kids to break the rules. We talked and it didn't happen again. Later, when other children would get caught at something, it would sound like Joseph put them up to it." He sighed, weary at the telling.

"Like what?" Donovan pressed, knowing specific examples would help their assessment.

"One of his best friends, Katie, got caught stealing, but she hadn't stolen anything she would want for herself. She'd stolen for Joe. She got in trouble, returned the item and worked it off. But I found the same item in Joe's room later. Joe had a lot of things, material possessions that he said the other kids just gave to him. Kids who hung out with our Joe wound up in trouble, they broke their arms and legs. But Joe never got in trouble."

Mrs. Baxter spoke, this time talking to Eleri, as though she would be the sympathetic ear when talking about a child. So Eleri put on her concerned face—not hard to do as she was getting actually concerned.

"The whole church raises the kids together. So other parents kept their eyes on Joe. They didn't keep their kids away from him. When they caught him, they confronted him, they punished him But it was only minor infractions. William Anderson overheard Joe telling the other kids how to sneak out of the house at night. When he pulled Joe aside, he was contrite, said he wanted the kids to know how to get out if there was a fire. Will couldn't prove anything, couldn't get him to confess to a lie. So he let it go." Tears streamed from her eyes in silent memory of something Eleri didn't yet understand. She was grateful when Mr. Baxter patted his wife's hand and continued the story.

"Three weeks later, Tom Anderson, Will's boy, died. He fell from the roof of the school, at two a.m. Everyone scrambled, the kids with him said he was pushed but no one saw who. When we started looking around, Joe was home, in bed. The only kid in his group not out that night. None of the other children would tell if he'd been there or not, but they all seemed to be lying."

Keeping her expression nonjudgmental was difficult, but it

wasn't as hard as not looking over at Donovan to see if he was managing the same. She wasn't ready for Mark Baxter's next words.

"Sarah Keller disappeared two years later. No one ever found her. She was one of Joe's best friends. Everyone fretted and grieved over the disappearance, but Joe told us to have faith in God, that maybe she was with Jesus now. Then Mrs. Murphy, his teacher at the time, died. She was strangled. By then we openly suspected Joe." His voice hitched at the belief his son could do something so outside his belief system. But Eleri had seen worse. She nodded.

"Three days later, Joe left the church and we never saw him again."

Mrs. Baxter's head was low. Eleri almost didn't hear the words. "I'm ashamed. I'm his mother. But we didn't try to find him." Then she looked up, eyes wet but clear. She stared right at Eleri, brooking no lies, no evasions. "Is that why you're here? Did he hurt someone?"

6

E leri sat on her bed, papers and pictures spread before her, her laptop open and lit up. The timelines didn't match. At least not to her suspicions.

She wanted Joseph Hayden Baxter to be the man who was running City of God. She wanted him to be the one. It was the name they'd been given to investigate, a name that had come up several times in sifting other cases, and it was up to Eleri and Donovan to put it together. But it wasn't fitting together.

Ruth was at least twenty-five years old—that was the age she gave to the hospital. But the nurse recalled it was not really believed. There was even a note in her chart. The nurses esti-mated she was closer to thirty-five. But they also thought it was possible she was a hard thirty. There were no cultural references to go by. Ruth didn't recognize TV shows or comment on any current happenings. She didn't react to references to older things. And the nurses tried. It had become a game to find out Ruth's real age. But it was a game no one won.

Still, the age created a mismatch. There was no way Ruth was twenty or under. Baxter had disappeared from Zion's Gate at age sixteen. Even if he'd founded City of God as a near kid, within days of leaving home, there was no way he could have been there for Ruth's childhood. Thus, Ruth's lack of vaccination was not due to Baxter's city or preachings. Had Ruth changed cults midstream? That would be odd.

What Eleri knew was that certain personalities were attracted to cults, cult life, and zealous worship. Thus, if one cult folded or was disbanded, this person might easily end up in a second cult or even actively go searching for one. Research pointed to the idea that zealots didn't need particular beliefs; they just needed to have something to rally around. But generally they didn't leave. So where had Ruth been that she wasn't vaccinated as a child?

When she considered Jennifer Cohn, it became even more of a mess. Both Jennifer and Ashlyn Fisk had the same man's fingerprints at their abduction sites. But if it was Baxter, then he'd been very young when he started, before he even left Zion's Gate. It wasn't out of the question, but it was unlikely.

The problem was that the middle of Texas was a great place to hide. Plenty of open space where gunshots wouldn't be heard. The neighbors wouldn't mess in your business because that was Texas culture, and besides, there were no neighbors. When lush weather was factored in, it was enough to keep even the brownest thumb alive off the land.

The City of God could have its Eden just a few miles from here and no one would know.

Donovan must have been thinking the same thing; her phone chirped at her. "Do we drive around tomorrow?"

Yes, they had to. "Come over?"

It sounded like more of an invitation than it was. They were in each other's pockets for the duration. While she'd hoarded herself in her room to get away and be alone for a while, it wasn't going to happen.

Soda in hand, Donovan was at her door when she opened it. There was a connecting door between the rooms, as they had requested they be side by side, but that was more than she was ready for. She'd known this man for less than a week. Still she wasn't surprised by the soda. He ate rare steaks, thought potatoes were a vegetable, and consumed quantities of food that made all her physiology coursework invalid.

Eleri ignored the informality of it all. For a girl raised with more rules than breaths, having a man in her hotel room, both of them in jeans was nearly a declaration of war on her upbringing. Not that she was above petty rebellions. She'd done plenty of those. "We have to triangulate the area. There's too much area, too many dirt roads. We could easily drive by and miss it."

He nodded and closed the door behind them before either said a name, uttered anything that could be overheard. "Baxter could be anywhere. But given the dead girl probably didn't get too far, we should use her as an epicenter."

Donovan looked on the map of the state she'd pulled up on her screen. Pulling the laptop over and not asking permission, he quickly typed in coordinates for where the girl was found, making a red dot appear on the screen. Zooming in, he showed Eleri that it hovered over a road banked by old-growth trees.

"Are you sure you have the numbers all correct?" A minor error could cause a huge problem.

He pulled a post-it note out of his pocket and while he double-checked, her brain churned. Old trees meant undisturbed growth. The road was nearly covered by the trees, another indicator of a place that was far from modernized. Scanning the area on the satellite image, she saw no other evidence of human life for miles.

It was hard to tell from the images they captured, so she pointed. "Let's run a line of equidistance between her position and the hospital, see if there's anything in between our Jane Doe and our Ruth."

Focusing the image more, there was no evidence of activity in between. But dense growth could disguise old homes, particularly if there was an effort made to not disturb the foliage. Most new construction leveled the trees, then the builders ironically named the streets after them. But if you were careful you could build under existing trees and keep the shade and avoid exposure to both the sun and passing satellites. This could also happen if the builders were hand building, using only smaller equipment, like, say, a church group.

She sighed. Nothing was easy. Nothing had been since the year she was ten. So at least she never expected easy. "Use the girl. Do a forty-mile radius from the coordinates. See what that nets us."

Eleri had given up thinking about getting her laptop back from him. He'd simply taken over. His inky eyes looked up at her sharply. "Forty's a lot for an injured person."

Eleri shook her head. "I don't want to go too small and miss it. Besides, she was strong. Her bones indicate that she'd carried muscle mass for years, she was used to being strong. She would keep going. She was injured and fighting for her life. She could do forty if she had to."

Donovan conceded, but clearly he thought she was over-shooting.

Eleri didn't.

This was his first FBI case. He was an ME. He only saw the dead. Only saw them after they gave up, after they lost. She had seen the survivors. And survivors accomplished inhuman feats. All for the goal of staying human.

DONOVAN DROVE THE RENTAL CAR. He went for miles in near silence with Eames looking out the window, sometimes with binoculars, sometimes with the laptop open and the sat-map scrolling.

She shook her head. "Nothing."

They'd stopped for lunch after passing a sign welcoming

them to the "Town of Mullin, Texas." Donovan thought Mullin was overstating its case a bit by calling themselves a "town," but they did have a diner where grease was the main ingredient in everything and he loved every bite.

As they ate, Eleri laughed more than usual. She chatted with him about everyday things, asked after his house outside Columbia—how did he like living on the edge of a national forest?

At ease with her, letting the conversation lift the pressure of the investigation, he spoke more freely than he usually did. If they worked out, they'd stay partners for . . . forever. Donovan wasn't sure how long he could handle that, but he had to gain her trust.

Over hot apple pie and cold ice cream, she asked him about his strangest cases and didn't seem to mind the talk of guts and gore while she ate gooey, chunky food. Then she chatted up the waitress, and he realized she wasn't being nice to him at all.

The conversation had nothing to do with him, with her wanting to get to know him better. She was working the waitress, establishing the two of them as a friendly couple, maybe just friends, but here to just enjoy lunch. So it wasn't threatening when she asked if anyone had heard of the "City of God."

Her strawberry blonde ponytail bounced and twisted as she put a hand at the edge of the table, displaying manicured nails and leaning forward for a confidence. "I mean is it a place you can visit? It sounds so pretty."

As though it were a tourist destination.

The server apologized for not knowing but had no apprehension about answering the next question.

"Is there somewhere around here I could go ask? Someone who knows the surrounding area well? I'd love to say I came to Texas and saw the 'City of God.'"

Donovan offered his own supportive smile, but the server wasn't paying attention to him. Thank God, because he was fighting the urge to roll his eyes at Eames. In the end, they paid the bill and thanked the server for her help, then walked out with instructions to head toward the courthouse-slash-post office and ask for Bill.

Eleri wanted to drive when they could have walked the four blocks, but he didn't protest. She didn't seem to bear the heat as easily as he did. She wilted a little on the way in but stopped dead and looked around. She whispered, "Where are the security guards? The metal detectors?"

Small towns, he thought. They knew everyone, trusted more. It was harder to get away with anything when everyone knew who you were. It was a lesson he and his father had learned the year his dad took a job in a small town. They didn't last long there; it was a lesson Donovan had taken to heart.

It turned out Bill had not heard of the City of God in any capacity, though Eleri gave him a smile that would have made most men make something up. Eleri feigned resigned disappointment and they got back into the small car that still made Donovan's nose twitch with the smell of cat.

They crossed the back roads, both of them looking out the window. He stayed behind the wheel. Eleri's eyes were possibly better than his in daylight. But he didn't say anything about it, and they continued gridding the area as best they could even as evening set.

As they stopped at a small, one-off gas station, Eleri's shoulders visibly slumped as she scanned the surrounding emptiness. Aside from the house behind the station, where the owners clearly lived and ran their tiny, run-down oasis, there was nothing around.

Eleri was reaching for the passenger side door when he stopped her. "Want to drive?" He was tossing the keys to her and trading places before she fully agreed.

Using the excuse that he'd driven all day, he took advantage of not having to pay attention to the road. His eyes were better in the dark, his night vision excellent. Though the day was still warm, he rolled down the window a bit, even though his senior partner frowned at him. "Put all the air on your side if you need."

When she wanted to retrace their steps, he insisted on a roundabout route. She might not be able to do much in the dark, but he was far from out. "Turn here." Though she looked at him sideways, and though she took the turn slowly because of the combination of fading light and poor quality of road, she did it.

It was slow going and full dark a half hour later.

Donovan breathed deep.

"I smell it."

7

Donovan had to get rid of Eames, but he didn't know how.

She was his senior partner. They shared one rental car. So how did he get sole use of it? He couldn't take her with him—not for this.

On his own, he could get close, maybe even get into the compound with no one the wiser. If Eleri came along, he would never be able to explain. She already had more clues than anyone ever had.

Donovan lived his whole life with his cards close to the chest, rarely telling people even about his sense of smell. Every once in a while, someone would catch him sniffing an organ or getting his face close to a body. Mostly they commented that he didn't gag.

Last night, they'd driven into the oil smell from the shirt. There were more scents overlaid with that, helping him to be more certain they were driving close to where the dead girl had spent her time when she was alive—at least her T-shirt had been there.

There were oil wells all over Texas burning off leaking natural gas, so there was nothing truly unique about that. But the dirt of an area, the plants, often contributed to the local scent. Each place had its own fragrance. Most people recognized it subconsciously, but he was a special creature. Or maybe just an odd one. It depended how you categorized it.

He and his father were genetic mutations. He'd studied himself extensively. It wasn't a coincidence that he'd gone to med school; Donovan needed to know how he worked. He never intended to become a doctor in the traditional sense. He didn't have the people skills. Luckily there were other professions for people with MDs, and he found a good fit in the medical examiner's office. He found a great fit in Columbia. And he found a house that backed onto a national forest where he could run.

Why had he gotten bored when he had it so good?

Eames had them up and working early the next morning. Just to get out of the room, they went to a chain store with Internet and hooked into the FBI database. Immediately she opened with the news. "The DNA results are back. The bones don't belong to Jennifer Cohn."

It was good and bad news, and Donovan took a moment to absorb it. They had DNA samples from both parents on file, so they didn't have to ask each time. He still thought of the girl with both the first and last name. It helped to keep her at a distance.

Eleri apparently didn't need his time to think about the news.

"I think we should use drones to get closer. The satellite imaging isn't showing much out there." Eames hadn't dismissed him the way he expected her to. Maybe her own admitted bad sense of smell left her open to the possibility that he was just that good. Though he was, he couldn't tell her why.

"Does each place smell different enough to make it worth spending the funds on this?" There was no doubt in her expression, just the question itself.

He shrugged. "The short answer is yes. Places smell different enough from each other that each one smells different to me. The long answer is no." He didn't want to tell her this, but it was safe. There was nothing in this kernel that opened the whole story. Still Donovan remained wary about handing pieces to a person who was great at putting them together. Eames was not only an FBI agent, but she'd been part of an elite profiling team before moving to NightShade and taking on a junior partner. He hoped this bit of information wasn't too much. "My dad and I moved around a lot. Each place smelled different, each building—home, school, after school care. Each town. Different parts of town."

Her frown spoke before her words. "So why the doubt?"

"Well, I've never used it to really *find* a place before. I've never asked anyone else to invest money in it and I've never been into this part of Texas. So I have no idea how much of the state smells like this, maybe exactly like this. Or even how big the area is."

She nodded slowly, her gaze clinging to the distance for a minute before it came back to him. "But when we drove around yesterday, you didn't smell it all the time. Just that one section. That says to me that all of middle Texas does not smell the same and maybe we get a drone and take a look."

They didn't need a drone; he'd rather go out himself, but he didn't know how to say so. "How do we do that? How long does it take?"

"I'll talk to SAC Westerfield and see if we can even get one. We might have authorization by this afternoon. We're split distance between the Dallas and San Antonio offices, so if either of them has a machine, we might get to use it, unless someone else needs it." She threw her hands up. "Basically, I have no idea at all."

Laughing at her exasperation, Donovan nodded and pushed ahead. "Can I get a second rental car or just take the car out by myself tonight?" It was an odd request and he knew it. If she pushed back, that would be the end of it.

"Got a hot date?"

He knew he should say yes. That would make it easy—might

even explain him having the car out until close to sunrise. But the thought of flat out lying right to her face churned his stomach. "No, I wanted to do some recon."

There was a protest forming on her face. In the name of steering the situation so he didn't have to lie, Donovan jumped in. "I'm a hiker and a runner. I can go farther on my own. I also have excellent night vision and I'm the one who can smell the area."

"You're also the one who's untrained."

"I'm trained." He was something else, too. "They'll never see me. Never know I was there. I promise."

Her pause gave him hope.

And the opening gave him rope. So he grabbed it, knowing full well the thing about rope was just how often it got used to hang you. But he took it anyway. If he was going to do this—be an agent—he was going to do his best. Even if his senior agent didn't know how that was going to happen. "This isn't cockiness over my Academy training. I was a young kid in bad neighborhoods. Always on my own. I live on a property next to bears and cougars and I run with them all the time."

Her hand went up. "Bears and cougars are far kinder and more logical than some people. And we have reason to believe that the people you might find are exactly the ones that make the wildlife look friendly."

Donovan was out of ideas. Maybe he could just rent the spare car himself. She wouldn't know anything, maybe not even know that he went out, and he'd come back in the morning with solid intel.

His chest ratcheted down on his heart and he realized for the first time why he left the ME's office, why he joined the FBI readily when Agent Westerfield had shown up and asked: he was tired of being alone. He needed a partner, someone to force him into communication with the living rather than the dead. Someone—a boss, an agent in charge—to be responsible to.

For the first time in a long time he wasn't the one who knew his job best. In the morgue he answered to administrators, doctors, investigators, but none of them would look at him and tell him how to improve an autopsy. Most of them didn't even understand it well enough to ask him the right questions.

His father had isolated him as a child and he'd isolated himself as an adult. Only now, sitting in this mid-scale food store, did he even realize what he'd done. He'd put himself into a chain —below Westerfield and Eames. And he wanted that chain to work. So he asked her about the car, rather than just taking off on his own.

She was staring at him through his epiphany, her expression thoughtful. Donovan was forced to ask himself if she was profiling him. If so, what did she see? Should he be worried?

Her words came as a shock. "You'll have to stay in constant communication with me."

Damn. "I can't."

She rolled her eyes. "Why not? You want me to send a new agent out into unknown territory on his own and cut communications? I don't think so."

"Any noise is problematic. Any light can be seen far away. How would it work?"

"You're right." She conceded and he breathed a sigh of relief, but it barely formed before it froze at her smile.

"We'll GPS you!"

How in hell was he going to take a GPS with him? Unless he could swallow it, the result of which would be just too disturbing to think about.

Eleri shook her head, exasperated at the obvious turn of his thoughts. "No lights. You'll carry it in your pocket." She was proud of herself. "They vibrate, so I can signal you if need be. No light, no noise."

He had no idea, but he'd make it work. He would figure it out. "I'll be out, I won't be able to come right back, but I'll pay attention and you can track me."

It was the best he could do. Still he held his breath waiting to be struck down. Thoughts of his childhood came rushing back with sudden clarity. Asking his father about sleepovers, if he could ride the bus to a friend's house . . . and always being denied. He was a kid, so he learned slowly that letting go of the hope was easier. For years it tormented him; each time he asked, thinking this time he'd get what he wanted. Later he realized it was better not to ask.

Eleri was nodding to herself. "Am I off base here?" She didn't let him answer, which was good, because he didn't understand. "When I was a new agent, I wanted to do what I did best. Which was not what my senior partner did best, and thus not what he understood. If you add to his issues that I was young and female, he didn't let me do much."

Yes, she was on base.

She kept going, showing just how on target she was. He bet she'd been a great profiler. "You're older than me. You aced defense and maneuvers at the Academy and you have a ton of skills I don't. But I'm responsible for you. So I'm between a rock and a hard place here. If you really think you can come back safe, then let's do it."

"I can come back safe."

She was staring right at him. Pale green eyes boring into his head, trying to read the hieroglyphs of his thoughts. He wouldn't let her, but she tried. Finally, she sat back. "Good, because if you don't, my ass is fried."

"Your ass will be fine." He said it in all sincerity before he realized he just commented on his senior agent's ass. A younger, female agent's ass.

Her head snapped back so fast he thought she was having a seizure. The gulping for air didn't help, and he almost whacked her on the back before he realized she was laughing. Hard.

The rich throaty sound caught him off guard.

It shouldn't have. But it was so at odds with the clothing that screamed of money and taste. The posture that spoke of classes for deportment overlaid with hours of logged firearms and defense training. The long swimmer's muscles, the feminine disposition, the straightforward speech, even her unusual facial features that he couldn't quite put a finger on. Eleri Eames was a mass of contradictions.

Donovan would have been beet red if not for his darker coloring. He tried to drop the thought from his mind, too, but the best he could come up with was that at least she wasn't offended.

Focusing on planning, Eleri continued to gulp for air as she laid out the day.

She slept the night before with Jane Doe's box in her room. Even he didn't invite the dead into his bedroom, but Eames seemed undisturbed by it. "We need to get her to a field office and into the hands of a real forensic anthropologist or pathologist. And we need a drone from a field office. Let's go get you a rental car." She started shutting things off, talking while she made her work almost literally disappear into the plain but beautiful gray bag she carried. "Then you sleep today, because you're going out on recon at night."

He only nodded because that's all she gave him room for as she kept going. "I'll take the current car and head out to whichever field office has what we need. Hopefully a drone I can work, or an agent to work it, or . . . well, we'll see. So I'll trade Jane and Jane's artifacts for whatever I can get and I'll come back here to meet with you."

Slinging her bag over her shoulder, signaling that this little meeting was done, she looked him in the eye again. "You don't go out until you and I have met and we know we have a working GPS system."

They were in the car before he thought of his question. "Are you going to stay up and monitor me?"

"Maybe." It was the best answer she would give. "I may catnap and pray things don't go horribly wrong for you while I'm out."

He didn't believe that for a hot second, so he asked questions about the GPS while they drove. A short while later they headed off in opposite directions. Donovan needed a mesh backpack, a dog collar, duct tape, and rope. He bought more than he intended, checking out in two batches—what he could expense and what he couldn't figure out how to explain. Then he headed back to the hotel, drew the shades and forced himself to sleep.

Later that night, he sat in the rental car inhaling the air.

Eames had run tests on the GPS, syncing it to her system, making sure she could find him within a ten-foot radius. So he sat in the dark in his car, smelling that he was in the right place and stuffing his supplies into the pack.

He couldn't start here—it was too open. Anyone could see.

Turning the lights off, he stepped out, pocketed the keys and slung the pack over his shoulder. At first, his world was a nebulous mass of darkness held back only by the sliver of moon overhead. With several blinks, his eyes adjusted and the terrain turned colorless but clear.

It was one of his mutations. The human eye had two kinds of neurons—rods for black and white vision and cones for color. He had more rods in his eyes than a human should—far more. His color vision was passable at best, but in all but total darkness, he was a predator, seeing clearly over long distances and easily picking out prey. Now he just had to follow the scent to find out what was going on in the City of God.

Donovan walked an easy mile into the dense growth. Here he could smell the earth, the oil-and-burn combination that was the same as Jane Doe's shirt. Here he would make base camp.

Stringing the rope up into the tree, he hooked up the pack, his things all tucked neatly inside. The GPS had been his biggest concern. He couldn't leave it; Eleri would come looking for him if it stayed stationary. But he had no pockets. When he mentioned this she frowned and shrugged at him as though everyone had pockets. Not Donovan, not tonight. He'd been itching for a good run, but he wondered how it would feel with the GPS device duct taped to the collar he now clicked around his neck.

He felt ridiculous, though it should at least work.

Peeling all his clothing, he folded it neatly, sliding it into the pack, piece by piece. When it was all in there, he used the rope to tie it off the ground. He didn't need anything sniffing at it or chewing it while he was gone. That would be a hard one to explain come morning—he knew from experience.

Just an hour ago, Eames had wished him luck, told him to go track.

Donovan rolled his shoulders into place and cracked his spine, slightly altering the arch. He felt his breath open up and his feet hit the ground. Muscles stretching, unused for too long, he loped off at a steady pace. He could smell the oil-and-burn on the wind and he turned toward the scent.

He was tracking.

8

Eleri rubbed at her eyes. Donovan may have napped all day, but she'd driven miles upon miles, handled political negotiations, and worked her way through a good-old-boy network.

Mentally, she conceded that the good-old-boy network wasn't as "good," "old" or even "boy" as she wanted to believe. It was simply red tape and limited resources, but when other agents called her "honey" or "darlin" it was really easy to blame it on an inside club. Eleri had never been anybody's darlin'.

When she asked for a drone, she'd hoped for a small team—an agent or two—to run the flight. She imagined men in suits, wilting in the hot Texas sun as they launched the drone. They would roll up their sleeves, work the system, and record everything.

Instead, she was given a box. Her drone came in pieces to be assembled. "Easy Peasy" the agent had told her.

Eleri didn't think she'd ever heard an agent use quite that terminology before. She also hadn't used a drone before—she'd seen them, but never worked one herself. Maybe all the sweet words were just a response to her strawberry blonde hair, freckles, and facial features that contained no sharp edges, making her look young and sweet.

She didn't open the box. She had a tracker to track and she had to stay awake.

When Donovan left in his compact rental, Eleri headed the other way. Trusting in the computer to show her where he was when she returned, she went straight to Grounds for Thought, a little coffee shop she'd noticed earlier. Relatively frou-frou and located in the heart of a nearly permanent heat wave, she knew they had to serve cold drinks with massive quantities of caffeine. She left with a full tray. A frozen caramel latte thingy to start. A coffee and a tea and a massive cup of ice waited to be fed into her mini-fridge for the wee hours. Or for the next morning when she had to haul her sorry ass out of bed again. Eleri believed in being prepared.

When she returned to the hotel and her perch on the bed, she took her first huge sip of the frozen latte and stopped dead. Damn, that was good. Then she booted her system and prayed her partner hadn't gone out of range or lost signal or any of the other things that could have gone wrong. Things she could never imagine reporting to a superior and having to say, "I was getting coffee, sir."

Luckily the red dot pulled right up. Donovan was within a mile of where he said he smelled the T-shirt scent. Good for him.

Sipping at the coffee—a perfect blend of sugar, caffeine and cold—Eleri kept only half her attention on the dot and the other half on some truly terrible television. She briefly considered catnapping, but Donovan could start moving at any time and she wanted to keep a weather eye on the tracker, see where he went, what the pattern was.

The way he talked he must think he was some kind of Indian warrior? Who knew? It hadn't seemed arrogant, simply confident. That, combined with her own memories of being held back by agents who didn't see that her skills were different from theirs, led her to put her faith in him. She sipped again and hoped it wasn't misplaced.

As she watched, the red dot started to move.

It was disturbingly fascinating, and she stared at it, her brain zoning out. In slow motion, the dot tracked Donovan's position. Stats updated moment by moment on a panel to the right. Coordinates—which she could read from her Academy training—held rudimentary information. The map itself told more about the terrain, the flora, the things she was interested in. Her partner moved in odd lines, the map constantly shifting under his path.

The constant updates now kept her glued to the screen, at odds with the slow motion movement that nearly put her to sleep more than once. Still, she could see where he was and tell where he was headed.

As her head snapped upward and out of near sleep and her body jerked, Eleri made the decision that the drone was not going out bright and early tomorrow. No, there would be sleep. Tired agents were bad agents. Tired agents didn't make good first impressions on their inaugural cases with their new elite division. Yes, sleep was definitely on the docket. She just had to fend it off until Donovan got back.

The low rubbery sound inside her head each time she blinked and the slight burning sensation around her eyelids let her know that was much easier said than done. The coffee cup left a wet ring on the bedside table and she wiped at it, thinking a big sip might perk her up. She then gathered the whole setup and moved to the desk. Waking up, curled on her bed, with the red dot that was her partner nowhere to be found was a potential nightmare. She was better off in the chair. If she woke with an impression of her keyboard on her face, well, that would only be what she deserved.

The TV turned then to an infomercial but Eleri left it on behind her, hoping the perky voices would keep her awake. Academy training had involved exhaustion and long periods without sleep. Agents often ran for more than a day or even two with no breaks, but the negotiations and the heat had sapped her today. She was warm, it was dark outside, and she had the deep, saturating need to curl up and give in to sleep.

Eleri fought it.

Donovan had balked at the GPS, brushing aside her comment about just sticking it in his pocket. She laughed about it now, thinking, you try getting women's clothes with pockets. Still, what did she know? Only that in the end he thought he figured out how to do it and she was happy. He needed to keep it with him. She had to know if he stopped moving and she had to be able to find to him. So she needed to stay awake. Just in case.

The numbers scrolled down the right side. He was keeping up a pace of eight miles per hour. She quickly did the math coming up with an impressive seven-and-a-half-minute mile.

She could do that—for a short while, but only a very short while. Then again, she was a swimmer. Her running days had been almost entirely at the Academy. She passed the time trials only seconds before the failure mark and even then only managed that pace by imagining homicidal maniacs chasing her. In water, she was fast, outswimming most of the men. But running? That was clearly Donovan's forte. His pace was solid and superbly impressive given the terrain. She would never be able to maintain that rate or even keep up in the woods that separated the road from the open spaces.

There were open areas between the towns, places farther from the water sources where the trees didn't grow as tall. As the red dot approached the edge of the forest, she was left wondering what he would do when he hit the flatter field. Donovan was a tall man, how would he stay low enough to not be seen?

Four minutes later she watched in awe as the dot went straight from the forest into the field without stopping at all. There was no change in movement—as though he were just striding through the tall grass, plain as day.

She frowned and sipped at her coffee, only to be affronted by a gulp of air and a hissing noise. Great, her coffee was gone and her partner—extraordinary tracker and self-proclaimed man of stealth—was just strolling through an open field near a compound that housed a leader who likely killed three people before he turned sixteen.

She waited for the dot to stop dead and wondered if she'd hear the bullet crack from all the way out here. But the dot didn't stop its forward progress. In fact, the mileage increased by half a mile per hour. Did the man think he was better off going faster in the open space rather than skirting it? What the hell kind of stealth was that?

Debating whether to trust him or buzz him and bring him back in occupied her next thirty minutes. By the time she didn't decide, he was safely across the open area and into another patch of dense forest where his pace slowed just a little back to the earlier rate. The man had been holding an eight-minute mile for two hours now.

Her head buzzing, Eleri tried to calculate it. Marathoners held that pace, for several hours even, but they did it on flat ground—not in forests with protruding roots and thick underbrush. The winding path may have been Donovan following a trail that was already established, but even that wouldn't explain the speed he held. And he'd gotten faster in the field. While it lacked the underbrush, it was full of tall grass and that couldn't be easy to run through. Aware that she wasn't a runner and wasn't up on the finer points of wilderness jogging, Eleri still couldn't make logical sense of it.

Forty minutes later, the pace of the red dot changed drastically.

She had just pulled the tea from her little fridge, using standing and stretching and even the short distance walked to keep awake. She made a production out of pouring the tea over a cup she filled with the ice she'd brought and giving it a good shake. A caffeine-heavy mix of black tea and some fruit flavoring, it hit her senses with a bloom, bringing her awake and recharging her a bit. So when she sat down to look at the screen again it had catalogued a few changes in the numbers.

Donovan looked like he'd come to a block. He veered almost a full ninety degrees to his left—west—and his speed dropped. She wondered if he'd worn out. But that wasn't her concern. If he was upright, if he was moving, she was going to let him do what he claimed he could do.

An hour later he'd made most of a circle.

DONOVAN SNIFFED the air but didn't detect anything. When he arrived, he knew he had the right place. This small cluster of homes must be the City of God. Whatever it was, it was where the dead girl had come from: the T-shirt smell belonged to this place.

Now though, he couldn't smell much of anything. It was as though the air had been cleaned. Still he stalked the edge of the compound, mentally recording every bit of information he could. All in all there were twenty-two buildings, most looking like homes, although about five appeared to be more for common use or storage and several of these were farther away. Some had security measures around them: razor wire in the grass, nearly invisible over the fescue that grew up through it. Fences made of spikes driven into the ground at intervals too small for a person to squeeze through.

A number of small generators were scattered around the compound, chugging softly in the dark. Since they didn't seem connected to anything, Donovan figured there was an underground wire network. This in turn would indicate a sophisticated system that wasn't quite as primitive as it looked.

The houses and buildings were parked under large trees, all but obscuring them from overhead view. They were painted camouflage colors, so satellite pictures could show the house but you might still never see it. A few buildings—those more out in the open—were earthen in one way or another. One was half-buried into the rich soil, only two sides of the building exposed, so that from several angles it looked to simply be a hill. Another two buildings were painted in the same camo shades but sported grass rooftops. These sod tops were benefits for heating and cooling as well as making sure they weren't found. Eleri and her drone would have fun tomorrow.

In the dead of night, the little hidden village seemed peaceful, but closer inspection made it clear all was not as it seemed. Concerned with the lack of smell, Donovan sped up his pace. The GPS not only knew where he was at any given moment, it would trace his path. If he could get all the way around, he would clearly show the boundaries of the compound when Eleri pulled it up.

Armed guards—about five of them—traipsed through the City. They walked a path only they saw, checking the outer edges of the homes before criss-crossing their way back through the center of the compound. Though they all carried guns, they left them at their sides. Donovan watched them as he skirted the edges. Relatively lax in their watch, they didn't see him, so their patterns should be relatively normal.

He tracked the perimeter without coming too close and as he was deciding to finish the job or leave the area, the wind changed. It must have cleared his sinuses because fresh smells slowly came back to him.

Frowning, he thought he detected blood, so he followed it. As a faint scent, it didn't mean much. It might mean someone cut himself working recently. It might not even be human. In a place like this, the scent of blood should be everywhere. Unless they were the only gun-toting vegetarian cult in Texas.

The wind shifted again, bringing a fresh wash of the blood scent. This time he knew it was human. It wasn't a huge quantity, but it was fresh and overlaid with fear—deep, bone-chilling, anyone-could-smell-it fear.

Searching for the source, Donovan sniffed around in a circle. He had just caught the scent when he heard the sounds to his right. A quiet cacophony came from another part of the compound. Something was wrong but not quite wrong enough to wake everyone.

Donovan was watching the mess intently, when one of the guards suddenly spotted him.

Dead on, gun already raised, the guard stared him in the eyes.

9

Donovan felt the weight of the guard's stare as the man sighted him down the long barrel of the gun.

One good bullet and Donovan would be dead. Then again, he figured he was hard to hit. He made a bad target.

Staring back, he offered what he could of a smile and waited. It was his only gambit. Everything was up to the guard now.

With a swear word harsher than what one would expect of the godly, the man lowered his gun and turned away. Resuming his path, the black-clad guard turned the corner of the nearest building. All Donovan heard was the soft sounds of his feet in the low grass as he walked away, dismissing what he'd seen.

Donovan turned away, too, the circle around the camp not yet complete, but the GPS would clearly define where this little self-contained mecca lay. The scent of blood was compelling and he followed it.

In colorless clarity he saw broken branches and the set of footprints leading into the woods in uneven patterns. A smattering of larger booted prints swarmed the area at the edge of the tree line, telling him the soldiers had looked for something they hadn't found. A long time ago he'd learned to quit asking how others couldn't see it. Clear as day, the first set of prints went the direction they checked, but it seemed they made it to the woods and lost the trail.

Donovan knew he wasn't supposed to form judgments without more evidence, but he was glad the one had gotten away. Loping farther into the woods and checking for signs, he found the first drop of blood.

The smell had been there, but the tracks erased the visible drops, scattered the condensed smell. Here it was then, the first drop. Dirty blood. Not a clean arterial spurt of a dying animal. Had the tracks of shoes not given it away, the smell would have. It was definitely human. And definitely recent.

Picking up his pace a little, he followed along. But his speed only came in spurts—he was following a trail and sometimes it would disappear. The wounded person wouldn't bleed for a while, and Donovan was stuck wandering and sniffing until he found another drop, spotted a broken branch, or smelled where the person had rubbed against the landscape as he blundered through. Wounded, there wasn't much more the victim could do but leave a wide and relatively well-marked path.

Donovan wondered why the people at the village didn't have dogs. While he was thinking, he almost put his foot in it.

He bet dogs didn't have this problem. They probably just got curious and followed a smell, but here he was, thinking about all the little issues and almost stepped into a disturbingly large puddle of human blood.

He should have been paying attention; he should have smelled it. Something like that, a concentrated source, and the odors came up the way the smells of baking wafted from a kitchen. The way skunk hit you long before you saw it. He'd caught the scent, but then again his mind was elsewhere and he almost stepped in it.

Suddenly, this wasn't a search for whatever he would find. This was now a man hunt. The blood was a puddle, not a drop.

He sniffed harder; the runner was a boy, not yet a man and he stood here and bled for a while. Maybe he pulled away a bandage or stabbed himself a second time. It still wasn't high velocity, not arterial, but it was no longer the drip of a man running with something as simple as a cut hand.

This was fresh, very recent.

Since there was no body here, this person must still be alive, still moving. But it was clear he was leaking too fast to stay that way much longer without medical help.

Donovan stopped. Listened. Slowly turning his head, he monitored the woods for sounds from any direction. Alive around him, the forest had its own white noise and he picked out specific sounds. Behind him he could still make out the faint chug of the generators. He could hear the rustling movements of a community asleep—branches on windows, feet on patrol—but not what he was listening for.

To his right, a large animal moved.

Cat. It smelled of large feline. Puma, maybe ocelot. They were both out here. He'd scented them before; they'd crossed the path he was taking tonight more than once, though he hadn't seen them. Now he saw the movement in the distance, between the trees, up in the branches.

It smelled the blood, too.

Donovan redoubled his efforts, sucking in air through his sinuses. Using all his senses, he added together the smells, the broken branches, the visible blood still actively soaking into the dirt. And he moved faster.

No longer quiet, he took his chances. The cat now tracked him, pacing off to one side, and he wondered if she was willing to fight him for the prey. Pausing, he turned his head, sniffing again as the cat got closer. Puma—dammit—and she was nursing. She had cubs to feed, which would only make her more aggressive.

In front of him, the woods were thinning out and there was a quality to what he sensed that he couldn't put his finger on but he could identify it. Roadway. It must be the tar or additives they used. These back roads baked in the sun and gave that heat back at night. They radiated chemicals that oozed up and into the air like steam off a hot lake.

Ahead of him, he heard sounds. Grunting, stumbling noises. Muttering.

The young man was talking to himself, telling himself to keep going. Stumbling again, yelping in pain, and scrambling back up.

Still Donovan trailed. This kid—it had to be a kid—wouldn't know it, but Donovan was by far the better option. The puma would not hesitate to take out a wounded child.

Beside him the cat started her own lope. No longer in stalking mode, she sped up to a full run, her strides clearing the ground cover and closing the distance. Donovan had to pace her or she'd get to the kid first, tear him limb from limb, and feed the parts to her cubs.

Stretching, he reached for every leap, pushing a little further, until—at the same time—he and the cat cleared the forest edge. Between them and the road, a boy, early teens, screamed at the sight of them rushing him.

As Donovan watched, the boy stumbled, went down on his ass and scrambled back up. At this point the fear kept him from noticing that one arm didn't push, didn't work. One pant leg was soaked in blood, and the cut there screamed of fresh meat.

The cat's mouth opened, long teeth glinting, catching the bare amount of moonlight and framing the screech that emanated from her. She was taking those last bounding steps to close on her prey. She leapt even as the boy was running into the road, screaming. He waved his arms as if anyone came along this road in the daylight, let alone at night.

There was no answering drone of tires on pavement, no purr of an engine, no faint spot of light rounding the corner to save the boy. There was only Donovan.

So he threw himself at the cat, catching her side mid-leap and not quite able to keep her claws from reaching the boy. Donovan braced, and though he kept the worst of it from the kid, he wasn't sure if he would survive her claws himself. There were rumors that men like him healed fast, were immortal, could only be stopped by certain metals. It was all bullshit. She could kill him as easily as she could kill the boy.

But he got lucky. She rolled onto her back and didn't like it there.

Donovan shoved himself off her, his main goal to escape her claws and teeth. Given the way they tumbled, it left him handily between her and the boy. However, the boy was screaming his fool head off. He'd worked so hard to get away from the little city, but everyone would likely hear this. Then again, maybe not; he had run for miles.

Rapidly regaining her feet, the cat stood her ground, hissing at the broken kid, wanting dinner for her cubs. Donovan faced her. Just taller than she was, he could intimidate a bit by height. His mass was greater, too; she was a big girl, but adult female pumas clocked in around one hundred pounds. Donovan was double that. He bared his teeth and waited. He'd rather not fight. Puma claws were nothing to balk at, and he did not want to explain that one in an ER. Or to Eleri.

When the cat didn't move, he let out a low growl, speaking a language she understood. You didn't live on the edge of thousands of acres of national forest and not learn a thing or two about big cats. Getting back to her cubs alive was more important than getting this particular meal.

Still, she was pissed as hell. Hissing at him, she backed away, ass in the air. As she melted into the forest, Donovan entertained the fleeting thought that she was beautiful—or she would have been if she hadn't been trying to fight him and eat a wounded person.

He turned back to the boy—who took one look at him and promptly fainted dead away, cracking his head on the pavement.

Shit.

What was he supposed to do now? He couldn't communicate with an unconscious kid. He could bring pointy sticks so the kid could defend himself until Donovan could get the car and bring it around. Or he could hang out. But the best he could offer was a naked man, and a naked man wasn't much help. He literally didn't have anything on.

Anything but a damn dog collar with a tracking device.

Shit.

He brought the sticks. The sharpest ones he could find. He wished he had a gun to leave, but then again, as soon as he put a gun in that one working hand, there was every reason to believe the kid would take aim at him. So, pointy sticks it was.

Then he nudged the kid awake.

The tall boy—blonde haired and with saucers of blue for eyes —took one look at him, screamed, clutched his arm, and passed right back out.

The thoughts in Donovan's head became less flattering. "You have to stay awake kid. Or that cat will come back and you won't wake up until she drags you away. There won't be anything I can do then."

He nudged the boy again.

This time the kid screamed, but scrambled back away. Once he was firmly on his ass, he reached for one of the branches and brandished it at Donovan.

"Good boy," he thought.

He could leave now. He had no idea how long it would take to loop back around, but he had a good idea where he was.

With a single nod at the kid, Donovan aimed toward his car, creating a large triangle on the map and without thinking what the GPS would show, he took off like a shot.

~

ELERI BLINKED RAPIDLY. Her vision was thick, her brain trying to shut down. For a moment she thought she actually was asleep.

The red dot now left a blue trail on the map. Learning the system was a good way to stay awake at two-thirty in the morning when you were watching a tiny dot move on a satellite photo of the wide-open Texas landscape. Staying awake was important as she watched the map coordinates change, number by number, each time the right side of her screen updated. No wonder her brain was telling her to shut down.

But Donovan was out there. Not only did she not believe in leaving him to fend for himself when she specifically told him she'd be watching, but she was also his senior officer. It was literally her responsibility to bring him back safely.

She enjoyed the irony of being responsible for the older, better educated, physically larger agent. The only thing she had on him was FBI experience. They were a good team, that much was true. However, it depended on her keeping things working, on her eyes sticking to the red dot and making sure everything didn't go to hell sideways.

The dot had tracked northwest originally, zig-zagging its way through underbrush and across fields. After about ten miles of that—Eleri used the mapping feature to check the distance—the blue line wrapped around what must be the City of God. It was something roughly circular he was skirting there. The only question was how far out from the compound/town/whatever was he? Likely it was just a few homes, the circle wasn't that wide. After that he took off almost due east. Once again moving side to side, slowing down, speeding up.

Then there was an odd cluster of activity.

Eleri frowned. She must be asleep. According to the computer he'd gone almost twenty-two miles. That was a marathon—in three and a half hours. Many people didn't complete the marathon in that time and they sure as hell didn't do it in the woods.

It was her brain; it must have shorted out, or else the computer had. Either way her brain wasn't awake enough to fix either. She discounted her desire to bang on the side of the screen as though bumping it would actually put the right pixels and bits back into place. She almost laughed.

Yes. A sure sign she was losing it—sitting by herself in the middle of the night, laughing at her own stupidity. Traipsing to the fridge, she got out the second coffee. Clearly she needed it.

It was a production, scooping the ice, pouring coffee from one cup into another, not spilling the sticky sweet liquid on the carpet. She wasn't at her best, but she got it done, double-checked the lid and turned back to the screen after chugging a cold shot.

Her eyes opened fully. She was awake now and the blue line still showed that he'd walked a tight space repeatedly. Only now she noticed that he was roadside. Was he talking to someone? Why would he pace like that? Given the map size he was going ten, maybe twenty, feet away and then coming back. That was odd. It was too big to be a signal to her that something was wrong.

Thinking it through, she tried to imagine scenarios that might explain it. If someone found him, they wouldn't let him go that far. He wouldn't move like that if someone was chasing him, or had a gun on him. He couldn't figure it out.

Her forehead had a knot on the front; Eleri could feel it. She was thinking hard and trying to make sense of it all when the blue dot shot out. Heading southwest, back toward the starting point.

Eleri almost took the flat of her hand and bumped the side of her head, as though doing so would realign her own pixels or bits. None of this could be right.

The screen updated.

The numbers made her head pop forward and her heart race.

The GPS was moving through the woods at thirty-two miles per hour.

10

Scrambling both physically and mentally, it took Eleri far too long to yank the cords and grab her bags. She almost forgot her jacket. Not that she needed it for heat, the ground was still radiating from the day. Donovan was out in thick stands of trees and underbrush. Contrary to what she thought Texas should be—desolate and brown—this area was lush and green. And that meant lakes, standing water from rain, and bugs. Lots of bugs.

She was likely going into the woods to retrieve her partner. It wasn't going to be pretty. Given the pacing of the GPS—it held a steady thirty-plus mile-per-hour rate—it was just as likely it had been taken from Donovan than that he was still with it.

Eleri tried to stop her brain; she needed to stay calm. If she showed up with missing pieces, she would be of no use. Checklist: gun, holster, and two spare magazines. Jacket, long pants that she could move in, socks, and sneakers. Hair! She rushed into the bathroom and pulled it up into a ponytail, then looped it up and around. It wasn't pretty, but it wouldn't catch on anything.

Scanning the room, she spotted her small weapons bag and quickly strapped her hunting knife to her ankle. Computer:

check. Backup battery, cord for the car. She needed the laptop *on*. She still had to track Donovan, hopefully where he was now but maybe just from where he'd last been. Shit.

Everything in place, it still took her two trips to get it all to the car. Though she was jacked up on adrenaline, she took the coffee with her and shoved a power bar into her face while she drove. She didn't know what she'd be called upon to do or how long it would be before she ate again. Luckily the area was deserted this time of night, because she was constantly looking at the laptop she'd left open on the passenger's seat.

The drive was long enough for her to suck down all the cold coffee and even make her way through most of the ice. The blue line—the GPS—was headed back toward his car still at thirty-plus miles per hour, so *something* was wrong. Eleri couldn't tell if she was going to beat him to the car or not. Also, there was no telling if she would meet up with Donovan, Donovan with someone else, or just the GPS. It was entirely possible that some bird had eaten the transceiver and was flying off with it. Though the likelihood that the bird ate it then headed straight for the rental car was slim to none.

As she got closer, Eleri used her left hand on the wheel and with her right she checked her weapon, pushed her spare magazines into her pockets—another good reason for a jacket that would be too hot to want, but not too hot to need. Who knew what she would meet up with at the rental car?

The blue line burst faster, somehow picking up speed then stopped at a point in the woods just beyond the road.

So it was not a bird or a big cat—those were no longer possibilities. Nothing like that would wait just beyond Donovan's car. This couldn't mean anything but trouble.

She turned off the headlights about a mile away and let her eyes acclimate to the low light. She had great vision, but it took too long to get accustomed to the thin light of the moon branching through the trees. She crept the car forward, using her right hand to hit off all the interior lights as well. Glowing like a beacon when she opened the door was not only foolish but target-worthy. Parking well before reaching Donovan's car, Eleri figured she was much better off coming up stealthy and on foot as she had no idea what was making the GPS run that fast.

Holding the door handle up, she quietly pushed it closed, wishing she could take the laptop with her. Her brain muttered choice phrases about agents running off into the woods at night and agents who trusted them, but she kept the sounds vaulted. They might be running through her head at top volume, but they weren't running from her mouth.

Step over step, gun out, safety off, pointed at the ground in front of her, Eleri approached. Listening hard for anything of value, she stopped and finally heard a rustling noise from where she'd last seen the GPS on the screen. As she stepped into the tree line for cover, she heard him.

"Eames! Eames! It's me. Go to my car!"

Donovan.

He was safe and at least alive enough to yell for her.

Did she trust him enough to just do as he said? What if someone had him?

With the right incentive, even the best agents turned. It was more than possible someone had him and they wanted her, too. Could he have been coerced?

It was a chance she would have to take. She had to trust her partner.

"Run!" He yelled at her.

Shit.

She bolted.

Angling out of the woods, heading toward the spot where she knew his rental to be, Eleri prayed under her breath. "Bon Dieu, keep me safe. Bind me from trouble. Aida-Weddo, protect me from this forest I walk." It was an old prayer her great grand-mere Remi would chant as Eleri fell asleep at night. The forest was metaphorical then; tonight it was literal. Eleri muttered it again, not sure if she believed, but sure it wouldn't hurt. Grand-mere had believed and hopefully that counted for something.

She burst out of the tree line to see Donovan opening his car door and motioning frantically to her. His clothing was odd, disheveled, and he carried a cloth bag she hadn't seen before. But she did as he said and frantically inserted herself into the passenger side of the car. His lights didn't come on either. Academy training. But he shuffled a bit, shoving something in his pocket, buckling in and trying to drive at the same time.

Eleri tried to listen. He was talking a mile a minute over the sound of the tires peeling away on the hot asphalt. The car lurched forward and she didn't understand much of anything. "Kid" "cat" "road" were all she could make out, but clearly he was driving toward something. In a moment she realized he was headed back to the point where his tracks had connected with the other road.

"Donovan, calm down. Tell me what happened." She turned toward him, looking him up and down.

"I was skirting the edge of the compound—"

So he found it.

"And then I—I took off after some blood and a trail leading away from the houses."

There were houses. Interesting. Nothing showed via satellite. Wait. Blood?

"It was a kid, about thirteen? Fifteen? Beaten. His arm is broken. There was a puma there."

Holy shit. "And you left him there?" Why hadn't he signaled her? She could have gone straight to the kid.

Donovan was shaking his head. "I didn't have anything on me. Nothing with me. First I ran the cat off, but then there was nothing I could do but go for help."

Which he'd done crazy-ass fast. Maybe even thirty miles per hour fast. She wasn't wrapping her head around that yet.

Her partner wasn't done. "I gave him a few big sticks to fend off the cat. But we have to get back to him."

Eleri agreed. "Med kit?"

"In the back. It's why I wanted to take this car. I always bring a serious kit when I run in the woods."

He was starting to calm down. They were coming closer to where the line had intersected with the boy. This time, Donovan turned the lights on bright and slowed down. Eleri knew she should be looking for this mysterious kid. Another escapee from the City of God. This one alive. One who could talk. They needed this.

But she couldn't peel her eyes from the man driving the car.

He was poorly put together. Dirty, bloody, and . . . *wrong*. Her brain had been working the puzzle in the back of her head while she listened, while they drove.

Why hadn't he stayed with the kid? He could have signaled with the GPS, drawn her an X. A circle. Something. She would have figured it out. Then again, in the heat of the moment decisions weren't always clear. Maybe it had made sense at the time to go back to the car, get the medical kit, not wait for Eleri.

Still, that didn't explain everything.

They turned the corner and watched as the boy jumped in front of the car, right into the headlights, blinding himself in the process. He waved one arm, clutching a branch, and turned his eyes away from the light. Eleri could hear him—hoarse from screaming, he used what voice he had left to yell at them. He worked frantically to flag them down, unaware that they had come specifically to find him.

Donovan hit the brakes, throwing her sharply forward and making her glad she'd buckled in. He was out of the car and running toward the kid before she could open her door. As he dashed into the light of the high beams it hit her full force.

The blood on him, the dirt smeared in, it was all *under* his clothing.

Donovan looked the boy up and down. The kid was on his feet again, tall for his age, or . . . Donovan corrected himself, maybe just older than he'd thought. He would have been able to tell better if the kid was dead, but he just wasn't good with live children.

He was chagrined to think he didn't quite know what to do. Sure, he understood that he needed to splint the arm, stop the bleeding and before that, get the kid out of the road. But he didn't really know *how* to do it. Didn't like the idea that while he tried to remember his training, the boy suffered. Donovan didn't treat wounds that could kill, only wounds that had succeeded.

"Help me! Help me! They'll kill me!" Trying to scream, the boy pushed the words through wounded pipes. His broken arm hung limp at his side, making Donovan wonder if maybe the shoulder was dislocated, too.

It was Eleri who reached out for the kid's good hand, held it without insinuating that he drop the stick, and asked a reasonable question. "Who is trying to kill you?"

"Abraham! Belinda!" He sucked in air. "The mountain lion!"

This made Eleri look around. Maybe she hadn't believed him when he told her in the car. Then again, he might not have believed himself either. Donovan nodded. "Puma. About a hundred pounds." He didn't add that she had cubs.

Breathing heavy from exertion, he couldn't ignore the cat's scent. She was still there, lingering nearby. He wondered how many times the kid had to fend her off since Donovan left.

"Holy shit." That from Eames as she searched the woods.

The cat wouldn't come out now. Not with three of them there. She'd have to be rabid to try that, and she wasn't. The way the kid had been crazed and out of it, his strong memory of the cat was indicative that she'd been back. Thankfully the kid had stayed awake and alive.

The boy blubbered now, falling apart as Eleri talked over him, her bottle green eyes earnest as she tried to soothe him enough to make a real connection. Donovan knew what she was doing; he'd learned the same thing at the Academy, but he didn't *do* it as well as she did. Maybe because he had nearly a foot on the kid, was dirty, and acting hypervigilant. Maybe because he'd always been bad with people in general and kids in particular.

Scanning his surroundings, he tried to stay sharp, but the night had been long and exhausting. The run had done him good, at first. But at the end, the all-out dash back to the car, the pounding of his heart, the concern for the boy, had tapped him.

Something grabbed at his brain, tugged his attention back into the woods.

Turning sharply to Eleri and the boy, he hissed, "Shut up."

"What are you—" She was starting to ask, but she stopped abruptly when she saw his face. Donovan duly ignored her as he turned back to the trees, his eyes searching. Unfortunately, his night vision had been blown out by the headlights on the car. The three of them stood there, trying to calm the boy, keeping watch, standing like targets right in their own spotlight. There had been no reason to worry about that, they were miles away from where he'd seen the houses. But the sounds, the woods—now Donovan wasn't so sure.

"Get in the car, Eames. You too, kid." He didn't know what to call the boy; he only knew he needed to be obeyed. He heard footsteps. Human footsteps.

The cat was long gone. Other smaller creatures scattered at the boy's frightened and frantic pass through the woods. He'd crashed left and right, then hollered at the road and into the night. He yelled until he was hoarse. Sane animals didn't like that.

So the noises coming from the woods weren't made by creatures. They were from people. Several of them. Heavy footsteps. Men. Possibly the armed ones from the camp. Probably.

"Get in the car." Keeping his voice low, he glared at them. Why hadn't they moved?

Because no one heard what he did. The boy—who should have been listening like his life depended on it—was too busy blubbering. Eleri was soothing the boy, thinking she was relatively safe here on the road. But Donovan heard them.

They were too far away to see anything.

So he slid into the car and softly pulled his door shut. Contemplated turning his lights off, then thought the abrupt change in lighting might be more of a signal to those who came than anything else. The engine started quietly, and he was grateful for the newer car. It was all he could do not to peel out.

No one came out of the woods as Eleri far too slowly coaxed the kid into the back seat. She looked to Donovan in the rearview mirror, questioning him. She would have to trust him a little longer. The men were coming for the boy.

But they hadn't seen who took him.

Donovan hoped.

11

They couldn't take the boy to the Brownwood Hospital; there had already been one patient from the City of God there. Better to spread them out. Eleri tapped Donovan on the shoulder and pointed him toward Hamilton.

She still didn't know how she'd walk in the Hamilton Medical Center with a dirty, bloody grown man and a dirty, bloody boy whose name she didn't even know. She would flash her badge and that would have to do. Westerfield hadn't been kidding when he said NightShade was going to be different.

Eleri had been a field agent and she'd been a profiler, but the arrests had been cleaner than this. Neater. Simpler. Though she'd stayed up all night fueled by candy and caffeine plenty of times, she'd never run an agent through the woods with only a GPS or picked up a broken child on the side of a deserted road at four a.m.

Now that they were all reasonably calm, the roadway before them dark but open, she decided there was work to be done and turned first to the boy. "What's your name?"

"Jonah."

"Where are you from?" She wondered what he would say, especially when he looked out the window and didn't speak.

Cradling his clearly broken arm, he sat still, his head turned away from her. In the dim moonlight, she could barely make out the tracks on his face. Dirt had smeared in, tears made trails, blood crusted at the side of his lip. It looked like he'd been punched in the face, but Eleri held back that judgment. Open mind. Gather evidence. Give a little.

"I'm Eleri Eames, and the man driving is Donovan Heath. You're safe here. We're FBI agents." Slowly she pulled out her badge and placed it in his good hand. Now was not the time to flash credentials like she was kicking ass and taking names.

Jonah flipped the standard black leather cover open and read her info.

Eleri catalogued everything: Jonah could read, easily. Aside from being beaten and broken, he looked healthy, well fed and mentally stable for the situation. "We're about thirty minutes away from the hospital. I can look at your arm if you'd like? And your leg. I'd like to stop some of the bleeding."

Startled, he knocked her badge off his lap and into the footwell. He gasped at the sight of his own leg, his already wide eyes going wider.

"Let me look?" She truly wanted to take care of him. He was just a kid, clearly in a bad situation. If he was another sociopath like Baxter, he was hiding it very well. At the same time, she had to squash the urge to coddle. Jonah was a material witness to something, possibly to the very thing they'd been investigating.

She looked him up and down, checking out his wounds. Nothing appeared animal in origin, it all looked like the results of a standard human fight. "Your leg?"

Nodding, scared, he held the leg up to her. Though she knew it must pain him, he didn't make a sound.

Peeling back the fabric of what she now saw were flannel pajamas, she tried to carefully extricate the wound. Crap. Blood was everywhere. The pants were plaid, but his blood had soaked through the pattern making the fabric a uniform shade of black. She needed plastic to protect the car and collect evidence.

Gingerly, she pulled a clear panel of polyfilm out of Donovan's kit and laid it over her lap and under Jonah's leg.

"He needs water. Get him drinking." The first words from Donovan. He'd been busy watching the rearview mirror and scanning the sides of the road. "He's in shock."

Donovan didn't ask, just diagnosed, but Eleri assumed he was right and dug out a bottle of lukewarm water. It was the best they had. She almost handed it to Jonah, then at the last minute realized he wouldn't be able to get the lid off. Opening it, she pushed the bottle into his hand, making certain he had a firm grip, then pulled back as he shocked her by greedily chugging almost the entire thing.

His thin chest heaved with the exertion. His eyes leaked slow tears that made new tracks in the various substances caking his face. Her heart nearly broke, and she shoved aside her worries and her own memories. But she went to work on the leg, cutting open the seams in the flannel, slowly peeling back the fabric, and trying to ignore the hiss Jonah let out as she did it. The blood was clotting into the cotton—that was good; it meant he wasn't bleeding uncontrollably, but it couldn't feel anything but awful.

His leg was cut, a diagonal from the outside of his calf across the front of his leg. She could see the white of bone through the gap in skin—at least it looked intact. "What did this?"

Maybe that would be an easier question for him to answer.

It was. "Shovel."

Just the one word. Quietly spoken. Followed by a sniff and a blink of memory.

Opening bandages, she laid them on her lap and went for the squirt bottle of saline. She could wash it out a little. "This will hurt."

No response.

Not adding that "this will also collect possible evidence," she washed the deep gash just a little, then pressed the bandages along the fresh red wound. It was worse than she'd thought. The bone wasn't deep at the shin—just slice through the skin and there it was, but his calf was flayed. She could see striations in his muscle. Someone had been trying to stop him and had no desire to stop themselves. Eleri didn't make any comments.

She was reaching to check Jonah's arm, though she was already certain it was broken, when Donovan spoke a second time. "His shoulder looks dislocated. You shouldn't move his arm at all. Just bind it to his torso."

Clear, concise directions.

She followed them and Jonah allowed her. Already handing back the water bottle, empty now, he stayed silent as she completed what must be painful tasks for him.

"Can you tell us where you live?" She tried again. Soft voice. Simple words. Same question asked a different way.

This time he answered.

"I used to live at the City of God."

His phrasing was certainly odd. "And now?"

Again he looked out the window, but this time he shook his head and she strained to hear the single word. "Nowhere."

Eleri's eyes connected with Donovan's in the rearview. Jonah could be a jackpot.

Donovan's voice came through again. It was sterile sounding, straightforward, and she wondered if that was his idea of soothing. He clearly wasn't comfortable. "We're about ten minutes from the hospital. We'll get you right into the ER."

Eleri heard the undertones loud and clear. Ten minutes to get the information they needed now. Then Jonah would—rightly—fall under the care of physicians and possibly surgeons for a good period of time.

"I don't have any money." Jonah shook his head slightly.

Wanting to set her hand on his shoulder in reassurance, Eleri found there was nowhere to touch him without hurting him or being just plain odd. She settled for leaning closer. "We're with the FBI. We'll take care of it. You're in good hands."

Blinking, Jonah looked straight into her eyes for the first time. The grief there would have overwhelmed her had she not dealt with the likes of it herself before. She didn't wait for him to ask for clarification, she just gave it. "It's all covered. You won't owe us anything. You need medical help and you'll get the best of it."

Something passed behind his eyes, something dark, and Jonah stared her down. He spoke with the conviction of a child on the brink of manhood. She remembered it, that moment when you realized you could make your own decisions, when you understood your family's beliefs didn't have to be your own. His words confirmed her perception.

"Joseph doesn't believe in medicine. Only prayer."

She was about to ask what Jonah believed, but she didn't have to.

"I don't believe in Joseph anymore. I'll go."

HER BODY CONVULSED, bringing her instantly awake from depths darker than she wanted to remember. Eleri's eyes flashed open, scanning the area for threats. When she found none, she checked for people who might have seen her thrash herself awake.

The hard chair of the waiting room only emphasized that she was alone. At ten a.m. she would have thought there would be more people here, more surgeries scheduled. But it wasn't a big hospital, and anyone else in surgery right now didn't have anyone waiting in this lonely box of a room with its right-angle chairs.

She wouldn't have thought the nightmares would come here —not in the waiting room, not in a well-lit place, not in the morning. But Jonah had consciously reminded her of Emmaline; it was no wonder her subconscious had run with it.

Eleri dreamed often. Weird, nebulous runs of thought and idea. People morphed one into another and she, the dreamer, thought nothing of it. Her dreams of Emmaline were always starkly different from that. Her sister would stand before her, still frozen at age seventeen while Eleri got older and older as time passed. Emmaline often spoke in relevant sentences, told her secrets. When Eleri awoke she would still hear her sister's voice, feel the brush of breath on her hair, in the shell of her ear.

This time Emmaline had not spoken at all. She simply walked toward Eleri, the two of them in a field, surrounded by old, twisted trees. The wind had kicked up, and Eleri felt it. It grabbed at the cotton fabric of the shirt she wore, a pale-blue button-down made out of T-shirt knit. Her shoes had squished in the mud as she walked toward her sister. And when they met, Emmaline hugged her. Eleri felt it. It was too real.

When she spoke, the voice and the words were real, too, as she asked "It's not a dream, is it?"

Emmaline shook her head and hugged Eleri tighter.

Her sister's dress was white linen, cool to the touch. She was thin, fragile, but strong, her wide mouth smiling—something Eleri had not expected. Her skin was warm, her blonde hair whipped as the winds played with the strands, and Eleri held tight, knowing even if it weren't a dream, it was fleeting.

She fought the tug that worked to yank her from her sister. Grasping tighter, as though she could hold on, stay asleep forever here in the field where her sister was. But in the end, it was Emmaline who ended their hug, pushed Eleri away. It wasn't mean, but it was clear. It was time for Eleri to go. One step back. Her heel squished into mud and dead hay. The loss of touch was deafening, numbing. Her body convulsed. Waking her. Dumping her here.

Sucking in air, Eleri now fought the memories. Just here . . . Emmaline was just here. Eleri would have thought she'd be better at this by now. It wasn't the first time she'd seen, touched, interacted with her sister while asleep. She never got better at it; each waking was as devastating as the one before it. And as comforting.

Footsteps in the hallway made her shake her head, straighten her shirt, and wonder what was available in the vending machine. She was standing, stretching, and trying to remember which corner of the hospital maze held the candy bars and soda when a doctor appeared in the doorway. Stopping all motion, she looked at him.

"Are you Agent Eleri Eames, here with Jonah?"

She nodded. They still didn't have a last name for the boy and she fleetingly wondered if even Jonah knew it.

"He's out of surgery and in recovery now. It will likely be another several hours before he can speak." The doctor was turning to go before she got a word in.

"His arm? His leg?" She cared. Jonah might not tell them anything, or he might be jackpot gold. Either way, someone needed to be concerned about the bruises, gashes and breaks he'd suffered. It pissed her off that the doctor assumed she only wanted to pump the kid as a witness.

"Oh." As though he was surprised. Maybe he just thought she'd be cold because he was. "Well, we set his arm. He has two metal rods aligning it now." In his monotone, he went on explaining the basics of the human skeleton to her as though she had no idea what existed inside her own body. Maybe most people didn't. But he'd get so much further if he'd just ask people to start with. Something like, "How much of this do you already understand?" Eleri would adopt that herself—because there was nothing like listening to Dr. Doldrums here explain that there were two long bones in the lower portion of the arms. Had he looked at her, even attempted to get a gauge on her take of things, he'd have seen the droll expression. Instead, he rolled on.

"Jonah's leg was sutured at three layers. He had a stab wound at his hip that luckily didn't hit anything vital. Another gash on his shoulder—probably caused by the same weapon that laid open his leg, but not a knife. He had seven bruised and four cracked ribs."

The more she listened, the less irritated with the doctor she felt and the more concerned for the child.

The doctor finished his litany and left just moments before Donovan came in. Now he was clean, freshly shaved, and looked rested. Which was more than she could say for herself. "That was about Jonah? Is he going to be okay?"

Scrubbing her face with her hand, she explained everything. "He will be okay, but for now, he's really beat up." That was an understatement. She looked up at Donovan. "Did you see anything? See what he got himself into?"

He shook his head, a troubled expression on his face. Eleri didn't wonder about it. They had back-calculated the time. Given when Donovan started out for the night, Jonah must have suffered his beating sometime either right before or during Donovan circling the compound. They must have soundproofing or else Jonah had never screamed. Wouldn't Donovan have heard something? The path he traced was relatively tight, he wouldn't have been too far away? Or would he?

Her brain circled the thoughts, revisiting the same spots in her questions over and over and not reaching any conclusions. Never hitting a moment where two things came together.

She must have looked as bad as she felt—though not as bad as Donovan had looked earlier—because he dangled the keys to the rental in front of her. "Your turn. I filled up the tank for you, too."

Eleri didn't think she'd ever been so grateful. She only whispered the words, told him the doctor's name and when they expected Jonah to wake, and she shuffled down the maze of corridors. She should be back before Jonah woke, but she was about past the point of caring. She needed a nap, too.

It was nearly an hour between the hospital and their hotel in

Brownwood. That was a good thing—the staff wouldn't overlap. The fewer people who even had an inkling into the investigation, the better. They still didn't know if the City of God people kept to themselves or if they had feelers into the nearby towns.

She was in her hotel room before she knew it. Shaking off the fear that she'd driven the distance mostly asleep, she hit the shower before gravity could pull her onto the bed. She cranked the heat and scrubbed herself in record time. Not thinking much of anything, she crawled between the sheets and disappeared into the void.

The noises pulled her out.

Sucking in air and fighting for reason for the second time in a handful of hours, Eleri was grateful that this nap had consisted only of sleep. This time, it wasn't her sister pushing her out, but the phone call—Donovan—pulling her.

"Yes?" She croaked the word out and checked the time.

Shit. She'd been out for nearly two hours. And she knew what Donovan was going to say before he said it.

"Jonah's awake."

12

Donovan looked at his phone. Eleri said she'd fallen asleep, which meant she would be about an hour getting here. That was good. He couldn't officially question Jonah on his own, and it was probably better if he didn't, given his people skills, but he could find out some preliminary information.

Since they now needed to move locations, Donovan had already packed up his room. Now Eleri would check them out of the hotel in Brownwood. It would add to her time. Jonah—although awake now—was still in recovery and had to be moved to a private room before Donovan could talk to him. There might only be a narrow window to ask his questions without Eleri there. He would need it.

Pacing the waiting room, Donovan was restless and feeling out of his skin. He often felt that way if he didn't get to completely crash after a good run. He'd burned a ton of fuel and eaten three full drive-through breakfasts this morning. Already it was gone and Donovan was itching for a snack machine. This diet was crap and he knew it, consoling himself that he would eat better at home. Or next time. Right now he needed anything with calories. And a chance to talk to the boy.

He'd located and consumed a candy bar, a pack of peanut-butter crackers, and a whole bottle of water before he saw them wheel Jonah by. Discreetly Donovan slipped in behind the team steering the bed and boy down the hall and was right there to ask at the desk when he could go in to see the kid. At the last minute he remembered two important things. Flash badge. Smile.

"Oh!" The nurse almost smiled back. She seemed unsure if he was flirting with her or merely requesting information. He wasn't flirting. He didn't really know how—so he couldn't be doing that. His second expression must have shut her down, because she quickly shuffled papers and then frowned. "Agent Heath, do you have Jonah's last name?"

The *agent* title still threw him some, but especially when he was standing in a hospital. Doctor. In his cells he felt that he should be addressed as "Dr. Heath". It would take some getting used to, and he turned back to the nurse.

"No. I'm not sure he even has one." Putting his hand over the edge of the counter into her field of view, he attempted to get her to look up at him. It worked, and he kept his expression blank. "It's best if people don't think there's anything unusual about him. We found him on the side of the road, and we're trying to learn more. If something is wrong, please let us find out before someone else does."

He put all the emotion he could muster into his eyes. It must have worked because she nodded solemnly. "From the way he was worked over, it looks like you'd best protect him from whatever did that."

"I'm trying." A beat later he realized that maybe he should have said "ma'am." He was in Texas. Then again, he lived in South Carolina and didn't use "ma'am" or "sir" much at all. Well, that might not mean anything since he didn't interact with live people much at all.

Standing in the hallway, waiting, Donovan crossed his arms and leaned against the wall, generally letting it be known that he was ready as soon as Jonah was. That he wouldn't be put off.

Earlier, when he got to the hotel room, the first thing he did was fish the dog collar out from where he'd jammed it in his pocket. The last thing he needed that night was to explain why he'd duct taped the GPS to it. As it was, he spent a good amount of time cleaning the residue. Though the task had eaten into his nap time, it probably considerably lengthened his stay with the FBI. Now he just had to find out what Jonah remembered. Not that he'd be able to ID Donovan, but . . .

The doctor came out of the room at such a clip that his coat billowed just a bit behind him. He stopped short with a curt nod. "You can go in now. Please don't upset him."

Donovan only nodded in return. He always wondered why they told people not to upset the victim. If the FBI was there to interview you when you came out of surgery, you had plenty to be upset about, harsh questions or no.

When he strode into the room, Jonah looked up at him, unsurprised. The kid seemed sad, but accepting, and most importantly, lucid.

Deciding to go for an easy opening, he asked "How are you feeling?"

"Lonely."

Okay, not an easy opening, actually a stupid one. Physically, the kid was obviously feeling beaten up. He was not in good shape to start and surgery was just another kind of beating. Sure it helped more than it hurt, but first it hurt. Emotionally? Well, Donovan had no education to prep him for any of that. "I'm sorry."

Jonah looked out the window, and Donovan was secretly glad the kid ended that part of the conversation. "I was curious what you remember about . . ." How did he put this? "After you went into the woods?"

The blonde head nodded a little. "My arm hurt and I fell a few times. I automatically put my hand out to catch myself. I didn't scream though. I had to stay quiet. I think I might have hurt it worse than it originally was."

His eyes were vacant at the telling. Donovan found himself biting his tongue to keep from saying, "It's better than being beaten to death." Instead he prodded the story along. "Do you remember the puma?"

It was a loaded question. The Academy taught him to ask a question he already knew the answer to—it was a good check for liars. But Jonah wasn't one of them. The kid nodded, then looked at Donovan. "There was a wolf, too. It fought the cat and brought me sticks."

Well, that was a pretty clear memory. Donovan only nodded and let the kid go on.

"I thought I was hallucinating that, because I thought the wolf would fight the puma then eat me itself."

"Actually, you did hallucinate it. Or at least part of it." Now was the time to get the story straight, before Eleri showed up. "I saw the puma, I think I saw the wolf, but I brought you the sticks." He paused, trying to be sure that everything worked before he spoke. "I didn't have anything on me, no supplies, not even a phone. So I brought you the sticks and ran for help."

Jonah nodded, buying it hook, line, and sinker.

Donovan wasn't sure Eleri would be as susceptible to minor rewrites in the story. But he needed her to be.

For the first time in his life it didn't sit well that he was covering things up. Unsure whether this was due to his age, the lack of contact with his father, the switch in his career, or to Eames herself, Donovan only knew that the change was upon him. As certain as he'd been of anything, he knew he had to form some kind of connection. He was living the life his father had laid out for him—a solitary existence with security for his oddness. It was suddenly crystal clear that this was not the life Donovan wanted for himself, but he simply had no idea how to change it. So he was greatly relieved to hear Eames's footsteps coming down the hallway and he made a tentative first step.

Turning to Jonah, Donovan asked something that he didn't need to, started a second conversation here that would have been easily initiated by his senior partner. But who else to attempt his social skills on than this awkward, downtrodden kid?

"Agent Eames is on her way in, do you feel up to answering a few questions?"

Two hours of sleep were not enough for Eleri. Being pulled from the black pit below dreams by the ringing of a cell phone in broad daylight? That didn't help either. But the frothy, frozen coffee did. She figured she was burning calories faster than she was consuming them, even if she was consuming them at an alarming rate right now.

She had to be alert, find out what Jonah knew without scaring him. Tease out any answers he might hold back out of loyalty or terror. It was a tightrope, and she did not have enough sleep to walk it well. The question was: did she have enough coffee?

The phone had woken her, and she'd had the whole conversation with Donovan before she'd fully come awake. Sitting there in the hotel room she'd been confused. Even after she hung up the phone, she thought she was at Foxhaven.

The bed, the sheets were wrong. They didn't feel like Foxhaven. The air was wrong, too. But something pulled her thoughts to North Carolina. She expected the familiar tall windows with tiny panes—ridiculous in a beach house, but state of the art when the house had been designed. She expected wide, slow ceiling fans, but found none. She expected salt on the air and breathed in, instead getting a lungful of heat overlaid with Freon. She wasn't at Foxhaven.

It took her a minute to place that she'd fallen into the bed just moments after showering. That she'd used the hotel shampoo and something in it smelled just like the beach house. It was a mean trick. She'd slept in wet hair, wrapped in the scent—which she was paying more attention to now that Donovan said he could smell *everything*—and she'd been fooled.

Alert now, she wished she was at Foxhaven instead of walking down this long hall, finishing the last of what she would get from this cup. She'd have to throw it away, because that was no way to start an interview, taunting this poor broken kid with what was essentially a milkshake then asking him to relive what was clearly a nightmare so she and Donovan could sieve the details for gold flecks. Tossing the coffee—still half full—into the lone trash can on the corner, she headed for the room the nurse had pointed her to.

She was surprised to see that Donovan had pulled the chair close to the bed, leaning forward, elbows resting on his knees, talking to Jonah. Eleri expected him to be waiting outside for her to start the interview not voluntarily holding a conversation with someone he didn't know.

Immediately suspicious, Eleri tamped down the feeling that seemed to be just part of the job. So she simply smiled and let the conversation go on for a moment without her. Had he started the actual interview? He didn't have any visible recording device—no pen or paper even—so she hoped to hell he hadn't. His next words soothed her.

"Eames is here." He didn't use the "agent" part and she wondered if that was on purpose. Given Jonah's own lack of surname, it might be a good idea. "We can get started."

Stepping fully into the room, she offered a smile amid the bleak situation. "Call me Eleri. Please. How are you feeling after the surgery, Jonah?"

"Like I have metal screws in my arm and enough stitches to

become Frankenstein." He tilted his head as though none of that was any big deal.

Since she couldn't fault his logic, Eleri only nodded. "How is the medicine helping?"

She could see he started to shrug, then stopped. That was enough of an indicator about how it was working and his words only confirmed that.

"I had a concussion, so I can't have any of the good stuff yet. It helps a little, but mostly I'm muddling through." Then he grinned. "Apparently, the concussion was a doozy because I hallucinated a wolf bringing me sticks and fighting off a puma."

Crap. Looking to Donovan, she found there were no better answers there. He must have picked up on the fact that Jonah's hallucinations prior to surgery made him a less credible witness. She would interview him even though his testimony might need a liberal dose of salt.

Donovan shrugged. "I saw the puma, and it did try to eat him. And there was a wolf. Then the kid passed out and I brought him the sticks—I didn't have anything else but to run for help."

So the error in memory was minor.

Still the issue with Donovan "running" for help was still there. Unfortunately, her curiosity was not the priority and now was not the time to address it.

Settling another chair on the opposite side of the hospital bed, Eleri started as gently as she could. Asking Jonah if they could get him to tell his story. Asking if they could record it. Setting up the small recorder unobtrusively, Eleri tried to make the setting as non-threatening as possible. She'd never upgraded from her old recorder, didn't want to use the computer. She wanted small, discrete. She wanted an unhackable copy. Old-school. Private.

Maybe it was the medication or maybe he'd just gotten fed up, because Jonah was a fountain gushing information. He knew the City of God.

His eyes were round. "Yes, I could take you there. But I won't. I won't go back."

Shit.

This led her right into the question she most dreaded. If foster care was Jonah's future direction, then he might clam up, but she didn't know a way around it. So she asked, "Do you have family outside of the City?"

"City people are the only people I know. I've seen and read stories about people who have a single mom and live in a family that's just the mom and the dad and the kids, but I don't know which woman gave birth to me, or which man sired me. No one ever says. We're all one family." He looked out the window, as though the trees wouldn't judge. Neither did Eleri. She'd seen and heard some weird shit in her time, but she never held it against a child. "Once I got older, I figured a lot of it out. I mean, Ruth was pregnant, then she wasn't, then baby Rachel was around. You know, two and two makes four." He shrugged with one shoulder as though it was just a "thing" and her heart nearly broke for him.

She didn't want to mention the government, foster care, any of it. So she shifted the topic. "I'd like to ask you a favor. Could you work with one of our artists? Describe what these people look like? Name them?" It was manipulative, but the wounds still on his body and his lip, swollen more since they'd found him last night, only served to instill that they needed everything he could give them. "There are other children in there. We need to keep them safe."

Jonah nodded at her, his expression grave.

Whatever had happened, his switch had been flipped. He'd been a teen on his way to becoming a full-fledged loyal member of the City of God, and now he was ready to take them down.

His smile came out of nowhere, and Eleri was concerned that he'd cracked mentally, but his words stunned her.

"I don't need an artist. I can draw it. I'm right-handed, so it's okay." He flexed the fingers on his good hand, showing that—despite the bloody knuckles where he'd fought back—he could still function. "I won't go back. But I can draw you everything."

13

Eleri was exhausted. In yet another room that would have looked much like the first except it was clearly set in a smaller town, she felt that bone-deep knowledge that she was "on the road."

It was a traveler's conundrum—the ability to see the country, but probably not enjoy much of it. When people asked her if she'd been to a place, she often answered, "Not really."

"I was on assignment" was a phrase that all kinds of travelers understood. And Eleri understood it now on a cellular level she had managed to forget.

Here, they sprung for the "suite" type rooms. A king bed—a godsend to restless FBI agents—and a desk/sitting area. She'd already taken over the desk; it would have looked like she made herself right at home, except that no Eames ever chose peeled birch furniture. A flat slab of an old tree trunk was planed and polyurethaned within an inch of its life. Four legs from saplings made it a desk. The chair matched and would have been comfortable if she didn't have to look at it.

So many travelers complained that all the hotel rooms looked the same. Not true. This one would not let her forget that she was in Texas.

No mini fridge here. No gourmet coffee shop down the street. It would be even harder to pass unnoticed in this even smaller town. For a moment, Eleri contemplated moving Jonah to Dallas. More people meant more anonymity. It would have to happen, but not today. But it wouldn't be long before all of Hamilton knew the FBI was in their midst.

Jonah had been given a drawing tablet and a series of art pencils. Donovan had gone two counties over to find them. Currently, the kid was sketching away, page after page of the City of God. Donovan had checked in and sent pictures of two of the first sketches. They had asked for a likeness of Baxter first, to use as a reference regarding Jonah's skill.

They shouldn't have just told Jonah okay. What if he'd drawn stick figures? Or even art that was very good, maybe even the best in his whole community, and they couldn't be used to ID anyone? She blamed the lack of sleep for her poor decision making.

But they'd gotten damn lucky. Donovan had checked in on the kid after they posted a police officer on the ward—plain-clothes, in case someone showed up—and they went back to their own rooms. But so far no one had come for him. Each time he visited, Donovan sent her pictures of Jonah's sketches.

The kid was incredibly talented. Which was good for him. He'd need a way to earn a living out in the world.

His sketch of Baxter was spot-on when compared to the few old photos they had of the man. They asked for Ruth next. Jonah had quietly and reverently drawn the woman in three-quarter profile. Intense in her expression, kind in her eyes. The nurse at Brownwood had already used the drawing to match the woman they had treated earlier that month as "Ruth."

Eleri's heart broke for the kid.

According to Jonah, Ruth was dead.

That was what had made him snap. The men in charge of the

City had gotten so mad about Ruth seeking treatment that they incarcerated her upon her return. For three weeks she'd waited, punished before convicted, held in a closet with rare restroom breaks, no light, and little food.

Jonah had started full conversion away from Baxter's teachings then. Clearly forming a sharp logical streak of his own, he'd begun to question the interpretation of the Bible that the man ran his colony by.

In a farce of a trial, Ruth had been publicly convicted, placed in front of a wall and stoned by the citizens of the City of God. There had been no room for appeal.

She had walked miles, ill, seeking treatment, had been returned, cured, and killed for her efforts.

Jonah wanted no part of it. Eleri wanted no part of it either. But it was her job to stop it. They had to find proof. They couldn't go in on the story of a minor—a minor who had clear memories of a wolf bringing him pointy sticks and fighting off a puma for him.

When Jonah protested the stoning of his friend, Baxter turned on him. Wrapped his body around the smaller teen's and picked up rocks, putting them in Jonah's hand, making the boy hurl them at a woman who raised him.

He cried openly when he told them that some of the others turned on him, beating him, breaking his arm, bloodying his lip. It was their sick zeal for Ruth's last moments that distracted his tormentors enough for him to get into the woods.

Donovan had shaken his head. He should have seen or heard some of this as he approached the area, he said. But he had nothing.

Jonah then told them the main building had a basement. And Donovan agreed that worked, in theory.

There was no evidence of a basement, but none against it. They had no body. He didn't detect any of this while he was there, but clearly the City of God was literally trying to stay off the radar. Publicly stoning one of its citizens under the big Texas sky would have gotten the attention of some satellite or other.

Having recorded two hours of Jonah's story, they had to take a different attack. Jonah was drawing faces, places, everything he could produce before he was given the go-ahead for stronger pain medicines. What they needed was hard evidence, something to back up the kid's story.

It was broad daylight and it was time to get out the drone.

She and Donovan rode out in the opposite direction, away from the camp, put the drone parts together, and did a test run. Always a test run. She sent Donovan out in the heat and followed him with the drone. Had him duck under trees, tried to find him. When he took the controls, he danced the machine around the car, seeing how well he could control it, how close he could get. They both agreed that coming drone-to-face with a City of God citizen was not a good idea. While the thing was relatively quiet, coming out in the open or being obvious would blow the whole thing wide open. They couldn't afford that.

So there would be short, furtive runs. Their goal was to gather data quickly and get out without getting seen.

Their plans and good intentions didn't change the fact that they stood in a field by the side of the road. The temperature had climbed into the upper seventies, which wouldn't be too bad, except that the humidity had no respect for life. They had a drone, they had a witness, they had secondhand information. But they had no evidence.

Standing in the heat in her lightweight jeans, she wished they made lighter-weight jeans and shaded her eyes with her hand even though her sunglasses had already turned as dark as they could. And she looked up at Donovan.

"Are you ready?"

DONOVAN PUT his head in his hands. Eleri had called time of death on the drone mission.

They had done their job.

They now had aerial footage of the City of God—or at least of a cluster of camouflaged houses in the location that Jonah and Donovan had pointed them to.

There were a few relatively clear, telephoto shots of faces that matched the drawings Jonah had produced.

And they had managed to not get caught. That was maybe the most important thing.

So they had a group of people in the middle of Texas with no incorporation papers. The land was registered to a Marcus Aebly, but there was no current record of him. He hadn't paid taxes in years, other than the land taxes. He might live in the City of God, or he might not live at all.

They knew Jonah had been in the group, that he ran—bleeding—away from the homestead on Thursday night prior. They had a few matches on faces. But no hard evidence to support any broken laws.

It was frustrating.

Before they gave themselves away, they left.

Eleri had dunked yet another steak fry into ketchup and looked him square in the eye. "It's only a matter of time. We stand out. We're newcomers and not even related to anyone around here. We have frequent trips to the hospital, and you know that second officer won't keep his mouth shut. We have to leave before we tip our hand."

He thought the steady diet of steak fries might be tipping her decision, but he didn't disagree with it. He was a steak and potatoes man, but fried, fried and fried didn't make anyone run well.

Jonah had amicably moved to Dallas. His easy agreement might have been morphine induced, but Donovan didn't look at that too closely. Another agent from the Dallas office was getting involved with Jonah. Agent Bozeman was a nice sort, but again, Donovan couldn't tell much.

Robert Bozeman had made the transition easy for Jonah, coming to Hamilton and escorting him out. He'd even done it wearing khaki shorts and a Hawaiian shirt. Donovan didn't trust people in Hawaiian prints—he never had and didn't know why. But Eleri liked the guy. Said she'd worked with him before and he was good people. Donovan tabled his feelings and let it go.

He was glad to pack up and get out of the deer-head-heavy Inn at Circle T. He didn't like woodland creatures watching him from dead eyes. And he'd rather suffer a generic print of a forest or a lake than a metal cut-out of a praying cowboy, complete with horse, hanging over his bed.

They went home.

Eleri to hers—which he still didn't know where it was. And he to South Carolina.

Though it was five p.m. when the car delivered him to his doorstep, he dragged his luggage inside, showered in his own shower, fell into his own bed, and slept like the dead for twelve straight hours. Then he'd eaten enough eggs to empty a henhouse and walked right out his back door, through the wooden gate and onto national park ground.

And he ran.

Hikers passed him, though he tended to stay away. A bear lumbered across his path once, but they'd stared at each other and went their separate ways. He didn't know how many miles he covered, but he loved every minute. This was his humidity. The smell of loam was his dirt, his area. The cypress knobs he leapt over were ones he recognized. And his heart settled squarely into his chest.

At thirty-four he was just now learning what he was made of, what he wanted, and what he needed. And he'd needed this.

Reaching out was something he started, but he needed to pull back, too. As much as his father had been wrong, Aidan Heath had been right, too. People like them, they had to keep their secrets.

Eleri had called the next morning and they spent the day working back and forth. Donovan dug into Baxter's background more. Eleri worked with the drawings Jonah had done and tried to create matches to missing persons.

She reported back that his drawing of "Charity" certainly could be a ten-year age progression of Ashlyn Dakota Fisk. But it couldn't be definite. Growing changed faces, sometimes dramatically.

Two hours later, Eleri came over the computer system again, this time sending him files as she talked. "What do you think here?"

She sent five files in rapid succession, making him turn off the stupid notification blurp that his computer made. Then she sent a drawing that was clearly Jonah's.

Donovan blinked. The kid had real skills. He was well educated. He wore jeans and a cotton T-shirt. And he grew up in a community that stoned a woman to death for seeking medical treatment. Donovan could not wrap his brain around the incongruity.

After the amazing portrait of Ruth featured her in partial profile, they'd instructed the kid to draw the faces straight on, thus making it easier for him to compare these pictures to the "missing" photos. "Maria Parker. I think we follow this up with the agency that investigated her initial disappearance."

That was his vote.

He could hear Eleri breathe in. "Me too. The age matches. I called and asked Jonah about her arm, and he confirmed she has a mark where her parents noted a burn scar. He wasn't confident that it was a burn, but he also said he didn't know what one looked like. Bozeman is showing him burn marks as we speak."

Donovan cringed. Lucky Jonah. He escaped. But now he was the key to unlocking the City of God and—willing or not—he was going to suffer for it. No kid should have to look at burn marks to identify a missing girl. It wasn't in the job description of being a kid.

It put Donovan's own lonely childhood into perspective. At least he hadn't been kidnapped. At least he hadn't been raised by a cult. At least he hadn't been beaten. Just told not to have any real friends. Just uprooted every time he started to settle in.

Throughout the day, Eleri made preliminary matches on two other missing kids, a girl and a boy, patching the photos through to him for back-up decision making. He worked just as hard though he couldn't say he accomplished as much, but he did find some signs of Baxter after he left Zion's Gate. JHB had been arrested in Pecos County by the Fort Stockton Military Police, but it was a sealed juvenile record. Donovan was having fun chasing that down. Apparently there were better and worse ways for an agent to get information out of other government organizations. Whatever he was doing was not the better way.

Luckily for him, his "boss" said they needed at least one normal work day in this whole mess and said she was signing off at five p.m. sharp and he was welcome to as well.

Not needing to be told twice, he cooked up a pot of rice and hamburger, and watched some mindless TV before heading to bed. It was nearly three a.m. when he woke up. The moon was high and only somewhat thicker than it had been when he was out in Texas.

It was easier to open the gate first and simply run through. His own yard was safer. A naked man was not thought of well in the woods. It nearly hurt his sinuses to pass through the gate at first, but he'd gotten used to it. Three tries it had taken him to figure out how to leave the gate open but protected. Three tries and a family of raccoons and then a bear in his yard and too close to his home. But he didn't want to have to shut the gate.

The lion urine had been a stroke of genius he thought. Obtaining it had been harder, but the Internet being what it was, things could be had. In the end, he'd only had to go as far as his local zoo once a year. He told them the truth: that his yard bordered the national forest and bears liked to wander in. They gave him a mason jar of the stuff for free. He didn't ask how they got it.

The first time he put it at the posts for the gate. That had made his eyes water. He'd learned to put it at the outer corners of his property. On the park side. Putting it out there still killed him; he was nearly blinded when he opened the jar, but there was no way around that. At least the gate was now much safer and could be left open.

He passed through, steered clear of the reeking corner, and headed southeast. The trees above filtered the moonlight, almost as though the beams were the source of the constant high-frequency static and not the crickets and frogs. Deep croaks and the occasional plop of a fish followed the very slow moving river on his left. Donovan tracked it, staying just far enough off shore to not get muddy and to give the mink chances to scurry away from him.

The air here was clean, though he could guess that the Texans thought the same of theirs. He wasn't much for traveling, but his new job would require that. He'd adapt. He always had in the past. Only now he had a home base. He had a safe—well relatively safe—place to run. And though he hadn't yet solved his first case, he had a sense of satisfaction he hadn't felt since the early days of medical school.

He was making a loop but was still far away when the sun came up.

Time to head back and log onto the computer again, get back to finding out what was in Baxter's sealed juvenile records. He aimed straight for home and picked up speed.

He was maybe ten feet from his back gate, forty feet from finishing his run, when he heard it.

The side gate at his house unlatched. The large wooden door

swung open. He hadn't oiled it. He knew that squeak. That meant someone had come into his backyard.

All the maintenance—the meter readings, everything he didn't specifically request—was in the front. On purpose. He trotted through the back gate thinking *who would come in here?*

He knew before he saw.

There she stood, looking right at him. Eleri Eames was planted in his backyard staring like she had no clue what she was seeing.

She didn't.

14

Donovan stared back at Eleri, knowing she didn't recognize him—thankful she didn't recognize him. His mouth was open, his breathing heavy, as he'd run most of the way back.

"Donovan!" She stared at him but hollered as though Donovan would come out and help her.

Well, he couldn't.

Shit.

"Donovan?" This one wasn't as strong, but that made sense since Eleri was clearly no longer expecting her partner to come help. Her hand was reaching for the Glock she held at her side.

Holy shit. She wouldn't shoot him, would she?

Of course she would. If he attacked, moved in an aggressive manner, she'd lay him low. He wasn't inside the gate though. And thinking through his options left him a very short list.

He could stand up, change in front of her and freak her the hell out. Then he could tell her she hallucinated it. He just had to hope that she would stay passed out long enough for him to get some pants on.

Or he could leave. Trot off, wait her out. Eventually—hopefully soon—she'd realize he wasn't home and go do . . .something.

Last option, stare her down. But her gun had slowly cleared the holster and her hand wasn't shaking.

Option two, it was then.

Lowering his head in the universal sign of submission, Donovan backed away from Eleri. She surprised him by stepping forward, only one step to each of his two, so he was gaining distance and she was allowing it. But he was surprised that she was moving toward him. Or he was surprised until she moved like lightning, striking, slamming his gate shut, and making him sigh with utter exasperation when he heard her latch it.

Great. Now he was locked out of his own yard.

Thankfully, he'd installed the latch at the very top of the gate, with the intention that he could reach over and unlatch it from the outside. The one time they had a yard onto woodlands when he was kid, that was how his father had done it. Of course, they'd latched the yard and gone into the woods, hiding and stringing up their clothes. His new method was much easier, lion urine and all. Unless, of course, someone came into your yard and latched your gate.

At least none of the trails came by his house, something else he'd checked before buying the place. It was no good to have random people coming by and seeing what you could do. There was a reason his kind was still considered myth after all these centuries. The few who had come out had been badly treated, and Donovan had no reason to suspect his welcome would be any different today.

He lingered on the other side of his fence, listening for her to leave. But she didn't. Instead he listened as she called him. Left him a message, exasperated that his car was there and his gate was open but he was nowhere to be found. She also told him that she saw a wolf coming into his yard and maybe he shouldn't leave the gate open, then ended with, "I've been trying to get a hold of you since six a.m."

He could almost hear her ire as she hung up on his voicemail.

Surely she would leave now.

But she didn't.

Instead, she stopped, listened, and called him again. This time she waited through his message and only said "Test" before signing off. Then she stayed very still.

Why did he have to join the FBI?

She heard his phone beep inside the house. So she knew his car was there, his gate was open, wild animals were trying to get into the yard, and he was gone without his phone. It all made perfect sense to him, but it wouldn't to her. So of course she was banging on his back door, hollering out for him.

When that didn't work, she worked her way around the house. He could hear her checking the window latches, the door-knobs. He locked them. He lived in the country where most people didn't, but he'd seen enough strange deaths and enough people killed by someone just walking right in, that he locked his doors and windows. Always.

Despite her attempts, Eleri didn't find a way in. She only found no running water—clearly he wasn't in the shower where he couldn't hear her. No loud TV or music—he wouldn't come running to the door not having heard anything. And it didn't help that when she circled back to his car she would see that he hadn't moved it since he got home.

He knew she was looking in windows. He just knew it. He was also pretty certain that his time was limited before she popped out a pane of glass and broke her way in. He was at plan D.

So he backed into the woods, far enough away that she wouldn't see anything and he sat on the ground. It was the easiest way out. One leg at a time, he popped joints, pulled muscles into their new locations. Rolled his shoulders back into the places they were expected. As he put himself back into proper form he watched as the hair virtually disappeared.

The rest of it, he'd figured out. It was really just minor variations in skeletal structure—most mammals had the same basic skeleton and similar musculature—along with a specific set of double-jointedness. All of that made perfect sense. It was logical, clear. Weird, sure. But nothing amazing. The hair still got him though, and he ran his finger over the scar on the side of his thigh. In medical school, he'd headed into the lab, taken a needle full of Xylocaine and a scalpel and took a biopsy of his own skin. He'd stitched it up and tried to make the hair work. But he never could. He dissected it. Found the hair shafts unusually long compared to his dermatology texts, mostly buried. And the best he could figure was that it operated like piloerection—hair moving to stand on end in the cold—in normal humans.

None of the rest of the myth was true. It was, in fact, baldly ridiculous. And the truth was that he was now walking through the woods, bare-ass naked. He wanted to close his eyes and sigh. He wanted this to not be happening. He debated using her first name or her last.

"Eleri!" If he was going to ask her to throw his pants over the fence, a first name basis seemed inevitable.

ELERI WAS KNEELING beside his car, growing increasingly alarmed when she heard Donovan call her name. Relief deluged her, entirely out of proportion to the situation. But in her world, missing partners were not acceptable. Missing people triggered severe emotional reactions. And his car hadn't been moved in several days. Since she'd spoken to him at five p.m. yesterday she knew he was alive then, and healthy, but that was nearly twenty hours ago.

"Donovan!" she called back to where she'd heard the sound—

the other side of the tall fence. She looked up at the top of it and gauged it to be eight feet tall. Shit. The wolf. "There's a wolf on that side."

She was already running for the back gate, ready to reach up as high as she could to flip the latch and let him in. "It walked in toward the gate, toward me. It might be rabid—"

"Don't open the gate!"

Was the wolf over there with him? "Do you want my gun?"

She didn't open the gate; she didn't panic. She was trained for harsh, strange situations, and she was trained to listen to what her fellow agents said and react as a team, not as a lone, panicking person assuming whatever they thought was best for the situation should be done. It had been one of the hardest parts of training—to hold fire when another agent said so, to not bust down a door when your team was in peril on the other side. But she'd learned. And now she paused, waiting for further instructions from the person who could see the situation on his side of the fence.

His voice was remarkably calm. "No wolf." There was something sardonic in the tone, but she still called back.

"Keep an eye out. He was right here." Some of the tension that had snapped back into her at his sharp command began draining again. "What do you need?"

His request surprised her. She'd expected maybe a rope or help climbing over, she really didn't know. But not what he said.

"There's a key to the back door here." His hand appeared over the top of the fence, holding the key. No ring, no identifying marks, he must have carried it with him. But when he dropped it to her at her word, she found it cold to the touch. "Go into the mudroom and bring me the jeans there? Throw them over the fence."

Her mouth opened. Thank God she'd already caught the key, because if he'd dropped it right now it would have fallen right past her. "You're out there running around in your underwear and you won't walk into your own yard?"

No, that made sense: she was kind of his boss. Not really the boss, but his ranking officer so to speak. Turning to walk away, she almost missed his next words.

"Nope. No underwear."

Holy shit. "You're running in the woods in the altogether?" Her brain did not process that and her mouth opened, letting out the first thought that came to her. "What about ticks!?"

He laughed, deep and rusty, and though she'd heard it before, she got the feeling that it wasn't a common sound. "Ticks and mosquitoes don't like me."

"Well, I wish I had that problem." She muttered under her breath. Then again, even if they didn't, no one was going to find her running naked through the woods. "Give me a damn minute." She was fetching pants for her new partner. Stranger shit had happened, but not that often.

The key slid easily into the lock and luckily a pair of jeans, neatly folded, lay right in the doorway. Swooping them up as she leaned over, Eleri turned in one motion and marched back to the fence. She was not opening it. "I'm throwing them over now. Watch out for that wolf." Then she muttered, "Hope he doesn't eat anything important to you."

He laughed again, this time a chuckle as his hand came over the top of the fence, lifting the latch and letting himself in. "I'm very familiar with the wildlife here. It's why I moved here."

"So you can run around naked on national park land?"

She was surprised when he looked up over her head and thought about it, then simply said, "Yes." After a pause, he added, "It's a bit of an old family tradition."

"Well, you make sure your family is wearing pants before I meet them."

Unable to help herself, she added, "You know, wild animals approaching humans or clearly human areas is a sign they aren't mentally stable. Possibly even rabid. And you're out there with that thing, with . . . everything available for bites." She waved her hand up and down at him, realizing she'd dug herself a hole with the direction her sentence was heading. "Anyway."

He turned then to close the gate and latch it. In only his jeans, his bare feet melted into the grass and he seemed completely at home. "I usually walk in the gate, in the back door, and right into the shower. Key?"

The change of topic startled her from her examination. But she handed the key to him, not paying attention as he put it back in some secret spot at the top of the fence. "Donovan."

"What?" He was turning to face her, but she put her hand out, turning him, keeping his back toward her.

"Your scapulae, they're both larger and narrower than normal." She was almost reaching out to touch them, forgetting he was a person and not a specimen. He looked normal—right— at first glance. Anyone else wouldn't know it, but she was trained in forensics and biology. She knew the human skeleton, how it worked together, how it gave evidence to the life lived, how it decomposed. And she was seeing so many tiny aberrations in him. Eleri couldn't stop looking.

The curvature of his spine was shy on the lower portion of the usual S. It was within human range but definitely at the end of the spectrum. His neck muscles were relatively thick, his jaw longer than average—that was clearer now from this angle—his hips narrow for a man of his height, but he had a taller hip girdle than normal.

She was still frowning, examining, when he turned around. No longer laughing or even smiling, his ink-dark eyes looked at her sternly. "Are you done?"

"I'm sorry, I—" There was nothing she could really say. Something about his eyes was bothering her now, too, though she couldn't place why. But more than that, he was angry and she'd caused it. "I'm sorry."

"Why are you here, Eames?"

No more "Eleri" then. Sure it was "Eleri, throw me my pants," but one comment about your scapulae and it was Eames again. Her brain sharpened. She'd been distracted, but she was here prowling around his house, pissing off her naked-in-the-woods partner for a reason.

"There's another City of God escapee. She calls herself Charity. And she's asking for Jonah."

15

For a moment, Eleri just stood at the one-way glass and peered through at the girl sitting huddled on the chair. She was shivering beneath a blanket despite the raging heat of the day and the moderate interior of the Brady City Police Department.

The municipal building was a squat thing, the bricks multi-sized and at one time quite the trend. The single story, flat-topped design made the building look as though the heat had pushed it down, stunting its growth. The girl inside looked like she was getting pushed down, too.

The police officer handling her case was a sweet, slightly pudgy woman with abnormally bright red hair. Eleri liked her within moments of arriving. Detective Cassa Brinks wouldn't let them see Charity any closer than the window into the holding room, her fierce protection of the girl evident in every move. She did let them see that the department had already provided drawing paper, a stuffed animal, the blanket, ice water, juice, and a meal—most of which Charity hadn't touched.

Cassa shook her head. "She won't eat and I keep hoping she'll just fall asleep. She's clearly exhausted."

Eleri positioned herself strongly despite being the shortest one there. She wasn't taking over the investigation, but she was firm that she needed information. Hoping to keep everything friendly, she asked, "Do you have time to talk to us about what you know?"

"Of course." The woman led them down a short hallway and into a room designed more for conferences than for holding people. It took a minute for Eleri to place that this building held more than just Police Services and this was a joint-use room.

"I'm sure you'll want a copy of the file we already have started, Agent Eames, Heath." The red hair bobbed as she nodded at each of them briskly.

"Please, call me Eleri. This is Donovan." It was the least she could do, since the other woman had told them to use her first name before she even shook their hands. "And yes, anything you can share is helpful."

Cassa carried the file along with her, but Eleri could see it was woefully thin. The detective said they fingerprinted the girl and kept a scan of the prints on file. When Donovan raised his eyebrows at the standard fingerprint card—old-school, paper-and-ink style—the officer explained. "Our chief will scan the cards, but says ink is still the best capture system."

While some of the light-scan programs were finally getting better, for use in a situation like this, the Brady Department had it right. "Is the original card headed to the AFIS team?"

Cassa nodded. They'd given it to someone who would run it through the national database and hand check the ink against possible matches the computer spit out. "Since she's a minor, we gave it priority."

Given their location, they had pulled someone away from a serious backlog to match the prints. That person was likely three counties away which meant someone was driving it over there. A lot of the specialists swore by the old ink-and-card system, said they could be far more confident of a match with a real print. The timing sucked, but it often did, and a child huddled under a blanket at a police station with only a first name to go by deserved the time to get it right.

Cassa offered them drinks, and Eleri's original intent was to give a blanket "no, thank you" but Donovan beat her to it. "We're fine."

Out of the corner of her eye, Cassa poured several cups from a standing water cooler. "You should drink even if you don't want any. This heat will dehydrate you faster than it feels like it will." With that, she handed them the water they had already refused.

Not able to not drink it now, and knowing Cassa was right, Eleri wondered if they'd passed the required small talk and could get down to business. Pulling out one of the wheeled, padded chairs, she made herself at home and leaned forward. "Can we ask how you found her?"

"Of course, but I have to ask to see your badges first." She acted as though it was a shame she had to do so, but Eleri appreciated the check. She pulled her holder from her purse as Donovan was pushing his across the table. They had different models, hers with the actual gold badge on the outside, ID and commission on the inside. His was all interior, though both were black leather. Eleri wanted a red case, or something less drone-like, then she learned that people don't respect an FBI agent with any sense of style.

As they sat there, Cassa Brinks inspected the badges and radioed the front desk. In just a moment the office girl came forward, snapped pictures, and returned to call in to the Dallas field office to check on them. Again, Brinks looked chagrined at the procedure. "Protocol."

Offering a smile, Eleri only said, "I appreciate it. It's the way things should always be done. Don't apologize."

A return smile was the only segue before the woman launched head first into the story. "I input her to the system. I was out with an officer in a black and white, when this truck driver pulled up and stopped us. Said the girl had flagged him down outside Mills."

Donovan held up a hand then, a cross between a classroom question and an interruption, "Where is Mills?"

With deliberate movements and a tug at her pants, Cassa stood and moved to the cabinets at the side of the room. Unlocking one with a key she produced from seemingly nowhere, she pulled out a tablet and turned it on. In a moment she had an interactive map up and was showing Donovan all the small towns between. "He says he picked her up about here." She pointed. "And that she said she wanted to go to Austin, but he was headed this way. She decided having a ride was more important than going the right direction."

Brinks then opened the manila file and showed some of the slim pickings inside. Pictures of Charity's face, arms, legs. All bruised. Eleri's heart squeezed even though it shouldn't. Getting beaten was bad enough, but treated like meat to get photographed by the police—officers she may not trust, strangers definitely—that was often just as bad. Eleri wanted to check the wounds. While they were fresh, one could glean all kinds of information, but it could be as invasive as the original round of photos, and the girl didn't know Eleri from Adam. Instead, she asked the question she could. "Did she say where she got these?"

Nodding sagely, Cassa showed another set of photos. Fists, held out side by side, large fingered with faded tattoos stretching across knuckles that were arthritic but intact. "Driver's hands. Girl and driver both say she had the injuries before she got in the car. She had a bad headache, and we had a doctor check her for head wounds but found none. The trucker waited around to be sure she was okay and we photoed him as evidence. He agreed readily, knowing that a photo now saves him trouble in the future. Both said he's the one what talked her into coming to an officer."

Donovan nudged her, but she ignored it. If they started doing hand signals or that head-tilting-thing to signal each other, it would only look bad. When he nudged her a second time she nudged back to stop him, keeping her attention on Detective Brinks. "So you brought her in, turned the driver loose?"

"Yes, we had all his information and no grounds to hold him. He had a delivery, had really gone out of his way already for the girl."

"Of course." Eleri nodded in agreement. She wanted to come across as sincere and she hoped that was easier because she was. Despite the accent and the occasional word misuse, Cassa Brinks was sharp, though Eleri guessed the officer was often underestimated. "What else have you learned from your interview?"

Brinks also seemed to know that she was playing with the FBI, and she wasn't going to be able to leverage her knowledge against theirs; there was no quid pro quo expectation here. At least she didn't seem to mind. "Only that she calls herself Charity —says she has no last name, none of them does—and that she wants to see her brother Jonah from the City of God."

Giving one of those exasperated blinks, Cassa missed the shock on Eleri and Donovan's faces as she rubbed her eyes and continued. "She's been here five hours now, won't say anything. Someone beat her up pretty bad. She's clearly a kid though she doesn't know her exact age—says they don't celebrate birthdays." A head shake punctuated the next line. "We don't have a lot of folks from those religions in this part of the state. You know, the God-doesn't-like-birthdays kind. We're really more of the God-loves-a-good-party-and-a-good-beer kind of people. . . . But we can't help this girl if she won't help herself. Keeps asking for Jonah."

Eleri and Donovan didn't speak. Donovan hadn't spoken the whole time and she didn't know if he was listening, sniffing the people and hallways, or just tired and checked out. She, at least, was trying to get Cassa to continue.

The detective shrugged again, pulling her shirt tight with the motion. "I asked her everything I could think of. If she knew that woman, Ruth, the one that come in about two months ago? Charity didn't answer, but she stiffened real bad, so she knows something she's not telling me. I asked her if Jonah was that kid over in Hamilton, got beat up real bad and saw wolves and she seemed really excited—"

"How did you know about the kid in Hamilton?" Donovan suddenly joined in, leaning forward, pushing, coming on stronger than Eleri would have liked. While she thought she already knew the answer, she waited, wanting to hear it from Cassa.

A sweet, pitying smile crossed the almost too red lips. "Where are you from, sweetheart?"

Eleri grinned. She didn't think anyone had called Donovan "sweetheart," maybe ever.

"Just outside Columbia, South Carolina. Why?" He seemed taken aback that his home place mattered.

"Where'd you grow up then?"

"All over." He was still frowning, though Cassa was now nodding and clearly understanding his lack of comprehension.

"Well, honey, there are no real secrets in a small town." She splayed her pink-painted nails on the table in front of her and leaned forward. "We don't have to find out what happened— everybody already knows—we just have to prove it. We're all related, too. My sister's in Hamilton, works as a nurse there. My brother's a cop in Dallas—left us for the big city, but I'm detective here and he's still on patrol. Seriously, the best kept secret in the state is that I'm not as dumb as I look."

Donovan nodded slowly and Eleri put together what she'd known but not acted on: there were no hiding places. Bringing in the FBI made people speculate. Bringing in the locals meant soon everyone knew.

He asked what Eleri wanted to. "So why doesn't anyone know about the City of God?"

Cassa sat back, sighing, shaking her head at that one. "None of them are local from what I can tell. They don't venture out, don't call their mamas, and don't celebrate birthdays."

"Apparently, they also beat their kids." Donovan was clearly disgusted, not with the detective, but the situation. Eleri hoped Cassa could distinguish that herself. Her next statement made it seem like she could.

"Is that what happened to Jonah, too?"

Eleri bumped his knee with hers under the table. Senior officer, she would be called to the mat for leaks in information. She leaned forward, too. "Seriously, Cassa, how well can you keep this information under wraps? I mean, if we give you something to follow, can you dig without letting other people know what you know?"

The bright smile burst into guffaws of laughter. "I planned my Daddy's fiftieth birthday party, brought in people from five states, and he didn't know dick about it. Oh, and he's the mayor of Temple, two towns over. My sister's husband came to me to find out what engagement ring she wanted. I didn't know, but I got it out of her and she still had no clue a proposal was coming. And my chief is the only one who's seen my test scores. If you need more than that, well, I can't give it. But I understand that helping these kids takes priority over bonding with my sisters." She sat back, apparently resting her case.

"Yes. That's what happened to Jonah. Only Jonah was worse: broken arm, cut on his leg down to the shin bone." Reaching into her bag, she made a decision to tell more, and she made it based on her gut instinct about the woman. As she grabbed one of the photos that had slipped to the bottom, she saw that Donovan had leaned her way a little, bringing his hand near and giving her a surreptitious thumbs-up, though she didn't know why. Popping back up, Eleri held her arsenal in her hands. Cassa was trustworthy. Eleri *knew* it, even if she didn't know how she knew. "Jonah told us about Charity, as well as other adults and children there. He's an amazing artist —we didn't need to bring in a professional." Eleri smiled. "The kid has a career ahead of him. This is his drawing of Charity."

Sliding it across the table, she watched the detective's eyes light up.

"Oh, wow. He is good. She's beautiful."

Eleri was beginning to wonder if that wasn't part of the problem. Maybe Baxter liked pretty kids. Some were born there, some were brought in, but she scrubbed the thought from her brain and stayed focused. "This is Jonah's drawing of the man who leads the place." She pushed that one over. "We believe this is Joseph Hayden Baxter. He was raised outside Nolan in a small cult called Zion's Gate. We met with them and they seem open and friendly."

"A good cult?" Cassa's eyebrows disappeared under all that red hair.

With a sigh, Eleri gave the best answer she could. "The best we can tell, yes. They gave us a full tour, cleanly answered our questions. There's no sign of abuse, they educate all their kids. And we've tracked down a few people who left and they tell much the same stories. But Baxter's parents told us two people died and one went missing while Joseph lived there. He left when he was sixteen."

That bit of bad news made Cassa jerk back. "Straight up sociopath?"

"Looks that way. Until the third incident, they didn't have a clue. But with the third, and his subsequent disappearance, they started putting some of the coincidences together."

Eleri made another decision. She pushed her print copies of Jonah's art across the table, the whole stack. "You can keep these, but don't share. Not with anyone—I'm trusting you to keep it to yourself. Anything you can find will help."

There was a moment of silence as Cassa tapped her finger on

the top drawing, a pretty landscape of the hidden houses, but she didn't look under it at the other sketches.

Eleri had done what she could here, so she pushed the chair back. "We'd like to take Charity with us."

It was couched as a request, but they all knew it was a statement made with the full authority of the FBI behind it. "We'll take her to see Jonah. But we'll have to question her more first, before they see each other. If you'd like to come along, if you think you can help, we'd like that."

"I don't know what my chief will say about that." Cassa shook her head and Eleri understood. There was old blood—both good and bad—between local precincts and national divisions.

"I can make it an order if that helps?"

Cassa shrugged. "Let's see what Charity says. Lord knows I haven't slept in a full day. So if she's willing to go without me, I'm happy to end this damn shift."

Eleri understood that one far too well, so she just smiled and nodded.

They rearranged, packed up papers. Brinks put her copies of the sketches into a file folder so she could walk them down the hall without flashing them. Charity's file was duplicated, and Brinks explained what would be happening, but the girl stood and went to Eleri and Donovan of her own will. She opened the door and stared them in the eyes. "You'll take me to see Jonah?"

"Yes." Then Eleri went with honesty, knowing how it would ultimately help. "But first you'll have to tell us everything that happened. If you don't, we can't take you to Jonah."

"Is that blackmail?" The girl stepped back.

"No." The voice startled both the females. Donovan had stepped in and Eleri figured he had a reason, so she let him go on. "We need to have a statement from each of you. If you both tell the same story, it helps us show that you are innocent and that the bad guys are bad. It helps the evidence if you two don't have a chance to get together and make up a story first."

"I wouldn't do that." She didn't seem offended or anything, just stated it as fact. Though looking in her eyes, Eleri was more convinced than ever that she was looking at Ashlyn Dakota Fisk. She wondered why the girl didn't tell anyone about that name; surely she remembered it.

While Eleri tried not to stare, Donovan stayed on point. "I believe you, but the protocol is this way so we can prove it. After your story—which will probably take several hours, because you know a lot more than you may even think you do—we'll take you to see Jonah. I promise."

Oh, "promise" was a bad word, Donovan. Eleri smiled to cover the sigh that wanted to escape, but all those concerns were diverted when Charity said "Okay!" and grabbed the stuffed animal and the blanket and headed out the door.

Nearly two hours later, they were on the road, Charity in the back seat, answering questions on record, when Eleri's phone rang. Holding up a finger and turning off the recorder, Eleri took the call. It was Brinks.

"This Ruth woman. I know her."

16

Donovan drove the three-and-a-half hour trip to Dallas mostly staying quiet. He listened to Eleri talking with Charity in the backseat. The recorder on, his partner asked her questions, figuring the car was as good a place as any.

This way they could finish the interview and get her reconnected with her friend as soon as they arrived. Agent Bozeman had been alerted of the development but instructed not to tell Jonah of Charity's arrival. Eleri and he agreed the best thing was to see how the kid reacted to the new addition. They both expected it to be a welcome arrival, but how this meeting went would tell a lot about the two.

Charity handled the interview well, answering questions clearly and without Jonah's innate outrage. She was quieter, more accepting of her fate.

He heard Eleri asking if the girl had ever had another name and noted the pause that followed. He was confident the prints would match Ashlyn's and he wondered how it would feel to tell the Fisks their daughter had been found after five years. And how it would feel to tell Westerfield they still had nothing about Jennifer Cohn.

The phone call from Cassa Brinks had changed things.

Unfortunately, the detective didn't remember exactly where she'd seen the woman, but she knew her as a friend, years ago. The woman who now called herself Ruth had been much younger, giving Cassa difficulty placing the memory. But she assured them she hadn't ever lived out of the area, even for college, so Ruth had been close. She would, of course, tell more when she remembered it. Donovan thought it would likely pop into her head about three a.m. when he was good and asleep.

Eleri went back to interviewing Charity, who thought for a while, then said yes, she'd once been called "Ashlyn" but had been told if she ever uttered the name again, she would die. Then she turned to chatting cheerfully again, painting a story of a happy community, growing vegetables, getting raised in a group of kids, going to school, working hard, building, weeding, worshiping.

But lately—she couldn't really tell the time, a year? Maybe two?—Joseph had been getting meaner. The punishments for infractions had gotten harsher, the justice swifter. Then Jonah had started gathering the children.

Donovan couldn't believe what he was hearing. Baxter ran the cult and Jonah was starting a cult within the cult. From Ashlyn's telling, the kids were all turning to Jonah for leadership.

She said Jonah believed in a kinder God. He cited the Bible as being more full of love than hate, that God would not punish them for being too good to each other, but he would punish them for judging, for meting out judgments that were God's and God's alone to give.

Donovan had never had a bible, a church, a group. He saw the value in the community and the support, but didn't understand the rest of it. He was a man of science and strangeness but couldn't maintain a grasp on the idea that one could blindly follow something intended to lead people in primitive cultures and assume that it applied today. To his way of thinking that was like reverting to a Mesozoic-era cookbook, eating found plants, only cooking over open fire, and drinking unfiltered water. Then again, he'd been hearing of people doing exactly that. He was equally baffled by both.

His own longing for a community was the only thing he could pinpoint, that maybe the group was so wonderful it was worth following any law to be accepted. As a man who'd never been accepted by any real group, he tried not to judge. He had no meter for it.

It was clear Charity loved Jonah and worshipped at his feet before Baxter's.

Was that part of what had led to Jonah's more severe beating? That the kids were following him rather than Baxter? What little psychology Donovan had studied didn't give him any insight.

Eleri would know more, reams more, but he couldn't ask with the girl in the car.

Charity told how she was held in the basement after Jonah escaped. Baxter became convinced she helped Jonah—and she had, but she now readily admitted to lying to her leader about it.

She also knew she was held in the open because Baxter believed that a variety of aids had been snuck to Ruth during her incarceration, and he believed that keeping Charity where all could see her would reduce that. According to Charity, it really hadn't. The women brought her extra food. The kids came and asked her about Jonah. Any time she wasn't where Baxter or one of his men would see and report it, someone was helping her out: feeding her, walking her to the restroom, playing games. Then Sarah, one of the women, told her Baxter wanted to make an example of her, and in the next hour, the man had come in and beaten Charity for her insubordination. She was released from her punishment and the others were told not to help her in any way, just let her hurt. So the girl had limped to her own room, as the others stared.

Donovan's heart twisted with the thought of this poor child, now going on fourteen, on this ultimate walk of shame. Broken, bloody and bearing the weight of the grief of her community. He braced himself for the story to get worse.

Instead, she said the women packed her a bag, gave her food, extra socks, the jacket, money and told her what to ask for when she found someone to help. They said one of the men knew Jonah was first in Brownwood and had later been moved by the FBI. The women picked Austin for Charity, thinking the men would expect her to go to Jonah first, which meant Dallas or San Antonio, where the nearest FBI offices were located.

Donovan cringed at being predictable, but Charity had played it smart. Got herself into a police department that was far enough away to protect her and was capable of getting her to Jonah without leading Baxter and his men to the boy. Someone inside the cult, an adult or group of them, was playing a dangerous game and Donovan wondered when they would push the next kid to the border and what it would take to trigger that. He wondered if the next kid would make it.

Eleri managed to achieve quite a bit on the trip. She convinced Charity to eat something and got them to stop for a late lunch-slash-early dinner. Donovan was soon convinced the girl had a hollow leg.

Unfailingly polite, she still scarfed down the meal, offered to pay for her own ticket, and said, "I haven't had a burger like this, ever. Thank you."

Only his partner had any scraps of food left on her plate by the time they paid the check. Then they loaded back into the small car and were set with a recording and notes of everything but the initial abduction or confirmation of Ashlyn Fisk's identity by the time they pulled up to the safe house where Jonah was being kept.

Agent Bozeman was on duty, probably on purpose and he opened the front door before Donovan even put the car into park. Recognizing them on sight now, he didn't make them flash badges. Still, while they got a more formal greeting, Charity got a winning smile and a sweet introduction.

Bozeman turned on charm Donovan wouldn't have guessed he had. "Us agents have been talking and we've decided it's best and safest to keep you here with Jonah."

The girl's excitement pulsed through the air and Donovan could almost feel the wave hit him.

"He's here?" Her voice went breathy, her heart floating up into her eyes.

Telling her no would be like kicking a puppy, but Agent Bozeman simply reached for her hand, as though she were a small child and not a girl on the brink of womanhood. "Yes." Leading her inside, he left Donovan and Eleri trailing. "And he doesn't know you're coming. It's a surprise."

Again, Charity became more excited and tagged behind Bozeman until Jonah came into view. He was sitting at the main table, this time working in watercolors and obviously in the zone.

"Jonah?" Her voice was tentative, but the kid's reaction was not.

Despite the crutches at his side, he stood sharply, clearly recognizing her voice. Hobbling to her, he engulfed her in an embrace the likes of which Donovan had never seen before and certainly had never experienced.

He wondered if the pinching in his chest was jealousy.

DONOVAN RODE BACK to Hamilton under a wide dark sky. Eleri didn't let him drive this time, so he laid back the passenger seat, and simply agreed with what she said the infrequent times that she spoke. He let his mind wander and contemplated what he'd seen, what Charity had spoken of.

He considered himself an introvert and figured that explained his lack of social skills and his subsequent lack of desire to develop any. But Eleri and this whole FBI job were opening holes in his theories about how his life should be.

Deep in his own thoughts and tangled in the conundrums coming to light, he was surprised when Eleri turned the car into a chain restaurant for a late dinner. Then again, maybe he'd agreed to this at some point. Oh well, he wasn't against another burger.

He found himself seated at a dark wooden booth across from his partner, who was looking at him expectantly. He had to ask, "What? What did I miss?"

"I suspect the entire last two hours."

Nodding sagely, he added, "Did you say anything important?"

"Nah." She shook her head, and when the waiter appeared a half moment later, she offered her entire order and then looked at Donovan expectantly.

He pointed to the most appetizing picture and said "A Coke, too, please." Then wondered what he had ordered. It looked like chicken. At least chicken wouldn't hurt him any, not after the baconed and sauced double burger he'd had at lunch when Charity had attempted to out-eat him.

"Are you paying attention now?"

Nodding yet again, he focused. It was the only appropriate thing to do.

"So if Cassa knew Ruth a while ago—" She was cut off when her phone rang. "Well, speak of the devil... Cassa?"

A fleeting, furtive movement of her eyes indicated she was checking to see who could hear and Donovan did the same. By the time his gaze landed back on the table, Eleri was putting the phone on speaker and placing it in the middle of the space. "Cassa, you've got Donovan on the line, too."

"Oh, hi Donovan." There was only a slight pause then, "I remembered where I knew Ruth. We attended several years of college together. I was straight out of high school and she was an older student but our writing classes always seemed to overlap. She was in a theology program while I was in CJ."

At the initials, Donovan frowned at Eleri, who mouthed back to him "Criminal Justice."

Cassa continued on, unaware of their brief exchange. "Part of the problem was that she wasn't Ruth then. She was Robin. Robin Jennings."

"You remember her last name?" Eleri smiled and Donovan could hear the return smile in the other woman's voice.

"See? No one credits me with the smarts I've got. I have a great memory. Get a pen." And she proceeded to give them the dates she'd overlapped with Robin Jennings at the college. She gave the name of the school, the location, two professors they shared, and even the name of a dean who had been in position when they attended and was still there. "I hope that helps you out."

"I'm sure it will."

Eleri hung up with a smile as their drinks arrived along with chips and salsa that Donovan didn't expect. Grabbing a chip, Eleri grinned at him. "You really should pay more attention. You said you liked it really spicy, right?" She scooped a disturbing amount of salsa into her mouth and nearly moaned at the taste.

No. He didn't like anything spicy. Not too much anyway. His sense of smell and taste was too sharp to handle it. He was stuck watching while she ate several more bites before taking pity on him. "It's mild, Donovan." She sighed and scooted the bowl closer to him. "I know you don't like spicy foods."

Yeah, he should pay closer attention. It was bad form and she was his boss. He almost apologized but instead dug into the chips, suddenly ravenous again after the long day.

The food arrived and they ate in silence for about five minutes before Eleri looked up at him. There was something feral in her gaze, and he was bothered before she spoke, but not as bothered as he was after she asked her question.

"So Jonah saw a wolf, a pure-black wolf, that delivered pointy sticks to him at the roadside. Sure, he was crazy and out of it, but his delusion is quite clear in his head. You said you saw the wolf, too; what color was it?"

No, he definitely did not like where this was going. But he shrugged, tried to play it off. "I don't really remember, I was frantic. There was a puma."

"But really, what color was the wolf?"

He shrugged again even as he remembered not to do anything three times. That bit of information from the Academy stuck with him; it was from the "how to spot a liar" class. "I don't know. Dark? Wolf colored?"

"See, the thing is, I then saw a wolf at your back gate. A wolf you didn't seem very worried about at all."

Shit. He had a brain fart. He forgot for just a moment in his attempt to cover the issues with Jonah, that she had seen the wolf, too.

"The wolf I saw was black. All black. Just like Jonah said." She picked up another chip and began playing with the salsa more than she seemed to be getting ready to actually eat it. "So I got online—"

Immediately, he interrupted, wondering if his redirection would work at all. "Oh yes, the Internet, source of all things reliable."

It didn't.

"I trust the Internet on this. There are no black wolves in this area. So I asked Jonah to draw me what he saw."

Donovan swore to himself. This was not good.

Eleri continued, "There aren't any black wolves that look like what I saw—which is identical to what Jonah drew for me. In fact, there aren't any in all of North America . . . or anywhere."

17

E leri slept hard that night. It was their last night in Hamilton, and if she had her way it would be her last night ever in a room with antlers. Despite the fact that her father was a hunter and despite the fact that she ate meat herself and had no problem with it, she did not cotton to dead things as decor. Even the furniture looked like trees that had been slaughtered and taxidermied.

Although she was pretty certain the antlers were resin and not real, it was still too much to take and she was shocked she slept so hard with the remains of the dead around her.

While she slept hard, she did not sleep well.

In the beginning she was back in the hospital. The nurses handed her medication after medication and told her she was "healed." In the dream she wondered if she had actually healed at all or if the cuts had simply scarred over—there was a difference, she knew.

Eleri made mistakes in her last assignment. She dug too deep, letting the profile get its claws into her. During that chase, she hadn't slept for fear of missing something—a clue, a sign, a thread to pull. When she was being honest with herself, she admitted that she didn't sleep for fear of what she might see.

In her dreams she saw the man they chased. She saw him with the women he stole. And she was helpless to stop. She could describe his job, his lifestyle, that he lived with his mother—how typical—but no one believed. There was no stake in dreams.

So it didn't matter that she learned how he got them into his car. That he was small, unassuming, but trained. The bruises on their necks were not marks of strangulation but of systematic and repetitive pressure designed to make them pass out, to make them malleable. He needed only the strength to lift them, to move them, not to fight them. Some of these women should have been able to take him.

Then there was one missing woman who confirmed all of Eleri's suspicions.

Eleri's profile assessment was so dead-on that she was brought in for questioning herself.

It wasn't unheard of for legal agents, officers, lawmen to go rogue. When they did, they knew just how to do it.

Eleri should have remained calm. She should never have put the details in her report in the first place. But she wanted this guy, wanted him bad. While hard, angry agents spent three days interrogating her, he had abducted another woman. Just like she said.

She screamed, she railed, she did everything wrong.

So now she slept below the fake antlers and dreamed of her months in the hospital. She got the guy. She was absolved in the end. But at how high a price?

Agent Westerfield brought her and Heath in on this. He put her in charge—something she'd never expected to be. Westerfield knew her history, knew what she'd done, but called her back into the field anyway. Now here she was again: the more they worked the more she saw the beaten kids, the more she thought of the dead Ruth and the bones from the girl on the side of the road.

Then the dream changed again.

The familiar field formed around her, block by block, surreal in the setting, dusk dropping even as the pieces of landscape clicked into place. The wind accosted her and Eleri turned as though she could ascertain its source, and when she came full circle Emmaline stood in the distance.

At Lakewood, Eleri had told her doctors about Emmaline, the dreams, all of it.

Another mistake.

She tried not to think of that now. Avoided the memories of holding Jane Doe's bones and first determining that it wasn't her sister. Only when Eleri had been positive of that fact, could she begin her assessment. She pushed all those thoughts aside as her sister walked toward her in the dreamscape.

Emmaline wore the same white linen dress as last time, only she wasn't alone. Eleri knew she couldn't move. So she waited, watching her sister and peering at the dogs that walked calmly alongside.

The wind came again, whipping Eleri's hair in front of her face, making it a constant struggle to see. But time passed easily and before she knew it, her sister stood in front of her. It became clear the dogs at her side were dreams though Emmaline herself was real. Despite the solidity of her sister, Eleri found herself frowning.

Not dogs. Wolves.

One of them black as ink. Black fur, all over, black eyes. While she stared, both wolves sat, drawing her attention to the other one. This one was brown all over. Slightly smaller than the black one, its eyes were hazel. Eleri's head snapped back when she saw this. It was all too odd; something was off with their faces. When she gave up trying to place it—what did she know about wolves anyway?—she looked at her sister again.

Emmaline simply reached out and took Eleri's hand between both of her own. Eleri stared. She drank in as much as she could of Emmaline's face. It was so infrequent that she got to see her sister. She stood still, letting her hand be held until she woke up.

Light bled in around the corners of the heavy curtains. Horses walked myriad ways on the thick print as though they, too, were trying to escape the room, Eleri thought. The alarm clock told her she'd woken just five minutes before the beeping noise would start and she'd best get up. She had to pack, had to leave this place, get away from the antlers and the praying cowboy and the horses trapped on the curtains.

With the efficiency borne of too much practice, she put her bag together. Rolling certain pants for space, folding tops, tucking shoes into corners of her suitcase. She dressed and packed in sync, the second dream of Emmaline within a week disturbing her more than she wished to admit.

The two wolves with her sister weren't that hard to figure out. At least part of it could be easily sorted: Donovan had neatly evaded all her questions. And she had—eventually—let him. Clearly, he did not wish to tell her what was up with that damned black wolf. Just as clearly, something *was* up with it.

The previous night, before she packed up her computer, she nearly fell asleep on the keyboard, she'd been so busy looking up black wolves. Had she been limited to only her own memory she might have dismissed it, but she also had Jonah's sketch. In the sketch the wolf was positively glossy, black from tail to tip, but it was the face that got her. Though all-black wolves did exist—a mutation normal to the breed, like redheads—none of them looked like the wolf she saw in South Carolina. Which was somehow exactly like the wolf Jonah saw in Texas.

The wolf she saw didn't really look like any wolf on any continent.

The coloring could match to some wolves. The eyes could match to some. Jonah had drawn the mouth open and the teeth were wrong—not as pointy in the front as the images on the Web.

These were flatter, more Mongoloid. Shovel-shaped. Like she'd learned in forensics. The brow was higher, the face not as long.

When she looked at the drawing, when she searched her memory, she immediately thought *wolf*. But as she looked online, she realized that every piece of it was off in some way. Eventually, she gave up and crawled into bed, but the dreams chased her.

She didn't call Donovan to see if he was up, just expected that he would be. She wasn't mad, exactly. There were things she would evade, too. Still this one was biting at her. Eleri sighed to herself, knowing if the situations were reversed she would want him to back off; she let it go. For now.

She found him standing in the hall, bags packed, waiting on her.

They didn't speak as they walked down the hallway, looking like the Feds they were. They each had a rolling bag, hers in red, stacked with another bag. They each had a shoulder bag for electronics—again, hers in red. Their not speaking wasn't out of anger. The air didn't hold that vibe, it was simply too early in the morning. It was simply that they had once again packed everything into small suitcases and rolled out of one place only to know they would roll into another later.

Eleri wanted to go to Brady, but there were already enough small towns around here getting familiar with the Feds coming by and staying for a few days. As Cassa Brinks said, the locals were all related and they all talked—all except the City of God people.

Donovan stood back as Eleri handed in their room keys. She was slipping the paperwork into the folder she kept in the front pocket of her suitcase when she saw Donovan tipping his head toward the breakfast buffet.

"Buffet" was a very loose interpretation here. Warming dishes appeared to hold two meats in one dish and the other had thin, stacked servings of eggs. Eleri shook her head; she couldn't handle perfect pancakes of eggs that folded into quarters.

They were on their way to Dallas. There was an FBI building there—so they wouldn't stick out so badly and so they would have access to the things they needed and maybe get some work done. They would check satellite images of the area they found, do heat readings. See if they could match the number of kids to the numbers Jonah and Charity talked about. Check some forensic evidence from both kids.

The Fisks were being flown in today. Not shockingly at all, Charity's fingerprints had been a perfect match. Agent Bozeman reported that as soon as he informed the two escapees of this, they started singing like canaries. Telling more about how Charity had been "acquired." Unfortunately, it appeared there had been drugs involved—not willingly on Charity/Ashlyn's part —but it changed the dynamic. It meant the Fisks could not be completely reunited with their daughter until they had been re-questioned, now that there was more information about how the kidnapping happened. Eleri, desperate to be in the room for that, hoped there would be clues to find Jennifer Cohn.

Her chest tightened at the thought and she could almost see the words in her FBI file—"no children." So why was she put on this case? She was starting to get attached to the idea of finding Jennifer.

It meant she had six hours to beat Charity's parents to Dallas. They had a three-and-a-half hour drive and she wanted a real breakfast. Thinking they'd find something on the way, they watched the town of Hamilton rapidly fade at the edges, leaving them on small, back woods highways with no food in sight. They suffered the occasional random traffic light or even stop sign as they crossed another road and Eleri became willing to down-grade her expectations and eat somewhere that had "and bait" at the end of the name.

About an hour later, her stomach growled loudly as they

spotted a large truck stop named only "Larry and Sue's" and Eleri gave up. Some of these dives had great food. It was a crapshoot, she knew, but one she was now willing to take.

The waitress, Amy, was wearing a perfect polyester reproduction of the old Mel's Diner uniform. Though the place was too crowded to get away from everyone, Eleri accepted a table at the back and took the primary seat, able to look out the large front windows. While trucks parked or fueled up, truckers walked by toward the convenience store behind her. She trusted Donovan to keep an eye out in that direction while they spoke in low tones, taking notes about what questions to ask of the Fisks, maybe Charity and Jonah, too.

Hoping the sheer volume of patrons was an indicator of quality and not desperation, Eleri ordered a large breakfast. She was able to pick from three kinds of fried potatoes, but the only fruit or vegetable she could find was a frozen blueberry in the pancake mix. She went for it. Donovan, of course, outdid her.

While they waited for drinks, she tried not to look at Donovan oddly. His evasion of the questions she had already asked, as well as the stockpile of questions she hadn't yet gotten too, didn't add up. Though she struggled with it, she aimed a different direction. "So we got word last night about Jonah's fingerprints."

"Did he match?" Donovan's head snapped up and he stared right at her. Something about his eyes bothered her, but she pushed past that thought, too.

"No. They've exhausted every database they can think of. As a male, his numbers are lower to check against, and while there are too many missing kids who aren't uploaded due to backlog or whatever, he should be in the system. Given everything we know, he couldn't have been taken that long ago. So AFIS is calling it as a 'no match'."

Donovan nodded sagely, already refilling his coffee from the thermal pitcher left in the middle of their table. It was some of the best coffee Eleri had been served in a long time, but the mugs were small enough that Donovan looked to be serving himself shot after shot rather than getting to actually drink any of it.

She went back into her conclusions. "So I started thinking. Jonah said some of the women got pregnant, babies appeared. We believe that not all of the kids at City of God were stolen. So I thought about the players we know and who might have been there fourteen years ago. Then I tried looking through the pictures he gave us." Pulling out a straight-on photograph of Jonah, she laid it on the table. Then she put Jonah's own drawing of Baxter next to it. Next to that, she laid out the picture Mark and Lilly Baxter had given them, taken when Joseph was sixteen.

"Holy shit!" Donovan blurted it, then stilled, his eyes comically darting one way then another.

Eleri was more subtle in her perusal of the area but she didn't see anyone reacting to his swearing. "Exactly."

Already shaking his head, her partner returned to his normal self and started fixing another tiny mug of coffee. "But there's no way we'll get Baxter's blood to check for paternity."

His eyes opened with comprehension even as Eleri spoke. "But Mark and Lilly Baxter will gladly test to see if he's their grandchild."

"And Jonah wouldn't go into foster care."

"*If* he's a match."

Donovan was smiling widely at the new development. "I would say that's a very small 'if'. Those pictures are quite compelling."

She agreed, but Eleri couldn't stop staring at his teeth. A uniform shade of white with a hint of blue, they were perfect rectangles in the front. A bit shovel-shaped, indicating he had some kind of Asian background. From the color of his hair and eyes, she was thinking India, but the forensic recognition of the teeth grabbed her.

Not too big in the front, his bottom teeth were smaller. All were nearly perfectly spaced and she noticed for the first time tiny gaps between each. More disturbing, his canines were long, both top and bottom.

She could see with perfect clarity, the teeth on the wolf of her dreams last night because they were smiling at her right now. Well, they had been smiling at her, but now he was frowning and the wolf-teeth had been covered by his pinched mouth. "Eleri?"

She couldn't answer him. Her brain was working too fast to produce actual vocalizations in English words. The teeth. The eyes. They were the same. The hair color, also the same—and she looked now up and down his arms, seeing that he was a little more hairy than the average guy, but clearly not enough that she had even noticed it before. The hair on his arms was, in fact, as black as the hair on his head.

Still frowning at her, he leaned back a bit, breaking eye contact and stopping her perusal. Clearly, he was uncomfortable, but she still couldn't explain.

Staring out the wide front windows at nothing, she kept adding pieces. He ran in the nude. She met the wolf at his back gate just moments before Donovan appeared—naked. He refused to take the cell phone when she tracked him, and the night he found Jonah she'd sworn she saw him shove a dog collar in his pocket. The blood and dirt that night had been *under* his clothes —consistent with running in the nude and getting dressed after.

And he'd run thirty-two miles an hour.

She'd double-checked both the system and the GPS and they had no errors at any other time. She hand calculated the distance and divided by time. She got thirty-two miles per hour, too.

But it couldn't be.

If she thought that, then she was buying into an old myth.

Maybe she was more ready to buy in than even she thought. Eleri knew monsters were real. And myths often had origins in truth. Could Donovan really be what she was thinking?

The truck she was staring at blindly pulled out, leaving her gazing into open space. As she blinked, trying to put the jumble in her head together in a way that didn't leave her where it was leaving her, Eleri ignored Donovan repeating her name.

As she watched, a new truck pulled into the space.

A truck with an orange cab and blue flames painted across the front.

18

Donovan saw that Eleri was looking at him oddly, and he suddenly realized that in two and a half weeks with her he managed to reveal a secret he had successfully kept his entire life. He would have to tell her something. Maybe not the whole thing, but she wasn't one to let it go. He already knew that.

Her eyes bored into him, even though she wasn't looking at him so much as looking through him. She might as well be speaking, her thoughts were so clear. She recognized his teeth, she was looking at his eyes, she'd already alluded to the fact that she and Jonah had seen the same wolf—the wolf that didn't exist in nature, or at least in recorded nature.

Donovan knew all these things. No one had studied him more than he had.

His father had been content with just being, embracing himself and his son as magical beings. But there was no magic to it, and Donovan had always been a child of science. Absently his finger went to the scar on his right leg. He believed in the science, even if it didn't always believe in him.

He swallowed, getting ready to say—to confess—something, when Eleri's whole body snapped rigid.

Suddenly very worried for her, he followed her line of sight. Turning around, he saw nothing. Just trucks coming and going. Fueling up. Parking. Leaving. Exactly the same as it was when the two of them came in. However, Eleri's shift made it clear something had changed.

He leaned toward her, though even that didn't pull her attention from the plate windows in the front of the store. "Eleri, what is it?"

"The truck. The driver." Her eyes never wavered.

"Which one?" He was nearly whispering, probably because she was.

"Orange truck, blue flames. Round driver, white hair, saggy jowls." Her words were clipped as though recalling them, rather than describing what was in front of her, but Donovan easily spotted the man she spoke of.

"Why him?"

"We need to question him." She still didn't peel her eyes away. The trucker was going to run off if he caught Eleri staring; she was positively trance-like, so Donovan touched her hand hoping to break her out of it.

It worked. Maybe a little too well.

Eleri jumped sky high. Something about the movement made it look as though her soul had been dropped back into her body with a jarring motion. Donovan ignored all of it. "Don't stare at him. If we need to question him, we will, but staring won't help us."

She knew that and she nodded, but still wasn't entirely her normal self. Scrambling for a pen and a napkin, she jotted down what he realized was the license plate number from the truck. "Keep your eyes on him." She hissed and got up to go to the ladies room, pen and napkin still firmly in hand.

About as subtle as the Mac truck she was stalking, she made a wide berth by the front window before disappearing down the hallway. Donovan had to stop watching for a moment when their server came back, her arms laden with enough plates to indicate that about five people were having breakfast.

He only smiled and said thank you, then swung his eyes around again, immediately catching the man at the counter and almost as quickly spotting Eleri coming back out of the ladies' room. She barely spent enough time in there to wash her hands, let alone anything else. He just hoped no one but him noticed.

Actually, she was pretty furtive. He figured it was only because he knew exactly what she was doing—was trained to do the same thing—that he saw it. He was relatively convinced that she memorized the truck's registration from the print on the door as she went by and probably spent her time in the ladies' room writing it down. She would re-check on her way back.

Sure enough, her eyes darted to her right, scanning the truck and Donovan almost smiled. The older man didn't seem fazed at all, and as Donovan watched he was led to a long table and given a seat with other truckers coming and going solo.

Good, he would be here for a while.

When Eleri made it back to the table, she was still tense but hiding it much better. He grabbed her wrist, nearly pulling her into the booth as he spoke. "Why do we need to interview him? Am I missing something?"

She still didn't answer. Not for a moment. "Let me just say that I think he's a key witness and we need to ask him a few questions." She wasn't looking Donovan in the eye, instead surreptitiously scanning the area, keeping watch on the truck driver.

Why that one? Donovan couldn't distinguish anything about this guy that set him apart. Eleri had snapped when the man got out of the truck, or maybe when he pulled in. Donovan didn't know; his back was to the front window.

No longer paying attention to their food, the two of them ate, alternately keeping an eye on the older gentleman. His food arrived, the waitress winking at him and pouring his coffee—as she did with many of the men and the few women at the long table. So far, there was nothing special about him except Eleri's reaction.

For a moment, Donovan stopped and savored the food. As horrible as it was health-wise, taste-wise it was disturbingly good. Several times he found himself too busy enjoying the meal and not keeping his eye on the man at the long table. Eleri was suffering from a decided lack of vegetation, but Donovan's system had always been fine on large quantities of meat and starches. He wondered more than once if that was because of his alternate physiology. But there was no way he was doing a GI biopsy on himself. The scar on his leg was as far as he was willing to take it, and he was willing to admit that might have been too far.

They finished their meals—hers picked over, his cleaned down to the white Corian—and waited. As the man started to stand, so did Eleri, but Donovan held her back and watched. As he expected, the white-haired man made his lopsided way to the men's room hallway and Donovan nodded to Eleri.

They paid their check at the front counter and headed out. First, Donovan moved their car to block the truck then Eleri posted herself near the cab door.

When he came out, he saw them and ambled forward, his eyes focusing more as Eleri came into view. Donovan hoped maybe she didn't look as much like a Fed as he previously thought. The resulting frown on the man's face, the way he turned to Donovan as his shoulders sagged, told a different story.

She hadn't even flashed her badge.

ELERI WATCHED as the snowy-haired man changed in front of her. He went from proud, if old, to saddened in a single blink. He nodded as though accepting his fate, then went so far as to ask if she had a car.

"Yes, my partner is parked behind your truck." She had to make this more formal. "My name is Agent Eleri Eames with the FBI. My partner there—" she motioned toward the car, "is Agent Donovan Heath. We're hoping you can help us out."

The old man looked at her suspiciously from the sides of his eyes, as though he didn't trust her suddenly. But he got into the back seat when she offered him the door and before jogging around and climbing in behind Donovan, allowing him to chauffeur.

Suddenly, she was at a loss. The old man was agreeable to helping them, but they were in the middle of nowhere. She didn't even know what to ask him really. How would she say "Did you give a ride to this woman? And did you know she's dead?"

Then again, maybe that was exactly how she had to do it.

Watching the man for weapons or sudden moves—though she suspected the latter would be hard for him—Eleri checked her phone and then leaned forward, asking Donovan to take them to the Brownwood Police Station as their planned route to Dallas had them heading right through the small town where they'd started. The station would let them use a conference room.

The silence in the car suggested the old man was resigned to his fate. Whether this was because he knew something of value or because he simply hated authorities, she couldn't tell. The quiet pushed at them, the only sound the road under the wheels, then the gathering traffic—if it could be called that—as they passed the city limits of Brownwood.

Though they had stayed here several days, they had only been in the PD once to introduce themselves. Instead of achieving their feeble attempt at making nice, they announced their presence and probably sparked a good handful of rumors, hurting their job here more than they helped. Too late to re-think that one now. Eleri wished they had met Cassa Brinks first.

When Donovan pulled the car up to the bright brick building, no one recognized them, and they had to go through the ritual of flashing their badges again and explaining that they simply wanted a conference room to speak to the gentleman with them. The trucker stiffened at the offer of an interrogation room but was obviously relieved when Eleri declined. His name was Bernard Collier, but beyond that, Eleri had shut him down, preferring to wait until the recording device was on.

Her heart jittered. What if she was wrong?

The orange cab with the blue flames had simply been part of a dream. Then there it was at the truck stop. And this was the man she saw in the dream helping Ruth into the cab. So on some level something was correct, but what? It was too big a question to dive right into. It was too big a coincidence to leave alone.

Several raised eyebrows and phone calls later, they were seated at a nicely appointed conference table and even offered beverages. She suppressed a sigh at the trappings of hospitality that prolonged their start time.

At her glance, her clear desire to get started, Collier began to look even more concerned than he had before. Eleri had no idea what to make of him. So she went through the motions, asking his permission to record the meeting. He granted it.

She set up the recorder, noting all the details ad nauseam before asking him to state his name and occupation.

"Bernard Worley Collier. Independent driver for Diesel One Truck Lines." He went on to describe his route today, passing Mills and coming through Brownwood on his way to Sweetwater.

They asked about his usual routes, and he told them he hit El Paso regularly, coming from the east as well as the west. The company gave him several stops there. He operated out of Austin, often running a different route through Dallas or a third option through Amarillo.

He was nodding as she asked him about Brownwood, Hamilton and Zephyr. How often did he pass there? With each answer, he became more nervous. Sweat began to bead on his forehead, Collier successfully ignoring it until one drop ran down the side of his face.

Eleri was mid question as he reached up to wipe it away and something about the action broke him.

Interrupting her, he blurted out, "This is about that dead girl isn't it? The one I buried in that field?"

19

Donovan had not expected to be out sniffing in a field today. He hadn't expected to smell another death.

He used to perform autopsies on dead bodies all day long. Sometimes they arrived fresh from the hospital or a home case. Sometimes they were pulled from the side of the road or an alleyway, fished out of a river. He knew death and all its smells. And he could smell the girl under the ground.

Collier hadn't done a good job of burying her. It seemed he'd gotten her just deep enough to give the scavengers a challenge. One look at the man's arthritic hands and it was clear even this shallow depth had been hard for him.

It indicated some level of care for this girl.

Another smell hit him, bluebonnets.

Though they had passed a field on the way, there were no bluebonnets here. Donovan smelled them anyway.

Donovan's mind raced. Did Collier kill this girl? Was he a serial killer? The middle of nowhere Texas, small towns that people rarely leave but teenagers run from, a trucker with a route past the area: it was the perfect setup, even if Collier didn't seem like the kind of guy to do that. However, in Donovan's mind, that would make him the perfect killer. Who would suspect the round, slow-moving Bernard?

In the interview, when Collier finally spoke, it wasn't to say what Donovan expected.

"I saw this woman on the side of the road about three years ago." He pointed at Jonah's picture of Ruth. Eleri had added more Jonah originals to her collection as Agent Bozeman kept her up to speed on things. Still, there had been no more clarity on Jennifer Cohn.

Collier had spoken quietly the whole time. "She said she needed a ride, and so I took her into Hamilton, I think. That was it. I dropped her off. She said her name was Ruth and that she would find a ride home." His chest heaved with the effort of a deep sigh. Then he looked them in the eyes. "I know she made it home, because I found her in about the same place about six months later and gave her a ride toward Dallas that time. After that, I told her my schedule. All in all, I think I drove Ruth about five times. Four times away from where I found her on Farm Road 16, and once she flagged me down outside Zephyr and I took her back."

Donovan tried to stay calm despite the revelation. "Where exactly did you drop her off?"

It might give them insight into what was going on.

Collier agreed to show them the exact location if they would drive him out there. Donovan had a clear picture in his head of an old newspaper headline reading: FBI Agents Slain by Notorious Serial Killer After Driving Him to Kill Site. But Eleri agreed to it, and he knew the protocol—they would call it in, make sure someone was tracking them, check in regularly. Basically, be harder to kill.

"Last time, I took her to Brownwood and she was real sick. She needed medical help, but though she was barely upright, she insisted on walking into the ER herself." He looked up at them expectantly. "How is she doing? I checked later and heard they released her."

Oh, shit. Eleri nodded at Donovan and he took a breath in. "She did improve, she headed home."

"That's great."

But Eleri had nodded at him. It was a go-ahead; probably she wanted to see how Bernard would react, too. So Donovan gave him the dirt. "We have word that she died after returning to her home."

"What?" He blinked. It looked like this was news to him. Or else he was a stellar actor.

Donovan went for the next jab. "We don't have evidence, but we do have two corroborating stories that she was beaten to death by people in her group."

He'd kept his language purposefully vague, avoiding words like "stoned to death" "cult" and "murder" so he could see if Collier himself added them to the conversation.

Collier added nothing; he simply broke down and cried. "She was such a nice lady. So friendly. Very religious but not pushy." His shoulders heaved and he buried his face in his hands but didn't try to hide the fact that he was openly crying over a woman he'd met only a handful of times.

A few looks passed over Bernard's back between Donovan and Eleri, so Donovan felt safe with his next question. "Is it Ruth that you buried in the field?"

That at least stopped the crying. Face tear-streaked, the old man looked up, confused. "No. Ruth was a grown woman and I didn't know she was dead. The girl I buried was a girl. And she died while she was with me. I didn't know what to do." He looked away, shook his head, exhibited classic truth-telling tics.

Eleri nearly interrupted Collier, though he was looking out the window at the clouds rushing by and didn't seem to notice or at least he wasn't offended. "Tell us about the girl you buried."

He thumbed through the pictures again, pulling out another

girl, late teens. Jonah had ID'd her—on the back of the picture—as "Faith." Collier tapped the nose in the picture. "This girl. She's the one I buried. Said her name was Faith."

The older man's sadness played into the interview. The reaction of the person being interrogated changed how the agent proceeded. If the agent was any good at all, it was by conscious decision and not reaction. Eleri appeared to be very good. Her voice was softer now, soothing, probably in an effort to make Collier more at home, get him to give more details. Maybe let a secret slide out because he didn't know or wasn't paying attention. Donovan was paying attention though, taking mental notes at Eleri's kind tones and wondering if this girl had been Jennifer Cohn or if they were barking up the wrong cult.

"When was the first time you met Faith?"

"About a year or so ago. Same thing." He shrugged. "There were two others, too."

"What?" Donovan had reacted. Bad choice. He glanced quickly at Eleri and saw that she didn't fault him for it.

"Ruth I carried most. I think she told the others." He looked away again but kept speaking in that gravelly voice underlined by a faint wheeze. Donovan could smell a medication on him, menthol from his skin, but also the sharp undertone of albuterol for asthma or emphysema probably. He didn't carry even a faint tinge of cigarette smoke, but he might have given it up years ago or simply spent too long too close to the engines of the big trucks. Collier looked back at Donovan. "My truck is very recognizable. I don't think I am, but the cab is. One girl found me in Zephyr and flagged me down. Said Ruth told her my route and my truck and that I'd carry her home. So I did."

Placing her hand over his, Eleri pulled his attention back toward her. If Collier had any idea Agent Eames was directing the conversation as she was, he didn't show it. "Is her picture here?"

In the end he pointed out three women and an unidentified male he'd given rides to. Someone not in the pile of drawings.

He'd carried two of the girls, alone, in or out of the area. Neither had given him names. Collier stated that he hadn't pushed them to.

Eleri then steered him to a description of the boy—obviously wondering why Jonah didn't have the drawing in the pile. They had asked him to first draw portraits of every person in the camp. It had taken a while, but Jonah had produced. There were forty-two faces. But none of the boy Collier described.

While his partner asked more pointed questions about the boy, Donovan rummaged through her bag. Behind Collier, he held up the photo of Jonah to show her. Understanding dawned in her eyes and she asked the man, "This photo my partner is holding, is that the boy?"

Turning took longer than recognition. "Yes, that's him. Is he okay?"

"He is." Eleri smiled.

Jonah had not drawn himself in the batch.

Collier said he had suspected something like an Amish community, deeply religious, overly protective of their children. He wondered if what he was doing was right, but felt—hoped— that it was. When Faith died on him, he realized he had no alibi. He didn't know where to find her kin or how to keep from going to jail for a crime he didn't commit, so he buried her.

So while Eleri called the Dallas office to check in and create a backup system, Donovan called Bozeman and told him of the new development. He apologized about the Fisks and emailed the questions the two of them had come up with last night. "It looks like you're on your own."

"Nah," Bozeman sounded as laid back as ever, a trait Donovan was beginning to get jealous of. "I'll call another agent in from the center. I won't go solo with distraught parents. How in hell did you find this guy?"

He almost stumbled but in the end got his voice together.

"Lucky break, I'll have Eames tell you about it later." Yeah, right after I have Eames tell me.

After borrowing an officer from the Brownwood PD, then making her wait in the car with a book, they traipsed out here at Collier's arthritic pace. Donovan wanted to run ahead; he could easily find the body. Knowing he couldn't say anything in front of the trucker, he instead held back. Catching Eleri's eye, he made a phone motion to her.

She shrugged in return, like "call who?"

He mouthed, "The team." Then he pointed toward where Collier was heading and pointed toward his nose.

Yeah, she got it now. But then she didn't. Using her actual voice, she called ahead. "Are you still headed the right way, Mr. Collier?"

"Yes, ma'am." He kept high stepping as best he could, rolling forward through the tall grass.

Then Eleri held back a little, allowing them to at least whisper with a modicum of privacy. As long as Collier's hearing wasn't as good as Donovan's they would be okay. "What do you smell?"

"A rotting body." He wasn't sure how much more specific he could be.

Eleri was. "Can you be sure it's human?"

Ah, yes, a rotting cow carcass would not be worth dragging the FBI's site team out. "Yes. I know the smell of dead human flesh, and it's about sixty more feet in front of him."

She swept her hand by him, palm up, indicating that he should go with Collier. Turning, he saw she was moving farther away, pulling out her phone. He caught the first strains of the conversation as she called in the team, telling them approximate coordinates from where she stood and saying she would give them an exact location as soon as she had it.

He was surprised by the pride that swelled slightly in his chest. Though there was no visual on the body yet—nothing but an old man and Donovan's word—Eleri had just mobilized a full site team.

His moment of positivity was cut short by the wheeze of Collier's voice calling back over his shoulder. "It's right up here. I brought her flowers just a few days ago."

Bluebonnets.

He'd brought her bluebonnets. They were starting to rot, too. Donovan knew it moments before he saw what was now just a smear of purple in the near distance.

Collier pointed, his finger misshapen under the faded tattoos and his arm shaking slightly. "It's right there."

At his side in a moment, Donovan grabbed the man's shoulders, keeping him upright and his lungs as open as possible. Too damn many live patients these days. He was going to have a dead one if he didn't act fast.

Collier began coughing, or trying to.

"Sir, do you have your inhaler with you?" Bernard Collier, leather-tough truck driver, turned cherry red and nodded, reaching toward his back jeans pocket but not making it. Donovan pried the small apparatus loose and put it to the man's mouth. Quick bursts of the medicine escaped around his lips. It always did. Albuterol had a bite to it, a scent that bordered on taste, and that would cling to the back of Donovan's throat until he drank something strong.

He gave the man a second dose but couldn't let him sit. Settling him into the very grass that was shrinking his bronchi could kill him. Instead, he held the man upright, Collier's weight not insignificant, and yelled for Eleri. In half a moment, she had hung up on the team, called the backup officer, and arranged an ambulance.

Eleri's expression as she handed Collier over to the arriving backup officer was dark as night. "Fucking everyone will know about this now."

Donovan agreed but was almost more shocked by the use of the f-word.

Eleri walked a tight circle in the grass, muttering "Fuck, fuck, fuck, fuck" as the other two walked farther away. Nearly a full minute later, her head popped up, her eyes clear of the angry rage that had shown there a minute before, making them appear nearly black in the midday heat. "Okay, I have that out of my system. Now that we know Collier will be okay, let's get to this shit before the others do."

She started off in the wrong direction, but Donovan corrected her quickly, pointing out the bluebonnets, ripped from the ground, gathered in a bundle and dropped on the marred surface of the earth. It was a good thing Collier hadn't seen this.

Animals had been at the gravesite. Dig marks showed in several places. A hand snuck out from exposed earth, a foot—sneaker still intact—was twisting out of the ground in another spot.

Donovan pulled gloves from his back pocket as Eleri did the same, the snapping sounds of latex popping oddly in the still air.

When they were a few feet away, Eleri stopped dead. "I figured it was long hard work for Collier to drag a body out here. We aren't that far off the road, just far enough not to be seen. But he couldn't even walk it. He started wheezing and keeled over before he made it to the site."

Donovan was looking at her, the body in the ground almost at his feet, begging for inspection. But Eleri held her hand up.

"How did he do it?"

20

Eleri was mad. She thought she was onto something—how could old, nearly-hunched, asthmatic Bernard pull a dead girl's body out here then bury it? He couldn't even *walk* all the way to the site.

But Donovan sighed at her and the whole theory went away.

"He may be wheezing, but he's strong. The arthritis will definitely cause him pain, but never let an arthritic person tell you they can't do something. The pain itself can be physically limiting, but when they can push past that, it doesn't often cause other hindrances. This was not a fine-motor-control situation." He waved his hand at the ground despite the fact that she was clearly pissed. "Also, Bernard's asthma is in response to allergies. You and I both know it wasn't this bad last week. All we have to do is check the date Bernard says he buried her. Cross-reference that with her decomposition and check the pollen count. Add in adrenaline and I'll bet it plays out entirely like Bernard said."

Just in case she wasn't pissed enough, she sneezed right then. As though to punctuate his total breakdown of her theory.

Fine. Bernard buried the girl. Eleri bought that now, but they still had to dig her up, be sure she was what Collier claimed she was. Right now they could only see a hand and a foot. So they weren't even certain they had a girl. These parts could just as easily belong to a boy or an adult.

She knelt down on one side of the grave, looking, but not wanting to disturb anything before the full team got there. Donovan knelt on the other side of the grave, looking much like a child on Easter morning, told he couldn't yet touch the basket, but almost able to peer inside. She tried to give him the benefit of the doubt. Surely he was excited because this was what he was best at.

As she watched, he gingerly moved his hands, placing them flat on the earth several times in slightly different positions. It wasn't until he leaned over, using his arms to brace himself from falling on the girl, that she realized he was trying to get close enough to smell the body.

All of the things she'd thought, all the pieces she put together, the accusations she was almost ready to make came flooding back. For a moment she imagined the black wolf hovering over this girl, sniffing at her hand, and Eleri's brain sprang back into action and she analyzed the area of the disturbed earth. "Something dug at her!"

Donovan looked up slowly from his precarious position. "Yes."

"So why didn't it eat her?" She didn't let him answer. "In shallow-grave situations like this—spring time, creatures are out with babies to feed—scavengers will come and make use of what they can find. They scatter the bones over miles. But she looks intact! You could smell it, so could they. Why didn't they eat her?"

Carefully he tipped himself back on his heels and pointed at the exposed hand. "She was sick."

Looking more closely, cataloguing what she hadn't yet paid attention to, Eleri realized he was right. The skin was gray with a slight pink hue. It should have been nearly black at this stage. The girl should have passed into the active decay state, but she seemed slow to turn despite the heat and humidity of the early Texas summer.

"Larvae?" She asked Donovan rather than looking for herself. After all, he already stuck his face near the body.

He shook his head in response. "I didn't even see any eggs. But look." He pointed several times at the back of her hand, moving his finger slightly with each jab in that direction.

It took a second for Eleri to see he wasn't pointing at the hand itself but at the mottling and—more specifically—at the small dots marring the smooth skin. She looked up. "Measles?"

"I think so."

She almost whispered, though she didn't know why. She hoped the team was coming soon. They would have to bring in the flood lights because the day was already heading into the last phase and this would keep them most of the night. "Can you smell it?"

"Sometimes." He tilted his head as if trying to figure out how to describe it. Eleri wondered if it was like describing color to a blind man. She had only the most rudimentary reference when it came to smells.

He offered what he could, "The last case of measles I came across had a distinctive smell. But it was a hospital death, in quarantine. There's so much else around here that it's all overlapping." He waved his hands a bit as though that helped explain. "But this has the same tone as that one."

She nodded. "You remember the smells that well? You can classify them better than 'I like it' or 'I don't like it'?"

His nod was small and hard to follow. But it was there.

Interesting.

He looked up and over his shoulder, "The team is here."

She couldn't hear anything, but she had already reached the point where she trusted that he could. Sighing, she pulled out her camera. "I'll get some active light pictures. Can you call and just see where Bernard is and what's happening? I'd like him sent to

Dallas and let Bozeman get his hands on him. Get a full formal interview, since we really didn't get to finish."

She got high shots, making sure her own shadow didn't get in the way. She took low shots, lying on her belly in the grass and ruining a few with sneezes. When she looked closer she saw that tufts of long hair had been dug up. The strands caught in a small breeze, lifting as though still attached to a living person.

Stepping a few feet away, she rummaged through the kit she had hauled out here. Given the walk and Bernard's certainty of the situation, it had seemed easier to just bring it than have to return to the car.

After the preliminary photos, she pulled out her tape measure, laying it out along the body. She staked bright, tiny flags at the visible corners of the grave. There were five, as the grave was not rectangular, which she mentally attributed to Bernard's lack of practice and need for speed. Once she was set up, she took several more shots from each direction, wanting extras to be certain at least one had readable measurements in good light.

She was itching to get out her small trowel and begin digging, when she heard the team finally walk up. For a moment she tried to back calculate how long it had been since Donovan told her they were coming and how far away he must have heard them from. Whatever it was, it was significant. And it was another piece of evidence about him. Forcibly, she pushed her focus away; there would be time to consider Donovan's oddities tomorrow.

Eleri held herself back from digging at the body—the right procedure was tedious. She knew that criminals were put away or turned free based on the minutiae that came from proper processing. Still, she itched to just dig.

The team said hello from a distance and faster than she could pay attention they erected a closed tent, emerged in paper suits and began staking out lights. One of the members came with a clipboard and took statements from her and Donovan.

How had they discovered the site? In what condition had they found it? What had they moved?

Eleri fought to keep her eyes from narrowing despite the fact that she had asked other trained agents those very same questions herself in the past. It was annoying even if it was necessary. What if there had been some reason to move something? Often there was.

The agent then asked for a hair sample from each of them.

Eleri offered it but pointed out that hers was relatively red, whereas the girl's was brown. Also, hers was in a ponytail. She was an FBI agent, so wherever she was could become a crime scene at any moment. It rarely ever did, but today she felt vindicated when the investigator agreed to get a sample later if they needed a cross match.

Donovan had likely shed all over the scene. Guys often did. Any man with any real arm or leg hair couldn't help it, unless he wanted to shave everything—eyebrows included. That look usually meant hard-core swimmer or serial killer. Donovan already admitted to being neither. For a moment she imagined that look on him. Her face pulled into something distasteful as Donovan voluntarily plucked a hair and handed it into a baggie.

Frowning, the agent held the bag up to the light, squinting his eyes for a better look. "Wow, your hair will be easy to rule out. It's thick!"

Donovan clearly didn't understand. "Lots of people have thick hair."

"No, not the volume, the shaft. The hair itself is almost twice the width of normal human hair." He was grinning now. Something new for the lab.

Donovan was not grinning, in fact he looked worried. Eleri shook her head at him, wondered how to convey that it was highly unlikely the lab would put the whole thing together on the basis of a single hair sample. How did she tell him not to worry about something she technically didn't know yet? How did she get all that across without speaking it out loud in front of the agent who was all happy with a new anomaly to play with? She couldn't.

Turning back toward the body, Eleri saw that the lights were up and on, the sun already starting to ride low in the sky. Sunset took a long time out in the open, the trees the only thing to thwart it before it hit the horizon. Accepting a paper suit from one of the techs, she climbed into it, oh so excited to add another layer of clothing out here in the Texas heat.

She donned her face shield and turned to get to work.

SEVEN HOURS LATER, the body was out of the ground. Eleri sat back on her heels, or she hoped she did. Everything from her butt down was mostly numb.

The majority of the work had been performed on hands and knees, carefully scraping and bagging dirt, stopping for photos and water breaks. The techs had a timer to tell them when to rotate people out; they had mandatory amounts of water a person had to consume in order to stay active. They had been working scenes in Texas for years and knew that the heat kills. Not wishing to become part of the scene herself, Eleri followed their protocol.

The girl's body was extracted with the same care an archaeological team would use to pull a dinosaur out of rock. They used tiny trowels to avoid disrupting her skin, which at this point would break easily, oozing decomposed fluids and disturbing the scene. They cleared her piece by piece with tiny brushes, took swabs, and sealed them in closed containers as she was slowly exposed. Donovan occasionally surreptitiously sniffed at her.

When her face was revealed, it was as Bernard had stated. They received updates from Agent Bozeman periodically, learning that Mr. Collier buried her face up, head toward the trees, hands at her side. More details came in, all proving true. They sent a few questions back for verification, and the trucker answered each correctly. Her shirt was red, she wore jeans, no jewelry. One shoe had come untied when he dragged her. In the end, it all showed that Donovan was right: Collier had buried the girl.

With the front of the girl exposed, Eleri spotted something and stopped the team for a moment. Using gloved hands and another person to brace her, she reached out and gently moved the neckline of the plain red T-shirt. It was on backward, the tag now in the front reading "100% Cotton."

Had she dressed in a hurry?

The tag nagged at her for a little while, tugged at far portions of her brain, telling her the jeans were important, too. The team was carefully lifting the body from the ground, commenting how intact she still was after nearly two weeks out here, when it came to Eleri.

No mixed fibers. There was a biblical mandate about wearing clothing of only one fiber. She wasn't sure it was important, but despite the jeans and sneakers, Baxter's cult was following some archaic rules.

All the evidence said this was Faith, Jonah's friend. Her face, relatively preserved, looked enough like his drawing to make at least that verification. Bozeman had sent Charity through all the pictures; she corroborated every name Jonah had given them. The question was: was she also Jennifer?

Following the team the short distance to where they set the body on the bag laid out on the gurney and waiting, Eleri was lost in thought. She almost missed the comment as one of the team members moved the clothing around for a better inspection, "Something odd is happening here. She's still preserved, maybe has some drug or chemical in her system? But look here," He pointed and Eleri looked, too. "She was beaten pretty badly, just before she died."

21

Exhausted and weary to his bones, Donovan climbed into the driver's seat of the small car. Somehow Eleri managed to be relatively graceful despite the fact that she claimed her ass was asleep and that she managed to slide like raw meat into her designated seat. While he didn't think he was at his level best, he was in better condition to drive than she was.

"Do we find a place in Brownwood?"

She had pointed out earlier that they needed showers. Though their paper suits had been peeled off and tucked into evidence bags, the two of them still smelled like they'd just dug up a rotting corpse. Her comments reminded him that most people found that smell to be extremely unpleasant.

He leaned back, watching as she did the same and thought that the smell of cat that had been in the car when they got it was going to be the least of the rental car company's concern now.

Her body may have draped listlessly in the seat, but her voice was firm. "Oh hell no, we are not spending another night in this town."

He almost laughed but couldn't quite summon the energy. Eleri's comment also reminded him that they were homeless. Their bags, their equipment, it was all in the trunk of the car. Donovan had checked on it before climbing in—he'd become suspicious when traffic on the lonely back road had picked up about four hundred percent after the ambulance came out to fetch Collier.

It was inevitable. Having lived in several very tiny towns over the years, Donovan had come to understand that the reputation of the residents breathing gossip wasn't exactly true. When everyone knew everyone else, gossip was as much a way of keeping up with the goings-on as it was about telling fish stories. Still, news traveled fast in small towns. The dispatcher sent out two EMTs with the ambulance, which meant that everyone at dispatch and everyone at the station knew what was going on. If they said something to their families at the dinner table or called to say they'd be late, that they had to pick up a truck driver with asthma in a field off Farm Road 16, then everyone knew.

He understood why Eleri didn't want to stay in the fishbowl. Why she didn't want to walk back into the lobby at the Hampton Inn in Brownwood. Anyone in the lobby, anyone in the parking lot, the mother of the kid who worked the nightshift would know the Feds were back. And if the agents smelled of dead body?

They had to get out of here and get relatively far away. Dallas was the best bet. The field office keeping watch on Jonah and Charity—or Ashlyn again?—was in the area. He aimed the car roughly northwest looking to turn onto State Road 183.

The sun came up over his shoulder while he drove, and while the road exhibited plenty of weather damage, it didn't have many gaping potholes. Which was good because the repetition of noise and gentle jostling on the shocks was about to put him to sleep.

When he checked on his partner because she was quiet, he saw that she'd already succumbed. Uncomfortably backed into the corner made by the seat and the door, she appeared to be held upright by the seatbelt. She also appeared to not care about any of this.

Maybe it was good that she was asleep, because for the moment there was nowhere to shower. They could only drive the remaining half hour into town, stinking up the car. At least in Dallas they could go to the FBI building and use the locker rooms. There was no point checking into any hotel smelling like this. It would only draw attention.

The day was bright by the time he pulled into the parking structure at the building that housed the Dallas office. Leaning over, he nudged Eleri, who blinked and frowned at him.

Putting the car in park, he said, "We're at the Dallas FBI building. I'm hoping they have showers here. No hotel we're willing to stay at would even allow us in the lobby."

She blinked a few more times before looking down at her knees. Despite the paper suit, she'd managed to grind dirt into them. Her first words—spoken mushily—were "literal field work."

He had to laugh as he popped the trunk. The building was beige concrete, geometric, reinforced, and well within spitting distance of Waco. These architects had not forgotten Oklahoma, they weren't messing around.

Eleri stood at the back of the car, one hand holding her luggage upright, the other rubbing her face. Fighting the urge to comment on what germs she might be forcing into her eyes, he led her to the elevator. Inside, they flashed badges and made their way through security. When Donovan asked where he might find showers, the guard pointed and said a few terse words, but it was clear Donovan and Eleri were not even the worst he'd seen since starting his shift a few hours ago.

The locker room provided shampoo, conditioner, and soap in carefully labeled dispensers. Towels were just outside the concrete-sided stalls. Even naked and wet, he felt relatively safe here. Now if he could just catch some sleep. The soap smelled faintly of pine trees and he wondered if it was intended to be ironic in this land of horses, leather oil and grass everywhere. He only needed to get into his bag for a change of clothing.

He emerged, Eleri only two minutes behind him. She didn't say anything, just held her hand out for the keys. "Food or sleep?"

Oh God. He had not yet thought about food but the mere mention of it sent his stomach into fits. It growled loud enough for her to hear, and it seemed she was awake enough to smile over it. "Your vote has been duly noted."

At the car, he leaned back in the passenger seat, now ravenous and nearly in pain. Eleri took the turns sharply, winding on and off freeways and access roads, driving them up onto overpasses high enough to make a good roller-coaster drop, and turning their direction completely around about three times before pulling into a place that looked a little chi-chi but like they could conjure a decent breakfast.

As he unfolded himself and climbed out, he noted that she'd brought them directly into the heart of restaurant central. Though by that measure, Dallas had a minimum of five hearts. He'd never seen so many mid-level chain restaurants in one place. The extended cluster of high signs was interrupted only by low-level taco joints and high-end steak places. He guessed if he didn't like Eleri's choice he could probably walk to a seafood place, two steak places, a chicken place, or something Tex-Mex.

"I don't think they're open yet. It's still only nine-thirty."

"McDonalds is."

Only one side of her mouth smiled. "Feel free to walk."

"No way in hell." He caught up to her with a few quick steps and momentarily found himself in a padded booth in the only open restaurant considering breakfast. Eleri had ordered a coffee and a fruit plate before the server even got her name out.

Ah. His partner needed green things. He only nodded at her and ordered the crab cakes.

Eleri sighed and it turned out he'd been reading her mind. "I hope our next assignment is in New York. They have organic everything, lots of veggies you can find easily, and even soda machines with no high fructose corn syrup drinks."

"Not so much here, huh?"

"I'm having trouble with the concept of salad here." She stirred three packets of sugar into her coffee, and he wondered if she was one of those who thought it didn't matter what she ate as long as it was "natural."

He'd been hungrier than he thought and his crab cakes disappeared quickly. They were chased with pineapple pancakes and pecan syrup. Eleri even finished all her food for the first time, including a whole Belgian waffle. Apparently she needed the fruit but it wasn't enough. No surprise though, they hadn't eaten since breakfast the day before—random granola bars and twice hourly forced water breaks notwithstanding.

She paid the check, stood and said one word. "Hotel."

Settling in, he barely pulled the shades and set his suitcase into the closet when he heard the knock at the door. The peephole revealed the top of a strawberry blonde head, the hair only just now drying. His keen sense of observation—not at its best, he could admit—deduced that it was his partner. Had she not been senior to him, he might not have opened the door.

"I can't sleep. Maybe too much coffee?" She came in and made herself a seat on the second bed.

He sat on the one where he had already pulled back the covers. Not having the same problem himself, he decided silence was the better part of valor.

"So," Her eyes were clear and bright now, direct. She'd slept in the car and it had apparently revived her. They'd told him at the Academy that he'd learn to do this. Donovan had scoffed, he'd been to medical school. He could sleep anywhere, revive and perform surgery on ten minutes rest. But he'd either lost the touch or he had performed some very bad, very arrogant surgeries in the past. He waited.

Eleri didn't disappoint.

"Tell me about the wolf."

ELERI SAT CALMLY WAITING for her answer. Between the coffee and the food, and probably the nap in the car if she was being honest, she'd hit her second wind.

But Donovan just stared. Clearly he'd heard her. Just as clearly he had no intention of saying anything. So she tried something a little bolder. "So, you're a wolf."

Had he been drinking something, he would have spit it out.

Eleri couldn't quite believe she said it. She was thinking it, had been for a while now. She was still blinking when he spoke.

"So you think I'm a werewolf?" Suddenly, he seemed perfectly alert and together. "That's ridiculous."

"Not so much." She should have brought a drink or candy, maybe popcorn—something to do with her hands. Something to put in her mouth to maybe make her think for a minute before she spoke. But she hadn't thought ahead, and here she was, sitting in his room, accusing him of being a mythical creature and pretty convinced she had the right of it. "There's a scientific basis for many of the creatures we thought were just stories in the past. Why can't you be a werewolf?"

"They don't exist." His facial expression was blank. He wasn't outraged that she accused him of this. He wasn't shocked. He didn't look at her like she was crazy. He just looked blank. Which meant he knew more than he was—or wasn't—saying.

"Why not? Are you a god and know all that science has yet to tell us? I find that much harder to believe than that you can transform into a wolf and *run thirty-two miles an hour!*"

Leaning back onto her hands, she bounced her foot and tried to look calmer than she was. At least she tried to look like something. He looked nothing but empty until she threw the number out there. "You had the GPS on. The machine isn't broken. I double-checked everything. So how did you do it?"

"I'm a fast runner." "You broke human land-speed records for the hundred-meter sprint and maintained that rate for miles. I find it easier to believe you're a wolf than that you dust the fastest man in the world, do it over terrain that is only beaten for horribleness by sandstorms, and that you—a proclaimed runner— aren't out winning medals." She leaned back on her elbows this time. "Oh, and no one sees you and the wolf at the same time."

"You have me mixed up with Clark Kent."

She tipped her head, watching him. "You're very funny." She delivered the line deadpan, but paid close attention. He hadn't moved one bit from where he sat.

He also hadn't told her 'no'.

Eleri waited, convinced she was backing him into a corner. It was tough business, getting him to confess. But she wasn't going to throw him in jail, study him, anything. She just wanted the truth. She knew how to interrogate and she was really good at it. The problem was, he'd just graduated the Academy, so he knew at least the basics if not the nuance of the techniques. Which pretty much shot them all out the window. Maybe she should tell him she only wanted to know, she wasn't going to do anything with it. She was lining up her ducks, figuring out how to say it, when he delivered a counter blow.

"So, how did you know to bring in Bernard Collier?"

22

Donovan didn't like this game Eleri was playing with him.

This was exactly why he stuck with his previous job for so long. He almost wanted to cry. All his life, he managed to successfully hide his condition. Thirty-four years—most of it moving around, some of it finally, blessedly, stationary in South Carolina—and now in just a few weeks, she managed to ferret him out.

His brick wall had sprung back up rather quickly when the words tumbled out of her mouth. She looked like even she was surprised that she said them. Everything he said to her was true: the very idea was ludicrous. That didn't reduce its factualness at all.

Turning the table at least startled her.

Truthfully, he expected nothing but an impasse.

This would be it. Just a few weeks in and his career with the FBI would be over. He would leave while she still had only suspicions, before she had proof. Before she could hold him up to the powers that be so they could study him.

His father had told him horror stories. There were no

boogeymen for his kind. There were fanatics, true believers, hunters, even groupies, but nothing good. People didn't understand, and when they didn't, they made up tales to fill in the blanks. Silver bullets, full moons—he'd read it all. And he'd hidden it all his life.

Eleri was thinking, not blank like he'd tried to be. Her stance changed. Her fake-relaxed position was abandoned and she sat up straighter. Her hands twisted a bit before she realized what she was doing, and she laced her fingers and looked at them for a moment before lifting her gaze to his. The directness was unnerving.

"I dreamed of the truck. About a week ago."

"What?" That was not what he expected. He'd suspected she was holding out research on him and never thought this could be the issue.

She nodded, confirming her words without saying them again. "I have clear dreams. I see things that seem like dreams, but they're real."

He leaned forward, suddenly engaged in her story rather than his. The brick wall never even tumbled, it had simply disappeared. "Maybe you saw the truck before? And put something together?"

Her smile was sad, and worse, it traced that bleakness all the way into her eyes. Her words were flat, scientific—she'd put thought into this. "That's possible. Though, since I never met the man before, I'm not sure how I would have deduced that. We never drove by that road where he buried her, so I couldn't have seen and subconsciously matched the tire tracks."

"Maybe you overheard something?" For all his oddities, he believed in science. He was a mutation, certainly, but mutations themselves were not abnormal.

Her head shook softly from side to side, denying that possibility. "If I overheard a conversation, then you should have, too. We've hardly left each other's sides."

He didn't know what to say.

She did.

"I dreamed that the orange truck with blue flames saw Ruth on the side of the road. I saw Bernard help her into the cab." Eleri frowned and looked into the distance at the telling of it. "Ruth opened the passenger door, but Bernard leaned over and helped haul her in. That's when I saw she was sick. She could hardly climb in." A long, low sigh punctuated the story. "Of course, when I dreamed that I already knew that Ruth hitchhiked into town to get to the hospital when she was sick. I only thought he could give us some information about . . . I don't know. More information. I was shocked to see him, nothing about the dream seemed to be anything but a dream mixing up elements from the case."

"Maybe it's coincidence. Maybe your subconscious put together some pieces for you." He'd studied that a little in med school. There had been classes on healing, on patient attitudes, and how to deal with the different personality types.

She didn't look at him. Instead, she studied the slim strip of carpeting between the beds as though it was fascinating. "I would dismiss it if it were the first time it had happened."

"What?" Something inside him melted.

She looked disconsolate. Lost. Like no one understood.

He needed to hear what she said. Needed to put the empathy that he felt in its place. He didn't do empathy. He didn't do feelings at all if he didn't have to. But his shell was dissolving. Eleri—normally so bold, strong, smart, even sweet—looked hollow and alone.

She looked like he felt.

Her words only knit the ties tighter.

"When I started with the FBI, I was a field agent for the first year. I think I was pretty average in most respects. I'm a good marksman, I pass my tests easily, but I wasn't winning top honors. In the Academy, I got called out as much as anyone for my mistakes. I wasn't the first over the wall or through the course, but I was never the last. But on a case, I was great at thinking ahead of the suspect."

She blinked as though trying to hold back tears. Donovan could see the gap between them was larger than the space between the beds. Theirs knees were about a foot apart, but he couldn't reach across. He had no idea why she would look like she was about to lose it when she was describing something she was good at—something that made her valuable at the thing she'd chosen to do with her life.

After a breath or two, Eleri kept going. "I was really good at it and they moved me to the profiling team where I became a star. I was the best. I could tell you our perp's make and model of car. I could tell you what his house looked like and how neat or messy it was. That he would keep magazines stacked on the corner of his coffee table. Or she would have a drawer stacked with tiny shirts from the babies she'd stolen from the hospital."

Oh, shit.

He saw where it was going. He saw in her face, in her eyes, before she spoke it.

Donovan didn't know what to do. He'd never felt *for* anyone before. His father kept him from others. There were just the two of them—a growing boy who was denied friends and left only with the company of a cold man who often drank more than he should have. Donovan had built his walls early, and he'd built them high and strong. Now he wanted them back. He had his own pain, his own shit to deal with. He didn't need Eleri's. But it assaulted him, piercing him as surely as silver bullets.

Silent tears rolled down her cheeks. "I dreamed them. I dreamed them all. Sometimes I just had a hunch. Maybe it was something I dreamed and forgot. I don't remember everything when I wake up."

Her fingers were twisting in her lap, to the point where Donovan realized she wasn't paying attention, and he was getting concerned that she might inadvertently hurt herself. Finally reaching out, he settled his hand over hers, thinking it would break the spell she was weaving. It only stopped her hands.

"I saw the woman take the babies and I couldn't stop her. I could get ahead of her and we returned six of the kids to their homes. But four of them died. Three were taken while we were on her tail. Five were stolen from different hospitals—despite those silly store-theft tags they put on the babies, she still got them out. It took two more to triangulate her and it took three dreams. Three dreams where I saw how two of the babies died in her care."

There was only a beat, only a moment where Donovan could have said anything but he was too slow.

"I saw the Trail Killer take two of his victims. By then I knew what was happening. I knew my dreams were predictive, *real*. I knew what I'd seen and I knew no one would believe me. So I had to gather evidence, work up a vague profile, send the agents in the right direction."

He interrupted. He was prepared this time, hoping his question would break the chain, disrupt the ride she was on. "Doesn't the FBI understand that hunches are valuable? Especially from people who produce consistently good ones?"

She nodded. "But how do I tell them I have a hunch that he put a sticker family on his car specifically to be more approachable? How do I tell them that he chose his parking lots to have several cars, so it would look inhabited, even if there were no people in earshot? That he would stand next to the car and play with his phone and act frustrated? He'd ask to borrow theirs then Taser them, take their keys, push them into their own car, and drive off with it . . ." She looked up at him, her round features red-rimmed with the tears that slowly made tracks down her face, her eyes wider and greener than usual, and so bleak. "How am I supposed to save anyone when I can't tell them how I did it?"

His internal organs sank to the bottom of his ribs. He ached for her. It would have been easier to admit to her accusations than to hear this. He could have stayed cold and given her the facts about himself. But this was killing him.

Eleri's next words came at a whisper. Harsh and biting, they tore through him.

"So I told them. I saved the women he would have attacked. We pulled the last one from the basement where he taped her to a chair and . . ." She didn't finish the sentence. Donovan had read about the case; he didn't need the details. What he had read had been chilling. Imagining that Eleri *saw* it as it happened was sickening.

"She's a mess, but she's alive. And I spent eleven days in holding. I was interrogated up and down. Barely fed. I asked for a lawyer, but as an agent, I was told I had to be accused of something first—"

"What!" They held her?

"They didn't formally accuse me of anything. They were just questioning me." She looked at him as though he didn't understand.

They thought it was her?

"I had airtight alibis. I was with a senior agent during two of the abductions. But they still thought I knew more about it than I said. That maybe I knew Jeremy Kite personally and was trying to gain credit for turning him in like I was a rockstar or something."

Donovan tried again to shift the subject. "Was this the agent you told me about? The senior agent you like?"

"No, that was my senior partner when I was in the field. In Profiling, we often worked in groups rather than pairs. So I didn't have a specific senior agent there." Always Eleri, she headed right back on track. "They eventually cut me loose. There was no evidence against me except my overwhelming knowledge of Kite."

"You stopped the Trail Killer. You should be proud." He understood the burden of what she saw, but he didn't understand why she still carried it. "Your balance sheet is firmly in the positive. That's good."

"They pulled my assignment from the Profiling division."

"But you were so good at it!" These people were his new bosses?

"Too good. And too crazy." She looked away. "They put me in a mental hospital for treatment. And I actually kind of liked it there."

Donovan didn't like this. For a moment he fantasized about standing over a dead body. Lifting a heavy liver and smelling the poison there. He imagined writing the order for the tox screen, weighing the organ, noting the color, bagging it. He imagined making an incision into dead flesh. Popping his shoulders into place, his hips, his face and running wild through the woods. He didn't do connections, but he was connected now, even if he hated hurting for her.

His eyes were closed when she spoke again, though now the whisper was gone. Her words were clear, strong. "You should know. You should know that I was in the hospital until three days before I met you. I was pulled out to run this case."

Holy shit.

She seemed so normal. Not at all like the basket case she described. Not like an agent that should be questioned for days at a time, stripped of her badge and tossed in the bin. He didn't know what to say. The words that came out of his mouth shouldn't have been said. "But you were declared sane, right? That's why you're here now?"

He would have been good if she'd said yes.

"No. I wasn't. They weren't ready to release me. Westerfield signed me out against medical advice." She looked him dead in the eye, as though she wanted to be sure he knew what he'd gotten himself into. "He wanted me on this case. Apparently, he handpicked us. Since the hospital had signed off my adjustment over—" she raised her hands and made air quotes, "—'the Jeremy

Kite incidence and the subsequent questioning,' Westerfield decided I should join NightShade."

"If you were declared better, then why were you released 'Against Medical Advice'?" Patients left AMA all the time. He knew that. But better was better, not AMA.

Again, a big pause. A big sigh. A look off into the corner. "Because while I had apparently cleanly adjusted to what happened with Kite and my stint as a profiler, I made the mistake of telling my doctor about my sister."

This could not be good. He didn't even really want to know. He was her junior partner. Under her thumb, and now he wondered if she was batshit crazy—though he'd seen zero evidence of that himself. All he'd seen was a series of odd incidences that, if he had to add them up, mostly supported what she said about her profiling days. She had something normal people didn't and, burden or not, she was using it to keep the FBI out front. Even when they slammed her for it.

He was already tied too tightly into this assignment. He was wrapped in a web he couldn't escape. He'd helped train the replacement ME at his old hospital in Columbia. He couldn't go back. He could only go forward. Right now, forward was with Eleri.

"What about your sister?"

23

Eleri had opened her fat mouth thinking that she should give a little to get a little. She told Donovan she thought he was the wolf. When he asked about Bernard Collier, she thought she would tell him just enough to make the exchange more even.

She did not expect the empathy she saw from him. Nor did she expect it to affect her the way it did. The words poured out, the stories coming like a flood, though she knew from her months of therapy that she was still attached to what she'd suffered—both what she saw and how she was held and questioned over it.

When she started talking, she promised herself she would give just enough to make him spill and instead, *she* did.

About three sentences in, she realized that she was simply bleeding herself. She was finally voluntarily telling someone about what happened, not having it ripped from her in an office with a doctor taking notes. Just telling Donovan. And damn him, he was as close to a werewolf as existed. He had to listen to her without judgment.

Simply stating how she'd been removed from her post and questioned sickened her all over again. But it was lessened a bit by the way he was outraged for her. Hardly a stranger, he was still hardly a good friend. They had common training—studying in biological fields, both working with the dead, going through the Academy—but even these paths only put their language and logic on the same road, they weren't shared experiences in the real sense.

Eleri got the feeling Donovan didn't have shared experiences with much of anyone. She was also convinced he didn't have shared feelings with a soul. His outrage felt all the better, all the more soothing for its rarity.

Empty by the time she made it through her work history, the story of her sister was already passing her lips. It wasn't so much that Eleri chose to share it, but that it would tell itself. Emmaline was a burden she'd carried in her soul for far too long. The resulting feeling of hollowness was itself a welcome relief. Hollow wasn't heavy.

Feeling her spine straighten and her breathing deepen, Eleri went almost into a trance. She didn't look at Donovan, just remembered happier times. "I was only two when my sister came along. So all my remembered life, I had a younger sister, Emmaline. I was named for my grandmother on my father's side, Emmaline for the grandmother on my mother's side. I don't know why. When I got older I learned that grandmother Emmaline had a drug problem and left my mother—just a girl at the time—with my grand-mere Remi to raise her.

"My Emmaline and I grew up in my father's family and culture. The Eameses trace back to the first families of Virginia, having settled there before the US became the US. His mother was Eleri Hale, and the Hales were a first family of Massachusetts. We can trace that lineage back to the 1500s in England. Emmaline and I were brought up mostly outside Charlottesville, Virginia, at Bell Point Farm. We traveled back and forth to

Kentucky a lot though. It wasn't our home, but we have a house there, too, Patton Hall."

Donovan frowned at her. She knew he hadn't grown up the way she did. Money wasn't even discussed in her home. Eleri didn't really understand what money was, other than something her father complained others wanted from them, until she entered high school. She had come up the polar opposite from kids like him, but she had become aware as she became older. Surely he did, too.

"You had multiple houses? With names?"

Ah. She nodded. "Bell Point was in my father's family forever. I think his father or grandfather purchased Patton Hall in Kentucky when the Pattons lost everything. The way the story is told in my family, the sale of the house saved the Pattons from destitution." She said it before she realized the Old Kentucky family's idea of destitution was probably still miles above Donovan scraping and saving for running shoes for the cheapest sport he could find.

He laughed at her, not in humor but in that "oh, God, I should have known" kind of way. "Any other grand homes with names?"

"Just one." The wrong thing to say, given the way his eyebrows climbed. "A beachfront home in Hatteras. Foxhaven." Done with listing her family properties, she went on. "We were at Patton Hall in Kentucky. I was ten when we lost Emmaline."

His breath sucked in. "I'm sorry." He shook his head. "I lost my mother when I was seven. She died suddenly and unexpectedly." Death and the pain of it were universal, and he absorbed some of hers. "I know you never get over that really. At least my mother was an adult. She'd had a child and a life. I can't imagine a child dying."

He didn't have the right of it though. "No. We *lost* her. Literally."

Eleri's eyes burned. They always did, the pressure at the back of them leaking forward. Though she tried not to cry outright, she could never stop the jagged pain that accompanied the memory. "We were out for a riding lesson, Emmaline and me. We were with David, our instructor. It was my turn to take a run, and I went over some tiny jumps that I thought were so high, and David told me to do it again. So I did. By the time I got it right—or right enough—we told Emmaline it was her turn and she was gone."

She saw the horror in his eyes. Missing children were the bane of the FBI. The Feds were brought in on any case that was a legitimate abduction and only the coldest agents didn't cry themselves to sleep, even when the child was returned relatively safely. Even in the best cases, you stood at the end when the reunited family walked away and tried to hold the shreds of yourself together.

And she wasn't the attending agent in this case. She was the sister. She was partly responsible, though she told herself over and over that she wasn't. She was ten. She was with an adult. Sometimes these things just happened. It didn't change the fact that her heart still stopped beating at the very thought of that day.

"We looked for her for about half an hour, yelling for her and for Biscuit, her pony. But we got nothing."

Donovan's face fell. Eleri knew why. It was exactly the wrong thing to do. People looked for their missing kid first, sometimes for hours, before notifying the authorities. The police loved finding kids who had wandered off, but a time lapse like her family created allowed predators to get farther and farther away. Allowed the trail to go cold before anyone even knew to look for it.

"David bucked up then and told my parents. They came out and looked, too. It was another hour before they called the police. The police questioned me and David and then my parents. I didn't know anything. I was ten. I was petrified." And no one had paid any attention to her. Authorities knew differently now. At the

Academy, she had received the very training she could have bene-
fited from. She knew exactly what should be done and exactly
what had not been done for her when she was ten.

Her mother had looked at her wild-eyed and demanded to
know why she'd let her little sister out of her sight. Now, of
course, with the distance of time and adulthood, she knew her
mother was mad out of her mind and not considered that her
remaining child, obviously safe in front of her, was just as
distraught as she was. Eleri had been questioned, locked up tight,
and shoved aside.

"They hunted for days. It was years before my mother could
leave Patton Hall. She was so afraid Emmaline would return
home and no one would be there to meet her."

Unable to handle any more, knowing she was close to losing
the slight control that kept her from splitting into pieces, she
blatantly changed the topic. "Cheer me up. Tell me I'm right
about the wolf."

She was met with silence. Well, he had changed the topic on
her, too. She sniffed a little and tried again. "Seriously, I just
confessed I did a stint in a mental hospital. It's not like I'm going
to tell anyone about you. Besides that wolf isn't a wolf except at
first glance. After that, I saw that it has your eyes and your teeth.
And that's just weird if it's not you."

He still looked at her, staring, that blank expression having
slid perfectly back into place. Suddenly she hated it. She had one
herself, a mask that shut out everything, but she wasn't shutting
out anything. She never told people about Emmaline; she sure
didn't tell people about the hospital. Even her perfect parents
didn't know where she'd been. She told them she was vacationing
with Wade, afraid anything else would break them. Since the FBI
picked up the tab—a good idea since they'd pretty much driven
her to the brink—there was no reason to tell them. Nathalie and
Thomas Eames had worked hard to return to their perfect lives. It
was enough trouble that their federal agent daughter refused to

marry and produce Eames offspring. They didn't need to know she was mental as well.

Donovan still didn't answer.

Having been through the wringer enough times, and being adult enough to admit that she'd put herself there and even turned the crank, Eleri stood and headed for the door. She was reaching for the lock, considering sleeping the day away and hoping she didn't dream anything else useful when she heard the word.

"Yes."

For a moment she thought that was all she needed. He obviously wasn't going to be forthcoming. And suddenly she was tired. She flipped back the U-bolt that was still in her way and nodded once before turning the knob.

"Yes, I'm the wolf. If you tell anyone, I'll deny it. If you convince them, they'll probably kill me."

Slowly, Eleri moved the bolts back into place. Kill him? Turning, she saw that he was serious. "Why would they kill you?"

He broke. At first she thought it was instantaneous hysteria of some kind, but she quickly realized it was real mirth. He threw his head back and laughed loud and long. All she could do was wait while his laughter pulled her back into the room.

Donovan was wiping his eyes when he finally found the voice to speak to her. "They'll kill me because I'm a monster. Silver bullets and all that."

"No one would do that. Not in this day and age."

He laughed again. "There's still a reasonable percentage of people who think that homosexuality in America affects weather patterns! Just because *you* wouldn't string me up doesn't mean others won't think the world is better without me. They'll become heroes, just for killing me."

"You sound like you know something about it." Her heart twisted. This time it was his eyes that held horrors past. Because his eyes were usually relatively blank, she found that concerning. As the thought hit her, she whispered her fear, "Your mother?"

"No." He was fast, solid in his answer. "My mother died, never knowing what my father was, what I was. I didn't even know it at the time. Back then, my dad was only hiding himself, but later, when I was ten, he took me to meet my grandmother."

His head tipped a little and Eleri read that as indicating the memory was not so good. Slowly she came back into the room and softly resumed her seat on the second bed.

"I had just realized what I could do, discovered some of it on my own. It turns out my dad was hoping it would skip me, since my mother wasn't one. His parents were both hybrids. That's what he and his folks called us: Hybrids." He smiled and his back straightened and when he started speaking, she realized he had transformed from Donovan, the poor kid with hardscrabble memories and the burden of being very different, to Dr. Heath, the scientist.

"I'm guessing my father is double dominant gene, as both his parents are Hybrids. And 'hybrid' is completely the wrong term —we're not half and half anything. We're . . . weird human I guess. It's a complex series of double-jointedness. Some people can contort and fold themselves into a suitcase, I can contort and fold myself into a wolf." He shrugged as though it wasn't a scientific breakthrough at all.

"Show me!" Suddenly, she felt like a kid on Christmas morning. A complete one-eighty from where she'd been just thirty minutes ago.

"No way in hell. You'll freak out."

"No I won't! I know what I'm in for." She was leaning forward, her hands braced into the soft comforter, waiting.

But he refused again, shaking his head. "Maybe someday, but not today."

She sighed. "So if you're not a hybrid—and I'm not suggesting that a wolf and a human got together, because that kind of cross species mating does *not* work, and I know it—then how do you explain all the extras?"

"Extras?"

Her mouth worked for a moment. How was she supposed to put it? "You don't just look like a wolf, you can hear like them, smell like them, run like them." Eleri waved her hands around as though that helped. It didn't. She was sure.

He nodded, absorbing her question and bouncing it back to her. "I can run like a wolf only when I'm shaped like a wolf. That's just muscle and physiology. The rest just seems to be mildly altered 'normal'." He ran his finger down the bridge of his nose. "My nose is long for a human, not out of normal but on the long side. It's short for a wolf. I have a larger nasal cavity inside my head than most straight-up humans. That alone accounts for a good increase in sense of smell. Some normal people can smell really well. I'm just a bit beyond them."

"How do you know your sinus cavity is larger? And I thought your nose was long because you were part Indian. Just a guess though on the heritage."

He was smiling, genuinely smiling. "I have tested, X-rayed and CTed every part of me every chance I could. I've drawn my blood while in human shape but full fur, trying to see if there's a chemical that runs that process—there's nothing I can find, by the way. And I am part Indian. My mother was from Calcutta. Good guess."

Not a guess. She was a forensic scientist. She didn't need to see the actual bone of his skull to place portions of his heritage, but she wouldn't have guessed "wolf" from what she did see. If she and Jonah hadn't both seen the creature, if Jonah hadn't been so lucid and spot-on about everything else he said, if the wolf hadn't walked so boldly into Donovan's backyard and looked her in the eyes the way it did . . . If it all hadn't happened the way it did, she would never have put it together.

Silence fell between them. His laughter and sudden-onset

happiness had sloughed off and in the wake of it his discomfort talking about himself settled back in. When he finally spoke, he shifted the topic yet again. "They never found your sister."

Eleri shook her head. It was all she could do. The crushing weights that had lifted for a little while settled back into well-worn grooves, almost comforting in their familiarity.

"So you never saw her again?"

That was the million-dollar question. "My parents never saw her, but I did. I dreamed of her all the time. I dreamed of the man who came. I saw him open the gate and lead her horse away. I thought they were just dreams. I saw her with another family, over the years. I watched her grow."

The tears came again and she didn't even try to stop them. "I didn't know." It was a confession, whispered, pushed through her soul before the words formed. "I didn't know the dreams showed me real things. I didn't know I could tell someone or find her."

Eleri couldn't breathe. She had failed her sister before her own life even really started. Before she became her own person. She had decided to join the FBI when she was twelve, just two years after her sister disappeared. Eleri was going to find missing kids and bring them back to their families, but when she was in college it all changed.

"Even though I sometimes dreamed other things that came to pass, it never occurred to me that I was really seeing my sister." Her hand came up, to wipe the tears so she could see.

Donovan sat quietly, unmoving, not interfering. It was almost as if he wasn't there.

"When I was nineteen, the dreams changed. They became . . . real." This time she looked at him, into his eyes and she could see he was terrified of what she wanted him to understand. She still didn't really understand it herself. She just knew it to be true. "Nothing was surreal. I could touch things, think clearly, smell, taste, hear everything. Emmaline came to me. She was seventeen, it was her birthday. She wore a white skirt and a white t-shirt and there was blood on her. On her shirt, on her hands, dripping down her leg, but she walked fine and she hugged me. And it was real."

Donovan looked at her as though he could see her soul crushing under the pressure of the vise she felt. She couldn't breathe for the weight on her chest, couldn't see for the tears clouding her eyes. "She's come to me like that in dreams since then. She wakes me before bad things happen. Tells me things I need to know. Emmaline is always real to me now when I dream her. She sees me, touches me, hugs me. But she hasn't aged a day since then."

Eleri was gasping for air, but she got the words out anyway. "She was alive. She lived with another family for longer than she lived with us. She died on her seventeenth birthday. And I'm the only one who knows."

24

Donovan searched the rabbit's warren of rooms on the fifth floor of the Dallas FBI branch building.

If he hadn't double-checked the number placard on the wall he would have come back from the vending machines and inadvertently joined another group working on an entirely separate project. Aside from his recognition of Eleri, he could easily have done it. This other group sat at an identical table, sorting pictures and documents and talking about a stalker. Wrong crime. Donovan smiled and waved his apology for interrupting and they seemed to recognize it. Maybe people walked into the wrong room all the time.

Eleri and Agent Bozeman were farther down the hall than he remembered. So Donovan kept walking, juggling the bottle of water he carried for Eleri and a second can of soda for Bozeman —a Dr Pepper, which seemed to be the state drink of Texas.

Eleri looked up, nothing showing in her face of the day before. After telling him about her sister—which Donovan had not seen coming—she had sighed, put her head on the pillow for a moment, and passed out cold while he watched. Too deeply asleep to disturb, Eleri lay unmoving on top of the comforter and didn't notice when he turned out the light and crawled into his own bed. Which was exactly where he'd intended to be almost a full hour before she marched in, accused him of being exactly what he was, then opened the floodgates on him about her sister.

He figured he deserved it for turning the tables on her.

But he'd fallen asleep for the first time realizing he wasn't the only freak in town. And he'd woken up alone. At some point, she must have crawled back to her own room, and he didn't see her again until this morning.

Donovan had gone running late in the day yesterday, show-ered, and walked the two blocks it took to find a steakhouse. It had been good to be by himself. Yet it felt surprisingly good to be here now, to be part of a team for the first time in his adult life.

He spent the morning at the autopsy of the girl from the field —currently identified as "Faith." Fingerprint analysts had matched her with nothing yet.

At first, he and Eleri had simply watched the FBI medical examiner perform the task, but then the woman smiled and offered him a scalpel. She even mentioned that she'd heard about him from his days in Columbia, that one of her partners had shipped him a body and Donovan located a test and noted an obscure poison for them.

He was startled by the recognition and happy at the mention. He spent so many years living, then working, in a bubble, to hear that he wasn't as isolated as he thought was mind-blowing. It had been a lot to absorb that he wasn't the only one. Now, he was seeing that others appreciated his freakishness, even if they didn't know the full extent of it. While it was good news—or at least interesting news—he still felt like he was pulled by a tide and thrown against the rocks. Each time he was relieved and swept back out into the nothingness, he'd be surprisingly bashed again.

When he and Eleri joined in the autopsy, though, it was a roundhouse the likes of which he'd never experienced before. Eleri pointed out photos that needed to be taken and walked the assistant through a series of shots. She led them to check inside the sneakers, look for marks left by the seams of the clothing, things he not often looked at in a standard autopsy. She pulled soil samples from under the nails and used forceps in pockets.

Dr. Madison didn't bat an eye when Donovan leaned closer to the liver, only continued acting as though this was perfectly normal. "You smell something I'm missing, don't you?"

Surprised, though he didn't know why, Donovan didn't really know what to say. Eleri stepped in for him. "He has a great sense of smell. Even better, he has a scent memory like nobody's business. I can barely tell you when cookies are baking!"

Madison had laughed out loud at that. "Me, too! I thought that was an advantage in this job—not being able to smell—but now I'm rethinking that." She turned her attention from Eleri back to Donovan and he started to tense. The two women were a dangerous combination.

One of them could ask sharp questions, since she was seeing him work, and being an ME herself she would know exactly where he deviated from the norm. The other one could answer truthfully about him. It was a concerning situation, and the excitement and collaboration he'd felt just a moment before began rapidly congealing into a knot of dread.

"Does the decay smell not bother you?" Madison turned to him, her head tilted, genuinely curious.

He was sorting out how to answer that without saying too much when Eleri beat him to it again. "It doesn't seem to. Or else he has a way better poker face than me." She'd turned Madison's attention away from him, even if the conversation was about him. "We pulled this girl up, the rest of us taking breather breaks, but not him."

"Wow." It was all the other doctor said. She went back to examining the body and working one of the most thorough forensic autopsies on the books.

At lunch, he'd retreated back into himself after being buffeted with group conversation all morning. In fact he and Eleri had exchanged only a few words past deciding where to go to eat.

Tense and worried, he asked her point-blank, "Are you going to out me?"

"Never." The answer had been swift and sharp, her eyes narrowing on his, her brow furrowing as if to wonder how he could ask that. "You have to tell people something or else you look guilty." She had the right of that, he knew, and he took a moment to nod and acknowledge how she'd manipulated the conversation this morning. She allowed him to do what he did without making it odd. She distracted Dr. Madison when he needed to poke at something, sniff something else. But before he could tell her he understood, even thank her, she volleyed it right back at him. "Are you going to out me?"

"Of course not."

That had been the end of all conversation until they came to the FBI branch building and met up with Bozeman. While Donovan and Eleri peered at internal organs that morning, Bozeman had the thankless task of delivering the news about Faith to Jonah and Charity. He and another agent had interviewed them separately, and Bozeman was delivering those results, joining the braintrust here, while the second agent babysat the escapees.

Given that he'd spent yesterday sleeping, Donovan felt they had accomplished a lot here today. They had a location for the community. They had several proven deaths. They had children, some with IDs. At least one confirmed missing child had turned up in the City of God, though there was no evidence that these were the people who had taken her. In addition to working those angles, the team was figuring out a way to exonerate Bernard Collier.

The three of them sat around most of the early afternoon on that one. It was unanimously considered that the man panicked when the girl died. He knew she didn't have any family connected into the grid, and he didn't want to get his friends in trouble. Further interviews had revealed that he had not picked anyone up again since then, and was unable to offer input on the City of God's feelings about the missing Faith. So Eleri, Donovan and Bozeman came up with a plan to take to Westerfield about giving Collier a way to clear his name, given that he did commit several crimes.

While Collier knew nothing about the City's reaction to Faith's death, Jonah and Charity did. Ashlyn Fisk was being slowly reunited with her family, and they weren't dragging her home and thus away from Jonah. Or away from the investigation where she was needed.

Both the kids were devastated to learn of Faith's passing but not surprised. Bozeman played a recording of Jonah—looking as distraught as he sounded—saying how Baxter told them Faith was likely gone, that she had been sneaking out and that God had punished her by making her sick. When others had gotten ill with the same disease, Baxter claimed Faith and Ruth had brought the punishment down on the group. The community had been smart enough to quarantine the babies and the kids didn't think any of the little ones had gotten sick. But because they hadn't seen the infants in a while, they had only the reports of the adults to go on.

By the time Donovan had finished his candy bar and drink, Bozeman had headed back to the safe house to check in on the kids and relieve the other agent for dinner. Which left Eleri and Donovan with the last of the material.

They put away the interviews from Jonah and Charity. They put away the Bernard Collier information, and they spread out all the print photos across the table, old school.

Grouping Faith's autopsy photos on the left, Eleri let Donovan sort out what they had from the dead girl found on the side of the road. Then he pulled out pictures of Jonah and Charity. Photos from when they first made contact with the FBI, with Donovan and Eleri. The Grady PD had taken Charity's photos, but Cassa Brinks had done an excellent job.

Under all the photos they lined up the paperwork. Sometimes there was a stack; sometimes just a page or two. Jonah and Charity each had hours of interview footage, but there was no way to put that on the table. Standing back, he surveyed the organized mess, wishing he had another candy bar. "Baxter is one sick fuck."

Eleri nodded. "Yeah, and we have no evidence against him."

"His own parents are glad he's gone. They think he's a sociopath." He shook his head thinking Joseph Hayden Baxter could not have come from a more loving couple.

"Yeah," Eleri sighed, echoing his internal monologue. "The Baxters seemed like the nicest people. Like fundamentalism done right, you know?" When Donovan only nodded in return, she kept talking. "Do you think maybe they were monsters? That they abused him in some way we couldn't see? We were only there for a few hours. And we were only there 'now.' I mean, we can't ever see how they were when he was growing up. Maybe they're different now."

"That's possible, but I have seen some pretty sick stuff. I'm sure you have, too." He shouldn't have said that. She'd seen her own sister for years after the little girl disappeared, and the haunted look on Eleri's face when she said it indicated her sister hadn't lived a happy life with a loving kidnapping family. He kept talking to cover his mistake. "I'm guessing JHB is your garden variety indication of the fact that sometimes monsters happen, and they are going to be monsters regardless of how they are raised."

When he looked at a dead body, sometimes Donovan got angry about what had happened to the person. Sometimes it was a bad physician who had screwed up and missed a diagnosis. He could forgive that, eventually. Sometimes it was the way the body was desecrated. The person died or had been killed and dumped, left to scavengers. Donovan couldn't abide by that; given what he did, the dead were to be revered. But sometimes it was about what happened before they died. That was the worst. But it was almost always only one body at a time.

Here he had four. Two were still alive, but those two were kids. The third—Faith—was a very young woman. He knew there was a common thread here, something that would tie it all together. He already knew that thread would sew up Baxter, too, though he also knew he wasn't supposed to think that way. While he was supposed to stay open minded, he couldn't. Not really.

And he couldn't see the damn thread.

Most frustrated with Faith's information or lack thereof, he tried not to stare at it. In general, time sensitivity in the ME's office was about the importance of the people who wanted the information—how much someone was willing to push to make results come back faster. Here, the importance was on lives, not wants. There were more children in the City of God, and who knew what was happening to them? Donovan worked hard not to think that Jonah and Charity's escapes might have made things more difficult for the remaining ones.

Donovan and Eleri stood side by side, shared stances and shared frustration. Eleri shook her head and her frown grew to match his internal anger. There was no solid evidence on Baxter.

As Donovan watched, she sucked in a breath and put her hands back on her hips. It didn't mean she had anything. No epiphany shone on her face. Her unusual coloring only served to highlight the scrunched expression as she walked around the table to get a look at things upside down. Not knowing anything better to do, Donovan followed her.

She was only a quarter of the way through her slow trek when her phone rang and she stepped aside to answer it, letting Donovan pass. Given the way her entire body stilled, it had to be Westerfield and there had to be news.

"Yes, sir. Yes, sir. . . . Yes. Of course."

It was all he heard and he tried not to pay attention, tried to focus on the photos and information before him until she slid the phone back in her pocket and turned to face him, her eyes shining. "There's a match. The girl in the red shirt, the bones. A family came forward from the missing files and volunteered DNA. It's their daughter."

His shoulders dropped. Bitter taste filled his mouth. It didn't make the girl any less human to be unidentified, but it did stop another family from entering the painful mourning process. They had probably hoped and worried for years about her. He wondered how Eleri felt about it, and he wondered why he was wondering how someone else felt. Trying not to let any of it show on his face, he jammed his fists into his hips, a much harder version of the "thinking stance" he and Eleri had adopted and he suddenly saw it.

Rapidly he reached across the table, pulling certain photos together, pushing others away, praying that he was right and that there was enough information here.

25

Eleri's heart was in her throat thinking about the family that had come forward. For a moment she wallowed in self-pity, torturing herself over the closure her own family didn't have for Emmaline.

Eventually, her mother gave up, decided that it was over. It took eight years to get to that point, and Eleri leaving for college had certainly helped trigger it. For Eleri, college had changed everything, too. It led her to this point, to standing here, getting news about another family too much like hers, and watching Donovan practically crawl across the table to rearrange the photos.

She was opening her mouth to ask what he was doing when he anticipated her voice, holding his hand up to stop her before she even started. He dug frantically through his bag, coming up with a grease pen, which he used to scribble something on the pictures. Not wanting to bother him, Eleri didn't move, but it meant she couldn't see what he was writing. It was several long moments before he turned to her, a look of triumph across his bold features.

"They were all hit by the same person." He pointed at the pictures he'd aligned.

Bruises, all of them. On Faith's upper arms, matching hand-prints. On her leg a fist, the faint outline now traced in red wax. On Charity's face, the same imprint. The left side of her face, matching the inner plane of Charity's right leg—indicating a right-handed punch. The size indicated a grown man, a good-sized hand. There were more matches, Jonah's temple, his lower right back, just above the kidney. There was a marker in the impression, in the third finger, probably caused by something like an old healed break. That finger didn't fold down quite all the way, didn't form a plane with the other carpal bones. Or maybe it was the pinky that folded down too much. Either way, it was a distinctive fist.

"Here." He held up the photo of the bones from the red-shirted girl. The clothing and the smell tied her to the City of God, though only the shirt was admissible evidence and even that was a bit shaky. But they had photos of the autopsy, and while her bloated state didn't help identification purposes, it showed the bruising relatively well.

Donovan's voice was clear, "It's not a match to JHB yet, but it ties them all together. They were all hit by the same man."

"Person." She said it calmly and even managed a little grin. "Don't be sexist."

"True," he conceded, allowing her to slightly lighten the moment as they looked at all the markers of pain and mistreat-ment on the photos in front of them. "But statistically—"

"It's a man." She finished. He was right about that.

Eleri was tired. She was still wrung out from the day before, when she'd talked for one hour and slept for twelve. Of course, they had worked the twenty-six hours prior to that interviewing Collier and then digging up the body—no mere vacation, that day. The twelve hours were warranted, the eight she added to it after her too large dinner, maybe not so much. Today she feared she had over-slept a bit. Anything over ten put most people into a dulled state that left them with a siren song from their pillow all day. Though the work in front of her was interesting, the lack of food and the fading light outside the large windows were signaling her brain to shut down. While she knew all the neural processes behind it, she was still having a tough time fighting the urge to find a soft place to sleep.

"I need dinner." She announced. "And we need to get to San Antonio."

"What's in San An?" Donovan looked up at her from where he continued to sort through photos.

"Westerfield. He'll be there tomorrow, wants to meet us in person so we can hand in our Collier report and talk about the next phase of the investigation."

This time her partner looked up. "There's a next phase? We don't have enough to implicate anyone yet."

Her shrug was somewhat exaggerated as she didn't know anything about that either. Unable to provide information, she provided labor and started gathering up the photos and paper-work. They would have to clear everything out of here. "Eat first or pack first?"

"Pack?"

"San An. Our meeting is in the morning. Pack and drive tonight or get up early. I'll let you call it." She had most of the pictures stacked, the bruises grouped together, writing on the back of each photo now clearly delineating whom it belonged to and what body part had been photographed. As she gathered them, Eleri realized they would need to print off clean copies to replace these. Oh joy. She could stay up late in her room setting up the photo printer from the trunk of the rental car. It came to her that she could just do it in San Antonio at the branch office. She felt better just thinking she didn't really have to haul out that little brick of a printer again and wait while it chugged out more photos.

"How far is it?"

"Door to door? About four plus hours."

"Ugh. Let's do it tonight then." Donovan looked like she felt.

Eleri had long ago learned to turn off any tracking feature on the GPS she used. She really did not want to see all the times she backtracked, all the ground she crossed three times, four times, ten times. It almost always seemed to produce a literal map of the investigation—interesting at the end with clear points of far reach and little knots of frustration—but nothing you wanted evidence of while you were in it. "Luckily there's a real freeway between the two cities."

It was disturbing they were both that pleased about it, but it would be a big improvement from the off-roading they'd been doing with their little rental.

Putting the last of the papers into the bag, Donovan ticked off their itinerary. "So pack, check out, get dinner, drive, check in, sleep, meet with Westerfield?"

"That sounds about right." Pushing the heavy door out of her way, she started down the long hallway. The building was quieter this late. The traffic buzzing just beyond the window had finally settled down, normal people were home with their families, having meals cooked in real kitchens. But no one here was normal.

For a flash of a moment, Eleri considered that she and Donovan were the most abnormal of all.

They were climbing in the car when he turned to her again. "So dinner? How about steak?"

"I hate you." She deadpanned. "I really hate you."

DONOVAN WASN'T PREPARED for Eleri's agenda in San Antonio. She came into the hall in the morning ready for the meeting with Westerfield and spouting plans for the afternoon. She had an old friend who had moved to the area and she was going to meet him for a late lunch.

Having not gotten to sleep until around 1 am and then not having slept well in general, his brain wasn't up to comprehending the logistics Eleri was laying out regarding dropping her off, picking her and her friend up. He hadn't had his coffee yet, so he trusted that because Eleri was normally good with planning and organizing, she had it all worked out.

"Coffee?" he croaked, and her answer was a smile and a nod. It was not fair hanging out with a person who slept that well in strange beds. For a moment he wondered if owning the variety of homes you lived in and not worrying about food or being ousted from your shelter made sleeping in a new bed all the time easier to swallow. Having been raised in as many as five different cities in one school year, he would have thought he'd sleep like a baby in a nice hotel room paid for by his job. But no.

Inside thirty minutes, she'd found them breakfast including fruit for her, coffee for him and a chance to sit a minute and open his eyes. Silently he thanked her for the time, since he had to be on his A game with Westerfield. Donovan had met the man only twice before, though there were additional phone conversations. Still his initial interview and subsequent introduction to Eleri were the sum total of his exposure. In both cases, though Westerfield wanted something from him, there were terms to negotiate. Now Donovan was returning as the employee, his plans pending approval.

So used to working for himself, answering to bureaucrats, but not so much bosses, this was a new concept.

They didn't review at breakfast, figuring they had everything set for Collier, and that Westerfield would come up with questions they weren't prepared for no matter what they did. So when Donovan followed the San Antonio branch administrator down the hallway, he wasn't nervous. He knew there was no way to prepare.

Westerfield waited for them in another room that looked both the same and different from the one they spent their day in yesterday. Though his hand fidgeted with a quarter again while he waited, the man looked impeccable in his suit and tie and for a moment Donovan wondered if his boss followed Einstein's model and had fifteen copies of the same suit hanging in his closet. Donovan wasn't sure but he might have seen the exact same tie before, too. Then Westerfield stood, shook hands, and said hello to them, breaking Donovan's train of thought.

Only as they all sat back down did Donovan see that all the blinds had been drawn. But he didn't get to think about it as they got right to business, Eleri laying out their proposal to put Collier back in his truck and on his routes.

They had already spoken to his agency—without letting them know one of their independent employees had picked up a hitch-hiker and then buried her on protected park land when she died. The trucking company was willing to work with the FBI to keep Collier on his regular routes, thus improving his likelihood of finding another City of God member out in a nearby town.

Westerfield asked only a few pointed questions. Wanted to know what exactly Collier got in exchange for his work and whether he would be kept on a watch list.

Donovan fielded that one before he even thought about it. "With all due respect, sir, the man is nearly seventy and set to retire soon. Had it not been for the burst of adrenaline I'm assuming he suffered, he would never have physically been able to bury the girl."

Eleri chimed in. "He became asthmatic when he showed us where he'd buried her, barely even able to walk back to the site. And the majority of the good information we have came because he volunteered it."

Donovan tried not to stiffen at her comment and immediately spoke, trying to steer the conversation in a different way before

Westerfield asked how they found Collier in the first place. "I think he's an asset rather than a threat to society."

Westerfield only nodded then went through the motions of granting formal approval for them to offer clemency to Bernard Collier, dependent upon his cooperation with their operation. Done.

Now all they needed was for Westerfield to let them in on this "next phase of the investigation" he mentioned yesterday and Eleri would be able to go meet her friend and Donovan could continue his research on just how many really great steaks a person could find in Texas.

Westerfield tapped the quarter on the table twice, as though to punctuate what he was about to say. "In addition to keeping an eye out for Jennifer Cohn, I need you to gather physical evidence, statements, whatever you need to find out if Baxter really is behind this. If he's killing his own people. Find out where his money comes from."

Eleri nodded as though in complete agreement, then said what Donovan was thinking. "We want that, but we don't have enough to get a search warrant. All we have to show that Baxter's DNA should be tested against Jonah's is a picture Jonah drew and our belief that they look alike. That's not warrant worthy. Also the land is privately held, and it appears the owner is living on the property with them. We can't even get them on trespassing yet."

Her shrug went unanswered by Westerfield. "You don't need a warrant."

"Yes we do." Her response was calm but solid.

"No you don't. You have reasonable cause. You can't barge in, you can't force, but you can collect for yourselves." Westerfield matched her tone, more matter of fact than his words were.

"But sir, that won't hold up in court." She kept going, obviously confused. "The chain of evidence will be screwed. Everything will be thrown out if we obtain the fingerprints without full cause and a warrant."

"You aren't going to court, Eames." Westerfield looked back and forth at them now, pointedly stopping at Eleri. "You're Night-Shade division. You tested into this."

"Tested?" Donovan had to ask. It sounded like Westerfield was reminding them of something they'd openly done, but he didn't remember anything specific. He'd been given what felt like thousands of tests, physical, skills-based, knowledge and psychological batteries. Which one was this?

Westerfield ignored him. Now he leaned forward on his elbows, ever-present quarter still clutched in his hand. "Night-Shade doesn't detain and provide evidence for prosecution."

"But that's what the FBI does!" Eleri almost blurted it, her calm starting to unravel a bit at the seams.

"Not NightShade. It's part of NightShade's security clearance. It's why we don't exist on the official roster. But we do the good work. NightShade balances the karmic books. Your assignment is to gather evidence and, if warranted, once you are convinced of the necessity, remove Baxter."

26

Although she walked out of the building to all appearances perfectly normal, Eleri was stunned.

She was trained to gather information under the umbrella of a warrant and to make sure she had all her paperwork in place before she moved. She collected evidence, detained, supported the prosecution, and smiled broadly when the bad guys were locked up. Sometimes people died during the investigation. Sometimes it was the good guys, often the bad, and Eleri tried not to lose sleep over it. But she had never openly gunned for one before.

Donovan didn't even question her when she stayed in the car, just sat in the parking lot and stared at the front door for a good three minutes.

Her voice came from nowhere. "I don't want to eat steak. I want one of those salad bar places. One of the places with five kinds of soup and a hundred items on the bar."

"I don't think they've heard of salad here." His voice was quiet, as though he understood it wasn't about the leafy greens. "They do sometimes have vegetables."

"Those things are vegetables the way a corpse is a person.

And I mean that as a pretty literal analogy." Other than their mouths, neither of them really moved. She breathed, but she didn't really understand.

There was something so seductive about being in charge of the balance sheet. It was tempting to make plans before she even decided if this was all acceptable. Westerfield seemed to think their tests indicated they would be fine with it. She remembered testing; she'd done a bunch of it at the psych hospital. Had it been at Westerfield's behest?

NightShade was a subdivision of the overall umbrella of the FBI. They had FBI IDs, FBI rights, and then some. She was so confused that she said the only thing she could think of. "What about Chinese?"

"What about your friend?"

"Shit! Wade!" She fumbled for her phone, jerking her conscious brain out of the haze, finally finding something normal to grasp onto. She dialed from the directory on her phone and was shocked how much she relaxed just hearing his voice come through the line.

"Eleri? Are you finished at the branch?" The cadence of the words righted something, the way the sound of a good friend does. He called it "the branch" because he'd worked for the Bureau, too. Only recently had he "sprung himself" as he called it and after eight years as a Fed went to work in the private sector.

"Yeah, we're done. My partner is with me, I can have him drop me off. I'll meet you for lunch now." Only as she said it into the phone did she realize that Donovan might not take kindly to being used as chauffeur. She was turning to apologize to him, but he was already motioning for her to hand over the keys.

Climbing out of the driver's seat, she popped around to the passenger side while she was still on the phone and gave Donovan directions by hand.

Feeling a hundred percent better, she found she was able to process things a little more clearly. Ready to ask her partner if he had been prepared for Westerfield's announcement, she instead wound up fielding a question of a different topic.

"So, how do you know this guy? Is he an ex or something?" Donovan had one hand over the steering wheel, the other on his leg.

Her chest loosened with a laugh. "No, not an ex. Old FBI buddy. He was a senior officer on a case, called in to consult. Science nerd. We just hit it off. You'd like him."

"Bio-forensics, like you?"

"No, physics. Amazing brain." She found talking about Wade allowed her to push Westerfield and Baxter to a compartment she could close the lid on, at least for now. "Wade can stand at a scene and tell you a body was staged, because the bullet couldn't have hit him from that angle if he'd been standing where it was made to look. And not the usual stuff either. Straight-up physics, trajectories, that kind of thing." She paused. "One time we were at the aftermath of a bombing. Wade points to one of the victims, says he's actually one of the perpetrators. That, given his distance from the bomb, and the location of the shrapnel on his body, he had to be turning away before the bomb went off.

"Wade walked up to the guy—who's getting treated in the back of the ambulance, acting like a victim—and Wade just pulls the oxygen mask off of him and says, 'Tell me how you triggered the bomb and we might keep you out of the electric chair.' I thought the guy was going to start crying right there." She grinned at the memory. She had been new, a freshly minted field agent, working her first multiple homicide. "I wanted to be Wade."

"Did you get there?"

"Hell no." She laughed out loud. "I did what I do best and wound up getting questioned as a suspect then thrown in the loony bin." She paused for a second, the memories changing from funny to somber. "He was the only one I told I was inside.

He came to visit every other week. Wrangled me a day pass each time and made sure I got to see the sun out beyond the gates."

They pulled up and parked in front of a pretty glass-and-brick building that screamed money and class at the same time. The words "Atomic Measurements Unlimited" graced the façade along with a logo of an atom exploding into a variety of items including alpha and beta decay, viruses, computer code and a handful of other things that even Eleri's geekiness didn't grasp.

Deciding she wanted Donovan to see that she had friends—or maybe at least "friend" in the singular—Eleri motioned him into the building with her. He'd be lost in the lunch conversation, but at least he could meet Wade.

At the front desk, the woman there greeted them politely if oddly, then showed them into the back halls where she knocked on doors to see which one was Doctor de Gottardi's. When Donovan asked for the men's room she flustered for a moment before pointing him in the direction she "believed it was."

Just as Eleri was thinking this woman wasn't the best receptionist, someone popped out from one of the office doors and stuttered, "Dr. Wilson! I am almost finished with that requisition paper. The university did not get back to me until this morning."

The panic in his voice indicated that Dr. Wilson was not to be trifled with, despite her easy smile for Eleri and the fact that she was playing receptionist. Eventually they found their way around the back loop of the hall, and the doctor sighed with relief as she knocked on the open door. Her tone let him know she was there, "Wade! You moved on me. I have visitors for you and I couldn't find you."

"New office. Windows!" He pointed at them as he grinned up at Dr. Wilson before taking in that only Eleri followed her. "It appears you also forgot how to count in single digits. Or was it so traumatic you lost someone along the way?"

"Option number two." Wilson grinned and turned away before Eleri could thank her.

Eleri greeted her old friend with a huge smile and, "She's a crappy receptionist." Which just made him laugh and pull her into a bear hug Eleri hadn't realized she needed. She was used to being on her own. She learned quickly after Emmaline's disappearance not to ask for anything. But Wade didn't wait for her to ask and maybe that's why she liked him so much. Well, that and the whole brainiac/walking-up-to-people-and-pointing-out-they-were-lying/bam!/physics, bitch! Kind of thing.

He settled back into an ergonomic chair that reclined farther than gravity should dictate and steepled his fingers. "How do you like being back in the Bureau?"

Wasn't that the question of the hour?

"It's good. When they signed me out of the hospital it was 'against medical advice,' but I seem to be holding my own. Even got a new Bureau ID card and everything." She didn't know why they'd issued her a new one, but she flipped the small wallet open in an exaggerated movement, like she was a gun slinger or something. She was laughing as she did it, but Wade didn't laugh.

Slowly pulling the leather from her fingers he checked out the card, his face pulling into a frown, making her own smile slide off her face. "What?"

"You're with NightShade." It wasn't a question. "It was Wester-field who got you out of the hospital early." He ran a hand over his short caramel hair, his gaze pulled off into the distance. His sigh was deep and told myriad things she didn't yet know but clearly needed to.

"What, Wade?" Eleri sat her ass down in the very orthogonal-looking orange padded chair—clearly more a marvel of physics than it was of comfort.

"NightShade's a whole different ballgame than you're used to."

"How do you know that? How did you know just by looking at my ID?" She reached out for it and grabbed it back to examine it. She didn't see anything.

"The line with the diamonds at the end." He pointed. "Not the standard border. The design is part of the coding for the FBI. If you know how to read it you can sometimes tell units and clearance."

Eleri saw the lines but hadn't realized they were different from her old ID. They must be though, because Wade had simply looked at it and pegged her. "I was told not to discuss the Night-Shade division, even with other agents. So how do you know?"

He only looked at her for a moment while her world spun. She was ten easy rotations past dizzy and about one more good turn from projectile vomiting. "Tell me, Wade."

He still didn't. For a moment he sat and stared at the tile "art" he'd put onto his wall. It was about as artistic as Tetris or the Periodic Table, but Eleri never said anything. If she hadn't known him better, hadn't known this was his thinking space and that he was better with numbers than words, she would have grabbed him and started rattling him. That wasn't in her best interests though. He was an ex-agent and she didn't know if he'd kept up with his training—it was fifty-fifty who would win.

Eventually he moved his feet, slowly swiveling the chair back to face her as though turning himself was out of the question. "Did it not occur to you that you shouldn't have been put back into the field so soon after they hospitalized you?"

Her stomach clenched as though that would stop the blow or at least soften it. She tried not to be hurt by it. Wade either didn't notice or didn't care.

"Are you suggesting that I'm not mentally fit for my job?"

"Not at all."

That helped. His response had been swift and almost shocked.

But the rest of it he didn't notice, just kept going. "You should have been let out earlier. You practically chose to stay. I don't know what went down after the first two months, but they did a one-eighty and kept you longer. It's not that. It's the FBI. You were in a mental hospital for a breakdown. They wouldn't put you right back in the field and certainly not before the doctors officially declared you better. You would be a huge liability."

"So why did they?" She hadn't missed the fact that he still didn't answer how he knew all this.

"They didn't." The bridge of his nose pinched and the corners of his mouth pulled. It was the exact opposite of the look he got when he was explaining quantum calculators. Those made him happy. Clearly, this didn't. "The FBI didn't pull you out. Night-Shade did."

"NightShade is the FBI." He was making less sense rather than more.

"NightShade uses FBI IDs, operates under the cloak of the Bureau, interacts with their agents but doesn't operate as actual agents. NightShade doesn't follow standard protocol. Or didn't you know that?"

"I just got my first inkling of that today." She sat for a moment, still as a statue, just breathing before she spoke again. "How do you know all this?"

"Because I was NightShade." He looked at her oddly, as though he couldn't figure her out.

Well, she couldn't figure him out either. "The whole time?"

"Yes. I never went into the actual FBI. I didn't apply, I was recruited directly into NightShade."

Like Donovan, she thought.

No sooner had the thought passed her mind than she heard his voice careening down the hall.

"Eleri? Eleri!" The sound was restrained but bordered on panic, so she stuck her head out the doorway and smiled at him. Glad for the distraction, she was worried by the look on his face.

"I'm right here."

"Get out." He said it through teeth that suddenly looked sharper. His shoulders were pushing back and downward and for a flash of a moment she could begin to see how he changed. His stride was purposeful and he was closing the distance rapidly.

"It's just Wade and me." Still she stepped backward, pushed by the way he moved the air in front of him. Propelled by the palpable change in him, his fighting instincts all on alert.

Donovan shoved past her into the office, turning her as he went by. Already on his feet, Wade stood his ground at the comer. But he stood it slightly forward, almost on his toes. His shoulders also pushed down and back, his head swaying low, extending his neck.

A deep, soft growl came from Donovan's throat. It was almost more menacing for its softness. "Eleri? Do you know what he is?"

27

Donovan fought the urge to extend his neck, push the center of his face out and really make his teeth useful. His shoulders were already rolling, already moving into place. He wouldn't look at his arms, afraid the hair had sprung up, changing in appearance from a slightly above average amount of male arm hair to a full, black pelt.

Eleri's hand was suddenly flat on his chest, and she was in between the two men before he even knew how she got there. "Can we stop this pissing contest for a second? I'm about to choke on the testosterone."

Donovan stepped back, his non-primal brain taking stock that this man was her best friend while Eleri seemed to have no clue what he was. Or maybe she did, she'd certainly figured Donovan out fast enough.

Turning to look right in her green eyes, ready to assess what he saw, he asked her again, "Do you know what he is?"

"He's a physicist and an ex-agent." She put her hands on her hips, apparently her standard position for anything frustrating.

Well, Wade was something else, too. "Eleri."

"Eleri?" It came at the same time from the other guy in the room.

Looking up at Wade, Donovan tried to assess what he was dealing with. Slowly he inhaled, testing scent. But nothing had changed. Wade was doing the same, subtly sniffing the air.

It was the scent that first alerted him. Donovan had smelled Wade from down the hall, then he'd been frantic, running to find Eleri. He was even more stunned to see that the smell led him to the very man she was meeting.

"He's ex-NightShade."

Startled, his head whipped toward her. Too many disturbing ideas jumbled in his brain, stirring around, trying to link up. Westerfield's directive to take out Baxter. Obtaining their evidence without warrants. Keeping his own balance sheet in the positive. Now this.

It hit him suddenly and painfully that maybe Wade was ex-NightShade for the same reason Donovan was currently in the division.

His heart was beating faster, too hard to just stand down when he felt threatened like this. He hadn't reacted like this since he'd run into that bear in the park out behind his house two years ago. Now was no different.

Turning to his partner, not sure what to say, knowing— suspecting—that Wade would hear him, he finally confessed. "I've never met another person like me. Not except my father and my grandmother."

"Okay." She drew the word out, standing cautiously between the two men who both remained on guard but no longer in each other's faces. She still didn't get it.

"Like you?" At first Eleri was clearly confused. Then he watched as understanding dawned and she repeated her words. "Like you?"

Slowly, she turned to look at Wade mumbling a whisper to

herself. Donovan thought it was "the brown wolf," but he wasn't certain. "Wade?"

She was looking at her friend, inspecting him from feet to hands to hazel eyes. Eyes that were boring a hole in Donovan. Apparently, Wade didn't like being outed.

With slow deliberate movements, Wade put himself between Eleri and Donovan, as though he was protecting her. Donovan thought it should be the other way around. He didn't know who this ass was except that Eleri called him an old friend.

Shit.

Eleri called him an old friend. And Donovan—not knowing how to react—had just outed her friend, himself, and who knew what else. Making a conscious decision, he shifted his thinking to trust Eleri's judgment. After all, she already proved herself worthy in that department more than once. Her gut instincts were spot on, so while she may not have known exactly *what* Wade was, she probably knew exactly *who* Wade was.

They stood that way for a moment. Donovan looking to Eleri, Eleri inspecting Wade, Wade standing his ground against all comers. Which was pretty funny when Donovan thought about it. The glasses, the plaid shirt and khaki pants spoke of thought rather than impulse. Whatever this guy did would be deliberate, but he was making his stand inside the beige box of his office. Unless he could do something deadly with printer paper, the best weapon at hand was a stapler.

Openly, Donovan stood down. Taking his eyes off the other predator in the room, he turned to Eleri. "He's like me. I smelled him from down the hall."

That the man was ex-NightShade made the new unit seem shady, for lack of a better term.

The conversation turned to a three-way as Wade finally looked to Eleri. "You know about him? You know what he is? What he can do?"

"I just figured it out. But yes, I think so." She was still looking

at her old friend with new eyes. Wary eyes. "And you're the same .
.."

The words trailed off, as though she was concerned, invested,
not ready to face the possibility.

Resigned, Wade nodded. There was something in the way the
two looked at each other, something about shared history. The
words were out of Donovan's mouth before he thought about it.
"Are you sure he's not an ex?"

ELERI FELT the tension snap and break. Her head flew back and
she saw and heard Wade guffaw about the same time peals of
laughter emerged from her own throat.

Poor Donovan was looking back and forth between the two of
them, confused as hell, probably convinced they'd lost it. To his
credit, it had been one hell of a confusing day, but she couldn't
get herself together to tell him.

Wade managed. He'd probably dealt with this plenty. "I'm
gay." The words came out in between laughs that threatened to
choke him. But he pulled himself together before she did.

Donovan still looked confused. "So it's just Eleri, then? This is
just what she does? Makes you tell her all your shit?"

"Yeah, pretty much."

"I'm standing right here." She'd had to hold her breath to get
the words out. She thought being indignant would help, but it
didn't make a difference. They kept talking about her.

"So how come she didn't figure out what you are?"

Wade countered with, "How did you screw up so badly that
she figured you out? You've known her, what, all of three weeks?"

"You know that?" Donovan was now completely ignoring her
and having a great conversation with his new wolf buddy. Great.

Inserting herself into the conversation, because she sure
wasn't going to get asked to join, she said, "Yes, he knows. We're

friends. We stay in touch. He knew when I got pulled back into the Bureau."

Donovan nodded at her response, but spoke to Wade. "I went on a run. I did some recon and I took a GPS. She tracked me at thirty-two."

He had the decency to look sheepish about it, but it didn't stop her from adding, "Also, this kid saw him, and the kid's an artist—an extraordinary artist—so when I saw him, I had a print to use to look up the wolf and cross-reference the species to the area. Turns out, there is no species like him."

Wade started nodding as though all the pieces made sense. "Actually, there is."

"What?" She felt out of the loop and running slow on everything since she woke up this morning.

In response, Wade only pointed at himself before again turning to speak to Donovan. "You didn't stand a chance against her. I knew she was keenly observant before I even met her, and I was never her partner, never had to change near her." He grinned. "You got screwed by the artist, but honestly, it was a just matter of time before she figured you out."

Fine, if they were playing two-in-one-out, she could do that, too. Turning to her partner, she relayed the earlier surprise Wade had delivered. "He knows about Westerfield and NightShade. He probably understands far more about it than we do."

Wade stuck his hands in his pockets, his universal gesture of waiting the situation out. She, on the other hand, was waiting for him to offer up some grand observation about the speed of the sound of her voice, the way the sun's rays reflected, something that would change the way she saw the world. Something that would make all the pieces gel.

Instead, he suggested lunch.

Despite Donovan's smirk, Eleri suggested Chinese and Wade drove them to his favorite hole-in-the-wall nearby.

After they ordered and rubbed their chopsticks together and

were served their soup, Wade started talking. Since they were seated near the back, most of the conversation around them was in Mandarin. Eleri didn't speak the language but she could identify it, so she felt relatively safe there.

"NightShade exists because there are certain jobs that fall outside the jurisdiction of the FBI. In the simplest terms, you operate more like the CIA, but since the CIA technically can't function inside the borders of the US, we have NightShade."

He paused when plates arrived and the waitress hugged him, as he was clearly a regular. Eleri wasn't surprised one iota.

"The badge gives you access and respectability. It also keeps people from knowing what you're really doing."

Using the large spoon to make friends with the moo goo gai pan steaming in front of her, Eleri leaned forward. "But what about the other agents we work with?" She looked to Donovan who shrugged; he didn't know any more than she did. "Agent Bozeman? He's not NightShade . . . I don't think. I'm pretty sure he's just a field agent in the Dallas branch."

"Probably." Wade was making short work of both the food and the conversation. "You're under the umbrella of the Agency. No one questions the FBI coming in and taking jurisdiction. You have the full support of other agents who believe you're standard Bureau, too, doing the same thing they're doing."

The chopsticks stopped partway to her mouth. "Like my fellow agents and I thought when we worked with you."

The nod was likely the only concession she was going to get to that deception.

After that, the conversation stuttered and stopped for a while. The only sounds were those of straws in plastic cups, the faint fizz of fresh sodas that did not constitute the traditional Chinese fare the restaurant boasted. The food itself was incredible—Wade could always find the best places—and suddenly she was starving.

Every once in a while, she would find Wade watching her, as

though he were looking for something he couldn't find. But when she made eye contact, he would quickly offer a half-grin and turn away. It didn't hide what he was doing, but Eleri had enough for one day and didn't want to deal with anything else. So she didn't ask.

In turn, Donovan watched Wade carefully, though she couldn't tell if he was studying Wade because of what he'd discovered or if he was still thinking he had to protect her from her good friend. For her part, Eleri was trying not to process that she sat at a table eating excellent food in a strange city with two men who were probably the closest thing on earth to werewolves. Nope. Did not want to even attempt to wrap her brain around it. So eventually she spoke up, turning the conversation easily to mundane things as everyone seemed to agree these were the topics that were safer to talk about.

How did Wade like San Antonio? She asked.

Donovan followed up with, "Where do you run?"

Great. Werewolf conversation. She tried again. "Do you have a new boyfriend?"

"I was seeing one guy, but it turned out to be nothing special."

"Is it hard finding a boyfriend?" Donovan brought the conversation around again.

Wade only laughed at him. "You date a lot?"

"No." It was spoken with a wry grin. "The dating pool is pretty slim, and you can't get too close to someone or they start figuring things out." With his thumb he gestured at Eleri whose mouth fell open at the implication. But she was soundly ignored.

"Exactly. Now reduce your dating pool by ninety percent."

"Damn."

Leaning her face forward into her hands, Eleri started muttering "I hate you both. So much. So very much."

When Donovan laughed at her, she glared back and at least he apologized. "Sorry, I never met anyone like me, not that I wasn't related to."

Done with her food, stuffed really, she pushed the plate away and decided if she couldn't escape it, she should dive in head first. "Why do I feel there's something more to NightShade? There is, isn't there? Even beyond the directive."

Wade sighed first, then answered, but not the way she expected.

"You saw Westerfield this morning, right?"

When she nodded, he continued. "After lunch, go back and catch him before he leaves town." He looked to Donovan, too, this time. "He can tell you a hell of a lot more than I can. But make sure you see him face to face, no phone. And when you do, ask him about the quarter."

28

Donovan was frustrated. Three days with no real leads. Westerfield had flown out of San Antonio before they even finished their lunch with Wade. Hearing that news, the physicist told them to wait to ask their question until they could meet with their lead agent in person. Thus they were stuck waiting on that count.

There had been no new breaks in the case and Donovan itched under his skin with the need for a run.

When he lived by himself, going into the ME's office on a semi-regular schedule, getting called during off-hours to work the occasional crime scene, he hadn't experienced the overwhelming urge to put distance under his feet, not with this kind of drive. Maybe it was that he was living in odd boxes—one hotel room after another. Maybe it was akin to the psychological urge for something unavailable. At his own home he could always take off on a whim, but this life was confining for a creature like him.

His world had been thrown out of whack on so many levels, and he could see that Eleri's had been, too. So it wasn't surprising that each of them had retreated to their own corners, trying to put new information into an old schema of the world. His didn't fit. Eleri's clearly didn't either if the darkening circles under her eyes were any indicator.

Her humor had fled, replaced by soft monosyllables and deep silences. He didn't think she was sad, just disturbed. Jumbled. Concerned.

Who could blame her? In case it wasn't enough that her partner had turned out to be what he was, her best friend had been hiding the same secrets directly under her nose— and far more successfully—for years. She'd been asked to kill a suspect. Told that her government was no longer her boss, and lastly that she didn't actually hold the job she trained for.

Donovan on the other hand was struggling with the fact that someone else was out there like him. He believed for so long that it was a defect unique to his family. He'd been told it went back many generations but had no evidence of that.

Had he finally stumbled across someone else like him because he was getting out and about and meeting many new people all at once? He'd been such a recluse that, had another creature like him passed nearby, it would have had to get in sniffing distance for him to know. There was a possibility it was just a numbers game.

But when he learned that Wade de Gottardi had also been actively recruited into the NightShade division, Donovan began to get suspicious that there was a lot less random chance in this meeting. Maybe NightShade needed a wolf in its ranks and he was simply the current candidate.

He wrestled with his Hippocratic oath. He was to do no harm, but he wasn't a physician anymore, not really. Honestly, he'd been a speaker for the dead more than a healer. The only thing he'd healed had been court cases. If taking Baxter out made people safer then it was a hard decision to argue with.

Though the FBI didn't advertise it, there were numerous cases when the Bureau knew who their man was long before they could do anything about it. Perhaps NightShade was the righting of that inability. But at what cost?

Donovan believed in innocent until proven guilty, but he'd never been behind the entire idea of standards of evidence collection. He knew something of it before his Academy training, given his background, but the FBI had drilled the methods into him. The agents at the training cited more than one case to the students where an agent had to make the decision to save a victim—sometimes a child—from a monster or leave them there until the appropriate warrants could be obtained. Usually they rescued the victim, but the evidence found in the rescue was often declared "fruit of the poison tree" and completely inadmissible in court because of the way it was obtained.

That evidence was no less valid in Donovan's mind. A killer or child molester would go back on the streets, when there was solid and known proof against them, but the court rules couldn't allow it. The next victim would have to be taken, have to be hurt, before proper evidence could be obtained. A perpetrator would have time to disappear, change methods. Maybe NightShade was the better way.

Donovan couldn't say for certain. The only thing he did know was that he wasn't going to solve his moral dilemma any time soon.

In three days, he'd eaten two meals with his partner. During breaks, he stared at the walls, then did it again when he was supposed to be sleeping and couldn't. Donovan watched stupid television, in real time. He'd gotten so jaded with his recorder at home that here he picked up the remote when the commercials came on and was surprised again each time that they didn't simply bleep away.

He and Eleri had meetings that amounted to nothing. They couldn't find any other evidence. Then yesterday, Eleri reported that Westerfield called her, wanting to know what progress they had made and she was forced to say "nearly none." After that announcement, they both stared morosely at the wall in one of the conference rooms at the San Antonio branch for a while more.

His restlessness was hitting epic proportions, so he finally gave up and knocked on the door that joined the two junior suites without even knowing if Eleri was on the other side. It was time for action.

When the knocking yielded nothing, he knocked again, then a third time simply because he had nothing better to do. So he was shocked when he finally heard footsteps and Eleri pulled open the door, frowning up at him.

She had a soda dripping in her hand. "I just went down to the vending machine. Were you knocking long?"

"No." He lied. "I have an idea."

She waved him into the room and sat back into one of the two chairs that went with the desk pushed up against the wall. As she gestured him into the other, he noticed the yoga pants and tank top. She must have been thinking about working out, or maybe just not working at all. "Tell me."

"We need Baxter's finger prints and we need to see his fist. I say I go in."

Until he said it out loud, Donovan hadn't realized just how invested he was.

"How will you do it? Just walk in? Announce you want to join? You'll never just walk out . . ."

The way her voice trailed off told him she'd figured out what he intended.

"We need a smaller GPS, attached normally to a collar. I need to look like an escaped pet." He couldn't believe he was saying that. To him, the wolf was a sacred being—protected, hidden from humans, seen only if necessary. He was risking himself. But he thought of the two dead girls, of Ruth, whose body was yet to be found. He thought of Jonah and Charity, and his new thirst for

Baxter made him believe that he could expose the wolf but still keep the secret.

A sharp click and fizz preceded Eleri sipping at the soda, clearly thinking about what he proposed, and she started asking the relevant questions. "What are you trying to collect?"

"Fingerprints and enough DNA to match him as Jonah's biological father if we can. Though I wouldn't think that would be top priority." His fingers twined and untwined unconsciously.

She nodded. "I'd like the DNA too, but not at huge risk. And once we get Baxter we can get it another way. All we need that to do is show the elder Baxters they have a grandchild and keep Jonah out of the foster system." Her gaze shot off again in a new direction. "We should also get confirmation on the fist. If you could see it clearly, that would help."

If only Baxter would oblige and make a fist without hitting him.

"So, how do you get his fingerprint? It's not like you can pick up a glass he touched, drop it in a bag, and walk away."

It was his worst idea ever, but he was willing because he knew what was on the other end. "Dog tag. I'm thinking he finds a dog wandering around, checks the tag. We get his fingerprint. Maybe I can inadvertently scratch him a little, get some DNA to bring back."

She was shaking her head before he finished. "It's great, but there are so many ways it can go wrong. Right off the bat, if I were looking at a dog's tag, I wouldn't touch the flat surface, I'd want to read that part. Plus, you're hardly a dog. You're a wolf. I did not for one second think that a dog had wandered into your backyard."

Impressed with how well she had accepted what he was, and even developed an ease of talking about it, Donovan pressed his case. "As for the wolf, well people keep wild animals as pets all the time. I'm sure I can get close and make contact just by acting friendly."

"Have you ever done it before?"

"No." He hated to admit it.

Her cheeky grin told him he wasn't going to like what she had to say. "Wanna do a dry run? We can get a collar and a leash and I can take you for a walk. Let people pet you?"

He thought he might retch. That was so far from the sacred right of the wolf. There was no way . . . . "I'll make it work. The collar will identify me as belonging to someone, I'll be friendly. The tag just needs something to make him give us enough of a print for an ID. We have a full set from his juvenile record."

Her laugh was self-deprecating. "Yeah, it needs a 'press here' sign!" Raising her soda can in a toast, she grinned at him.

He was with her. It had too many loopholes, too many places to go wrong. "They make tags that light up with a button. Maybe we can get one of those."

She was actively frowning at him now, and it wasn't because of the suggestion, he was pretty certain it was a helpful one. Sure enough, her next words cleared things up.

"You sure know an awful lot about dog tags. You're really sketchy about the idea of even wearing a collar—" she held her hand up to stop his interruption— "I can see it when you even mention it, your shoulders get tense. But you know a lot about them."

She knew too much already. She knew the big secret. What did a wish he'd never spoken out loud matter? "I wanted to get a dog, a running buddy. But my hours were too crazy, it just never happened. But I made some plans."

He wondered if it showed in his eyes that he had *always* wanted a dog. Even when he was kid, even long before he knew what he was, he wanted a companion like that. It seemed he would never have one, but it would pay off that he knew some things.

Eleri kept going. "A light-up tag means you go in under darkness, or at least dusk. What if they see your eyes and they shoot you? You said they patrolled with guns at the ready."

He almost answered, but she didn't let him. "What if that doesn't happen, and you're the perfect friendly dog and they figure you're lost and they try to feed you? Or keep you? If they get their hands under your collar, can they control you?"

Having never been around people in that state, he'd never even considered what wearing a collar would allow. Still, he had a ready answer. "You'll be there. You can distract them or something. I'm quick."

Her head maintained a back and forth motion. "How am I supposed to stay close enough to keep you in sight and not get detected myself? That's exactly what these guys are out there looking for. And if I'm far enough away, how can I stop them from doing something very sensical like locking you in a cage or a room?" She'd set the soda down by now and was just waving her hands to emphasize the amount of questions that were piling up. "I could mount a rescue operation, but I can't bring in more agents and take down a commune to get back a dog."

Admitting the reasonability of her protests, he sighed. "If we could get Baxter out alone, it could work."

To her credit, Eleri was a listener. Though she had wound up adamantly against his first plan, she didn't wave his second option away just for its similarity to the first. "Maybe. . ."

She was still mulling it over when her phone rang.

Her eyes lit up at the number and she answered with a sharp, "Hello, Agent Eames here," even as she hit the button to put the phone on speaker.

"Ma'am. This is Bernard Collier. I'm the one—" He sounded like he was going to go on, but Eleri smoothly interrupted him, and Donovan grinned at her.

"Oh, Mr. Collier, how good to hear from you." She smiled as she spoke the words, maybe so the sound would penetrate her tone.

"Yes, ma'am. Well, I just picked up another hitcher. Young

girl. She's real sick, too." There was a brief pause on both sides as Eleri's eyes flew up to meet Donovan's.

A break! Maybe he didn't have to wear a damn collar after all.

The thought was passing through his head as Collier cleared his throat. "Ma'am, where should I bring her?"

29

E leri was grateful that Donovan was driving to the hospital. Unfortunately, the woman Collier picked up was very sick. When Eleri asked the trucker to put the woman on the phone, he said she was moaning and rolling her head from side to side, complaining of a headache and coughing. Since Eleri could hear that much over the phone, and since Collier was doing this to get himself out of jail time, there was no reason for him to lie.

Fortunately, he was very close to the Brownwood Regional Medical Center. Sadly, Eleri and Donovan were much farther away. Also Brownwood, via roadways, was exactly in between Dallas and San Antonio—which meant even Agent Bozeman couldn't get there any faster than they could. They would have to rely on the Brownwood PD.

No matter how good the department was, someone, somewhere would slip. Dispatch would hear. Someone on a trucker radio would talk to Collier. If nothing else, some staffer at the hospital would say something to his or her mama and in a few hours the information would be everywhere. Eleri needed the PD to hold back the gossip for nearly three hours.

With Donovan driving, Eleri paid no attention to the road. Even before she was buckled into the passenger seat, she was on the phone, talking with Brownwood dispatch, getting put through to Detective James Hill. When they were in town before, she found him to be the best at keeping his mouth closed.

As soon as dispatch pulled him from duty, she directed him to the hospital to meet with Collier and his City of God escapee, then hung up and found the next number. Elaine Coates was the RN they interviewed about Ruth. Eleri wanted her on this case, too. Wanted her eyes looking for similarities in symptoms, test results, behaviors, etc.

Trying not to bark orders, since she'd clearly woken the woman up, Eleri attempted to stress the importance of both speed and secrecy. Coates was willing, but had just finished a shift, cared for her ailing mother, and finally gotten to sleep. She was coming around from a dead stop. Though Coates's brain wasn't quite at full function yet, Eleri had to ask her which supervisor could help get her back onto the floor and keep it from looking suspicious.

Eventually, Eleri was out of calls to make.

She and Donovan heard back that Collier had arrived, his patient passed out and barely rousable. For a moment the woman had spoken, saying her name was Grace, and making Eleri flinch at hearing her own middle name associated with the City of God. It shouldn't have grabbed her in the gut and taken hold, but it did.

Grace—a little older than Collier had made her out to be— was taken immediately into the ICU, only because it would be the easiest to quietly monitor her there and keep people out. They assigned one nurse to her case until Elaine Coates showed up. Since Coates wasn't an ICU nurse, even after she arrived the other nurse stayed on. Eleri felt her lips press together when she heard, but there was nothing she could do.

Word would get out. There was no way around it. Having an

extra nurse on the case—a nurse they didn't know from Adam—didn't help things. All Eleri could do was try to hold back the tide.

The drive was tedious even if Donovan did manage to convince her they should pull off for a fast-food lunch. Though her system balked at the thought of a burger, she agreed. They had to eat, and eating while they drove saved time. Passing out at the hospital would do no one any good.

Despite eating food that put her system into even more of a tailspin, Eleri didn't complain about it. When they finally arrived at the hospital—the last ones to get there, arriving a good fifteen minutes after Agent Bozeman—they found that the patient was resting peacefully. She was on IV fluids and antibiotics, electrolytes, and pain medications, not able to speak coherently even if she was awake.

Sighing in defeat, Eleri proceeded to round up the troops and manage a brief meeting before giving up and checking back into the Hampton Inn, sadly just a few rooms down from where she and Donovan had started this investigation a few weeks ago.

Pushing his card key into the lock on the door next to hers, her partner managed to be more optimistic. "We're here now if she does become lucid and that's important. Also, we're closer to the mark. It's time to re-think a way in. We need fingerprints."

She would have shushed him, standing in the hallway, talking about an ongoing investigation, but it was late afternoon on a Tuesday and she hadn't seen another visitor in the entire hotel. Eleri refused to be paranoid enough to think someone was listening in on hallway conversations. Who would even want to hear most of what went on here? Suppressing a shudder, she pushed her way into her own room and gave up, flopping back onto the bed. It was firmer than the mattress in the last place they'd stayed and it resisted her flop more than she expected, which was a fitting bit of punctuation for this day.

Flopping didn't help and Eleri found her breathing was still fast, her shoulders still tense, and her need to accomplish something still dangling in front of her even as the daylight drifted west. Despite Donovan's very logical points that they had gained a new witness and were at the ready, Eleri still didn't feel the day had yielded what it needed to satisfy her work ethic.

Attempting to accept that she wasn't going to get what she wanted led her to some deep-breathing exercises. With her eyes closed, she smelled the staleness of the room, picked up the fake-lemon scent of the cleaner used a little too recently and a little too heavily. Well, that's what you got when you checked in at three in the afternoon. Smells were followed by sounds of cars outside, not passing by with enough regularity to become white noise but often enough to be disruptive. She wondered if this was what Donovan's whole life was like—one smell after another, faint sounds coming from all sides, knowing things he shouldn't because to a certain extent he functioned like the only sighted man in a school for the blind.

Turning her attention to her muscles, Eleri then worked on ignoring her sensory input and one by one releasing some of the tensions she felt. She carried her stress on her shoulders—as though the pressure she felt was borne on a physical yoke—but even though she knew she carried it here, she couldn't seem to change it. Now she actively rolled her shoulders, twisting her head from side to side until she heard the small popping sound that simultaneously made her shudder and feel better.

It took a few minutes, but she achieved some semblance of relaxation. Though the bed was not soft enough and the air not fresh enough and the day not late enough, she just lay there, breathing deeply.

Eleri was on breath number five—she was counting—when her phone rang. Why had she left her phone on the desk? Because she thought she'd be more relaxed than if she was holding it in her tense little hand. But now she had to abandon her laid-back position and actually get up. She couldn't ignore it because she suspected it was the hospital or the police officer watching "Grace" and calling to say she was ready to talk.

Trying to hold onto the modicum of Zen, Eleri glanced at the screen on the phone and promptly lost all of it. Shit. "Hello, sir."

Westerfield barked through the line. "Three days. No updates. What's going on, Eames?"

Eleri admitted his tone was probably not as harsh as it seemed, but given her hard won and easily lost relaxation, his demands were incredibly grating. She scrambled to retrieve some of the calm she possessed just moments ago. It didn't happen. "We don't have anything to report. We're trying to figure out how to get into the City and get evidence on Baxter without getting caught. And the woman Collier brought out is on so much medication that anything she says isn't valid at all."

Silence came loud and clear from the other end of the line. Eleri knew she should be affronted by it, that Westerfield was probably upset, but she didn't quite have it in her to muster up the disturbance. She was battling her own concerns about the new directive, and she wondered how Wade had reconciled it all. Then again, it was turning out there was a lot more to Wade than she had ever known. So she too stayed silent and waited her boss out.

"Tonight. I'll be there. Get food and a conference room at the local PD—" he sighed audibly, "—if there is one."

"There is, sir."

Lovely.

Hanging up, Eleri laid back on the bed again. Her arms splayed out, her legs dangled over the side. This time the phone fell only inches from where her hand, palm up, had decided to land.

She stayed there a while, sprawled across the bed like a victim. This time she didn't want the phone to ring, didn't want the woman from the City of God to wake up and tell them anything, not tonight. Eleri wanted to meet with Westerfield.

Though she dreaded the dressing down she figured she was in for given their lack of progress these past few days, she also had some questions of her own.

Lying there, she tried again to find the peaceful state she remembered from her early childhood—the core belief that everything was fine and would be good in the end. Since she was ten, she hadn't been able to achieve it without the help of a masseuse or a strong prescription.

Figuring Donovan was attempting the same beyond the wall that was probably more plastic than plaster, she fumbled her hand around on the bed and when she finally located her phone set the timer for fifteen minutes of nothing.

It beeped at her almost immediately, ending her failing attempts to relax, so she peeled herself from the bed and knocked on the adjoining door.

"Whaaat?" the stretched word carried through the panel, Donovan clearly not any happier than she was with the development. The sound of dragging feet came, then he undid the lock. So she explained the logistics of the new meeting while he looked at her like she was trying to tell him the moon was made of cheese.

It was nearly an hour later when they came through the front doors of the Brookwood PD. This time they stood out even more than usual, their tailored suits incongruous to the plastic bags of Styrofoam and Tex-Mex they carried. Eleri balanced a drink tray with even more Styrofoam in the form of three large cups. Each was big enough for Eleri to bathe in and she had all she could do just to balance the things.

Westerfield was late. Not a surprise, but Eleri and Donovan were halfway through the meal when he walked through the door, the ever-present quarter walking across his knuckles. It quickly disappeared into his suit jacket pocket as he closed the door behind him, deftly seating himself in the remaining seat.

Always a meticulous man, he first arranged the to-go box and plastic ware and drink. Always direct, he then looked from one to the other of them and said, "Tell me why you're balking at taking out Baxter."

Donovan nearly choked on his enchilada sauce, but Eleri didn't flinch. "Because I don't just shoot people. I'm not a killer. I've worked hard to take the killers out of society. I won't become one of them, no matter the purpose."

The man stayed calm, her affront worthless to him. "This way you keep him out of society. He won't appeal his way back in. None of these people will have to testify at his parole hearings to keep him locked up. He can't disappear and pop up under another name in ten years, doing the same thing only worse."

Clearly Westerfield was convinced of the job. Eleri wasn't. "I don't have the information yet. All we have is hearsay. I can't just go in and take him out on that alone." She tried to stem the tide rising in her voice but she was pretty sure she failed.

She moved her meter to "definitely certain" when Westerfield sighed at her, sat back, and folded his hands across his chest. "That's the problem."

"Yes, it is. If I'm out of a job, so be it." She didn't want to be out of a job, but she would leave before she would simply execute.

Westerfield only stared at her a moment before turning to Donovan. "Do you feel the same?"

A brief nod was all her partner gave. Eleri had expected more. Hadn't he taken an oath? Could doctors kill if it saved more lives? She had no idea and her boss was staring at her, so she figured this—like so many things—could wait to be pondered another day.

"You have the job description wrong."

No, she was pretty sure he'd given her a kill order.

Eleri raised her eyebrows and waited.

"Your job is to gather evidence. If you feel you know that Baxter is the one behind it all and if you're certain beyond doubt that his removal will save other lives, then you have an executive order to remove him. That's it." He looked at her again. "This is not an assassination. You're right, we don't know about Baxter yet. But you are no longer stuck waiving evidence and losing opportunities because of structured methodology and evidentiary proceedings for future court cases. I've untied your hands. That's all."

She leaned back, her food no longer appealing and she was suddenly glad he'd been late. At least she managed to get a good portion of her meal consumed before he showed up and ruined it for her. Being judge and jury was both appealing and concerning, but better than the kill order she thought she'd been issued.

Until she came to grips with it, they were at a bit of a standstill. She and Donovan were still stuck on how to get Baxter out of the City, and they didn't know how to get one of them in—or at least how to get the one they did get in back out safely—but she pushed that aside too. Waiting until Westerfield started to eat again, she asked him, "What about the quarter?"

His sigh was nearly a laugh. "It's a NightShade rite of passage to ask me that question."

Suddenly she wondered if Wade had sent her on a fool's mission, a mild hazing passed from one generation of recruits to the next.

Westerfield didn't let her ponder that long. "I won't even ask who put you up to it. Usually the more senior officer tells the new one. We rarely put two rookies together." His voice trailed off as he pulled the quarter from his pocket and spoke in the softest, easiest tone she'd ever heard from him.

"Welcome to the NightShade Division."

The quarter, sitting in his palm to start, slowly lifted, and began to rotate end over end.

30

Donovan closed the hotel door behind him, still in shock. He and Eleri hadn't spoken a single word on the way home.

Oh, they had chatted up a storm with Westerfield, his senior partner throwing accusations at his boss like darts.

"That's a trick quarter."

"So give me one of yours." The man had calmly stated.

When that one acted the same way, Eleri suggested he was using magnets. Westerfield asked for something plastic from her purse. Less than thirty seconds later, she pulled out a bottle of medication, popped the lid, and pushed the white plastic disk into his hand.

After that danced like the quarters had, Donovan asked if that was the limit of Westerfield's trick.

"It's not a trick. Get a pencil or a round pen. Put it on the table."

Pulling the grease marker from his bag, Donovan placed it near him. After a brief twitch, it rolled to the far edge of the table. When Eleri flashed her gaze toward him, Westerfield looked at the pen again and it rolled back the other way.

Almost before Donovan could think it, Eleri shook her head, dipped low to look at the man's knees. "You're tilting the table."

Without a word, Westerfield stood, hands out, palms forward and walked backward until he was against the wall. The pen jerked slightly, this time rotating first and strolling off in another direction as though it had simply decided it didn't like the conversation and wanted to leave.

She pulled a pack of gum from her purse and smacked it onto the table. Westerfield rolled his eyes like a ten-year-old. That was almost more disconcerting to Donovan than any of the rest of what he was seeing. Still the gum twitched and in small fits and starts scooted across the table to sit right in front of Eleri, as though asking her to believe. Her frown indicated that she did not. Not yet.

She was looking around when Westerfield sat down and waited expectantly.

"You rigged the room." Her voice lacked the conviction of her first statements.

"You chose the room." He rebutted her. "Can we stop now? I'm getting a headache."

After reaching into her purse and pulling out the pills she had just shoved back in there, Eleri had practically slapped the bottle in front of him. It was both an insult and an offer of help. Westerfield, still looking too buttoned-down for the demonstration he'd just given, sorted through the colors of pills she had obviously stashed over time. He laughed when she said gruffly, "I think the unmarked white ones are breath mints," and he tossed the pill back with the last of his soda.

Bracing his palms against the table top and looking weary, the agent in charge nodded briefly in their direction. "I'm very tired. Report in as soon as you have anything." Then he left.

They had quietly thrown out the remaining food and walked toward the front of the building. Donovan had been the only one to speak, letting the front desk know they had thrown out leftover food in conference room B. The last thing they needed was to be known for leaving Tex-Mex to stink up the rooms.

She'd driven them in silence. The click of the key, the roll of the engine, the road under the tires were all disruptively loud with nothing to contradict them. The elevator made noises as though it was tired and wanted to clock out at the end of a long day, but neither commented.

In his own room, alone at last, Donovan slipped between the sheets and stared at the ceiling as he had for so many nights now —each night for a seemingly different but equally sleep-disturbing reason.

Looking back, he could see that Westerfield had done this many times before. The man was, if not content, resigned to being center ring of this little dog and pony show for a short while. Donovan figured that made him the dog. And what was Eleri? Eleri visited her dead sister in her sleep and when she wasn't doing that she was having revealing dreams. How had Eleri become the most normal one of them?

His eyelids pulled back, his eyes widening suddenly. Donovan sat up with the revelation. NightShade. How many more "agents" were there and what could they do? Westerfield was recruiting an incredibly elite group. How had he figured out about Eleri? Had he gotten into her hospital records? Had he done it any normal way?

How had Westerfield found Donovan?

Donovan smelled Wade from down the hallway. So if any other wolves had come around and smelled him, wouldn't he have smelled them, too?

There were too many questions to hold on to. Too many links that when put together more resembled the web of a schiz-ophrenic spider than anything organized or revealing.

He tossed and turned for hours it seemed. But he must have gone to sleep at some point, because he woke up at precisely 3 a.m. according to the red-lettered hotel clock next to him. It was pitch black but he got up anyway. He had an idea.

"You're nuts." Eleri shook her head at him.

"I've been up for four hours checking everything. It matches."

He was still nuts and she was still hungry. "I want breakfast." She didn't want to listen to him, but she conceded if they could go eat something.

He was dressed, if a little scattered looking, holding his tablet to his chest as though it were precious, as though it contained evidence. In the elevator, he started to say something, but she slickly cut him off.

"I'm not talking about this until I get breakfast." There was a beat where he nodded in agreement and she took advantage. "Until I get the breakfast I want."

She wanted the place that served fruit salad with two kinds of melon, pineapple, grapes and blueberries. Her mouth watered just thinking about it, and her head felt just a little less like it would explode. But that place wasn't in Brownwood. Sadly, it was far from here.

Resigned to the local fare, she drove them to the Red Wagon and was surprised by the crowd this time in the morning. There would be no place to sit and have a conversation. So Eleri took the next blow and agreed to take-out. She would eat—yet again —in a hotel room. The food would come—yet again—in Styrofoam. And it would—yet again—be less than it's hottest, the service would be non-existent and anything missing or needed could not be fixed.

She must have looked as despondent as she felt, because Donovan sighed. "Let's eat here. Get served, keep the coffee hot —" Oh god, that sounded like heaven right now. "—and we'll talk when we get back. It can keep."

She'd spent too many of the hours she was supposed to be sleeping trying to figure out Westerfield's tricks. In the end, she couldn't come up with anything on her own. Breathing heavily, angry at the world for being out of whack, she lay stiff in bed, wide-awake for about an hour, before she realized what she should do.

At 3 a.m., she picked her way across the room, plucked her phone from her bag and called Wade. As asleep as he sounded when he picked up his end of the line, he still managed to answer with, "Took you that long to get Westerfield to show you the quarter trick?"

"So it's a trick." Her heart released the mad rhythm it had held tight to, her shoulders drained tension like a jug pouring water, and her breath flowed freely out of her lungs for the first time that night.

"Not like you mean. It's real, Eleri."

Well, fuck.

"Are you shitting me?" It was not a phrase she used often. Not one she'd been brought up with, but one she'd gotten from her first senior partner. He'd taught her about cowboy boots, Colt .44s and colloquialisms of the Deep South. Agent J. Birkley Raymer was one of a kind; he also taught her why she should let people underestimate her and he taught her to call a spade a spade. "I find it hard to believe you, Wade."

"Have I ever lied to you?"

She met that with a cold, hard silence and a moment of evil joy that she'd pulled him from a heavy sleep.

"Yes, I omitted, but I never lied—"

"Such an art form." She cut him off, angry and letting it roll out the way she did with so few people. In her family, people were always happy and perfect and when they weren't able to fake it they claimed some modern-day malady akin to "the vapors" and disappeared. Agent Raymer had done her huge favors.

A sigh came from the other end of the line. "Have I ever lied to you about physics?"

"No." She had to answer that one. Wade thought Westerfield's talent was physics? "So he's manipulating magnets or something?"

"No, Eleri. He's manipulating energy. In a way the rest of us can't."

Damn. Wade was telling her he'd reconciled it in his perfectly quantum world. Her eyes squeezed tight with pain and pressure and she was suddenly very tired.

After hanging up, she crawled across the bed and dropped like a stone into the deepest pools of sleep. She awoke with neither dreams nor improvement to claim. And now she was eating a banana that was actively crossing the boundary of ripeness. It was the only fruit they could offer her, a rescue from the pile waiting to get to near rotting for their legendary banana bread. She muttered to herself as she ate the blueberry pancakes. "I'm going to Foxhaven after this case is over. I'm going to Foxhaven."

"Was that the name of the hospital?" Donovan tipped his head. It was a legitimate question, but she glared at him anyway.

"It's the name of our beach house. I'm going there after I escape this state with no fruit and I'm cutting the phone lines." She would check with her father first, in case he was there, but her mother never went. Though Nathalie Eames had faked her return to sanity, she still never strayed far from Bell Point Farm or Patton Hall—the two homes Emmaline had lived in.

Breakfast sat like a Civil War cannon ball in her stomach. If the food hadn't been so easy to chew, Eleri would have thought it might have been cooked with actual lead shot in it. After all, two men sat at a nearby table, both wearing Civil War army caps, one gray, one blue, having a normal conversation while Eleri looked on. Surely she was hallucinating.

"I assure you they are quite real." Donovan had followed her gaze as he sipped the last of his coffee, his plate once again clean and his expression revealing absolutely no gastric discontent. Donovan only shrugged. Suddenly she wanted to get out of there as much as she'd wanted to get out of the hotel in the first place.

On the drive back to the hotel, she spotted a grassy area with park benches. Cutting a sharp left and squealing the tires as she pulled into a spot, Eleri used all her FBI aggressive driving skills and earned some dirty looks from the moms and dads dotting the edges of the nearby playground. She stepped from the car and felt the warm air wrap her like a blanket, the day still too new to do too much damage. Marching away and figuring Donovan would follow, she planted her butt on a park bench. When he did the same, she turned to him and simply said, "Spill."

He nodded. "I'm going to do another recon run. We'll use GPS like before. I won't go in, won't make contact, but I'll see what I can find out. I can stop and listen in to conversations. See if anything has changed."

Eleri agreed to that. Though if it was rational and well planned or just the best thing she'd heard, she couldn't tell. She did know they had successfully sent Donovan on a run before; they had even gotten Jonah out of that event. This one would have to go better now that Eleri knew what she was dealing with.

"Also, we get the elder Baxters down here. We test them against Jonah. Screw JBH's DNA, we don't need it."

"Sure, but we don't need to bring them here for that." It was too much, they could mail DNA samples, and—

He cut through her thoughts. "But we do need them here. We install them in town. Send them to church."

Eleri saw where he was going with this. "And draw Baxter out."

His nod confirmed it. It also confirmed that he'd done at least something productive with his awake hours last night. She'd only harassed a good friend. She was mentally composing her apology to Wade when Donovan's next words cut through.

"And you start carrying Baxter's picture with you. Sleep with it. Look at it. Keep it in your wallet. Touch it whenever you can."

She knew she was looking at him like he was five kinds of batshit. Donovan held his hand up as though there was a logical explanation.

"When you were on the profiling team, you touched things all the time. Victims' clothing. Photos of the suspect. Evidence."

She really wished she hadn't told him all that. This was not going to be good.

He didn't seem to notice her disdain.

"I think part of what you are doing is called psychometry."

Eleri stared blankly at Donovan. Psychometry? He didn't know what he was talking about. And what did he mean "what you are doing"? He stared back, not comprehending that she was not comprehending.

A few weird predictive dreams didn't put her in the same class as him and Westerfield.

Donovan apparently disagreed.

The people in the park had decided to ignore them, probably since her wild driving hadn't resulted in an actual accident. She knew she should care. Pissing off the locals in general was a bad idea in a town this small. Chances were good that at least one of the parents monitoring the children on the playground was married to a local cop. Given that the obvious parental activity was gossip, her parking skills were probably the least of her worries.

The woman in the hospital should come around any time now—Eleri checked her phone, not caring that it was a bit rude to Donovan. Sadly, no one had called her so she could call back and be a little ruder.

Slouching back on the hard bench, Eleri crossed her arms over her chest. This sucked. There were too many things to deal with and too much to do, leaving her with no time for sorting the rest of it out. While she was originally just threatening to disappear to Foxhaven after this was all over, she was now considering actually tapping out for a while. She had a trust fund, and while she generally preferred to earn her own way, not going insane—again—had a lot of merit.

"Eleri," Donovan tried to get her attention. "You can do something amazing."

"Not on command. It just happens." She still didn't look at him, just stared up into the trees and listened to the sounds of the birds overhead. For a moment she worried that they would poop on her. Then she worried that it wouldn't make her day that much worse.

"But I think you can start to do it on command. Like everything else, it's a gift if you make it one."

"Not so much." She didn't like knowing her sister was dead. Not being able to tell her parents made the burden heavier. Nathalie and Thomas Eames already thought she deserved to be in the loony bin just for joining the FBI. They had no idea that she knew from a young age the life they had prescribed would surely make her crazy. What she hadn't known was that the Bureau would make her nuts, too.

"I spent hours reading up on it." Donovan's hands twitched as though he wanted to use that tablet, produce actual evidence and convince her. Well, he had her number on that one. But since she didn't want to be convinced, she didn't want to see this evidence either.

"Psychometry is actually one of the more common types of extra sensory perception. It's believed that the person touches an object and picks up on energy or 'residue' left by a person who handled that object." He paused as though letting her soak it in. "Precognitive dreams are actually relatively universal. Almost everyone has experienced a dream that, at least in some part, has come to pass."

"Shut up." She still didn't look at him. Eleri spent far too big a portion of her life being good. Staying close by, never being out of her mother's sight, and never complaining. After all, she was still there, and wasn't that supposed to be good enough? Appearing as if all was well was better than actually being well. So her odd dreams and the fact that some of them came to pass was nothing she ever told her parents. That she saw her sister, living with another family, being seated at a dinner table the likes of which a thirteen-year-old daughter of a first family had never seen, had never been discussed.

Eleri did what she was good at: she deftly changed the subject. "How do we get the Baxters down here?"

Donovan's head jerked back a little, as though affronted that she had ignored his great revelation. Then he got it together and joined into the conversation she was willing to have. "I was thinking by plane."

"They may prefer to drive. Do you think they'll talk to us over the phone or do we have to go back up there in person to convince them?" There were always more questions generated than answered.

This time, Donovan leaned back on the bench. Being taller than her by a reasonable margin, there was no way he could slouch enough to rest his head against the back slats the way she had. Eleri could not call her position comfortable; Donovan's had to be worse. Though she waited, he didn't cry foul, and in fact seemed to act as though he had committed to the position regardless of the pain. "I really don't want to fly back, but we need them here and we need them here under solid pretenses. I'm not confident of the best way to do that. Won't JHB get suspicious if his parents turn up right around where he's settled down? So I don't know if the tourist routine would work."

"I'm thinking we get them here and have them actively look

for him. If someone is getting word in and out of the City of God —and they must be, because they have guns and ammo and military outfits, which don't grow in gardens—then JHB should know relatively soon that they're here."

"Do you think we can convince them to help? They seemed to want nothing to do with him."

She had been thinking the exact same thing, which was why she was one step ahead. "I think they'll want to meet their grandson. And if, on the off chance he's not their grandson, they may apply to be foster parents and take him home with them anyway."

"You're matchmaking foster families now?"

"I think I'm reuniting a genetic family. And I think I'm putting a kid with a deep religious belief in the kindness of God into a family that shares that belief, and into a community not too soul-shockingly different from where he grew up." She felt her jaw clench and realized that she had bonded to Jonah far more than she should have.

Donovan saw that. "Shouldn't we leave that to the professionals? Don't you think that's out of our jurisdiction?"

Using her hands, she scooted her butt back into the appropriate place on the bench and sat up straight and tall. Her chest ratcheted down and she felt her eyes sting at the thoughts. "I think you're a fucking mythical creature. That's what I think."

He started to protest but she steamrolled him, paying attention not to his feelings or hers, but only to not being overheard in this sunny little patch of park that was getting far too warm. "I think I just saw my boss bend gravity. I think you just tried to label me as psychic and I think we don't have any jurisdiction at all anymore. So if I can't do this one good thing for this kid who really deserves it, then screw it all."

DONOVAN WAS STILL LEANING BACK on the bench, in no position to pop up, when Eleri stood sharply and walked away. He scrambled to follow her, nearly dropping the tablet he'd hauled around all morning for no apparent purpose.

She was hitching her purse over her shoulder, a normal enough movement if it hadn't been so stiff, and he saw that she already clutched the car keys in her hand. Not trusting her to not drive off, Donovan praised his long legs and her short ones and strode to catch up.

The engine was turning over as he grabbed the passenger side door and folded himself in. Not looking at him, Eleri pulled smoothly away from the curb. Only thing was, he hadn't quite gotten his car door shut.

Maybe he shouldn't have pushed. It wasn't like he had a lot of practice with tough conversations. But he felt *wrong*. His breathing felt tight, as though he couldn't move. Twitching his finger just to test his theory, he found he could do that much, but something had taken over any greater control and locked him down.

Eleri was mad at him.

Since he'd been a small child left with his grieving father, he hadn't known this sensation. Growing up, he sometimes was disappointed in himself, missed goals he set, underperformed during rounds in med school. But that was him against himself. It had been decades since he allowed what someone else thought of him to have this kind of effect. As an adult, he was left with no developed method to deal with it. His mouth felt dry and his skin hot.

"You should buckle your seatbelt." Her words scorched their way across his revelation—their very ordinariness and complete lack of tone disturbing.

"I'm sorry."

"I'll feel bad if I kill you in a car accident. And I'm not in the best mood, so if I'm going to have one, it will be today." She stared at the road, not him, as though she were speaking to the air.

He managed to do as she suggested, only then realizing she thought he was apologizing for not buckling in. It took a moment to sit up straight, to speak. It had been hard enough to get the words out the first time; doing it again was worse. "Eleri, I'm sorry I made you feel bad."

It was like he deflated her. Her shoulders sagged, her neck lost its ramrod stiffness and her head listed to the side, her eyes no longer watching the road. He suffered a moment of worry that there wouldn't be anything left when she was done losing structure. But she stopped. Sitting probably five inches lower in the seat, unshed tears held back by force of will, her voice was no longer strong, and Donovan thought maybe he preferred mad Eleri. "I don't want it."

"It seems cool to me. I'm sorry." His brain scrambled. "I wish I could do what you do."

"No you don't." There was a slight pause. "I see killers tormenting victims. I saw a guy burying a kid and using the shovel edge to chop off limbs while he did it."

"You also saw the truck. You got our big break in this case." It was a gift. "There are good things, too. You see your sister."

"That's a mixed bag." She was speaking clearly now. The tears having vanished, she sat a little straighter, even if she wasn't at full Eleri yet.

"You solve cases. You save lives." There was an upside and a downside to everything. "Don't you see good things, too?"

The bark she emitted sounded too harsh against his optimism. "What good things? My sister's wedding? The birth of her first child? My parents' anniversary? My parents are shells of their former selves and they weren't all that solid to begin with."

Jesus. The girl needed a dog worse than he did.

"And by the way, it's not real psychometry or precognition. I did get curious about it once." She took the turn into the hotel parking lot and found a premium spot in the shade. That happened in Brownwood at nine a.m. on a Tuesday. "I don't see the future. My dreams are clairvoyant."

Just then, she was interrupted by the ringing of her cell. A shrill sound, he wondered if she'd chosen it specifically to sound harsh or if she'd more liked that it harkened back to the old, corded phone models.

By the end of the call, she was relatively excited and making promises to the caller. "Grace is awake and ready to be interviewed. Eating solid food."

Eleri nodded to herself, but since she made no move to get out of the car, Donovan didn't either.

For a moment they talked, Eleri rattling off the to-do list they had. It was just three items: interview the young woman, coordinate and execute another run around the compound, convince the Baxters to come help find their son. It was short, but each task alone would have been more than enough to occupy them.

If he were choosing, Donovan would talk to the Baxters first. Set them in motion, since it would take a while to get them here. He would guess they were drivers and not big travelers. They would likely arrive a full day or more after they were convinced of the need to come—and who knew how long it would take to convince them?

He and Eleri would need to get to the hospital next, while the girl was awake and alert. Before she needed more medications, before she got tired and crashed for another twelve hours.

He was reaching for the door handle, itching to get started on something, even if Eleri had a different idea, but she still wasn't moving. He'd begun to understand how she worked. Eleri was a thinker. Sure, she blurted sometimes, but mostly she processed first. She was processing now, and the fact that she wasn't looking at him was a clue that there was probably something big about to come out.

He was not disappointed.

"I've been working on recalling the dream about the truck, about Collier." Another pause. "I saw him pick up Ruth. I saw him pick up another girl, too. Given Jonah's pictures, it wasn't Faith. . . . I had another dream about Collier, after we met him." She shook her head as though trying to shake something into or out of place. "If what I saw was true, then there's another girl he picked up, one he didn't tell us about."

Eleri turned to face Donovan. "I think he's been relatively eager to help us because he wants it all to be done. But I think more than that, he knows where one of them is."

32

Eleri was surprised by the elder Baxters. Anxious to meet Jonah, even knowing full well he might not be their grandchild, they were ready to leave Zion's Gate practically before Eleri even finished explaining. They had no issues with the DNA tests. Where Eleri had steeled herself for a full-on science-denial argument, they surprised her again with the core belief that God gave them science, it was just up to them not to abuse it. Using it to save Jonah from the foster system was what God would intend them to do. Eleri was about ready to pack up and ask if there was room for her at Zion's Gate. It would certainly be less stress than she had now.

Though Mark and Lilly Baxter had already agreed to help, Eleri felt obligated to tell them the whole deal before they committed. It would be a bit easier for her—for today—to let them travel, then spring the rest of the info on them when they got here, but she didn't have the heart for it.

It was Donovan who figured out the key that would hopefully convince the Baxters of the need to travel to central Texas and offer their help. But it was Eleri who got to repeat it on the phone to them. "Flushing out Joseph is important. If we don't have evidence against him, and if he is Jonah's father, he'll have a legal claim to the boy that none of us can break."

Mrs. Baxter sucked in a quick breath and it tugged at Eleri even across the miles. She was being a bit manipulative, but what she said was true. If they couldn't take down JHB, and he was Jonah's father, then he could take Jonah far away and forbid his parents from ever seeing their grandchild.

The long pause was full of thought and fear on both sides of the line. It was Joseph's father who finally broke the tension. "Ms. Eames, we know exactly what our son is. We'll help the FBI get him into a treatment facility or even a jail, where he belongs."

Ignoring the twist in her gut at the deception—there would be no treatment, no jail for Joseph—Eleri started to respond, but she was jumping the gun, Mark Baxter wasn't done yet.

"Is there any chance this boy, Jonah, is like our son?"

"No sir. I don't see it at all. I have an undergraduate degree in psychology, and I realize that doesn't make me certified to diagnose anything, but your son appears to be a sociopath. It's a random event that happens to a portion of the population and it doesn't appear to be genetic." She was trying to be helpful. To her, "helpful" was information that set things straight. She floundered, knowing the science behind it wasn't necessarily what the Baxters needed, but she tried. "Not being genetic means he can't pass it to his offspring. I've met Jonah, he's a great kid. The other children there look up to him, a natural leader." Of course Joseph had been a natural leader, too. Eleri scrambled to cover that, "They love him. He thinks of others first. You'll be proud to have him as your own."

She must have said something right. Mark and Lilly thought they could be on the road within a few hours—they had to pack, talk to Father Jim, say their goodbyes to the group and request prayers—but they were anxious to come. They were more than willing to be part of the process bringing down their only son. It was all she could ask.

Eleri just hoped the interview in the hospital went as well.

When she and Donovan walked into the ICU room, Grace was awake and alert with an empty food tray pushed to her side. Eleri remembered to put a bright smile on her face and nudged Donovan. He looked at the girl as though he was making the initial assessment over a cadaver, and Eleri poked him again as she said, "We're so happy to meet you, Grace."

Finally Donovan smiled and Eleri accepted it, even if he did look pained rather than pleased. After introducing the two of them, Eleri told the woman the purpose of the interview, and that they were with the FBI. Her tongue tensed as the words rolled off. It was partly a lie that she wasn't comfortable with yet. Still holding a grudge against her friend for keeping all this from her for years, Eleri decided to call Wade and ask how he had handled it. She made a mental note to call between two and four a.m. if possible.

Grace didn't seem bothered by their need to question her, and Eleri had to wonder if that was because Grace was trusting or if she'd seen JHB for what he really was. Maybe Eleri and Donovan seemed tame and trustworthy in comparison.

The interview started slowly. Name? Only "Grace." People at the City? She named the same list Jonah and Charity did. They laid out Jonah's pictures for her and she identified each one with precision and certainty. Then she looked up at them. "Jonah did these." Eleri nodded and waited and was rewarded.

"Joseph says that drawing faces captures the soul. He beat Jonah for drawing things. But Jonah is so talented."

Eleri noted all kinds of things. She spoke of JHB in the present tense. She didn't agree with the statement; it saddened her. Her next words confirmed it.

"Mercy and Sarah and Abraham liked to sing. They had beautiful voices. Joseph says it's all fine as long as they sing with others. As long as they don't sing out of turn. When he found them practicing together, he punished them. But they weren't being vain. They enjoy it. And we enjoyed listening to them." Grace picked at the thin woven blanket on the bed. "God gave them those voices." Now she looked up, clearly older than Jonah and Charity. Maybe in her early twenties, but she lacked their confidence. "Doesn't that mean God wants them to use it? To give us joy? To praise him? I don't agree with Joseph."

Understandably, the last statement was hard for her.

In most cults, particularly religious ones, the leader was God's voice on Earth. To go against Joseph, to form her own opinion, would be blasphemy and likely also carried a very earthly punishment. What she said, what Jonah and Charity had said, made JHB sound very typical in that respect.

Eleri did as she was trained and steered the conversation. Using a soft voice, and a lowered gaze, she asked, "What did Joseph do when they sang?"

It was hard to sit and nod at the explanation of beatings and blood. At the leader's refusal to let the others tend to the wounded. Punishment, he said, did not include sympathy. Grace looked up at the two of them, looked to Elaine Coates for confirmation and understanding, each time she said something against JHB. When she described his treatment of her fellow City dwellers, she looked down. Though Grace wasn't able to truly stand up to the man, she had developed her own opinions. They eventually led her to the roadside and the orange truck with the blue flames.

"Joseph said my illness was a punishment from God. But I didn't have the spots. The spots weren't visited on those who needed to be punished." She looked down again. "Or Joseph would have gotten them."

Grace had not had the measles. She'd had a harsh fever and evidence of several strains of bacteria that should not have gotten hold in a healthy girl. She'd had a severe headache and told them that one of the women slipped her white pills for a while. This woman had gotten these when she snuck out of the City, and she gave them out to the kids and other women who needed them. From the description it sounded like they were probably Tylenol, but there was no way to be certain.

"Never the men?" Eleri latched on to what Grace didn't say.

Grace shook her head. "The men all report to Joseph. He says God made men to lead and women to follow. But the women started leading. The men are . . ."

Eleri leaned forward, grateful Donovan was just hanging back and taking notes. She was glad that Elaine Coates and the other RN working with Grace were female. It meant the ratio of men in the room was small, because it appeared Grace was used to the men being a separate group and interaction being low. "What are the men?"

Grace glanced to the side, then back to Eleri, leaning forward. All her body language said that she was revealing something, something she was unsure of or didn't like. "All the men are going crazy."

Donovan did not like the collar. It felt stupid, a grown man wearing a dog collar in the middle of a hotel room.

Worse, it was an invisible fence collar, the kind that picked up radio signals from a buried wire and shocked the dog if he went out of bounds. Certainly Donovan wasn't going to get shocked. Eleri jury-rigged it—pulled out the prongs, then replaced the inner workings with the tiny GPS. It looked spot on, but he was still a grown man wearing a shock-collar. Not cool.

If anyone was monitoring them, this would look like a setup for something very kinky—made all the worse by the fact that Eleri did not look like someone who would go for that kind of kink. But here she was, examining his shock collar. Donovan wondered what his dad would think of him, but like always he pushed those thoughts aside.

"It looks good to go." She sighed at him and frowned. "Your neck will be a different size, won't it? Can we guess?"

"We're fine, it doesn't have to fit perfectly, just stay on so I can be tracked." Eleri was not going to be left at the road this time. Wearing several weapons on her person and her own GPS, Eleri would set up between the road and the City. Westerfield had been alerted to the operation, and Eleri was to call in with a check for both herself and Donovan each hour. If anything went wrong, Bozeman would activate local police SWAT teams to extract them.

Donovan wasn't much for prayer, but he prayed now that nothing went wrong. The last thing he wanted was the City of God going crazy and his own life in the gloved hand of some local officer who probably didn't think very highly of him. If that all went well and he and Eleri were rescued, he would likely be leashed and kept until Eleri could reclaim him and get him somewhere to change. Or else they would find him naked, hopefully having taken off the damn shock collar. Donovan prayed harder.

Who had thought this stupid thing up? Oh yes, that was him.

The interview with Grace had taken several hours and was incredibly interesting. She inadvertently gave them more things to look for this time when he went in. The young woman described the layout of the compound, including which buildings had basements dug underneath them. Donovan didn't know if he could get close enough to check things out, but it might help him account for where people came and went.

She'd also given him several locations where Ruth might be buried. Grace had told the same story as Jonah and Charity about the older woman. Then Eleri had asked for Grace's oldest memory. The words had come out on a whisper. "I was six, I was on the swing set with my little brother next to me. And I told my dad to push me higher."

She didn't remember her "dad" but no one called any of the men in the City of God "dad". And no one had a swing set. It was within minutes of that announcement that Grace became quite saddened. So it wasn't a surprise when she said she was tired and asked, could they finish this tomorrow?

Though Grace got to tap out for the day, they did not. When the two of them called Westerfield to discuss the run that night, Donovan had listened as Eleri requested surveillance on Collier and his wife at home.

"Did you find something else out?"

"Not really, sir. Just a . . . hunch." The stiffness in her neck made it obvious Eleri didn't like being called out for her ability. She saw it more as something that happened to her, rather than a gift she might be able to control. Donovan thought otherwise.

Apparently so did Westerfield. The man responded, "Eleri, you were brought into NightShade because of your 'hunches'. We'll post regular FBI on recon there and see what they report."

She hadn't commented after that, just offered a terse thank you and moved to the next topic. But that conversation helped cement Donovan's belief that NightShade actively recruited oddities. They hadn't met anyone else in the division yet, which in turn made Donovan wonder if they had to complete this first mission before Westerfield would introduce them fully or if there was more to it and they might always be on their own, two Night-Shades floating secretly through the realm of "regular FBI."

Eleri stared at him, the clock ticking on the day. Everything was ready except them.

Neither had slept well the night before. They were exhausted —and the intense interview with Grace didn't help at all. Donovan only hoped it served to get them both to sleep for the next few hours. They were going to have to sleep through some daylight in order to get up at midnight and be fully alert for this run.

This time, he would get in closer—pull the lost dog act if he needed to. If that happened, he needed Eleri nearby and he needed her sharp. Shoving the hated collar into his pocket for later, he turned to her. "It's time for bed."

She only nodded at him. What she didn't know was that he had thought about her talent. He told her to sleep with something Baxter had touched. But right now that was limited to Jonah and Charity, and they were not options. Plus, he'd read that people were not good psychometric objects as they brought too much of their own energy and would obscure anything Baxter left behind.

Donovan could obtain the red shirt from the first dead girl. The blood and the fist imprint were pretty convincing evidence that Baxter had in fact touched her, repeatedly and with energy. But that was too creepy. Instead, he printed out another copy of Jonah's drawing. He glued it to the back of Baxter's mug shot from the juvenile record they had eventually been given access to. A two-sided picture of Baxter, now and then, photo and art. Donovan had no idea if it would lead Eleri anywhere near a helpful dream, but he'd slipped it under her pillow when she stepped out of the room.

He felt bad about it, though not bad enough to confess what he'd done. Motioning to the window, he said, "Be sure to pull the blackout drapes in the back. They really work. See you later."

"At the witching hour." She responded, shutting the door behind him.

33

Donovan walked into the woods, having left the car behind, tucked into thick bushes for cover. The tire tracks leading to the car would be obvious to anyone who looked, but hopefully no one would, not in the dead of night.

He held the strap of his silly little mesh backpack for comfort. He didn't think it would fall off, but the feel of it in his grip anchored his thoughts as he picked his way through the dense brush. This time he carried no rope or anchors, he would leave the pack on the ground. Instead he carried a super compact table tucked under his arm—the kind professional campers used.

Even odder than what he carried was the fact that there was a woman behind him, traipsing directly in his footsteps as best she could, given his longer stride. Eleri carried a chair that matched the camping table, a shoulder bag with computer equipment, and a smaller thermal bag of food. And also bug spray, because no matter how dim she made the screen, she was going to be a beacon for a variety of flying and crawling things. She'd bought two different bottles of heavy-duty repellent in an effort to hedge her bets. Donovan had almost suggested she also get a gas mask, but he managed to bite his tongue on that one.

He was simultaneously soothed and completely freaked out by her presence.

Always alone until now, he was breaking a thirty-four year silence. Though he still wasn't ready to change in front of her—wasn't sure he ever would be—there was a level of comfort that someone had his back.

No one had ever had his back and it had taken him thirty-four years to realize he could affect his own change.

Seemingly his change came in the form of a secretive division of the FBI. A boss with a questionable set of skills and directives. And a partner, younger than him, whip smart, and battling her own demons. So he walked into the woods, picking his footing carefully, for the first time needing to locate a suitable spot to set up a computer tracking station.

Behind him, Eleri remained silent. She had on lightweight but sturdy pants that wouldn't tear or get ruined walking the underbrush, hiking boots, and a long-sleeved shirt that would protect most of her from the bugs. She must be the proud owner of a shrink ray to get all that into the one suitcase, but he didn't ask.

They had hiked close to five miles, the GPS indicating they were now two miles from the area where City of God was set up. Any farther out and he could get stuck with Eleri too far away. Any closer in and the patrols might find them. Light traveled far in the dark. Luckily there was a moon out tonight to mask the glow of her set-up.

Eleri tipped her head back to admire the white sliver hanging there beautifully. "It's nearly full." Then she frowned at it. "Clearly you can change at will. I get the whole 'monster' thing, though. For centuries people assumed anything they didn't understand was either witchcraft or Satan. Of course the prevailing fix for things we didn't understand was to kill them—

often in a painful way. But how did the whole full-moon myth come about?"

Donovan shrugged as he set up the table and found an area of flat ground, digging the legs in for a little stability. "The best I can figure is that's when we were seen. The rest of the month it was pretty dark. Are we good here?"

The unsegued change in topic wasn't coincidental. He didn't know much of his own history.

Eleri nodded at him. She was pulling the bag from her shoulder, opening the tablet with the tracking device, making sure it linked to the tiny keyboard. She didn't need him here, so he turned and stalked off into the woods to a point where the light wouldn't carry, where anyone from the City of God wouldn't possibly see him. They would surely mark him as Satan and shoot on sight.

Peeling his T-shirt, he stepped out of his shoes and socks and shucked his jeans. In a moment, he stood there in the woods, completely naked and hopefully completely alone. After folding the clothing, pushing it down into the mesh bag and cinching the top, he began. First he rolled his shoulders, setting them into their alternate location, the long scapulae Eleri had noticed now anchored at a different angle. He flexed his toes, watching as his feet lengthened from the stretch, his ankle now further back—though not reaching quite the distance a real wolf's would.

His head was last—had someone seen him mid-change, they would freak out, probably not mentally able to deal with what they saw. So he didn't linger. The base of his neck popped as he moved his head forward, the muscles sliding into place to create the thicker, front-carried neck of the wolf.

When he was completely altered, the collar sitting just a little loose and a lot demeaning around his neck, Donovan picked up the pack in his teeth and trotted it back to Eleri.

She looked down at him, an odd, curious expression on her face as he dropped the pack at her feet. She was starting to give him a thumbs-up when she frowned a little more. "I guess I can talk to you, can't I?"

Offering the best nod he could in return—aside from a few barks and whines she likely wouldn't understand—it was the best they could do without reverting to the full Lassie scenario where she asked random questions and he barked when she was right.

"Well, then—" The look on her face was still a bit unsettled, but she was getting there. Donovan was starting to think Eleri could deal with anything. "—The GPS is working. You're good to go."

Another nod and Donovan turned to trot off into the woods. As long as the GPS was transmitting and as long as Eleri herself was okay, she would do the check-ins with Agent Bozeman. At one point, she offered up the brilliant idea of a button Donovan could press that would transmit his own check-ins. Donovan had quickly nixed that as he would have no way to tell when he should check in. Aside from "morning" or "night", his internal clock wasn't the best. And because a wolf wearing a wristwatch would get locked up at the very least and likely killed.

His pace was solid as he headed into the thick forest. This time he didn't hold back, didn't wonder what Eleri would think of tracking him. Inside seven minutes, he covered the distance and came to a slow trot. Just outside of range of what the patrol guards would take notice of, he walked a wide perimeter, once again starting by observing their patterns.

Out beyond sight, under cover of trees and scrub, he scared away several deer. Of the guys with guns, only two paid any attention, but a brief head turn and an even more brief survey of the forest was all the disturbance bought him. They understood they lived in the middle of any number of wild animals. Noises in the forest at night were the norm more than anything else.

Lying down in the middle of the area he cleared, Donovan rested his head on his paws. For a moment he considered napping. The feel of the woods, the dampness of the air on his fur, the loamy scents of earth and trees all alleviated the itch he suffered these past days. But he had a job to do.

Careful to tilt his head and not let the light catch his eyes too much, he watched the comings and goings of the compound. The patrol guys appeared to have the same schedule as before, walking odd but consistent figure eights around some of the buildings. They carried their guns almost at the ready, upright this time, with two hands. Only one guard had done that before. For whatever reason, they were on higher alert now. One house to his right held odd chatter he couldn't make out, but the rest were quiet.

Convinced he'd sat there long enough to develop a sense of the schedule, Donovan waited until their pattern moved them away before standing, offering himself the small luxury of a stretch, then trotting off in search of the places Grace had suggested Ruth might be buried. Earlier, when they asked the young woman why she thought these particular locations were options, she told them the children were allowed to play in most areas of the surrounding forest, as long as they stayed together. When they went out, the older kids had been actively searching for gravesites for Ruth and Jonah. They had found nothing, so she was sending Donovan into the areas that were off limits.

He made an effort to memorize the map before leaving; it wasn't like he could carry one with him. Pretty sure he had a good sense of direction, he was finally putting it to the test. In the past he could run a loop and head unerringly toward home, whether he was wolf or man. He could easily find markers he had left behind—a scratch on a tree, the spot he'd run into the bear—on a later run. The woods just made sense to him. But he'd never tried to transfer map information into ground direction before. This was definitely a test.

Donovan was relying in good part on his sense of smell to help him find Ruth. Mostly, he wished he wouldn't find her. He'd hoped for a while that Charity and Jonah were mistaken and the woman wasn't really dead, just missing. But Grace was a bit older, and while she wasn't as assertive as the younger two, she seemed to have a better handle on the goings-on. She was a more reliable source for the information, which made Ruth's outcome less likely to be good.

He searched a large swath of area where Ruth might be, finding nothing. Once he decided nothing was there, he circled back to where he had started and passed that point. As he came in close to the edges of the City, he would slow, watch the guards, keep his head low so his eyes wouldn't be seen. But he kept tracking the perimeter.

Last time, he was three-quarters of the way around before he ran into Jonah and was diverted. This time, he was tracking back the last quarter he hadn't explored. It was one of the areas that Grace had mentioned was off limits to the women and children, though the men went there all the time.

Donovan found what he thought was the area she referred to, surprised to discover open space here, just beyond the trees. A short distance away he could see an oil rig, pumping to music only it could hear. At the top, the burnoff shot flames another ten or fifteen feet into the night sky. Donovan knew it wasn't uncommon to have natural gas mixed in with shale oil. He also knew that as the gas leaked it was customary to burn it rather than send it into the atmosphere. This flame seemed suspiciously high to him, but knowing that the practice itself was normal exhausted all his knowledge on the topic. It did explain the smell he got from all their clothes—this was definitely the source.

Watching for others watching him, he tried to grid off the land without looking like he was doing it. A wolf trotting aimlessly about in the woods was not a big deal at all, but one working a clear grid? Yet another thing that would get him shot for witchcraft—especially in this bunch.

Nothing out of the ordinary came to him; in fact nothing much at all came to him. The ground gave off a light smell of decay and clean water. He could scent mushrooms blooming nearby, but that was about it. The oil burn overpowered other odors in the area until his sense faded. Sticking his nose closer to the ground, he tried harder but got nothing.

Eventually he gave up and trotted away, thinking there must be smoke in the air, he was getting a headache.

It was his hearing that saved him.

Three small buildings nestled discretely under spreading trees. Even with the drone, Donovan and Eleri had missed these. Though no one was inside at this hour, at least not that he could tell, there were guards standing sentry and more guards walking the perimeter. These buildings were more fortified than the others, more protected both by mechanics and personnel. Whatever was here it was more important than the people of the City of God.

Blinking at the dull throb radiating from the back of his skull, Donovan crept forward. One of the buildings was less guarded; no one was posted at the door, and guards walked its perimeter only half to a third as often as the other two. Donovan aimed for getting close to one of the other two.

Even with his good eyesight in the dark, the trees obscured his view. It was hard to tell just what he was looking at until he got close. On the upside, the trees would hide him as well, and he slowly snuck in closer and closer.

Once he was near enough, he could see that these were metal buildings, mobile units, intended to be taken down and reassembled a few times. Tucking himself under a bush and scooting forward, he watched while the guard passed, gun down, occasionally sweeping out at an invisible attacking enemy. No one was there.

Donovan checked out the ground around the corners of the building. They were shimmed to level the floor on this very lumpy Texas turf. Since the grass was still growing under the propped corner, they hadn't been here long. It looked as though the group made use of the portability features and actually moved them quite a bit. Hearing the guard head around the corner, Donovan made a break for it and cut an arc that took him in close to the edge of the container.

"What was that?" The shout went up from one of the men, overlapping another voice.

"I heard something!"

Feet pounded behind him as Donovan made a dash for the cover of nearby brush. As quick as he was, he knew they were rounding the corners, guns ready, even as he took off. His heart pounded and he was suddenly frightened again. Usually one for science over religion, Donovan shucked every belief system he had and began praying to several gods at once.

He did not want to die here in the backwoods of Texas. He did not want to die at the hands of these odd, militant people. He did not want Eleri to find him, bled out, in wolf form. She'd never be able to produce his body for burial, not that anyone would really come to his funeral. So maybe that didn't matter quite as much as the fact that he didn't completely trust Eleri not to study him for the sake of science.

Hitting the edge of the brush, he kept going, pushing through the foliage. As he escaped he did hear one of them say to the others, "It's nothing. I saw it, just a coyote."

He loped away, putting distance between him and the small cluster of sheds, only this time he watched more carefully, tried to pay more attention to the smells, so he wouldn't be surprised again.

As he passed the corner of the small building he'd picked up on a scent. Several in fact, but the main smell was cocaine. He wasn't positive—something was clogging his olfactory sense—if there was actual coke in the building now, but there had been. Recently. Mixed with some kind of soft, fluttery scent. Whatever it was, he'd smelled it before. In the past, he'd smelled cocaine with other scents, too, and this seemed to be a common enough cutting agent.

That, then, was the money. He'd found it and he'd managed to not get shot. He'd also managed to get called a "coyote," which was just insulting, but as he wasn't riddled with bullet holes, Donovan could live with it.

He headed around to complete the circle, passing through another of Grace's off-limits areas. As he moved away from the oil rig, his sense of smell started to return. Donovan had to conclude that the burn must have overpowered his natural senses.

Large trees dotted the area. Huddling together as though afraid of the dark, their broad canopies provided cover for the dense shrubbery underneath. Though it was much the same as what he'd been running through all night, this area had more open spaces, less overall density. More points where he could stand on dirt or fallen leaves and look up and see clear sky.

He almost stepped on it before the smell hit him.

34

W atching the screen in front of her, Eleri bit into her apple, and a trickle of juice ran down her chin.

Shit.

In her bag she had a wipe, of course, but her hand was dripping juice. If she wiped her hand on her pants, not only would they be wet and sticky, but she had no doubt she'd find a swarm of bugs crawling all over that spot in just minutes. Even eating the apple had been a gamble.

She settled for wiping the dripping, sticky juice from one hand to the other and gingerly reaching the drier hand into her bag, hoping to touch only the foil packet.

Letting out a sharp breath, she produced a single wet wipe successfully. The game of Operation had nothing on late night recon in the woods with apples. Now safe with her "moist towelette" she turned back to the screen and listened to the crunch of her teeth against the flesh of the apple while she tracked Donovan.

While the tracer left on the screen was interesting as hell, watching it happen was about as exciting as watching grass grow. She could only imagine how dull it would be if he were human and going only half to one third this speed. Of course, if he were human, there would be no need for him to be alone, and she'd be in there with him.

Instead, Eleri got to sit still in the woods. At a makeshift table. With a small commune of gun-carrying loonies close at hand. She jumped when a twig snapped behind her, rocketing to her feet and grabbing her weapon. She stood there for probably five minutes before concluding that it was a false alarm.

Mostly she sat and watched the bugs hit the boundary of her cloud of bug repellent. But almost every hour, something would startle her, sending her on a slow grapevine walk around the perimeter of her tiny space. She kept her screen as dim as possible, stayed relatively still, and made no real noise of her own—except maybe biting into the apple. At one point, she took out her night vision glasses and scared the shit out of herself. She was trained for human predators not the herd of deer passing ridiculously close behind her back, not the large cat stalking in the distance, or the thousands of dark-haired "swamp rabbits" that ran wild around here, eating vegetation and giving themselves heart attacks when anything moved. Eleri was starting to feel like a rabbit as she sat there. She reminded herself to find some Zen. She had a job to do, an important one.

She cleaned the apple juice from her skin and stuffed the wipe and the wrapper down into the plastic bag she'd brought for trash. Then she stood for a ritual reapplication of bug spray, which she was already practically inhaling off her own skin. Unlike Donovan, she was not naturally repellent—just the opposite in fact. When she finished and sat down again, Eleri was stunned.

They had worked out a simple signal system. There were too many variables for most communication options. Obviously if the tracker went into the boundaries of the City of God, Eleri would mobilize. But other than that, he wouldn't necessarily be able to, say, sit still for an extended period, or move in an X shape.

And there was every possibility that he would need odd patterns as they came up. But they had managed one sign, and now the blue line on her very dim screen showed a track, circled three times around a small space.

It was the signal that he had found the body.

Holy shit. Donovan had found Ruth.

For a moment, she turned sad. They had discussed the possibility that Ruth had made it out alive, that the kids were mistaken. Then they had discussed the probability that scenario was dead wrong.

Donovan trotted off, gridding the area pretty damn well. His lines weren't perfectly straight; there were aberrations, probably trees, maybe rocks, anything in his way, but he'd done it. Aside from a few fast motions—his speed was noted on the screen by dashes in the line—he did exactly what he planned. And he hadn't gotten caught.

As she watched, he worked the grid, but then the line turned sharply before circling tightly again.

Another body?

The third time he made the loop there was no denying that he'd given the signal again. There were two bodies out there. Eleri gave up being good and reached for the donut holes she packed along with the apple. She munched until she honestly had no idea how many she'd eaten, then decided that she'd been so focused it was time to run a search on the perimeter of her area. Using the night vision glasses and keeping her Glock at the ready just for good measure, Eleri walked her own ground.

The deer had moved on. So had the large cat. Down low she saw mice and up high, owls and other birds of prey. All over she spotted the rabbits that had somehow managed to multiply in the last hour. But all was clear. When she returned to her spot, Eleri cleaned her hands with sanitizer despite the fact that she'd really touched nothing during the slow search, and waved them around to dry off. If someone were watching, they would conclude she was doing an odd dance in the middle of the woods and likely think she was insane. If they somehow knew her history, they would be certain of it.

Once her hands were dry, she popped another donut hole, sat back down and promptly choked on cinnamon sugar dust. Donovan had made another circle—already traced three times—and it looked like he was starting a fourth.

Eleri's mind was reeling.

There was a whole graveyard there. How would she and Donovan get in to dig them up? Without disturbing the City of God members? It was far enough away from the compound to make her think they should try it. It was also close enough to likely get them killed.

Checking the clock in the lower corner of her screen, Eleri was startled that it was already well after three a.m. Donovan had a dawn deadline. At the latest, he was supposed to start heading her way when he saw the first hint of the sun. Since she would see he was coming toward her, it would be fine if he wasn't exactly on time. But she didn't want to be sitting here, or even packing up and schlepping away in full daylight. She didn't want Donovan changing when someone was more likely to see him.

She ate another donut hole and started praying things went well.

Her fingers hit the bottom of the plastic clamshell and she cursed herself for eating the whole thing. As she stuffed the empty container down into her trash bag, she looked up to see that he had stopped circling bodies and was making a wide arc away from the compound. Unwilling to let her breath out until she knew more, Eleri watched, this time clasping her hands together to keep from snacking on anything, and was gratified to see the line slowly turn back her way. As he was now on the far side of the compound, he still had some miles to cover, but her clock showed his timing was good. He'd get back while it was still dark, and they would be gone from here long before the sun came up.

She couldn't dismantle the system until he arrived. Plus, Donovan would need some time once he got back. He had to change, which didn't seem to take too long, but he would want to get his bag, go away somewhere, and come back. Once she laid eyes on him she could start powering down, but until then, she had to keep it up. Even though she could see her partner was on a straight track back to her now.

Eleri was just considering a last sweep with the night vision goggles when Donovan made an abrupt ninety-degree turn. Having no clue what this meant, Eleri simply clutched her gun and her NVGs and watched to see what happened. He didn't go far before he turned a full one-eighty, tracing his steps almost perfectly, given the way the blue trail doubled back. As she watched, he passed his original point, the T where he'd turned, but he kept walking straight ahead, still perpendicular to his route toward her.

Her brain whirled with possibilities.

He'd run into someone and changed direction so as not to lead back to her.

Maybe he encountered some kind of barrier—though what that might be, she couldn't tell. Could there be a fence, a wall? Eleri didn't think a tree would stop him. That had to happen all the time; he'd be a crap wolf if he couldn't handle a fallen log, even a big one.

His path started to curve toward her again, and the relief that hit her was a bit of a shock. So was the surprise when it was quickly yanked away. He turned sharply and headed back the other direction, tracing close to his original path, but not quite. Watching the screen, she could see that he was making the third line of what was shaping up to be a curved zig zag. Slowly, he was moving toward her, but taking great pains to not come exactly her direction.

He was just under a mile away now. While he could have covered that distance in just a few minutes with relative ease had he been aimed at her, he was now aimed every way except at her. She could see the amount of ground he covered and the time it took him—his speed had dropped a large percent when he took that first ninety off his path.

Grabbing the night vision goggles, she held them up to her face, scanning the area rapidly, looking for a sign of anything. When that yielded nothing, she scanned again, this time forcing herself to go more slowly.

Eleri pushed her breathing into conscious thought, taking over the almost-hyperventilation her body wanted. She tightened her chest muscles and forced her intake to shallow out, knowing that this would help slow her heart rate and keep her from doing something rash. Something was likely wrong. She needed to make calm, informed decisions now—and she needed to do it even though she was neither calm nor informed.

Unfortunately, the second pass with the glasses also gave her nothing. The forest was too dense to see that far. Peeling the glasses away, she blinked to help adjust her eyes to the screen. Donovan was still repeating the pattern, but curving the ends of his arc a little more. He was tracing a partial circle one way, then back the other, tightening the radius a little each time and moving just a little closer to her.

It took her another minute and another rapid change of orientation, before she caught on.

Donovan was herding something.

Or more likely, someone.

35

Eleri pulled out her night vision goggles again, though she wasn't sure they would do her any more good now than they did the last time. What she had learned was that she had to keep looking, so she scanned the entire area.

Nothing.

Only the silent streamers of bright moonlight filtered through the dense canopy of the trees.

In her search, she crept away from the set-up, away from where she could track Donovan. She didn't want to bring the tablet with her—though it would allow her to walk straight to him, it would also spotlight her face, making her a target to anyone who was in range. Out here, "in range" was deadly.

She was the one trespassing on someone else's private property. She was doing this on land she knew full well was home to a militia-like organization. She understood Texas laws favored the property owner in disputes, which in turn gave those owners more impetus to shoot first and ask for ID later. While they might find her badge and know they killed a federal officer, in the end, she would still be very dead. Eleri tread as cautiously as she could.

Donovan was out there and he had encountered something.

The problem was, there was no telling what else was out there.

Slowly, she tracked back to her setup and examined the screen again. Donovan was still moving toward her, still making those sweeping arcs. If he was corralling someone, then Eleri could almost pinpoint the location of the person just by watching Donovan's path. If he was doing that on purpose, she couldn't tell.

In that moment, Eleri made her decision. Maybe Donovan wanted her out there to help bring in whomever he had found. If he wasn't signaling her, then she could just get out of the way when she got there. Turning the tablet face down to block its light, Eleri patted herself, checking for the weapons she had on hand—Glock, at her side; KaBar knife, strapped to her ankle; backup pistol—an adorable little thing that was perfectly deadly —nestled at the small of her back.

Stepping carefully, she periodically held the NVGs up to her face, but didn't keep them there. While they afforded a wealth of information, even these newer models still blocked some of her peripheral vision. Unwilling to sacrifice it, she instead wound up letting her eyes adjust back and forth.

As it was more important that she not alert anyone to her presence, her movement was incredibly slow. Pressing cautiously forward, Eleri considered what she might encounter.

At first she assumed Donovan had caught himself a guard, but after a brief thought, she threw that idea out the window. A guard would be armed. Donovan would not. If the wolf faced down one of these guys, they would simply shoot him, at the very least they would shoot *at* him. Thus, the person, or maybe thing, Donovan had was not armed.

She considered that it might be another escapee. And then she had to consider that luck. While she inched through the brush, occasionally lifting her glasses and still coming up blank, Eleri did the math. The City of God was hemorrhaging people lately—specifically women and children. Given the numbers they had seen, her belief that Collier knew of at least one more, and extrapolating for the ones they hadn't found, well, Eleri came up with a one-in-four chance of someone making a run for it. That was huge.

She and Donovan had been out here all night, between the compound and Route 162. They chose to come in that way because it was the best traveled nearby road, and thus it made this the right direction to run if you were fleeing Joseph Hayden Baxter and his odd-knuckled fist. By her numbers, she had a twenty to forty percent chance that someone was on the run tonight and she liked those odds.

Getting excited now, and nearly convinced Donovan had another one, Eleri tried to pick up speed. It worked for about fifteen steps but then backfired when she cracked a branch, the noise reverberating through the air around her, laying a target right on her location.

Stepping sharply to the right, Eleri tucked herself into some bushes, the best she could do at the moment. If she ran, she'd leave a sound trail much like an arrow pointing right to her. Tightening her chest muscles again, taking conscious control of her breathing, she worked to put herself back into a calmer state.

Eleri tried to calculate how far away Donovan was now. Tried to see if she could figure out when she would run into him or his prey. Should she try to circle around or come up behind it? Him? Her?

Circling was too iffy.

This time when she checked the glasses the green of the night scope revealed an odd pattern. Two oval-ish shapes glared bright at the ground, moving in a slow motion bounce. Mesmerized, Eleri tried to keep her ears open for someone trying to do the same thing to her. A slash of bright came through the goggles just above the moving ovals and disappeared as quickly as it came. It wasn't until the second time it happened that Eleri comprehended what she was seeing.

The ovals were feet, bound in white, probably fabric. As she scooted closer she could see a lumpy knot tied on the top of each foot. The slash she'd seen was the hem of a gown, probably in glaring, virginal white.

Sneaking closer, it became obvious why she hadn't been able to make out a person before this.

It was a girl or woman—her long dark hair was tied back in a braid, and Eleri couldn't see the front of her head. As best Eleri could tell, the movements were timid and non-confrontational, which would suggest a younger woman. She had a blanket draped around her. In this heat the mysterious "she" had to be sweltering. Eleri pondered that decision for a while before concluding the girl understood that her white gown would be a beacon in the dark night. Whether she realized that changing her shape was also a help—Eleri had looked right at her several times before recognizing what she was seeing—remained to be seen.

It all added up to another fleeing City of God resident. At least they didn't sleep in their jeans and T-shirts.

In the distance she could see a set of red eyes a few feet above the ground. They were demon eyes, staring the girl down and probably scaring her shitless.

Donovan. He was so focused, Eleri couldn't be certain he had seen her there. So—feeling stupid—she raised her left hand, the one not holding the Glock, and waved at him.

A small upward bump of his head movement was the only thing that acknowledged her presence.

Eleri had time while she snuck up to think about how to do this, so when she reached a space behind the girl, she was ready and made a hand motion to Donovan, who offered another slight head movement in response.

Breathing heavily and moving with a jerky motion, the girl

was clearly afraid she was going to die. Close in behind her now, Eleri was still undetected, but she could make out what the girl was muttering to herself.

"Please, God, don't let it eat me. I'm sorry, I'll go home. I shouldn't be here. I've learned my lesson. Please don't let it eat me . . ." She started through the whole round again. Standing still now, her eyes locked on the black wolf with the eyes glowing red in the night. It stalked a circle around her, trying to push her ever deeper into the forest.

Eleri stepped into the girl's line of sight, her finger already at her lips.

The girl still started to scream but managed to stifle it—hopefully before alerting the entire nearby town. Her mouth worked like a fish upon seeing Eleri, and Eleri cataloged a variety of things.

Here in the moonlight it was clear the girl was flushed and sweating under the blanket. Even though it wasn't heavy, the night was nearly eighty degrees. It had been cooler earlier in the week, and Eleri had to wonder what had pushed her out beyond the boundaries with this escape plan on such a bad night for it. Her hair was plastered to her face and her breathing was labored.

"Ma'am." She managed to push out on faltering breath, "There's a wolf behind you." Her hand came out as though showing her palm would ward off the creature she feared. She was nearly in tears as she pled, "Please be careful."

"I've got this." Eleri's voice was as low as she could keep it as she turned to Donovan.

It was strange seeing him like this. Logically, she knew it was him, but her brain was simply reciting that fact—she didn't yet recognize him or have that chemical reaction a body felt when encountering someone it knew. "Go away wolf!"

She made the sound harsh, glared in his direction, unsure what to do, but knowing that if she said "It's all good, this is Donovan!" the girl would pass out and become dead weight.

Since Eleri didn't have anyone with hands to help her carry the girl she didn't want that to happen.

Donovan must be thinking along the same lines as he stepped sideways at her command but not away. Eleri said it again, and finally took a few rapid steps in his direction, almost forcing him to back up.

"Shoot it."

The words were soft, a prayer not a command, but it pointed out to Eleri the danger of what they were doing. She did not raise the gun at Donovan, but he did turn and trot off, presumably making a circle and heading back to their camp. A thought raced through Eleri's head on an odd laugh, "No worries, wolf, I've got it from here."

The girl's eyes went wide, as though she was shocked by this turn of events. Eleri thought it made perfect sense. You were a pussy and the wolf tracked you, I stood up to it and it went away. But the large eyes staring back at her demanded more.

Keeping her voice low, she said, "I'm wearing a ton of bug spray. It probably didn't like the smell of me." And she offered the sweetest smile she could muster in the middle of the night, after eating a whole pack of donut holes and finding out that there was an entire graveyard just beyond the City of God.

Staying silent now, she motioned to the girl to follow her, and it took a few tries to gain any kind of trust and get the girl to come. She tried a whispered introduction. "My name is Eleri."

Then she waited, watching, motioning with her hand for a return answer when none came. Again using the silence, Eleri waited longer, finally garnering one word, "Mercy."

Hoping it was the girl's name, Eleri nodded and moved toward camp again. She had worried about giving Donovan enough time to change and be ready when they arrived, now she worried about making it the near mile back before sunup. Then they would have to make it to the car with this girl who moved like a glacier.

In a few more moments, part of why she was so slow became clearer—her feet were obviously hurting her. As Eleri stepped easily over and through the brush, Mercy followed gingerly, even wincing each time she placed her right foot flat.

Shit, Eleri sighed the word internally. The last thing this timid, God-fearing girl needed was her new wolf-repelling friend swearing into the night. She wanted to help, but she couldn't. Even slinging the girl's arm over her shoulder and supporting her wouldn't work. It would make them wider on the path. They couldn't be as silent and Eleri needed her hands free, just in case. Mercy would have to make her own way and Donovan would be more than ready when she arrived. Probably Eleri's chocolate cookies would be gone. Which was just as well, since she didn't need to eat them anyway.

Their progress was slow, so Eleri used the NVGs several times as they picked their way along. But she never saw the men coming. The only warning was a series of breaking twigs, which soon gave way to the pounding of feet on the ground.

Too close, a voice yelled out, "Merrrrrr-seeeeeeeee."

Anger permeated the sound: this man wanted this girl back. From the violent noises shattering the natural stillness of the woods, he wanted her back badly.

Where she had been flush, the girl now suddenly drained of color. Her face a stark white, she froze for a moment.

Then she did the worst thing she could possibly do.

She dropped the dark blanket, her gown catching every stray ray and lighting up like a signal in the dark woods.

Next she hit her knees and began praying in a harsh whisper. Her hands clasped together, her noises scaring Eleri to the bone. Whispers carried farther than low voices and Mercy was now calling out to everyone who might have missed the pristine white of her gown.

There were plenty more than two men coming, Eleri could tell from the footsteps. Donovan had reported last time that the men were heavily armed and that everyone he'd seen at night had been carrying at least one firearm.

Eleri's heart beat in rapid time, pounding to the beat of the approaching steps. Trying to stay calm, she faced the girl, throwing the blanket over her and shushing her as best she could. Wide eyes looked up at her, deathly afraid.

Eleri only caught a glimpse, but she thought they were Jennifer Cohn's eyes.

36

D onovan was almost dressed—jeans and shoes but no shirt—when he heard the men hollering through the forest.

For a brief moment, he analyzed his situation. The men were heading right toward Eleri and the girl he assumed was named Mercy. If these were the men he saw earlier, they were heavily armed and seriously paranoid. There had been nothing out there to cause them to swing their guns, but they were jumpier than they had been the last time he was out. While this could be due to the exodus of members since then, that would still mean they had their weapons ready in case they encountered the girl. That was not a pleasant realization.

He wondered for a second if he might better help Eleri and the girl as the wolf but quickly realized a gun and opposable thumbs would be far better. Slinging his shirt over his head, he shoved his hand down into the bag where his piece was stashed. The click it made as he chambered a bullet was obscured by the onset of loudly whispered praying.

Mercy.

A bright splotch of white appeared in the short distance as

she must have thrown off her blanket and that had to be her praying. Eleri would never sit there like a white duck and holler out her location, even if she were hollering to God.

He was heading toward them, as stealthy as he could be on his human feet when the noise abruptly stopped and the white disappeared.

His heart hammering, Donovan ducked behind a tree, grateful he and Eleri had worn darker colors and were ready for this. He had to stay hidden, unable to act until he figured out what was happening.

Running scenarios rapidly in his brain, he came up with three. One, the men got Mercy, and Eleri abandoned the girl to them, though Donovan thought it unlikely that Eleri would just let them take her back, given what they knew of these people. Two, the men captured both Eleri and Mercy, and he would have to track them back to the City, call in the Feds and blow the whole thing wide open. Or three, Eleri had somehow managed to pull the girl out of the way.

He liked that scenario best. It was also the most supported option right now, since everything had gone quiet. Either that or they had both been quickly killed or disabled. His stomach turned at the thought, but Donovan soothed himself with the lack of gunfire.

All he could do was stay tucked in the brush, safety off and gun aimed in the general direction of the spot he'd last seen them, and wait.

In the Academy, he'd been taught the necessity of patience and even trained on it. His heart had pounded during the exercises—but those had used nonlethal rounds, and he knew everyone would be safe at the end of the training. Here, his adrenaline-infused heart tried to escape the confines of his ribs. It pounded until he simply waited for it to give out.

Thoughts collided in his head as the men's feet beat out of cadence across the paths. They shook their way through the bushes and called out to one another; if they hadn't yet captured everyone they were looking for, they wouldn't still be looking.

In case his heart wasn't close enough to bursting, two of the men came right up near him. One's leg moved so close to the bush, it almost brushed the nose of Donovan's gun. Though they quickly moved past, they thudded all around his hiding point, calling out for the girl.

While Donovan was relieved they didn't yet have Mercy, it didn't mean that they didn't have Eleri, though there was no mention of another person, another woman, a redhead, an agent. It was hope, but it wasn't confirmation.

With every moment, he wondered when they would step on him, stumble across him, or just start shooting randomly.

Shouldn't they hear him breathing so heavily? He could hear them—hear the exertion in their voices as well as their inhalations. He could smell the sweat under the heavy camo suits they wore. The scent of gun oil came to him and the leather of gloves and boots that must be stifling on a good night and miserable on a hot one like this. And he smelled something else, but he couldn't place it.

His senses weren't quite as sharp this way, his nasal cavity smaller in human form, the receptors less open.

Though they moved away before stepping on him, they could easily stumble across the table he'd left behind. Though the tablet was face down and not producing light, one look and it was clear someone was in their woods, in the middle of the night, and that someone was tracking something. These guys wouldn't have to be geniuses to figure any of that out.

If they found out the equipment belonged to the FBI, all hell would break loose.

Slowly, Donovan turned in his hiding place, trying desperately not to shake the bushes. He debated whether it was better they find him or the equipment. He prayed to whatever god was accepting new converts that the men didn't walk that way and it didn't become an issue.

Some deity must have been listening, because they headed from his position, away from the small camp table and the chair. So much of the Academy, so much of that long six months of training, was for the eventualities. If operations always went as planned, the FBI could graduate new agents every two weeks. But it had taken six months to get through all the contingencies—all the mentions of things they hoped agents remembered in the field, things that would save lives. Things like shutting the lights off devices they didn't actively need, so they wouldn't become beacons. Things like holding your position for much longer than you ever thought necessary.

Which was why, when Donovan was first ready to emerge from his position, he stayed put. And why, when the men returned and said, "This was where I saw her!" he was still hidden.

The faint light of the dawn was pushing fingers through the holes in the moonlight before he moved his cramped muscles. He'd heard nothing from Eleri or the girl, and he could only hope her training—even better and more ingrained than his own—kept them safe until the men were in the distance.

Donovan waited until they were far enough that he could get up and safely flee if at any moment they turned and began shooting. As he slowly stood, the branches grabbing at him and trying to keep him in place, he spotted a rustle of movement in the distance.

Eleri emerged, her strawberry blonde hair and pale cocoa skin blending into the shadows in her own personal camouflage. Mercy, on the other hand, shone white, not quite as bright now that the sun was drowning some of her reflection. But the day would only get hotter, and they had no idea when some of the City guys would come back.

It was hours later; he was showered, shaved, and fed. He was clean and upright, if not fully alert.

Mercy—she had said that yes it was her name—was being treated at the hospital, only one room over from Grace. Neither woman knew that. Mercy should be out soon; she only had wounds on her feet, but the hospital might be the safest place to keep her.

Guards were already posted. As far as they could tell, the news of the strange detainees had not yet leaked into the Texas groundwater. During the very brief pass through the hotel to clean up, Donovan had expressed his concern to Eleri about Mercy staying in the safehouse with Jonah and Charity. Mercy and Jonah had both seen the wolf, and Jonah had unerring accuracy in his art. They could be certain they had seen the same nonexistent wolf. Just like Eleri had been.

Driving the car and having stilted the conversation with a stop at a coffee place she found last time they stayed here, Eleri was far too perky. She'd talked him into an iced coffee, which hit the spot. The caffeine was helping hold him together, but from the way she was chattering and perfectly alert, Eleri had ordered a shot of cocaine in hers.

Given what he'd seen in the City's holding barracks, Donovan wasn't so uncertain that Grounds for Thought might not be doing a little something extra to their brew.

Eleri's voice was too cheerful, but he tried to ignore that and focus on what she was saying. "We can't put them together. We already let Jonah and Charity talk a bit too much. But they're kids. Mercy is a bit older, not much, but . . . if they're all together the prosecution will destroy the case."

"There is no prosecution." He sipped at the coffee, the cold and the flavor incongruous.

For a moment, she looked like he popped her bubble. Then

she bounced right back. "Probably, but we have the right to decide, and if we don't choose to take out Baxter, or if his offenses aren't deadly, then we might need prosecution for less heinous crimes."

He nodded, marveling at her ability to use large vocabulary on four hours of sleep and that awful night in the woods. "How did you get Mercy into that bush?"

She blushed. Donovan stared. What?

"Triangle choke hold."

"What!"

Defensive now, she gave a hard shrug even as she pulled into the hospital parking lot. "She wouldn't shut up. She was bright white and loud as hell. So I knocked her out and dragged her into the brush."

"Ha!" He barked the laugh out, the thought having brought him around far better than the drink.

"I came out when you did. I was waiting, figuring your hearing was better, you would know when they were gone."

She grinned at him and the smile jolted him.

No one had ever accepted him the way she did. Apparently, the way Westerfield did, too. Not even his own father. His dad had wanted Donovan to be like him—a mechanic, traveling, hiding, staying paranoid. Donovan had tried to explain that he was, in his own way, a mechanic, but it hadn't been enough. Yet, in the space of a few weeks, Eleri learned about him and not only tolerated his difference, she embraced it. She counted on his unique abilities. Most people would rather suffer than admit there was something out of their scope of understanding. It was a fact Donovan always saw as self-defeating. There was always more to learn, always something you didn't know, and a good part of that knowledge would come from other people with different experiences.

While he'd always believed that, he hadn't gone searching for it. He'd only read the final information written in the flesh and bone of others after they died. He only learned another person's story after the ending had been written. Eleri was a living work; in constant progress, she unfolded in front of him and allowed him to do the same.

The epiphany was almost painful.

Donovan imagined many people had these same thoughts around age ten or twelve, but he was only getting to them now, only now learning how to make a friend. Only now learning that there could be give and take.

Trying to seem normal, he nodded. "I did hear them, they were pretty far away before I got up."

"Good." She'd counted on him.

And he'd delivered.

They parked at the hospital lot and trekked the parking lot. The humidity was high enough that the car's air-conditioning made them colder than the outside air, causing condensation on their skin. So even if they didn't sweat, they would look like it by the time they got in.

Snaking through corridors and up staircases they now knew relatively well, they headed to Mercy's room first. It was a brief interview, just enough to get started before they finished up with Grace. She ran away because they wanted to marry her to Zeke, an older man who had been through several wives and was "unkind" to all of them.

Donovan waited and let Eleri ask what Mercy meant by "unkind."

"He hit them. Yelled at them." Her eyes pleaded with Donovan as though he could do something about it. "A husband is not supposed to be like that. He's supposed to lead his wife."

Donovan entirely disagreed, but he nodded anyway.

He could see Eleri getting antsy. They didn't want to split up —two sets of eyes on the interviewee were better than one. Still they had to get back to Grace.

His phone buzzed at the same time Eleri's did. Something had come in.

Since she couldn't take it, Donovan made a motion and stepped back to check. Recon from Collier and his wife showed unusual activity: changes in gas consumption, grocery purchases, and other things. Donovan smiled at what a little hacking could bring. The recon Agent—Annie Kinnard—was much better than her sweet name suggested. She was ruthless. She subpoenaed the grocery receipts, watched the house, and concluded that another person was now living there. It took her two days, but she saw a young woman, blonde, early twenties, arriving and leaving with Mrs. Collier.

Since Mrs. Collier didn't know her from Adam, Annie approached them and started a friendly conversation. The younger woman was named Tabitha and was favoring her left side. Becoming more suspicious, Annie followed the two to a restaurant and made the waitress hand over the young woman's glass. She was cross-checking fingerprints as she emailed.

Holy shit. Two days. Annie was a recon genius.

As he turned back, he tuned in to the conversation at hand.

"Joseph thinks he has himself in control. He says God gives him that. But Zeke doesn't even try. He just turns red and yells and hits." She made frustrated motions with her hands as though she lacked the words to describe it, but from the looks of what she mimed, Zeke lost it.

Her voice was softer. "Zeke hits the hardest. He hits so hard that he broke his finger once."

37

Eleri didn't know what to do with any of it. She watched the girl's face the whole time, trying to see any traces of the young Jennifer Cohn. She wasn't sure of anything except that Mercy's comment about Zeke's broken finger was both enlightening and disheartening.

After Eleri got the girl to describe the break, it became even clearer that the fist they matched on all the victims wasn't Baxter's at all. Zeke was the primary source of the damage they had discovered.

As Mercy described it, they hadn't asked the right questions before. Where Jonah and Charity both said Joseph beat them, this new information meant that Joseph ordered the beatings and even participated, but it was Zeke who did the heavy hitting.

"Thank you, Mercy." Eleri stood, her legs stretching and nearly creaking after being held then released from odd positions repeatedly over the past twenty-four hours. "We'll be back to interview you more. We're going to keep you safe."

Twisting the blanket in her hands, Mercy's actions were a sharp mimic of Grace's but with enough vigor that Eleri was concerned for the safety of the blanket. She had to wonder what they were doing to these girls at the City of God that made them so afraid.

"Will I have to go back?" Mercy's eyes were wide, typical scared puppy, and Eleri only wanted to assure her, but before she could answer, Mercy spoke again. "If I go back, they'll beat me for leaving. Then they'll make me marry Zeke."

"You can stay here. You're safe now." Eleri took the girl's hand in her own, watching out the corner of her eye as Donovan hung back. Mercy clutched at her like a lifeline.

A nod, a few loose tears from Mercy, and Eleri gave a good squeeze and tried to disentangle. She needed to get back to Grace next door, and she couldn't tell either woman that the other was there. It took three tries before she finally broke the hold Mercy had on her.

As she walked out the door into the hallway, Eleri's heart about broke. It was Donovan who thought to turn around and explain that there was an officer outside the door. He called the woman over, pointed out the uniform, had the two introduce themselves. Mercy's relief was palpable, and Eleri wondered why she hadn't thought of it.

They were almost in the door to Grace's room when the officer stopped them. "Agent Eames, Heath." Her words were soft but not lacking in strength for the tone. "I just wanted to update you on something."

Stopping, Eleri nodded at her. "Of course." And if it gave her a moment to get herself together before she had to go in and face another emotional firing squad in the form of Grace's testimony, that was only a good thing. "What is it?"

Officer Pleasant—according to her tag, which made Eleri smile—looked each way down the hall and kept her voice low. "Updike and I are the two primaries on this watch, with occasional relief from Traynor."

Eleri nodded again, not sure where this was going. Unsolicited information was always a crapshoot, which was why the

FBI had tip lines. Here Eleri and Donovan were their own front line. She waited.

"So he was relieving Updike late this morning before I came on. Tells me to watch out for this stupid nurse who tried to walk into the room, just like Grace was his patient." When Eleri's eyebrows shot up, Pleasant jumped in. "Don't worry. We're good. Traynor stopped him. This nurse guy says he has the chart and he's supposed to check on the woman, but Traynor says no."

It sounded like a routine error to Eleri. It was her understanding that the nurses rotated patients, and that this situation —with the guard posted and only two nurses allowed to enter— was the unusual one.

But Pleasant nodded again. The small coils of hair escaping her tight braids had to be planned. "Anyway, I had the same thing happen to me. Nurse says he's supposed to check on this one—" she pointed a thumb over toward Grace's room, "—but when I tell him no, he mutters something and wanders off." She patted at her hair, but it was more a nervous gesture than anything. "So, I called Updike and ask if he's had this. And he has. And it's a man, too." Now Pleasant was into it. "Not that many 'murses' in Texas, you know?" Eleri nodded, even though she thought a murse was a man's purse, but she didn't want to interrupt.

"It's all the same guy we're describing. Since turning him away, we've each seen him at the end of the hall, he sees us and heads the other way. So I check in with the nurses' station. There's no male nurse by that description in this ward. There is in pediatrics, but Traynor and I check his ID photo and it's not our guy."

Holy shit. Despite the tall-tale method of delivery, Officer Pleasant had done her due diligence and was uncovering something very concerning. Eleri nodded again, thinking she was better off not talking and just letting Pleasant unravel the whole thing for them.

"Well, we haven't had a chance to look through all the

personnel files—well, I did, but that's because I'm on right now and the nurses here brought them to me—but I didn't find this guy in any of the ID photos. I don't think he's a nurse here. Traynor and Updike have to look, but they aren't on shift 'til later." She still looked a little nervous, like maybe she'd over-stepped her bounds. Eleri hated that officers thought that of the FBI, but she understood there were situations that generated it.

This time, Eleri spoke. "That's amazing. And really good work."

"I'm telling you now, as it's only about two hours since shift change, since Traynor first told me, and I realized I'd had the same thing happen." She shrugged. "I didn't think anything of it at the time. He wasn't pushy, but he did look in the windows of the room."

Now, when Eleri was nodding, it was because she was processing information. The most sinister explanation was that it was Baxter himself, coming to check on his escaped wards. "Does he have brown hair? Cut about here?" She motioned to where Jonah's drawing had indicated.

This time it was Pleasant shaking her head. "Short blond hair. Blue eyes."

Eleri turned to look at Donovan, who was ready to jump in. While he did, she shook off her own illogical leaps. Lots of people had blue eyes, it didn't mean Joseph himself had come. If he was smart, he stayed holed up in his City and sent his people out to peddle the wares he had stashed in his mobile barns.

Donovan was pulling Pleasant's attention away, and the officer was grinning at him, a smile of appreciation for a handsome man. For a moment Eleri fought off the shock. Then again, just because he was her partner didn't mean he didn't strike others as good-looking. Interesting.

"Can you write down a full description? And can you tell us what days and times you saw him?" Donovan almost flirted back.

"Already done." Pleasant earned her moniker, looking back

and forth between the two of them, a softly satisfied smile on her lips. "I'm waiting on Traynor and Updike to email theirs into me. I can forward it to you when I get them. What's your email?"

That last line was smiled up directly at Donovan.

Eleri, trying to keep her own smirk to herself, left him to make that connection. She was stepping away when she remembered the collection of drawings in her bag. Waving at Grace through the partially cracked shades on the glass room wall, Eleri reached into the bag and pulled out the drawings. "Officer Pleasant? Can you look through these and see if any are the man you saw as the nurse?"

One by one she sorted through the drawings, removing the women and children, handing over the men and even some of the older boys. Officer Pleasant shook her head at each one, every answer a no. Eleri was getting discouraged, but she was one away from the end when the officer stopped.

"This one, I think. The hair was shorter, much closer cropped." She used one hand to block out the hair, a common technique since length, style and color could drastically change a person's look. "This one." Her voice became more confident.

Eleri nodded and took note of the name on the back. Abraham. Yet another player in a game that was getting increasingly tangled. But it confirmed her worst fears—the City of God was out and they were watching. Donovan was close, listening. "Please keep that and show it to your other officers. You may want to keep a batch of the pictures so you can recognize any of the others if they come by."

Eleri handed over the entire set of drawings for the men and older boys; she didn't include the whole City because memorizing a batch of faces from drawings was hard enough. Eleri was hedging her bets. "This confirms that the City of God people not only know that at least one of these women is here but that they are trying to keep tabs on her."

"Grace." Pleasant offered up when Eleri looked at her oddly.

"They at least know about Grace. This man came by and tried to get into her room two days ago. It was before Mercy was here."

Shit.

Just then her phone rang, so Eleri stepped to the side and put away her hard feelings about the case. "Hello, Mrs. Baxter."

"Oh! Um. . . . hello." The woman clearly wasn't familiar with the technology that allowed a personal answer to most phone calls. But she gathered herself relatively quickly. "We're in town. We're staying at the Comfort Inn."

Eleri frowned. She didn't remember a Comfort Inn in Brownwood.

At the pause, Lilly Baxter filled her in. "We're in Zephyr, or outside it in Early."

"Oh." Only about ten or so minutes away. "Do you have everything you need? Have you practiced?"

"I'm nervous. But yes, we practiced the whole car ride down. We're as ready as we can be." Her voice wasn't as steady as the first time Eleri had met the woman. Then, she had been sitting in her own living room in her hometown and the past was almost entirely behind her. Now it was clear she was concerned about what she might learn. Maybe concerned that she might run into her son.

As of yet there was no evidence that JHB even left the compound at all, though clearly some of his men ran errands relatively often. Eleri couldn't say that, but she did try to soothe the woman. "Then take a nap and get settled in for today."

Eleri had considered sending them out with Jonah's drawing, but that wouldn't match the cover story of two parents looking for their missing son. The story had the added benefit of being true —something she thought the Baxters needed. They didn't seem the type to be able to lie well or maybe even at all. So she had them arm themselves with the last picture of Joseph from before he ran away. At sixteen, he had been mostly grown, already greatly resembling Jonah's sketch. The old photo should be enough for anyone who had seen him to recognize him. She wished the couple luck and turned back to Donovan who was struggling to end the conversation with the overly interested officer.

"I can't thank you enough for your information. Please detain this man and call us if you see him again."

"You have a warrant?"

"I'll have one." Eleri lied smoothly and opened the door to the other woman's room.

Grace looked up and smiled broadly. Probably she was bored out of her mind. Television sucked if you weren't used to watching it.

From the bones Eleri had seen, and the dead girl they had dug up more recently, all the stories corroborated: these people worked and worked hard. They turned earth, grew food, and built houses. Sitting in a hospital room—especially after she was mostly healthy—had to be near torture.

The sharp tang of hope in her voice solidified that idea. With the City people coming around to check on her, it was clear they needed to get Grace to a safe house as fast as possible.

"Agent Eames! It's good to see you again."

"Hi, Grace." Donovan offered the woman a smile. Though Grace wasn't as worldly or as forward as Officer Pleasant, Donovan's smile for her was real.

"Hi, Agent Heath." She grinned back, obviously in much better spirits today.

Eleri was afraid they'd have to dash those hopes. Despite the lack of free time, she chatted aimlessly with Grace for a few moments before getting down to what she needed. Eleri went through the usual steps of starting the recording and stating the pertinent information.

Grace—as always—cooperated, answering every question Eleri and Donovan posed to the best of her ability. Her words came through strong, clear, and certain. She corroborated

Mercy's information about Zeke's broken finger. They hadn't told her about the forensic evidence they had located from the photos, but her information as well as Mercy's matched what they had seen.

Eleri followed that up by asking about Zeke's first wife. Grace's information mostly agreed with Mercy's but added that the woman before Mercy—Tabitha—had been his second wife. His first, Joy, had died under City law. She had been caught with another man and had been put to death.

This time Eleri knew to follow up. No, Grace had not seen Joy with the other man. In fact, she didn't know anyone who claimed to have seen it. She only knew that Zeke reported it to be true. She also said that Joy was about as pious as they came, and everyone had a hard time believing the woman would have done what her husband claimed and an even harder time believing that she then lied about it.

Eleri asked more and more questions, every answer supporting exactly what the other escapees stated, which in turn supported one of two possibilities: either the City of God people were truly believers in faith and honesty or else the whole thing was an elaborate ruse, with ingrained practice and carefully planned stories. The second possibility got more remote with each piece of information she heard.

Next, Donovan asked several questions about Grace's older memories from her early childhood.

She was becoming more comfortable talking to a strange man, but the two of them had decided that these questions might cause her some pain and that was better coming from Donovan. They decided that Eleri's tie to Grace, the trust the woman had put in her, was best undisturbed.

Still Donovan handled it with compassion and patience, surprising even himself it seemed. Before he was done, Grace had called up some details that gave them a direction to get started— she had been taken from a park in the summertime. She didn't remember anything after traipsing into her family church to use the restroom. Though she believed she lived in Michigan, she wasn't sure. In the end, the young woman even agreed to be fingerprinted and swabbed for DNA.

Eleri resisted the urge to jump up and down for joy.

Because the questions were going well and the hard topic had actually seemed to have opposite the expected effect and endear Donovan to the woman, Eleri stayed back and let them continue as they had been going.

Inside of five minutes, Donovan had garnered some stunning revelations.

Baxter was not the first father of the City of God. Grace remembered when Joseph and his wife arrived with a tiny baby in tow. She had adored the baby though it had been rapidly shuttled off to wherever babies went, and she hadn't seen it much after that.

Eleri wondered if that baby had been Jonah—Grace's time frame was sketchy since the City residents didn't celebrate birthdays or regular holidays. Forcing her attention away from her nebulous math and back to what Donovan and Grace were talking about, she learned the other leader had been Isaac. Isaac had been a hard man with few words for the children. His wife was even more strict, and both believed that God put man on earth to suffer.

Isaac believed that he rescued the children from evil and put them to work in God's care. Grace had hated him. She had loved her first family, and Isaac and the others schooled her not to speak of the demons that had birthed and raised her. She had been scolded, isolated and eventually beaten until she learned to keep those thoughts to herself and become a pious worker.

She believed three summers had passed from when she arrived in the City until the year of "the event."

Isaac had told them all that it was time to meet God. Originally, the residents had been happy, thinking there would be a celebration. It turned out the celebration was to be a month of worship and no food.

A quick glance to Donovan revealed that he was thinking the same as she was: a month of serious fasting would kill them all. Was that the leader's intention?

But Grace's next information was even more disturbing.

Ten days into the "celebration" Joseph confronted Isaac. They fought verbally. The next day, a badly bruised Joseph declared himself the new leader. The people of the City—hungry and tired of their forced austerity—hailed him as the new leader. Isaac and his wife were never seen again.

38

D onovan sat in the direct beam of sunlight, unwilling to close the curtain and suffer the artificial light. The AC was cranked as high as it would go and chugged away from its spot under the window as though it could really do more than just take the edge off.

His legs were warm but he stayed seated there in the hotel room—Eleri's hotel room—crammed next to her at the small desk. Given that they were both trying to fit equipment there and see each other's screens, they wound up scrunched side by side, Donovan sitting in the chair he had dragged from the other room. It was all too crowded to be comfortable, but the information was coming in a deluge and comfort was not a concern.

"Look at this, Eleri." Annie Kinnard had sent updates on the Colliers to him directly, since he was the one who responded to her initial outreach. The agent had uploaded telescopic lens shots of Carolyn Collier and the woman he and Eleri now had as much confirmation as possible was Tabitha—Zeke's previous wife.

Donovan was checking pictures of the two women shopping, Tabitha still in her uniform of jeans and plain T-shirt. "If there was anything legal about Zeke's wedding to Tabitha, then he would be committing bigamy with Mercy."

"Grace said he was married before Tabitha. So he may already be a bigamist."

Agent Annie had uploaded a ton of pictures for him to sort through. The woman missed her calling, she should have been in the paparazzi. He was checking photo after photo, noting Tabitha's consistent braid or bun, that the Colliers ate with her at the dinner table, that she had become one of the family. It was so rapid and—from the photos—seemed so complete, that he was curious if they had known her before this escape.

Eleri's computer dinged, but he ignored it, engrossed in the photos, until she used the back of her hand to tap his arm. It was easy to do; they were so close she barely had to move. Pointing to her own screen, she said, "Bingo!"

"What?" He almost couldn't look away from the pictures. Was Tabitha pregnant? It was hard to tell.

"I rushed the DNA tests for the Baxters and Jonah." She grinned at him. "It's a match."

His breath sucked in on a sudden surge and Donovan was surprised just how much he cared about the results. He'd hidden his anxiety about it even from himself. Only the two of them even knew the test had been run, and only they knew what the results meant. The participants had been informed they were just checking DNA and ruling out suspects. The Baxters may have been suspicious, but their lack of technological skills didn't put that square into the "definitely" category for him. "Should we tell them tonight?"

She closed her eyes, squeezed them shut, the decision obviously harder than a simple yes or no. Her answer confirmed what was written all over her face. "Let's think on it for a while. I mean, what if there's a reason not to? It doesn't change that he'll get to go home with them when this is all over."

If they took JHB out of the equation. Anything shy of that and the sociopath would get back custody of Jonah or at least send them all into a protracted court case to free the kid. At fourteen he wasn't yet ready to be an emancipated minor.

Donovan stood up and walked over to the bed. Eleri had made it herself this morning so they could spread out what they had. On one corner sat the portable printer. All morning it chugged, turning out screen shots from Donovan's trek, latitude and longitude now marked for each of the grave sites. They also scanned satellite photos, Donovan digging through archives and trying to remember what he smelled at each gravesite. He could sense different levels of decay; though he wasn't a cadaver dog, he had worked with corpses a good portion of his adult life and he tried to rank the scents.

He combed through thousands of backlogged aerial photos and managed to find one set of pictures. Since they were over-head photos, it was hard to identify the men in them, but the jeans and plain colored T-shirts were clear. The satellite had taken a series of stills as it passed over. If he zoomed in on the earliest shot he could find, Donovan thought he could see them just emerging from the woods.

Later, there were images of the men digging, a long black bag laid out on the ground beside the grave-sized hole. Though there were no pictures of the men putting the bag into the hole, pulling back the cover to expose the corpse or even killing the man, it was relatively damning.

Now he had photographic proof—time and location stamped —of them digging in the exact location of a grave that would turn up a corpse. It had taken him hours to find it, but he was glad he did.

Turning to Eleri, he asked, "Any ideas?"

∽

ELERI SHOOK HER HEAD. She knew exactly what Donovan was asking about. How were they going to get those bodies out?

The graves were on private land, and they had no evidence except the scent of decaying flesh. Even that information was suspect because it came from a dog who didn't really exist and certainly wasn't trained to be a cadaver dog—aside from being an ME.

Her head hurt.

She swiveled her chair, bumping her knees into the side of Donovan's. Scooting back, she stood swiftly and declared a break. "Let's get out of here. Let's get out of this damn stuffy little room, do something and brainstorm."

"What is there to do here?"

"I don't even begin to know."

That was how they wound up talking about digging up graves while eating ice cream and sitting on a picnic table at Lake Brownwood. With the pavilion empty and shading them from the sun, the ice cream and the thought of having to return to the hotel room made it just bearable enough to sit outside and talk.

Eleri attacked the three scoops of various chocolates. It was about two scoops too many, but she ceased to care when she stepped outside and was wrapped in a blanket of humidity. She threw out her opening gambit. "Okay, any idea at all will be discussed regardless of merit. We have no shame here."

With a nod from Donovan, his mouth full with one of the last bites he was going to get, she threw out the starting pitch. "Okay, the wolf goes in and digs stuff up. Very under the radar, he can use his paws, no tools needed. If anything is discovered it's just animals digging up the bodies. All normal. Once the body is dug up all the way, I'll come in, bag it, and drag it away."

It was a bad plan right from the start. But she knew why *she* thought that, she wanted to hear what Donovan thought. He didn't disappoint.

"Why would animals dig it up now? I think the men originally put the bodies deep enough to keep things out, which is why we never saw a graveyard on satellite images." He set his empty bowl aside with the clack that sturdy cardboard cups made, and spoke again. "Also, if they catch you, they'll shoot you. And they'll know they've been robbed—probably by the next morning."

Shit.

She had thought about getting shot. She was even ready to wear Kevlar, but body armor was heavy, and every bit you wore slowed you down and restricted your movement, thus making you more likely to get shot. But she had not considered that, without a body in the ground, there was no good way to make things appear undisturbed. "Actually, even if we return the dirt, once we take the body out, the ground will depress."

He was nodding, but she continued.

"Even if we cut the grass, roll it out of the way like sod, and roll it back when we finish, there will *still* be a depression in the ground." She leaned back on her hands. "So even being as careful as possible, we can only postpone their recognition that their graves were robbed. Maybe by a few days, a week, but that's it." She sighed. "As soon as someone sees that series of bowls in the field, they'll know something is up. And they'll check."

With her, Donovan added, "It may be as soon as the next morning. They only need to dig up one to see the body is missing."

"So we need the bodies, but we can't take them. Not until after everyone is arrested and parceled out." Not until after they didn't really need the information anymore. Eleri tamped her frustration down with ice cream. "Even if we can figure how to get them out without alerting the men and getting killed while we do it, we have to cover our tracks so thoroughly to keep from getting discovered that there's almost no way to do that."

"Okay, other side then. What do we need from these bodies? What will get us the kind of evidence we can use?"

"We need the bodies. We need them to get the evidence!" She hated the knots in her stomach that told her it was all in vain.

Donovan tried again, "But what *specifically* will you get from those bodies?"

"Height, weight, ID."

"What if the body is so decayed that we can't see that? Some smelled really old, and these were non-casket burials, all of them are degrading rapidly. It's not going to be like a normal exhumation."

"I know. But if I can see the pelvis or maybe the skull, a few long bones, I can ID male or female, make a ball park estimate of age. If we have DNA, we can check against the parents' swabs from missing kids and maybe lay some people to rest. Maybe prove how they died and when. It may prove that Baxter or even this Zeke guy was involved."

Donovan stared off into the distance. "So what about GPR?"

Ground penetrating radar wasn't quite ready for what they needed. "It shows disturbed earth, where burials happened, but we need the bones. We already know where the graves are, we know where to dig. With your senses you can probably even estimate how deep. Since you can tell how old they are, you're already way better than GPR."

They were quiet for a minute, looking out over the water, watching boaters and wakeboarders off in the distance. Eleri figured there were probably a few bodies down there. The lake was big enough. Probably someone who disappeared, someone murdered and weighted and dumped over the side of a boat in the middle of the night. They wouldn't be found without sonar, she thought.

"Donovan! Sonar! Ultrasound. There's a new device, it uses the full range of waves and returns a picture." Excited now and popping up from her seat, she threw out fully half of her remaining ice cream. Now waving her hands, she went on. "It's experimental, but it returns a picture. It's better if things are shallower. The images get fuzzier at greater distance, but we might be able to get our hands on one."

Following her, Donovan threw out his empty container and added his two cents. "If we can find the bodies, we can take core samples without disturbing the ground. And we can do it relatively quickly."

"Yes! Then we can match DNA. If we can find the body and get a sample, that's good. If we can get a picture of the body, or the bones, that's better." Okay. They had something, she hoped. Lots of the GPR systems she'd seen had more resembled a heavy lawn mower than a metal detector. Though the experimental machine operated differently, she had no reason to think it would be smaller. Still it might work.

She was already making plans: she'd call the branches, see what she could requisition, how long it would take to get it out to Brownwood, and would they need a tech? A lesson? Her brain was churning and when her phone rang she answered absently. "Agent Eames."

"Miss Eames, this is Mark Baxter."

"Oh!" She stopped dead for a moment before remembering her manners. "Hello." Unsure if they were reporting something useful or just asking questions, Eleri stopped walking and focused on the phone call. These people were doing the case a huge favor and they were very out of their element; they deserved her full attention despite her own scattered thoughts. "What can I do for you?"

"Well, we went out like you said. Used the old picture of Joseph and sometimes that mug shot you sent us."

"Thank you again for that." She inserted the words when he paused, wondering if he needed to hear that he was doing it right.

"We went around Zephyr and then around Mills." Another pause. "We've found eight people who know our son. They say he comes by all the time."

39

Eleri was stunned.

In a little over twenty-four hours the elder Baxters had done far more than she had even dared to imagine.

The four of them were waiting on dinner—Mark Baxter had requested steak and Eleri didn't have the heart to refuse him—at yet another back table. For a moment, Eleri dreamed of sitting in a coffee shop right in the front, the sun streaming through a plate-glass window, maybe even greeting other patrons that she knew as they came in. It was a pipe dream. There were no places like that anywhere, not for her. While she could sit by a window and sip a coffee, there wasn't a single town where she knew the people well enough to say hello.

Her daydream only lasted a second or two. Mark Baxter clasped his hands before he spoke, managing to look pious even at the glossy thick wooden table, even beneath the cowboy art and horseshoes hanging on the wall beside them. "We did just as you said, ma'am." He offered a respectful nod toward Eleri, making her wonder if she deserved this man's deference in reality. "We showed the picture, said he was our son and that we were looking for him."

He sighed shallowly and his wife softly touched his arm, offering silent support. "I don't know that I could have lied about it. I'm not proud of the fact, but I couldn't say I wanted to see him again."

Eleri offered her own support, but she didn't offer a touch, she offered science. "We do believe that Joseph is a sociopath—his morals are simply nonexistent. But it's nothing you did. There are many studies showing that it's simply something that happens in a certain percentage of the population."

When she finished speaking, Eleri realized that wasn't necessarily as comforting as she wanted it to be. Since she didn't have anything else to add, she shut up.

Mark Baxter gave her the acknowledgment of a nod, pausing briefly before talking again. "The people who recognized him described him like in that drawing you showed us."

Which meant Joseph left the City of God recently enough that he bore the same hairstyle and look. Eleri pushed with that. "Did you find out when they last saw him?" She'd given them specific tasks, things to ask should they find anyone who had seen him. Operating under the assumption that JHB was running the show from the safety of the City, she assumed all of the instructions were just wishful thinking. Now Eleri was glad she pushed.

He nodded sagely, and his wife let him speak. They were interrupted by the delivery of the food, and Eleri found herself staring at yet another piece of cooked cow. The others looked at it reverently as she forced her own matching smile.

Mr. Baxter slowly ate a bite of steak, savoring every moment, while she willed her shoulders to relax, reminding herself that this man had the right of it.

The likelihood of anything being solved tonight was slim to none. The Baxters would give her the information eventually. She simply needed to learn to wait for it, and she needed to find the joy in another steak. Deciding she was going to hit the nearest grocery store tomorrow and eat lunch right there in the produce section, Eleri cut into the meat.

It took a surprising amount of effort to keep her attention where it belonged. The work was incredibly tense—people were being hurt, no doubt about it. But one of the key things an investigator needed to remember was not to live the case. Eleri was in danger of doing just that. It was difficult not to when she was stuck in a hotel room, and the only person she knew was her partner—and she didn't know him that well or in any capacity outside of work. While she ate, she added a second directive for herself, get to know Donovan a little better. It would help them work together. When they went to San Antonio to pick up the GPR, she was going to have that lunch with Wade; the one where just the two of them chatted and caught up. The one that had been replaced by werewolf conversation last time.

"They said he was there two days ago."

Jolted from her thoughts, Eleri slapped back to the present. "When did they first see him?"

Finally, Lilly spoke up, maybe only because Mark had his mouth full. "They didn't remember when they first saw him. Said he'd been a regular around there for a long time."

This time, Donovan turned and looked at her, clearly thinking the same thing she was. Joseph was out and about. He was doing something, the question was just "what?"

Lilly shrugged and gave a cute smile. "The towns out here are just so close, and so small. There were only a few businesses to check—you know, the post office, the diners. So we went on to Mills. Then back to Early. People knew him in each place." Another shrug. "Don't know about Brownwood. We didn't ask here. We wanted to wait and see what you thought."

Only able to nod through her churning thoughts, Eleri chewed her bite before speaking. "Tell me everything else they said."

She and Donovan ate and absorbed what information the

Baxters had stored. Lilly even commented that she made notes each time she got back into their car—recording the name of the person and location where they had spoken. She added job title and everything she could remember that the person said.

Eleri was about ready to choke on her dinner she was so impressed. When Lilly and Mark finally ran out of information—long after Eleri would have predicted—she turned and nodded to Donovan.

At his agreement, she offered them a return. "We have some news for you."

Lilly's eyes widened in fear, but Eleri rapidly quelled that. "The boy we told you about, we did a DNA test between you and him." She paused as the implications seemed to set in. "He is your grandson."

Voice smaller than she'd heard from him before, Mark Baxter put his hand on his wife's arm as though he were holding her back. "Joseph's child."

It was simply stated and left to sit there, like the dishes that were near empty but clearly now abandoned on the table.

Eleri again turned to science. "We have nothing to test against for Joseph, so we only know that Jonah is your grandson. But there's no other way it could be, as far as I know."

Eleri added that last phrase as she always did. She was no longer surprised by the number of people who had illegitimate children, second families, decaying skeletons in their closets. But both the Baxters nodded.

Mark Baxter followed up with, "What's the probability of error?"

No dummy there. He may be plainspoken and slow to respond, but it wasn't for lack of intelligence. "Almost nothing. Not only does he match the correct percentage of DNA to be your grandson, he also matches key markers—dominant traits—that are gene-wise identical to yours. Which means he got them from you or from one of your near ancestors."

Eleri didn't add, "Even if your wife had slept with your brother and that child had a child, the match wouldn't be as good." But she didn't think insinuating anything other than the most pious behavior for Lilly Baxter would go over well at all.

As she looked at the older woman, Eleri saw tears forming in her eyes. Turning to her husband, Lilly absorbed the shock. "Mark, we have a grandchild."

DONOVAN CLIMBED into the driver's side of the rental, grateful that the car had been parked close. Grateful that at nine a.m. there hadn't been a long walk, because even this early the heat was ruining his fresh feeling from the shower he'd just taken. He hoped the air-conditioning in the car would crank up quickly and the sickly, sticky feeling that had pressed upon him would go away. Just then, Eleri slid into the passenger seat and as she closed the door, the picture landed in his lap.

Shit.

Joseph Hayden Baxter stared up at him from a mug shot about fifteen years old. The tape at the edges told Donovan all he needed to know. This was the picture he had slid under Eleri's pillow the first night they had checked in here. He was just surprised it had taken her this long to find it, when she spoke.

"No, I didn't have any dreams about him. Sorry."

The press of her lips into a thin line told him she was far angrier than her relatively light tone and words suggested.

"I'm sorry." He almost wasn't. She was a goldmine and they needed her.

"Fuck off."

He was pulling out of the parking lot, but her words seared through him and he slapped the brakes before swinging the car into the only shady spot. Throwing the car into park, he left the engine and the air running; there was a shitstorm brewing in the passenger seat and he didn't want to melt or wreck while he figured it out.

Though she appeared outwardly calm, Donovan knew better. She smelled angry and he could see the tension in her muscles under the smooth outer skin. She was furious, and it rolled off her, filling the car while she looked out the window as if waiting for them to go somewhere.

Speaking softly, he broached the subject carefully. "It was just a picture."

"Physically, yes, you put a picture under my pillow. I finally let the cleaning service in yesterday. The maids found it." The fact that it was far more than a picture was left to sit between them in the words she didn't say.

"What you can do, Eleri, it's amazing. And you can help the case."

Finally, she turned to look at him. "Yes, but it's what *I* can do. It's *mine*. You don't get to do it to me." She looked out the window again. "I'll officially be requesting a new partner when we get to San Antonio. If you'd like we can switch the order of events today and go there first. I'll take care of the Colliers myself."

"I'm off the case?" Stunned, Donovan leaned back almost as though pushed.

Blinking as if that would right a world tipped horribly off kilter, Donovan fought to control his racing heart. It was a slap, a stab at him, certainly far more than was warranted. Until right this moment, he hadn't realized how much he enjoyed this job, how much he had needed the change in his life. Fundamental things had been missing and NightShade—particularly Eleri's leadership—had brought them to him.

His father had been a volatile man, and Donovan knew only one thing: don't have friends. Everything else was up in the air. He could get yelled at for making dinner as easily as he could for not making dinner. He could get in trouble for fighting, or he could take a beat-down for having taken one at school. He'd never known which way trouble was coming. The old skills of silence and stillness crept back over him.

His shoulders didn't move. His breathing shallowed. Though his brain wanted to ask questions—Would he just get a new senior partner? A new case? Or would this mean he was completely out of NightShade? Could he get shuffled into the regular FBI? And what would he do there?—his past taught him to shut down. There was no advantage to be had until he knew more. He knew the drill. Listen and nod. Take what came, do what you were told and disappear. Become invisible.

But he was now a grown man. In a tiny car. And Eleri turned on him, green eyes flaring into darker shades of jade. Her lush features pulling tight, somehow becoming sharper as she threw her anger his direction.

When she spoke it was almost as though she was casting a curse on him, binding him from her. Had her hair flown wild and her eyes sparked he wouldn't have been surprised. "You do not control me. You do not attempt to control me. You have no idea what you did."

"What did I do?" The words tumbled from him even though he knew it was wrong to ask. Even though everything he'd learned told him to stay out of it, he engaged anyway. Because Eleri wasn't his father. Because he had chucked his father to the far winds as soon as he was able, but he couldn't chuck this.

Seeming to realize she'd crossed some kind of line, Eleri pulled back, both physically and emotionally. For a moment Donovan wondered if this cool, icy version was maybe worse than the fire of the moment before.

"Did I ever put a collar on you and walk you down the street?" She stared at him, held his gaze and didn't let him break it. "Did I demand that you change in front of me? Did I follow you and try to catch you at it?"

He could only shake his head. He was starting to see what she meant. She hadn't crossed the line. He had. "I'm sorry."

"How sorry?" The ice cracked, just a little, and she seemed to genuinely want to know.

But Donovan had no answer. He was sorry because he'd pushed. He was sorry because she had treated him with more respect than he had shown her. He was sorry because she wanted him out and he would never have done it if he'd known she would feel so affronted and this would be the consequence.

When he didn't answer, she stared right through him again. "Do you know what I see?"

A small shake of his head was all he could muster. He was still cold inside, still deathly afraid that this was the end of the road for him.

"I have experienced a rape. I have been there when seven different people were killed—not in a car accident, though I've lived that, too. I watched seven different people get brutally murdered by another person. Twice, the killer wasn't even driven to do it, it was just for fun. Three of those people were children. I have been beaten and taped to a chair. I've been electrocuted, thrown in a hole, and left to die. I see it. All of it." Her voice hitched, and she was shaking with just the telling of it. Donovan realized for the first time that she never let people know the whole thing. No one would ever really understand.

"I feel it, too." She turned away. "And none of it actually happened to me. I wake up in the morning having been beaten bloody, but there's nothing to show. I have to brush my hair and get dressed and get to work on time. I can't prosecute the perpetrators because even they don't know what they did to me."

He couldn't breathe. It flooded him, the realization that it was all going to hell and it was all his fault.

Donovan almost flinched when she turned back to face him.

"I'll push you but I'll never force anything on you. *I* am aware that—no matter what you've confided in me—I'm not you, I don't live life in your skin, and I don't deserve to make your decisions for you. And *you* do not ever make those decisions for *me*."

Only one single short breath in and she kept going. Donovan felt every word like a physical blow and knew now that every one was deserved.

Her voice was quieter, the blows sharper and sliding smoothly into his flesh.

"In the past, I have abused it. I pushed myself for the case and at the request of others. And it landed me in a mental hospital. I won't do it again." Reaching up, she tucked her strawberry blonde hair behind her ear, as though it were any normal day, as though they weren't sitting in a running car, parked at the far end of a hotel lot. As though Donovan wasn't getting fired. "I'll bear what comes. I'll use it. But I won't reach out for it. Never again. And you have no right to invite it to my doorstep, because you have no idea what you're playing with."

40

Eleri stared out the window, the drive to San Antonio seemingly longer than it was last time. They drove through unexpected rain, fat drops falling from fatter clouds, bringing moisture the air most definitely did not need.

Angry and hollow at the same time, she thought about Wade. One friend. There was really no one else for her to call. Her mother was pretty good in certain situations, but her advice was always the same. It was also laced with liberal doses of "we knew this would happen." Eleri had bucked her parents' plans for her from the moment she left for college. Thus, when anything went wrong, clearly what was best for Eleri was for her to do as the Eameses had wished all along.

So it was Wade she called, to tell him she'd be there for lunch and that this time it would be just the two of them. She didn't speak at all again and neither did Donovan until they pulled up in front of the building where Wade had his office.

"I'm truly very sorry, Eleri." This time Donovan looked like he was sorry he'd done it, not just that he'd been caught. This time he understood what he pushed on her.

He shouldn't have spoken. It brought everything back to the

surface when she had finally managed to get herself down to a simmer. For hours, she'd been holding herself under tight rein, having found the picture after arriving back from dinner the night before. She'd been high on the details the Baxters had brought. They now knew Joseph was out and about, they knew who he talked to, and they knew he called himself James Denton. They also knew—as the Baxters had reminded them at Eleri's frown of memory—that was Father Jim's name at Zion's Gate. Eleri had also been high on the Baxters' joy at finding out something good had come from their offspring. Through dessert, she told them all about Jonah, wonderful things about his talent and his kindness and intelligence. Eleri was proud. Usually a case was about cleaning up messes, this time she made something.

Then she'd walked into the hotel room and seen the picture on the bed.

At first she was hit with terror, wondering if the men from the City had broken in. When she realized it was Donovan's handiwork, she'd turned furious. Keeping herself together, she didn't bust down the door and yell. She could have, even now she felt that would have been justified. Even now, looking at him, dealing with her own roiling anger, she stood with the car door open for a moment. She knew he didn't have his bags packed. That he wasn't ready to be cut loose. She knew he was shocked by her announcement.

Well, she'd been shocked by his betrayal.

Watching him through cool eyes, Eleri took in the dark coloring, knowing now the interesting details of his features were as useful as they were artistic. "It doesn't matter that you're sorry. It doesn't fix anything. You were careless and you were arrogant, and the effect is the same."

She closed the door quietly and walked into the building, stopping only to flash her ID before heading back to see Wade.

He stood up as she walked in, probably having smelled her as she came down the hallway. This time she assessed him more carefully. The same longish nose that Donovan bore hid behind his dark-framed glasses. His shoulder blades were long like Donovan's and she knew why now. Emmaline had brought her two wolves in the dream, and Eleri was glad now there hadn't been an entire pack.

He greeted her with, "You look like you need a hug."

"Actually, don't. If you do, I'll break."

He seemed to understand. He picked another hole-in-the-wall restaurant, this one Indian, and listened to her tell him what she could about the case. As he still occasionally consulted, his clearance was up to date and he was a wonderful sounding board. For a while, it was good just to eat and talk shop, not thinking about things falling apart.

She was pushing her plate away when he finally called her bluff. "Tell me."

Eleri explained, trying not to crack and glad that Wade already understood most of it. So she didn't have to explain like she had with Donovan. When her therapist initially suggested she tell Wade the truth, Eleri was convinced the woman was batshit. She almost proposed that the two trade badges; Eleri could be the sane one and this woman could wait in line for meds. But the doctor had been right.

"Don't request a new partner. Keep him." Wade's voice was ever calm, ever reasonable.

She jolted almost as if he'd given her an electric shock. Wade was supposed to support her, her decisions. Then again, he'd never been much of a yes man. Not saying anything, not knowing how to respond, she waited.

Wade delivered. "You didn't have any dreams from it. It didn't work."

"That doesn't make it okay—"

His hand came up to stop her, waving her words away. "I know. I know he violated your space and your trust and that you could have suffered greatly for it. I know you protect that carefully now."

She nodded, wondering how he understood all that but still suggested that she keep Donovan around.

"But all your other partners used you, too. They learned to trust your hunches, pushed you into things, and you let them. In the profiling unit, you opened yourself up, and they ran with it until they turned on you." He pulled his napkin from his lap and put it on the table, clearly looking for words. "What I'm trying to say is that everyone who even has an idea about this has tried to exploit it—including you. Your next partner probably will, too. The difference now is that you didn't get hurt, and Heath has learned. He'll never do anything like that again."

Eleri absorbed the ideas Wade was pushing on her. He was right, but was it the right thing to do?

As usual, he started back up before she could process things. His brain ran about three times faster than everyone else's, and he usually reached a conclusion while most normal people were back at the starting line. "Plus, you get a free screw-up with him. He owes you. Big time."

It was a half hour and a tall glass of Coke later before they left. She didn't think Wade would go to any restaurant that didn't have a coke for him—ethnic foods welcomed, cultural beverages be damned. But Eleri spent that time thinking and thinking hard, and in the end she had to agree with Wade. Donovan was a damn good partner; they worked together well. She needed to forgive.

Harder to do than it sounded, it wasn't just a switch she could flip. And she was never one to forget. If he did it again, he'd be out on his furry ass faster than he could blink. But she forced a calm and dialed his number. She offered no platitudes or niceties. "Where are you?"

"Eating." He offered none back.

"Pick me up?"

"Sure." It was resigned sounding and she wasn't ready to fix that just yet. If she was going to offer him his spot back, it would be face-to-face. If he suffered a while longer thinking she was going to kick him out, well, she didn't really care.

Eleri sent Wade back to work and was waiting just inside the front door when the little rental car pulled up, a grim Donovan behind the wheel. Sliding in, she took a moment to gather herself. She wasn't going to apologize. "If you want, I won't request a new partner."

There was a moment as the silence swelled and flooded the car.

"I'd rather you didn't." He swallowed audibly and turned his whole body to look at her. His imploring expression compelled her to look at him, too, even though she didn't really want to. "You have no idea how sorry I am. I won't do anything like it again."

She wanted to be done with it all, just go back. Forgive, not forget, but get back to things the way they were. Latching on to the first thing she saw, she pointed to the empty container with a napkin and plastic spoon shoved inside. "Ice cream again?"

"For lunch." He grinned almost apologetically. "I felt like complete crap and figured it wouldn't hurt."

She almost smiled back. "Let's get the sonar and learn how to use it. Then we'll drop a surprise visit on the Colliers."

THE REST of the day went smoother than Donovan expected. Eleri seemed to have lost most of her ire. But he wasn't quite sure if she really felt that way or if she was using that airbrushed veneer of social politeness on him.

When he learned she came from money, he could suddenly read the tinge of it in her actions—the slight tilt she could put into her smile, the softness she could wash across her features at a moment's notice, even though her eyes stayed sharp. Eleri was an interesting mix, and right now her lack of anger was keeping him on edge.

They traded out the rental car for an SUV, given the need to haul the good-sized device back to mid-Texas. At first glance, it looked like a small lawn mower or maybe a jogging stroller, but anyone who looked twice would realize it was neither. The tech referred to it as "the groundhog" without any irony.

It took an hour to learn about the workings. Running them through the paces, the tech made sure they could each steer it easily—which was a little tricky as the wheels were large, all-terrain things. She made sure they could both operate the screen and snapshot features. They learned how to uplink the photos, so they would save even if they had to abandon the machine. She walked them through dimming the screen and dropping the volume since, like most devices, it made a noise to let you know it had completed the task. Then she marked all the settings for them. This one was one-of-a-kind, specially designed for the FBI, and ready for stealth operations like theirs.

It took another hour to trade the rental car, and longer still to get the groundhog into the back and finally hit the road. Donovan had called the trucking company Collier worked for and found out the man had returned from a run yesterday. He hoped they'd be at home. If he and Eleri couldn't confront the couple quickly, they would either have to come back another day or postpone the graveyard shift.

The Colliers owned a modest home outside Leander, which was outside Austin and not at all on the direct path back to Brownwood. The road to their home was heavily wooded and relatively out of repair. Eleri, looking smaller behind the wheel of the big car, stayed quiet, leaving Donovan to wonder when the tension would completely ease. Along the way they passed stately brick homes, well-kept trailers, and places that looked like a hoarder was running a junkyard. All sat right beside each other, a stark contrast to the overly uniform gated communities that pooled out beyond the borders of Austin.

There wasn't much traffic in the area, so the two pulled off into the grass about a city block away, not wanting to alert the Colliers of the visit before they were ready.

Eleri's sigh was audible as she turned off the engine and reached for the door handle. "Ready?"

"As I'll ever be."

Walking down the road, ready to duck away should a car come up, Donovan was hoping his next assignment left them neck deep in snow. He could feel his shirt starting to stick and he wished he'd brought a water bottle, though they were trekking just far enough to scope out the house and see who was home, without pulling into the driveway yet.

As they approached, Eleri quietly pointed to the window. Despite the fact that it was barely late afternoon, the three were clearly eating at the table. Donovan raised his phone and managed to get a picture.

With a nod, they continued around the side. Though they had confirmed the presence of the people they wanted, Donovan had learned that you didn't stop there. Before entering, it was just as important to confirm the lack of presence of anyone else.

Once they made a loop around the property and it became clear that the Colliers were really having dinner and not prepping for a surprise attack, Donovan and Eleri headed back to the car. Inside, she cranked the engine and ran the air for a few minutes, reading his mind.

Plucking at his shirt again, Donovan opened the conversation and prayed that it wasn't stilted. "So, how exactly do we do this?"

41

Donovan held back as Eleri knocked on the Collier's front door. He could identify smells from the kitchen —venison and tomato sauce?

Eleri wanted to take the lead. She'd told him to be present, be clear that he could be menacing if need be, but not just yet. He wondered if he should push his jaw out a little bit and offer a smile with some fangs, but he didn't.

Mrs. Collier answered the door wearing an apron over her dress, clearly interrupted from her dinner. "May I help you?"

"Hi, my name is Agent Eleri Eames . . ."

He listened as his partner went on with a perfectly pleasant introduction. She could have been trying to sell household cleaners, her tone was so sweet, but at the word "agent" he watched Carolyn Collier stiffen.

"We were wondering if we could come in and talk to y'all?" Eleri ended.

Y'all? He wondered. Good one.

Still board straight, Mrs. Collier called over her shoulder, "Bernard, put *all* the dishes away. We have several *guests* here who wish to speak with us."

Her husband was clearly not catching on to her blatant hints. "Mother, can't we just leave it here for later?"

"No, sir. You make sure *all* our mess is put clean away. People don't need to see what we're having with us for dinner."

"Oh!"

Donovan fought a laugh as he and Eleri were invited into the small front room. Everything was worn but clean, the TV cabinet closed. Knick-knacks adorned every surface, all dusted shiny.

Mrs. Collier offered them a seat and called for her husband. As Eleri took a spot on the plaid couch, she gave him a soft nod. She was much better at this than either of the Colliers, who not only broadcast exactly what they were trying to hide, but completely missed every signal between Eleri and him. At least they were working well together, though he still felt the grinding of the gears.

Slipping into work mode, he knew he needed to do the job first and worry about his personal concerns with Eleri later. He was grateful he still had the job. "We'll need your guest to join us, too."

"Guest?" She tried to look confused, but honestly she sucked at it.

"Yes ma'am. The young woman your husband brought home with him. From—"

Just as Bernard came into the room, she interrupted Donovan. "I have no idea what you are talking about. My husband would never!"

But Bernard looked between the two of them, his expression grim, accepting. So Donovan kept his focus on Carolyn as he pulled out his phone and showed her the picture taken just fifteen minutes earlier. "Her name is Tabitha. She's from a cult nearby called the City of God. And she has been living with you for at least a week now. Would you like me to continue?"

She wasn't a pretty woman to start with, but her face had

been kind. Now it was pinched, offended at being caught in her own lie.

"Let it go, Mother." He then turned and called down the hallway, "Tabby, you can come out. These people already know about you. They're FBI agents."

As Donovan looked back and forth between the two older people, he realized that Bernard Collier had told his wife about the people he picked up—the escapees from the City—but that he had not informed her of his dealings with the FBI. Interesting.

He glanced sideways to Eleri, who tipped her head only so slightly, indicating that she'd caught the same thing.

As they waited for "Tabby" to appear, Donovan was pulled into a realization about his own stupidity. For the first time in his life he had a partner. Never married, never having a real girlfriend or anything that involved more than sex, the only person he'd ever had an ongoing relationship with was his father. His father had kept him clothed and fed—usually—and that was about all Donovan could say about it. Now he finally had someone who understood what it was like to be a freak, to hide the real you, and he'd almost fucked it away.

Never again.

If he and Eleri parted ways, if he left NightShade, it would be to pursue something better, because another offer had come along, but not because he screwed it up.

Shaking the revelation away, he watched as Tabitha approached. Upright and walking tall, if scared, it became clear that she was pregnant. No wonder she risked all she had to leave.

Another small nod from his senior partner and Donovan knew to back down—finesse now, not aggression. It was in Eleri's court.

Her opening shot was a wide smile. "We're only here to talk. We are not going to take Tabitha away from you—" she looked pointedly at the Colliers, then directly to Tabitha, "—unless you want to leave."

"Oh, no! I like it here. They're so nice—" the words gushed and probably would have gone on ad infinitum had Eleri not held up her hand to stop her. Of course, she smiled as she did it.

"I'm not going to argue or try to sway you. I'm just going to give you the facts." She nodded and waited for Tabitha to nod in return. "We have a safe house for you. Some of your fellow 'escapees' are staying with us. You'll have agents guarding you at all times, and you can come back here whenever you like as long as it's safe." She held up her hand again, warding off another interruption. "However, it appears that you're safe here, so the choice is yours. We don't have any reason to believe anyone else knows you're here, besides the FBI."

Tabitha finally sat on the edge of one of the two worn recliners. She twisted her hands together, asked first to stay with the Colliers, then asked after the others.

Another subtle nod passed between him and Eleri and he told Tabitha what she wanted. "We have Grace and Mercy, they are in the hospital—but they're both going to be fine."

White as a sheet now, Tabitha asked him directly, "What did Zeke do to her?"

"Why do you think it was Zeke?" He knew it was a rude tactic, but he turned the question back on her.

Tabitha looked away, her face angry now, her sigh one of pain. "I loved Zeke. Didn't believe any of the rumors about his first wife."

Eleri interrupted her now, "What were those rumors?"

"That he killed her. Beat her to death, buried her in the woods."

That sounded a little too plausible. Donovan wondered how they could find DNA to match a body.

Tabitha went on. "I thought she just lost her faith and left. That's what Zeke said. He was a good husband at first, heavy handed, but good. Then he wasn't." Another sigh punctuated a difficult story from any culture. "He just didn't love me anymore.

He said God wanted him to be with Mercy and then he said that God would find a way to make it happen." She was scrambling now, the story bigger than herself, "I talked to Joseph and he said the same thing: if God wanted Zeke and Mercy together, then God would create that. I felt so scared. And they told me I shouldn't be afraid of being called home. But it hurt so much when Zeke hit, and when I found out I was with child, I just knew."

Donovan waited.

"God wouldn't give me a child and then call us both before the child was even born. And I talked to Mercy . . . It turned out she didn't even want Zeke. She was as afraid of him as I had become." Tears were flowing freely down her face now, and as much as Donovan hated making her live it again, they needed the information. "I wanted Mercy to come with me. I went out one night, went to the hospital and got checked. They said my baby was fine, so I went back. I tried to convince Mercy to come with me."

It took her a moment to get herself together. While she did, Carolyn went over and put an arm around the woman. This didn't appear to be a woman held against her will.

"He only hit me in the face a few times before I cracked. I took the cooking pot and bashed him in the head and I ran. That's when Mr. Collier found me the second time. I made it to Brady on my own, but I was watching for him, for the truck . . . Please, tell me about Mercy."

Donovan complied, give and take. Clearly she was distressed and was beyond relieved to know that it was not Zeke that put Mercy in the hospital, just the damage to her feet that needed healing.

They questioned Tabitha about Joseph, about Isaac and the "Celebration." They asked her about Jonah and Charity, recording her answers. Donovan noted that everything corroborated. If these people were lying, they all had stellar careers ahead of them in Hollywood.

When they finally left, Tabitha's stomach had been audibly growling and Carolyn Collier had begun fussing over "the girl and the baby." Donovan was exhausted himself and ready for his own dinner.

After they ate, he volunteered to drive. Both he and Eleri had been on edge all day, but she probably hadn't slept much last night. It was his fault she was worn out anyway.

Sure enough, as soon as it got dark, her head turned toward the window and she fell asleep. Donovan kept company only with his own thoughts as he drove the dark SUV and the strange "groundhog" machine back to Brownwood.

ELERI FOUND some rest on the car ride from San Antonio back to Brownwood, but it wasn't deep and it wasn't enough. Though she woke up when they pulled into the parking lot at the hotel, she didn't have enough juice in her to stay that way. Knowing she was about to crash and crash hard, she suggested they sleep while they could and reconvene around one a.m.

If it took them several nights to complete their task, that was better than pushing things and getting caught. "Caught" meant more than just trespassing charges. These people thought they were above the law or at least outside it and they clearly had no compunctions about putting people into the ground.

While she needed the rest, Eleri didn't want to sleep deeply. The hard sleeps were when things came, when she couldn't wake up, when she would get trapped. She thought of this as she climbed out of the car, still groggy from her bent-necked nap as she carried their trash up to her room to throw away.

But she only threw out her own paper cup. The other she handled more carefully, tossing the plastic lid and straw, then washing the cup itself, drying it and leaving it on the counter beside her while she brushed her teeth. It sat there, silently accusing her of what she was about to do.

Eleri didn't even know if it would work, but by the time she had her pajamas on and was sliding under the covers, she had the cup in hand. She told herself it was to find out more about him, that it wasn't spying and that it wasn't almost exactly what he'd done to her.

Once for once, she thought as she felt her head hit the pillow and the darkness crashed in around her.

It wasn't long before her dream deposited her just outside a trailer, wind blowing cool against her skin, pajamas scant protection against the night. The loamy air and Spanish moss clinging to the trees told her she was in the Deep South. Shreds of toilet paper ensnared in the moss and the occasional old set of sneakers wrapped around a branch by the laces told her she wasn't in the best section of town.

An old brown Caddy careened down the street behind her. She no longer shied away, having learned that the people in these dreams couldn't see her.

Voices came from inside the trailer, or rather one voice did. It held a conversation though she couldn't hear the other half. The voice sounded familiar—Donovan's voice—though she'd never heard it like that. Full of gravel and hate, it tugged at her core, leaving her helpless against it. On a blink, she was inside the trailer, heart twisting, cold as an arctic storm. Her shoulders fought to stay low, to appear calm and unafraid.

She shouldn't have come. In her sleep, her hand twitched around the cup, and for a moment, in the trailer she could look down and see she still held it. Already she wanted to toss it away and though she tried, it seemed stuck.

A young Donovan cowered before her, his feelings and fears sliding into her like knives.

He'd told her that he didn't begin to change until he was around nine or ten, several years after his mother died. Given his size, she guessed this was about that age. Though her logical brain functioned perfectly, it offered zero protection against the onslaught.

His father pushed his anger into the night. He hated with all his might. He hated the boss who had fired him just a few hours earlier. He hated that he could still smell the blood on his own hands though he had scrubbed and scrubbed, though he had pounded back whiskey to blot the scent and the memory.

Eleri nearly vomited as she saw what was in his mind. He'd been let go from yet another job, by yet another man who thought he was better than everyone else. Aidan Heath had had enough. Never a man in true control of his feelings or actions, he'd snapped. After work hours, it was just him and the boss in the old building. He'd given the man another good day's labor and in return he was getting fired. He felt his chest contract, his shoulders shift and the burn across his skin as the fur stood on end.

She could see the other man shrink suddenly in terror, his brain unable to process what he was seeing, and she felt Aidan's jaw move forward, the sickening pop as bone clicked into place. The flex of his mandible as he stretched in his new space. Despite the fear that misted to him through the dank office air, Aidan couldn't stop.

He'd been fired—again. He'd been roused to certain anger. And now he'd been seen for what he truly was.

She felt the odd stretch in triceps and quads as Aidan leaped, covering the distance to where his boss sat in his ripped swivel chair. She felt the soft give of flesh, the resistance of tendon beneath sharp teeth as Aidan tore into the man's throat. Hot blood spurted into his mouth and onto his shirt as he jerked back —not fast enough, but suddenly aware of what he had done.

His anger fled, the damage done. The heat that drove him was replaced by ice. He was folding back into himself even as he pulled away, still watching as the blood pumped, slower and slower, from the jagged hole in his boss's neck. Shock still registered in the man's eyes, but in another second, that too was gone as they clouded and lost focus.

With a sharp snap Eleri was back in the trailer, the smell of mold replaced by stale beer and sweat. Donovan, cowering in the corner, smelled the cheap whiskey on his father but not the blood. He only knew that this was it. The end to another stay, he had barely moments to gather what little he had and follow this beast out the door and into yet another unknown.

Though he needed to pack and pack quickly, he couldn't move, because his father was venting.

Aidan Heath, drunk and angry and in the company of only his son, was a sight to behold. He roared, he yelled, he growled. His tendons stretched as his muscles clenched. His eyes turned dark and foul and his jaw opened wide, a maw full of sharp teeth and acrid breath.

Piece by piece he turned into wolf then back to man, as though the creature fought to come out and he couldn't quite contain it. But that wasn't what Donovan was afraid of, not the wolf trying to escape the boundary of his father. It was the man himself Donovan feared.

Eleri turned to the boy, regretting her decision to come here, wishing she hadn't looked beneath rocks. It accosted her, the turbulence in him he didn't know he was sharing. Beneath the calm exterior, he was both frozen and frantic.

To this day he didn't know what his father had done.

And there in the trailer in thick air of the Deep South, amid the night calls of birds and deep-throated anger of his father, Eleri saw that Donovan did not trust this man not to kill him.

42

Eleri met Donovan in the hotel hallway at one a.m.

Staying quiet as they slipped out the back entryway, they headed toward the SUV waited in the far corner of the lot where Donovan had backed the car in earlier. It looked as though he was seeking shade, while in reality, he'd been aiming the tail of the car away from the lot, hoping to avoid people getting curious.

There was a camera on the corner of the building, and Eleri figured the kid at the front desk—the lone employee on duty after midnight—probably wasn't watching the feed anyway. While there would be a record of them leaving, it was better than parading by the front desk.

Both of them were dressed in dark colors. Despite the fact that they weren't in all black, they were still pretty conspicuous. Eleri had cuffed her sleeves and her pants in an effort to appear less like she was about to rob a bank, but mostly it looked stupid. Right now it was keeping her from drowning in a puddle of her own sweat, so she went with it. She kept telling herself it would be just a little cooler in the woods, under the trees, rather than out over the blacktop.

The drive passed in silence and Eleri continued to regret her decision with the cup. Her sleep hadn't been restful. More than that, she regretted what she'd seen. She'd been on herself all day long to forgive Donovan. He'd pushed her, and while he hadn't outright lied, he did do something that could have had serious consequences for her.

Now she'd gone behind his back, too. Once for once, she told herself, but she suffered for it. While she understood his loner mentality, she resented Donovan's freakishness—his seemed easy. It didn't sneak up on him; he changed at will. He seemed to know how to deal with it while hers came with something new and usually devastating each time. The way he spoke of running free, his oddity was a release, a pleasure; hers was harsh and had to be dealt with each time she woke from it.

Today, she saw his oddity in a new light. It had less to do with the wolf and more to do with his upbringing. She shouldn't have sneaked into his past, but it was done, and the knowledge clung like spider webs.

As they bounced off the road and into the small turnout, Eleri looked sideways at her partner. She saw him now as a wild animal, a pet that only appeared tame and might turn back to its true character at any time. It was an unfair assessment, she knew.

The thoughts crashed through her brain, unbidden, as she rolled down her sleeves and tucked the legs of her dark linen pants into her socks, just in case she hadn't looked dorky enough before. Opening the car door into thick brush, she had to shove her way to the back of the vehicle before there was enough space to pull out the super-duty bug spray. Catching every bit of exposed skin, she liberally laced her hair with the stuff and tagged each possible entry point on her outfit. Across the car, Donovan suddenly launched into a severe coughing fit. She didn't apologize.

When she put it away and he managed to quit hacking, Eleri opened the trunk and together they lifted the machine out. It wasn't that heavy, just a bit unwieldy and she already discovered during the training process that it would be easier to tow it through the woods than to push it.

Knowing what they needed to do, the two stayed silent. They pulled equipment from the trunk, punctuating the songs of crickets and frogs with clicking and buckling noises until she and Donovan were covered in gear. Weapons were holstered but at the ready. The body armor was probably the worst—even as light as the engineers could make it, it was by its very nature restrictive. They tested batteries on night vision goggles and decked themselves out until they looked like they were ready for an art museum heist, but they didn't speak.

Closing and locking the car, they each pocketed a set of keys before Donovan motioned for the groundhog even though he already held the set of long poles that would click together then slide into the dirt, the pointed end boring a thin hole in whatever they wanted underground and pulling up a sample. Eleri gladly handed it over—he was taller, physically stronger and willing. Pacing behind, she watched the groundhog bounce along between them as he traced the path to the unmarked graveyard.

As she watched, he lifted his head, sniffed at the air, and occasionally stilled to listen. Eleri trusted his senses, but after what she'd seen last night, she wasn't sure she trusted him.

She couldn't say why. It wasn't just because of what he was. She still trusted Wade and Wade was the same kind of beast. There had been something feral in that trailer, in the way Donovan was raised. Could he outgrow that?

They encountered a fallen tree and she automatically grabbed for the groundhog, helping to lift it over and set it back down on the other side. The motion didn't interrupt the disturbing path of her thoughts. His father had been unfettered, a killer. Was that genetic? Was it simply part of the wolf? Maybe Wade just hid it better.

She should ask him if he hunted—if he killed—while he was

out. She should ask both of them. But now was neither the time nor the place to wonder. They approached the open grounds and were ready to start.

The tech had reiterated their standard evidence collection training—make a grid, only giving a closer look if the initial pass showed something. But they didn't need to grid. Donovan could smell it. They knew exactly where to go.

Though her night vision goggles were handy, Eleri didn't reach for them. The moon had passed full just a few nights before, giving enough light to her adjusted eyes and presumably even more to Donovan's adapted ones.

They stood at the edge of the trees, his signal telling her that, except for the bodies below, they were alone. Eleri now held the poles, ready to be snapped into place when they found the first body. Staying back in the shadows with the equipment, she watched as Donovan walked out into the open.

Fully man, his walk was still wild, more leonine than anything. It was there in the way his head slid forward to catch a scent, the way he would turn, literally following his nose. Eleri could almost see molecules floating by on small currents. When he was on top of the first body, he dropped fluidly to all fours and while he still appeared human she could see the wolf underneath as his head dipped close to the grass. His eyes turned glassy for a moment, his hands gripping the earth as he focused on the scents. When his head tipped up, the eyes that locked on hers were not those of the man she knew.

Confident that it was her mind playing tricks in the moonlight, Eleri came forward, poles in one hand, machine rolling along behind her.

Donovan stood, her partner again, taking the poles and stepping back while she ran the machine slowly over the spot. It did not produce a clean picture of the buried body, but it did give enough. The changes in ground density showed clearly where the head was, the legs, that the arms were folded in across the chest in a disturbing rendition of a hug.

Bone density was different than flesh, fresh tissue different than decay, and she could see now what Donovan could smell. She wouldn't have known how to identify it without the training yesterday. The tech had run them over a small batch of prep tissues so they could learn the difference.

"It's relatively fresh." She spoke softly, looking up to see Donovan nodding in response. The ground was flat, the grass grown back in, so this wasn't from a week ago, but it wasn't years old either. In a few moments she had a fuller picture and they began the tissue extraction. The two of them hovered over the groundhog, watching the screen send back images as the tip of the pole inched closer and closer to the body. Eleri was aiming for what was left of the liver. When Donovan removed the pole and collected the core sample of tissue from the tip, she directed him to go back for another. They were trying for muscle this time; she aimed for the quadriceps.

They worked slowly, her own muscles aching from the tension. They bagged and marked samples from three more bodies, one barely a toddler, before calling it quits.

She would have loved to stay and work more, but her watch told her they were approaching the dawn hours. They would be back the next night and the next, if need be.

Reversing the process at the back gate of the SUV, they peeled layers of weapons and samples, loaded in the equipment, and headed back to the hotel. Parking the car in another out-of-the-way spot, they entered the hotel through the same side door they had left from hours earlier. Quietly parting ways, heading into their separate rooms, Eleri presumed Donovan did the same as her and showered off the night. She scrubbed at the knowledge that she'd been walking through the woods with samples of decaying human flesh in her pockets.

Never mind that it was what she had come for. Never mind that it shouldn't give her the willies. It did.

Clean and tired, she pulled the blackout curtains though it was still dark out. Daylight was coming and she wanted to sleep through it. Eleri forced herself to read for a while, wanting to fall into a normal sleep. While she managed that beautifully, she forgot to put the Do Not Disturb sign back on the door and was awakened by the cleaning crew mid-morning.

Upright, in spite of the fact that she didn't want to be, Eleri set to work, calling into the Dallas branch and finding a courier to get the samples into the lab as soon as possible.

After fetching a plate of disturbingly rubbery eggs at the hotel continental breakfast, she parked herself at her computer for a while, culling missing children reports looking for Grace's family, and not thinking about the DNA she had sent from Mercy to check against the Cohns.' Her chest squeezed each time she thought about it.

As it had been the last time she searched the missing children database, the hunt to match Grace was also flooded with too many possible matches. Eleri had weeded out boys first, then children who went missing in non-summertime months. She weeded out the blondes. She weeded out children with single parents. She weeded out the possible runaways. And then she began hand sorting. Or she started to.

The list was still too big, too depressing. It should be manageable with all she had dismissed out of hand, but it wasn't. Her data was old and even more disturbing for its lack of completeness. Her list also was only comprised of the kids who were still missing all these years later. The facts were, a lot of kids went missing and no one had really been able to put a dent in those numbers.

More upset than anything, Eleri busied herself printing pictures. The face on the posters was only one of many in a police file. When she checked through the records, some had family pictures from the time of abduction. She printed them all, hoping Grace would recognize someone.

In the meantime, Donovan had woken up and messaged her that he was uploading and reviewing the images from the groundhog. He was manipulating the pictures for clarity, marking anything he could ID—like height, weight, estimated burial date, male or female—then sending them on to Eleri.

She let him work on his own, only occasionally stopping to think that he was probably sitting less than five feet away at his own desk, as his room was a mirror image of hers. If she looked at the wall, was he looking back from the other side? While she didn't think he could smell her, there was every likelihood he heard her walking around over here.

So he probably heard her put on a skirt that she unrolled from the bottom of her bag and slip on a pair of sandals and head out the door with a click that reverberated down the hallway.

Swinging by the hospital first, Eleri let Mercy know that she could move to the safehouse in just a few days. Charity's parents were ready to take her home, having been in Texas a week already, and Jonah would need the company. They had enough statements from these witnesses that this wouldn't damage any court cases. Regardless of what Westerfield said, Eleri still thought in terms of evidence and prosecution.

After spending only a few minutes with the girl and still not finding anything that suggested she was or wasn't Jennifer, Eleri headed to Grace's room. Grace was older, no longer a minor even if she didn't know her exact age. Reuniting her with her parents wasn't a priority for the FBI. But to Eleri it was. If she was going to pull the trigger on Joseph Hayden Banks, then she wanted to control where the debris rained down as much as possible.

It took longer for Eleri to introduce the pictures she wanted Grace to look at than it took for Grace to race through them. The shots were old family photos, click-camera versions, printed from actual film. Though they had been scanned, there wasn't the time or budget to touch them up. The clothing and even the tint to the pictures were from another era. Still Grace rapidly sorted out five possible matches, her choices making it obvious that she didn't remember her father very well, but the mothers all looked remarkably similar.

Eleri took a quick cheek swab to add to the next days' courier batch into Dallas and noted the five couples to test against. Warning Grace not to get her hopes up, she left the woman to her monotonous existence and went to check in with Officer Traynor, currently standing guard. When she asked, he informed her no one unusual had tried to get into see either woman.

Disappointed, and reminding the officer to arrest on the spot with the authority of the FBI, Eleri headed out of the sterile confines of the hospital, finally hungry. Doing what she'd wanted to do for days, she found her way to a local grocery store, but even that felt foreign. Every place seemed to follow Texas rules: lots of meats, lots of processed, pre-packaged food, few vegetables. Nothing organic.

Sighing and realizing it was the best she was going to get for a while, she grabbed a plastic basket and headed into the small produce section. She managed to pick up a bag of tangelos, promising herself she'd eat them all. Even more limited by her lack of a kitchen, Eleri grabbed two bananas and a bag of grapes, suddenly disproportionately grateful for the tiny refrigerator in her room. She snagged a Braeburn, the most exotic apple she could find. She managed carrot sticks and a small, overly expensive bag of weak-looking sugar snap peas, but she took it anyway.

She was drooling over her purchases when she turned around and spotted two men heading directly down one of the aisles. They moved with purpose straight through the store, pushing one of the larger carts, entirely empty. There was something else about them that tickled her brain. So Eleri followed them to the back, checking out the goods on the shelves as she went and adding two cheap cans to her basket as though she were actually shopping. After cautiously listening in, she figured out they were picking up a large special order of beef. Enough to feed the City?

When they turned around to talk while they waited for their order, she could see them better but still wasn't able to look at their faces clearly, not without giving something away.

While she hadn't come face-to-face with any of the men from the City, there was nothing to prevent the good people in town from talking about the two FBI agents who'd showed up. If these guys were good and paranoid, they would have at least an idea what she looked like, so she spent another moment studying cans before grabbing a third can she didn't need and walking away. But it had been long enough to see that one of the men had a cough and was rubbing his hands oddly due to a rash there. Both wore body armor beneath their jeans and T-shirts.

43

Donovan woke from a bright dream where he was caught in daylight as a wolf. That, in and of itself, wasn't the problem, it was the crowd of people standing around, all of whom knew what he was. Eleri was there, Dr. Wade de Gottardi in his plaid shirt and khaki pants, Senior Agent in Charge Westerfield, his buttoned blazer and full suit not bothering him in the Texas heat. Donovan panted as he scanned the circle closing in on him.

He spotted an unfamiliar face but recognized her voice as Agent Annie Kinnard, the one who'd done the recon on the Colliers. Several of the women and kids from the City of God were there. They, too, pointed as the crowd turned angrier.

On the verge of pure terror as the dream morphed into a good old fashioned lynching, Donovan woke in a sweat worse than any the sticky humidity had visited upon him.

Even when the dream began to recede, his thoughts washing it back like the tide, the things that replaced it weren't comforting. Though Eleri said she'd forgiven his trespassing on her personal space, they had never gotten back to their original camaraderie. He considered bribing her with fresh vegetables, but aside from stealing them from the gardens at the City, it wasn't going to happen. He kept offering her ice cream, but she turned him down each time.

Other than that, he didn't know how to get back into her good graces. They worked, they ate. In several weeks they hadn't had a break. He only knew what food she liked because eating was a necessity. She had mentioned her family home on Cape Hatteras more than once, but he couldn't buy that for her, she already had it, and he couldn't even send her there.

He was out of ideas, stuck waiting to see if she would come around.

On the other hand, information on the case was coming in almost faster than they could process it. They had gone out two more nights, collecting samples from the unmarked cemetery. The last night, as sunlight peeked over the trees, Donovan had gone on high alert, letting Eleri do all the work—handling the machine as well as the collection device. With the light, it was far more likely that someone was awake and wandering their way.

They became better and faster as they went, their motions complementary, each seeming to sense what was needed to complete the task. Eleri bagged and tagged the samples, while Donovan scouted the next gravesite. He stalked the perimeter, checking for danger while she scanned the body.

They completed six bodies the second night and eight the third, capturing samples from each corpse, and bringing the total to a disturbing eighteen. Given the way the dead were wrapped, they were retaining at least some of their tissue for a handful of years. The data was coming back that the oldest corpse was seven years dead—though that had an uncertainty of two years either way. Donovan's math said even the low end was a high death count for a smallish cult, even under conditions lacking medical treatment. On the other end, eighteen in five years was significantly higher if the results were off on the short side.

More concerning than that were the DNA matches.

The toddler they found the first night matched Jonah as a half-sibling and the Baxters as a grandchild—which meant this was Joseph's child, not from Jonah's mother. It also had Down Syndrome. Donovan wondered about the death, unable to avoid thoughts that Joseph would kill an imperfect child without compunction. So he examined the images from that small body more carefully. He asked Eleri to do the same—she was the forensic specialist after all—but neither could find anything convincing one way or another.

Several of the older bodies didn't match anyone. Not each other, not anyone they had tested. Grace, for example, matched to no one in the cemetery. She claimed she had no offspring but that all the members were her brethren. Genetically, that was not the case and she was definitely an import. Charity also matched to no one. On the other hand, Jonah showed relationships to three of the bodies—the toddler, a woman (probably an aunt, though they hadn't heard anything about Joseph bringing in his wife's sister), and a cousin, as it matched as the woman's child.

The odd chains of cross matches and solo tests got Donovan thinking. So far, many of the linked people had been raised there, and many of the unlinked were possibly kidnapping victims. But he wondered what the likelihood was of matching them to old records, whether it was worth the time. They certainly had a lot on their own table and that clock was ticking.

Mark and Lilly Baxter had decided not to leave for home until Jonah was ready to go with them. Jonah and Charity wanted to be sure their friends were safe before they left the area. The agents at the house reported the two were growing more anxious over time rather than calmer—the opposite of adjusting. Adding Mercy to the household had apparently not helped. Instead of placating the group, showing that people were exiting the City and finding safety, she brought agitation. They began to fear Zeke even beyond the boundaries of the City and they were growing more afraid for friends left behind.

Agent Bozeman reported that the group was holding prayer meetings several times a day, with the elder Baxters joining in and Charity's parents standing by, bewildered. Jonah had even picked up the phone and called Donovan on several occasions to plead with them to get the others out. Given his lack of phone etiquette and poor conversational skills over the line, Donovan was pretty certain the kid had never used a phone before. If, like the Amish, they believed links to the outside were links to sin, then the kid was pretty determined and thus very scared.

Mercy and Grace had said the men in the City were crazy and getting worse. When Donovan questioned them further—he and Eleri were working separately a good bit now—he asked specific questions and found out that things in the City had been steady for a long time after Joseph took over, but they had begun changing lately.

It seemed the men had started something that "brought God's bounty" to the group. The women said there had been more meat and more weapons, recently. And as the men had more success, they became more volatile, quicker to anger, more lenient in their interpretation of God's words.

His computer chimed with a pop-up message from "AAKinnard." Donovan read it hoping that the encryption held, that none of the City guys had computer skills or knew anyone who did. After downloading and watching the video she'd sent, he knew they had just hit endgame.

Standing, he stretched, avoiding his task for just a few moments longer. Eleri was on the other side of the wall, the two of them holed up in their hotel rooms for yet another day. Mostly, the workload was so heavy that it was engrossing and he didn't notice, but right now, he felt the walls pushing at him.

Knowing it wouldn't be any better in her room, Donovan knocked on the adjoining door and waited until he heard the noises of the chair rolling back on the small tiled area of the floor, Eleri's feet on the carpet. She hadn't put on shoes and was possibly even shoe-averse. So much he didn't know. But he heard her bare feet padding up to the door and the metal of the lock offering a slight song as it slid back. "Yes?"

"It's time." He stepped over the threshold. Though the carpet was exactly the same from one room to the next, there was a seam at the doorway, an almost invisible barrier, separating what was hers and what was his. But they had orders. "I just got a message from Kinnard. She's got three of the City of God brothers dealing bricks of coke to some local distributors. She tried to buy off them directly, but they sent her to another guy who was, quote, selling their shipment."

"Shit." Eleri's eyes widened. "That sounds like she tied it up."

"She knew exactly what she was looking for, who to follow and where to pick them up leaving the City. We gave her everything." He was grinning. That was the way the FBI was supposed to work, fieldwork led to stings or busts, which garnered arrests and takedowns. It was pretty ideal right now, but it was less than an inch from becoming downright ugly.

"What does she give us? I mean, besides the info. Specifically."

Donovan grinned. "How about video of three exchanges of drugs for money? She has the car—license plate included— leaving the privately owned property that the City is on. Same car at the deals, and when she spoke to them she wore a wire and took a pair of glasses with a small camera embedded. She got all of them dead to rights."

"Wow." Eleri sat on the bed. "What about Joseph? Was one of the guys Joseph?"

He sat next to her. "Of course not. She has him on other video, saying things that are pretty obviously instructions on the deals. But since it isn't plain language, he'll wiggle in court." Donovan had watched it all the way through, hoping for incriminating wording. Joseph knew exactly what he was doing, what he was saying. His men did not.

"Crap."

She looked off into the middle distance, beyond the walls with their textured wallpaper and sterile tone.

Knowing she was processing, he started loading her up with data. "We have dead bodies. We can place men from the City of God burying them. We have missing children—"

"None of whom seemed to go missing on Joseph's watch." Eleri was looking at him now, like him, building her own case in her mind.

"True, but he led the City for years, he had to know where they came from. He has stores of illegal drugs, some of which are getting sold. Tonight we go in. I'll make a run and check if they're still there."

Nodding absently, she was looking into nothing again. He could see she was calculating the odds, checking her numbers. She was the senior agent, it was her call. The only thing Donovan could possibly see changing their trajectory was if Westerfield pulled them from the case.

This time when she looked at him, she seemed more focused. "Let's assume the drugs are still there. The evidence is over-whelming at this point. We know—even if we can't prove it—that Joseph Hayden Baxter is a sociopath and that he's killed several people himself. We also have multiple witnesses corroborating that he's given kill orders in other instances." Her eyes glazed a little and Donovan wondered if she was struggling the way he was with their orders to remove Baxter. "We have to shut the place down. Standard FBI procedures state that we have to stop the drug trafficking unless we're keeping them in place for a specific sting operation. We aren't, are we?"

"Not that I've been told. There are no other agencies that I know of." He shook his head. He was about to say it when she did.

"Time to call Westerfield."

Pulling out her phone, she hit a few buttons and had the

phone on speaker and ringing before Donovan was quite ready. At least this call was her dog and pony show; he for one was grateful not to actually be in charge here.

"Eames!" the voice was hearty, pleased to be getting the call. Not at all weird and gravity defying, though Donovan couldn't shake the image of the quarter and the message that they were all freaks. "Is Heath there, too?"

"You're on speaker, sir. And yes." She spent just a few moments outlining the basic data, but she didn't get through all of it before the Senior Agent in Charge told them they had more than enough.

"Sir," Eleri started. "What if other agencies are investigating this group? We don't want to step on a Homeland Security inquiry or screw up a DEA sting."

Donovan thought maybe she just didn't want to be the one running the raid, one that would surely leave dead bodies in its wake. But it was time to pull the trigger on this and Westerfield put her concerns to bed quickly.

"That's my job. I checked all of this before you started. In fact, it's NightShade's rule not to overlap." He was calm and seemed to understand that Eames was balking slightly, but Westerfield wasn't giving her room to wiggle. "It's go time."

As Donovan watched, Eleri absorbed the words. Slowly she settled herself into the task. He could see it and he wondered if Westerfield could hear it over the phone.

Her voice steadied as she asked, "What do we have at our disposal to run this op with? And what tips do you have for taking out our target without crossing standard boundaries?" She paused just a minute before adding, "And by the way, sir, we found Jennifer Cohn."

44

Eleri woke in a cold sweat, clutching the picture of Joseph Hayden Baxter that she'd gotten back from Donovan. Opening her hand, she looked into the eyes of the crumpled face. She'd mangled the print in her sleep. She still hadn't decided if she regretted taking the photo into bed with her.

She didn't want to see, but felt she needed to. She didn't necessarily trust what she saw in dreams—the original dream about Bernard Collier had simply seemed like any ordinary dream. Until she saw the truck itself outside the truck stop diner, she'd had no idea any of that dream had been anything other than her subconscious stirring the stew of her daily thoughts for nighttime entertainment.

But the dream of Donovan and his father had been too real, too raw, too fascinating, too frightening. Because of it she both ached for Donovan and mistrusted his instincts, though she was trying to put those thoughts away. Nothing he had done while she worked with him had given her cause to think he would turn on her. Nothing in his previous professional reputation had been anything other than stellar, if reclusive. Simply knowing he was his father's son was concerning though.

So Eleri now clung to the picture. The cup had worked so well—maybe too well—that she figured having the photo in her hands might be the key. Though she had dreamed of Joseph ruling over his family, and she had dreamed terrifying things, she still wasn't sure she could follow orders and take him out. Dreams weren't evidence.

Still, what she'd seen was chilling. In her dreams, Joseph was King of the City of God, usually benevolent, but when she was close to him she could see inside.

Joseph Hayden Baxter was blank.

His decisions for benevolence—extra money for the gardens, even the seemingly simple and generous acquiescence to certain City members' wishes—were all carefully calculated. He had figured out the minimums he had to give in order to get what he wanted, so he gave sometimes. Sometimes he put up a fight just to be able to back down in the end, appear as though he truly listened to the City members.

And he was smart. He didn't pick wildly outrageous fights. He chose things that would make sense, then graciously backed down. Outside of the community, he ran cocaine all over central Texas. He used his men to sell bricks to distributors, never dealing directly. While he was at it, he sold lies to his own people.

Most of the men were true believers. Joseph told them God had directed them to come to him. He told them it was righteous to feed themselves from the gains of the sinners of the world. They couldn't be expected to live in evil, they could only live on top of it.

Despite the fact that he sold the American government as a nonentity to his followers, he knew he was breaking laws and he seemed to know exactly which ones. He was cautiously always in the back, setting his men up to take the fall should things go sideways on him. He didn't say certain words nor did he ever handle any of the product. His deniability came from his own capacity to lie straight-faced. It wasn't so much that he believed his own lies, it was that he believed there was no consequence to the truth. Joseph felt no guilt for the fact that he had an exit strategy if and when the drug-running collapsed. He felt no guilt for throwing his people to the Feds to take the blame while his plans left him scot-free.

To Eleri, his lack of concern about anything other than his own wants and needs was a revelation.

A freedom.

She craved his casual dismissal of the most heinous of his crimes.

For Eleri felt guilt for everything. It was a mantle she wore every day. Not so much self-imposed, she worked hard to shed every bit she could, but in her past and her present she saw so much that it was impossible to save everyone. She understood that.

It was like she'd told her therapist: it was the missed connections that brought the guilt. The opportunities she didn't take. The signs she hadn't acted on. Those weighed heaviest on her.

It was only since her stint in the hospital that she was beginning to trust the dreams. Only at Donovan's behest that she was trying to manipulate them. In the past, she simply saw what she saw, and only after several things correlated did she act on any of it. Even then, under full FBI protocol, she considered it her job to collect evidence, prepare the prosecution. She had to come up with a connection, a reason, that she followed a certain chain.

NightShade was the first time she'd been cut loose.

The first time she was told to follow the hunches, her gut, her dreams.

The first time she was weighted by the trust of those very same things.

She sat on the edge of her bed in the camp fifteen miles from the City of God, shaking, sweating, and reaching for her gun.

∽

DONOVAN WAS READY FOR ACTION. Unfortunately, his team's action was currently limited to listening to reports come in.

Three trailers housed fifteen FBI agents, mostly from the Dallas and San Antonio branches. Two other trailers offered support, one with food, amenities and weapons, the other with surveillance equipment. The entire unit was led by Eleri, and by all rights Donovan should be second in command. Instead, he abdicated the position, believing he shouldn't be any part of "in charge" on his very first sting. He'd laughed loudly when he resigned and Eleri soundly and readily agreed with him.

Inside of the next minute she managed to appoint Agent Bozeman as her second in command. They'd looked over Bozeman's record and he had operations under his belt, not only successful ones, but a few that had gone to hell in a hand basket —which Donovan fully expected this one to do. Bozeman had also spent as much time talking to the escapees as the two of them had. Of all the local agents, he had the best idea what to do, whom to trust, and who was most likely going to shoot on sight. So Donovan wasn't surprised when she set Bozeman into place then immediately requested de Gottardi.

Donovan also wasn't surprised by the look on the man's face when she handed him his gun and Wade looked at it like it was a spoiled avocado that he'd been asked to make guacamole out of. Fascinated, Donovan had watched the physicist—hopelessly out of place in his white T-shirt, khakis, and ever-present plaid button-down—as he maneuvered through the agents already stuffed into the trailers.

De Gottardi's hands almost immediately began the ritual of checking the gun. He slipped the clip out, tested the weight, chambered a bullet. While Donovan had developed the patterns via Academy training, on Wade it was almost as if the gun made his hands do it. It was fluid, point-by-point, a virtually uninterrupted dance despite the numerous agents who came up to him and welcomed him back.

Each time they asked if he'd re-upped, Wade smiled and answered, "Just consulting."

Only in the FBI did a man "consult" with a gun, Donovan thought, but he liked Wade. Didn't hurt that the other man understood something of what he went through on a daily basis and didn't seem to mind the odd questions Donovan wanted to ask. It also didn't hurt that Eleri seemed to trust him with her life and clearly with her sanity.

As he watched Wade and Eleri smile at each other and joke despite the gravity of the situation, Donovan realized that he could no longer tell himself Eleri was just under stress. He had to accept that she was actively avoiding *him*.

He'd fucked everything up with that picture. Even though she came back yesterday and asked for it. Even though he was pretty certain that she was sleeping with it, hoping for insight, even though it was his idea to do that in the first place. The idea didn't matter, his mechanism had been for crap. He screwed her over and he screwed up. No two ways about it, but they still had to work together tonight.

The agents took shifts in the different trailers. The sleep trailers stayed dark, the beds tiny cubbies stacked into the walls, blackout curtains ran on rods so each bed could be plunged into near total darkness. But Donovan couldn't sleep there. Not well.

He'd never gone to summer camp or been to sleepovers. He didn't even have a sibling. He could sleep in the woods, changing and practically burying himself, but he almost never slept with other humans nearby.

Of the fifteen here, only two knew what he was. Only two were NightShade. Donovan didn't think the others would take kindly to his reality. He didn't even usually sleep over with the women he had sex with, so he had no idea if he snored, kicked a lot, or tossed and turned.

The bunk was small and confining, and as soon as he would get comfortable, someone would come in and pull back their own curtain, the ball bearings on the sliders zipping as they opened. The cheap covers and cheaper mattress rustling as the person climbed in. Then everything would zip again as the agent closed himself into his little hidey hole and maybe drifted off into a nice steady snore.

No, Donovan hadn't really slept for nearly forty-eight hours.

Luckily, the finale was almost upon them, if the days' events went as planned.

He tried to sleep again in the afternoon. Given that the noises seemed to wake him up repeatedly, he must actually be falling asleep. He tried not to do the math, not to divide the number of hours—two—since he'd crawled in, with the number of times he specifically recalled getting awakened—five. It wasn't a good ratio.

Crawling out, deciding he should check the incoming intel just for something to do, Donovan pushed back the curtain on his sleep cubby and dropped to the floor. The whole trailer rocked with his landing, the noise mostly obscured by the generator outside.

The FBI had struck a deal with a nearby landowner and they set up the self-contained trailers, paid for use of the property and threatened the landowners with lawsuits should the couple reveal the agents' presence.

It was the only way to keep this many agents this close to the City. His and Eleri's travels in and out of town had been enough of an alert. Knowing what they did now—that Baxter and others from the City knew people in each of the towns—they couldn't put the agents in hotels without certainly alerting the men.

Two nights ago, just before they had set up this sting, Donovan had gone for a run around the City. Though the intensity of the smell revealed that some of the product had been moved, some was still there. Luckily, there was almost no way to package and move the product without leaving some kind of trace. So even if the barn was empty, the men and the building would test positive. Even so, the scents told him there should be plenty left to incriminate anyone they wanted to.

As usual, Eleri had tracked his run with the GPS. He'd gone straight for the sheds, waited for the armed men to make their loops. He noted that they seemed just as paranoid as they had before, then he trotted right up and past, sniffing as best he could before looping back. He'd been afraid, holding tightly to the FBI's rule of three. The third time would be the time you got yourself killed.

The first time you were on high alert, no familiarity with the situation. The second time you did a better job, enough knowledge to make things work. But the third time, you got complacent. Felt you understood things. Forgot to check your back and got dead.

Donovan stayed strung tight. He sniffed, he headed off.

He came back with a headache, but he came back. They had evidence. That was what mattered.

Now he walked the short distance between trailers, his new, non-Newtonian liquid body armor in place. Never mind that it was lighter weight than what he wore previously, he was happy he could move more freely but disturbed that they had been ordered—by Eleri—to wear it every time they weren't inside the trailer. Just in case the City boys got wind of the operation and thought they would come pick off some agents.

He didn't open the conversation about how the body armor wouldn't help if the City boys blew them up. Luckily, he hadn't smelled explosives or the chemical derivatives to make them any of the times he'd been near there. So he hoped this tiny encampment didn't blow without notice. He hoped bullets didn't come. He hoped the City boys had no idea they were being picked off themselves, one by one.

45

Eleri watched the various screens around her as information rushed in. It felt to her as though it came directly into her gut and twisted the workings. She hadn't eaten much in the past two days—not since Donovan had come back from his test run around the City, telling her that the product in the shed was mostly intact. They had known: it was time.

Joseph was selling drugs, the men were becoming meaner and more paranoid, and the women and children were afraid—with good cause. There was no time to wait, so Eleri effectively pulled the trigger on the operation and was now deathly afraid that she was going to have to literally pull the trigger on Joseph Hayden Baxter.

Though she'd shot a man before—more than once—she only had one kill under her belt. That man had been a pedophile of the worst kind and still Eleri lost sleep over his death. She wondered sometimes if she didn't have the most perfect skill for this job (her ability to see) and also the most imperfect ability (her ability to remember what she saw). Her guilt would live with her forever, even though she balanced her karmic tally at the end of each day. She had no idea how she would react to taking out Baxter.

Along with Agents Bozeman, Kinnard, and several others, they had created a plan to pick up the men in town, one by one. Hopefully they would leave each one unable to communicate back to the group regarding his capture. They needed to grab and detain as many as they could, as fast as they could. No matter how well they did, the City would be on alert by the time darkness was falling, but as many of the men as possible would be missing.

The agents planned to raid the City before full dark, before the remaining members became too worried that some of the men hadn't come back that day.

Right now Eleri watched her screen as details came in from a pair of DEA agents on the streets in Brady. Eleri and Donovan had invited the other agency in to handle the busts. It was probably already well known through the City that a pair of FBI agents was popping up in nearby towns and investigating the cult.

It was clear the men in the City at least knew that Grace was in the hospital and probably also that Mercy was. So having FBI agents swarm the streets was about as much of a red flag as the Feds could possibly throw into the air. They might as well distribute flyers with time and date for the raid.

As an alternative, they offered the DEA a trade—local dealers and implicating videos in exchange for running the arrests and handing over the men from the City. The DEA had been happy to step in on that one. In small towns like these, cutting the local hand-to-hand distribution as they shut down the pipeline could make a real difference.

There were already five men from the City waiting behind bars thanks to the DEA. Eleri just hoped the captives didn't put two and two together and realize the busts were linked to the FBI. She also hoped they had no way of communicating to the City itself, and thus there would be no warning other than some people who were late returning for the day.

She was pegging a lot on nebulous hopes. So she was planning for every worst case contingency.

As Eleri scanned the new information, she saw mug shots post of the two men they had just taken into custody. Once again, the agents were using Jonah's art to ID them, as the men refused to speak. According to the pictures, these two were Zeke and Job.

They had been distributing their brick to a local dealer who was now left in the same holding cell with them. The kid was flapping his jaws, waving his hands, and generally bitching about the situation. Though Eleri couldn't hear him, his movements made it clear he was not happy about being caught and he wanted to know what Zeke and Job were going to do about it. They stayed stoically silent, not responding or making eye contact with the dealer despite his growing antics. They didn't even look at each other, just sat quietly on the benches. It struck Eleri that they had done this before—cooled their heels in a jail cell.

Though the men had been processed in the standard manner, Eleri and Donovan had called in an AFIS tech who was ready to go. As soon as the fingerprints scanned, the tech started matching. It wasn't a fast process. She was still working her way through the fifteen possible matches for one of the first two men they'd brought in several hours earlier. Jacob had not matched to the only thirteen possibilities the computer had offered for him, and Paul had matched to none of the twenty options the system considered possible.

Seeing that they were already getting behind, Eleri called in a second tech. The DEA was arresting the guys faster than the fingerprint matching could keep up. The sooner they knew who these men really were the sooner they could lean on them for anything that would help the Feds get into—and out of—the City safely.

The day was wearing on. The other tech couldn't arrive until later as she lived several hours away, so they were having her work from her local office. She could provide computer-based matches, but Eleri knew that would only get them so far. The locals were using ink-and-paper prints and the local AFIS professional would have to confirm anything the distance person came up with, but she was doing a great job of sorting things. It was saving them a lot of time.

Eleri only wondered if it was enough. She was starting to lose hope that they would find a match to some crime that was big, or big enough. An old warrant for a petty B and E wasn't going to give them the leverage they needed to make anyone give up state secrets. Given that what she was seeing from the detainees in Brownwood, who were also put into a cell with a live video feed, they all knew what to do: keep their mouths shut and stare straight ahead.

Dammit.

It was four p.m. The men had been back by eight the previous times they went out, usually by seven or seven thirty, though they hadn't run like clockwork. Still, it meant by eight they would probably be missed. Today, it wouldn't just be a few that had gone out had not come back, it would be all of them. And at seven thirty it would only just be starting to get dark.

She had about three hours for something truly incriminating to turn up. If it didn't, the team would go in earlier and relatively blind.

Her stomach turned.

DONOVAN LOOKED to Eleri and she shrugged at him in response.

He was ready for this. His vest was in place as was his helmet. He had the heavy weight of his gun in his gloved hand. Crammed into the single trailer with sixteen other agents, he listened carefully as Eleri and Bozeman described the operation.

He wasn't ready for this.

He was a doctor. He'd taken the Hippocratic Oath even though he'd never saved a single life aside from med school. Even then he'd only suffered through the live patient rotations so he could get back in the lab, back into the morgue. Those were his kind of people: dead.

They didn't need anything from him except his quiet expertise. He could solve mysteries, be useful, help people without actually having to talk to them.

But it had been slowly killing him.

So he'd thrown himself headlong into this FBI unit, attended the Academy, took his first assignment, worked diligently to improve himself—only to see now he wasn't really the agent he thought he'd be. Standing here in the middle of a busy, multi-agency operation, it became very clear how out of place he was.

Though he hadn't taken his Hippocratic Oath with the seriousness and gravity that his classmates had, Donovan now found that it didn't throw away as easily as he expected it to.

He'd pulled the trigger in mock assignments at the Academy, but knew his bullets wouldn't kill. Today he knew no such thing. Cold weight settled in. Fear mixed with the determination to keep a steady head. Regret for things he had not yet done reminded him why he was here. Though he had personal goals, those didn't change the fact that the job was to tip society back toward the sane, the safe, the wishful. He couldn't let Baxter win.

Donovan reminded himself it was Baxter who decided this game was deadly, not him. It was Baxter who started this war. He ran drugs. He held kidnapped children. He refused medical care to the ill. He ordered beatings and murder and he hid the bodies.

Piece by piece, Donovan talked himself into pulling the trigger.

The voices came back to him in a hum. Agents were asking

questions, refining strategies. Eleri was reporting new information.

"One of the men in holding is known as Job—"

Next to her Wade held up Jonah's sketch and a quick print of Job's mug shot from a few hours ago. The agents all looked.

Eleri continued. "His fingerprints matched to those found at several kidnappings, around twelve years ago." Her gaze met Donovan's as she paused for a moment and even under the heavy gear, he saw her sigh. "DEA agents are leaning on him for us, but he's said nothing. Won't even ask for a lawyer. So we are heading in at six forty-nine."

She outlined the plan one more time though they had all heard it before. "We'll go in full gear, in small groups in civilian cars. Leave the roadways at designated points and coordinate entry from multiple directions simultaneously. Don't forget to keep an eye out for razor wire coils and spikes in the grass! Two stations will be set up for holding City members once they are out—X to the east and Y to the west. Any questions?"

As Donovan scanned the faces around him, Eleri spoke of the women and children. Reiterated that it was expected they would be unarmed, but the City was their home and they would probably take this as a personal threat from a government they didn't acknowledge. It was a grim reminder that the agents would likely have to fight against the very people they were trying to help.

Donovan would have said to leave them there, let them be. But Baxter was killing them off as surely as disease.

Eleri's words pulled him out of his morbid thoughts and into the morbid plans they were past making and well into executing. "Timing." She called it out and they all synchronized their watches. "X and Y, go. Start setting up."

The timepiece felt odd to him. He hadn't worn one in forever, but an agent on search and seizure couldn't be pulling his cell phone from his pocket to check coordinated timing. He had an earpiece hanging from a coiled cord down his neck, and he would push it into his ear, wear the attached microphone sooner than he was ready.

For just a moment he thought about raising his hand, asking if they could just come back and do this tomorrow, but before the thought even finished, Eleri made another announcement. "Far side groups have to leave now. Units F, G and H group-up, head out. D and E will leave inside of fifteen minutes. Dismissed."

The tightly packed group started to wiggle as agents near the door opened it, letting the cold air rush out. Breathing in the heat, Donovan suddenly began sweating beneath all the gear. It wasn't just him. It was actually from the temperature and humidity, or else all the agents were as nervous and sick to their stomachs as he was.

His skin itched. He wanted to become his other self and just run. He flexed his fingers, fighting the urge. Donovan was willing to bet none of the other agents felt that specific need. He was unit F, far side entry, almost due north. Agent Sweeney was his partner—female, mid-forties and smarter than him and Eleri combined from what he could tell, given his few minutes of interacting with her. She probably couldn't believe she'd drawn the rookie as her leader, but if she did, it didn't show.

Sweeney simply nodded at him and let him lead the two of them to the tiny compact car. They looped west, taking one poorly paved farm road after another until they came to the other side of the City of God. They didn't speak during the drive, and at six twenty-two Donovan reached their designated point, pulling the little car carefully off the road, grinding his teeth as it bumped and scraped.

Using the last few minutes to pull an energy bar from his pocket and a bottle of Gatorade from the cooler he'd stashed in the back of the car earlier, Donovan tried to calm his stomach. The erstwhile meal tasted like dust and sugar water, but he looked over to see that Agent Sweeney was doing the same thing, though with much less tension.

"That's the right thing to do, eating." She took another bite of her own snack before continuing. "I know you're a doctor, but you don't know about these things until you get into them. I'm going to tell you what my senior agent told me before my first raid: you'll be fine."

His laugh was a harsh, fast sound that forced its way out of his mouth. "Were you in charge of your senior agent on your first raid?"

She laughed back at him this time and his heart pinched. He could do this. He could have friends, or at least have friendly conversations. Maybe he wouldn't ever be really good at it, but with the right person he could pass for operational as a human being. The good news was tempered with the reminder that he'd fucked up what he'd already built with Eleri.

In that moment, he promised himself he *would* get out of this just fine. Just like Sweeney said. And even though he'd never had a relationship in the past, and even though every time before when he got close he dropped it in the dust and left, this time he was going to fight for it.

Sweeney's response came through to him. "No, I wasn't in charge of my senior agent, but you have to remember what 'in charge' means here. I'm likely going to be separated from you soon enough. I'll have to make my own decisions, but you're the one who knows the area. They said you'd even done reconn out here?"

He nodded but didn't go into detail.

"Then there's nothing in my experience that can supplant that. You should be in charge."

Her comments made him feel better, but just as he was achieving a little bit of calm, she smiled at him. "Earpieces in. We are go."

46

Donovan walked carefully through the woods. Their "go" signal had come about half an hour earlier and he and Sweeney had begun their trek through the woods.

There was no night to cover them; they traipsed in broad daylight, the trees their only cover, their uniforms mottled green rather than all black.

Drifting up to him was the scent of his own sweat, more unpleasant to feel than to smell. In his ear, soft words came, and as the units reported positions he could almost feel them converging. He was division leader here. Though he was not in charge of the op at all, it was his job to get units E, F, G, and H into position.

Though everyone had studied the satellite photos and maps, Donovan was the only one who had actually walked the area. No one questioned how. It was considered his specialty, to get in and out of places unseen, so no one called him on it.

He and Sweeney came up closer, guns in hand but not raised. They didn't want to be seen yet, didn't want to frighten the residents into reacting.

If this went according to Plan A—which was the operating

plan—they would walk in, calmly discuss the need to abandon camp, arrest those who had warrants, and move the others. Plan A was not going to happen. The men were jumpy. They carried guns. Their brothers had not returned yet today.

Plan B was to start with Plan A, show superior weaponry, training, and group cohesiveness, and to simply outnumber the remaining members, convincing them to surrender peacefully. Plan C involved gunfire. Plan D—Donovan didn't like to think about Plan D.

His groups were coming together and he reported in. "G, F, E in place. H one minute out."

Eleri's voice came back to him, to everyone, "A, B, C, D, in place."

Of course, all of hers were where they were supposed to be. He and Sweeney stood ready. He could see two other agents at a distance to his left, but only because he knew exactly where to look for them. H was further down, but as Donovan stood listening, the agents reported in. He relayed their position to Eleri, who called time. "Coordinated start in 3 . . . 2 . . . 1."

Donovan stepped forward, heart pounding. He was no longer in charge of anything. Now it all fell to Eleri, Bozeman, and de Gottardi, letting Donovan think about keeping himself where and when he needed to be. He hated the helmet, it blocked too many sounds, so he tipped it back the way de Gottardi had shown him. It was improper, didn't leave his brains covered the way they should be. But the two men, wolves—or whatever they were—agreed that hearing what they could was worth the exchange. He could almost detect the thrum of Sweeney's blood in her veins. Despite her years and number of missions on him, she was tight, tense, alert.

They were one of the first groups to start moving. Their position was visually blocked from the center of the City by one of the buildings. Only two guards were on duty now, and they only came around the backs of the buildings periodically. That was part of this plan, because Donovan and Sweeney were wide open, most of them were now approaching the City across open grass, no longer hidden by the trees.

A sharp sound came into his ear as Unit G reported in. The two of them had run across a lone woman in the woods. She was frightened, protesting, and as far as they could tell had no communication to the City—except for screaming for help, which she tried to do into the agent's earpiece. Donovan fought his own reaction even as he watched Sweeney wince.

While it was good to have one person so easily in custody, the trick was not to use two agents to one unarmed citizen. Donovan and Sweeney pressed forward, having to assume the others could handle moving the struggling woman to Station Y for keeping.

Five more precarious steps and the two of them were flush against the back of the building. If anyone had looked out the window and seen them, they had done so quietly and without getting noticed. Donovan leaned against the siding, the small house tucked under several nearby trees, unseen from satellites passing overhead. He was still the voice for Unit F and he reported their current position. In moments, other units came through with the same.

He was waiting for the signal to go when the tip of the gun came around the corner.

ELERI SLID INTO PLACE, an agent she didn't know by her side. They all agreed it was best to split up the agents who knew the case. So she didn't have Donovan or Wade or even Bozeman with her. This other agent was just part of the machine, called in to help with the takedown, something she had experienced herself on several occasions.

It worked because all the agents had full Academy training. They all had the same game plans and protocols. She wondered if Bozeman was looking around the City for the first time. He'd only ever seen Jonah's drawings. Hell, she'd only ever seen Jonah's drawings. And she wondered if Wade and Donovan were sniffing at the air. Neither had offered anything specific yet.

She waited just outside the compound, settled against the back of a building that Donovan had marked as possibly being important. Given that, she pulled a listening device from her gear and put it to the back wall.

The full minute seemed like forever, but all she could tell was that someone was inside. She would have guessed it was an animal, except that Jonah and all the escapees swore they weren't allowed to keep pets.

Eleri waited quietly, not letting her helmet knock against the siding, thus alerting someone that they were there. As long as no one came around the corner she and Agent . . . Agent . . . Karyeva should be able to stand there forever.

Listening to the chatter through her earpiece, she heard that the agents in Unit G had decided to gag and tie the woman they encountered, leaving her for Y to fetch her. As much as Eleri thought that was a bit much, the City woman was fighting and Feds couldn't spare an agent to stay with her, not at this stage of the game.

She heard a struggle from Donovan, and Sweeney's voice came over the line, causing Eleri to tense. "Unit F, reporting gunman. Engaged with Agent Heath."

The rest was cut off by Eleri's own sudden intake of breath at the thought that her partner—her real partner—was under fire. Holding her air while she listened and trying desperately to keep eyes on her own position so she didn't become a liability herself, she heard another several grunts.

Just when she thought it was over, the crack of a gun discharging burst through the air and her earpiece simultaneously, sending everything into chaos.

Eleri could only hope that Donovan was okay, because she

held her own position, her only movement to bring her gun up to ready, Agent Karyeva mirroring her movements. They were moving.

Beyond the house, closer to the center of the City, she could hear the disturbance the gunfire had set off. Doors banged, women questioned each other and male voices hollered to shut up and get inside.

Shockingly, the women did not do as they were told. Eleri had expected a meek female society here—the escapees all said the men ruled the place and the women and children followed along, second-class citizens. But the voices she heard spoke out.

"John! Don't you go out with that gun aimed!" The woman's voice was angry, not cowed at all. "You're spoiling for a fight, and I swear if you start one I'll kill you myself."

Well, shit.

Eleri spoke into the mic held at the side of her face, allowing her to be as quiet as she could. She said only one word, "Hold."

It was hard to stay in place while Donovan struggled. But had it been any other agent, the decision would have been clear. He had a trained partner and both were making noises, so both were still alive. No other gunfire came. For all she knew, it was an agent that fired. Eleri reminded herself she paired Donovan with Sweeney for good reason; she had to trust that the older agent would make up for any rookie errors of judgment.

More voices came from the center of the yard.

"Put that gun down, Naomi!"

"I will not! I know how to use it and I won't have you going off half-cocked."

A third, female, voice chimed in. "I've got you, Naomi."

"Ester! Not you, too." That was the same man. "Go inside."

Eleri tried to place them, figure out where they were going. How many there were. How to best ambush them without getting anyone hurt—agent and City dweller alike.

"Samuel and I have this." A second man, the sound of a

shotgun being cocked. The usual clicks and slides as more guns were readied.

This was not good.

Realizing she was holding her breath, Eleri consciously regulated her lungs, still trying to stay focused on what she heard. The voices were on the move, likely meaning they were ready.

Her counts earlier told her fifteen grown men lived in the City, including Joseph. They had seven in custody already. There were nine women left after the several that they knew of had escaped. There were twelve children left. That was barring anyone else leaving or joining since Jonah and Charity had offered up their counts.

There were fifteen agents out here in the active raid.

A grunt came through her headset, followed quickly by Donovan's voice.

Her entire body unclenched as he spoke.

"Sweeney has restrained the gunman. He's zip-tied and gagged." He breathed in, "She sustained a direct hit to the torso, her body armor is intact."

Just as Eleri was wincing and thinking that was going to leave a mark, Sweeney's voice came through the line. "They are shooting first and shooting to kill."

Eleri spoke then, giving orders. "Stay safe. More are headed your way, at least four, two men, two women. All are armed. Repeat, all are armed." She took a deep breath and gave the order. "Agents, fall into the center of town. Units A and D will go after the people heading for position H. We are live."

DONOVAN STOOD at the back of the house, his foot on the kneecaps of the man they had subdued.

He had rounded the corner, gun up. Despite the fact that Donovan and Sweeney lowered their guns slightly and held their free hands up, the man shot Sweeney, dead center. She'd blown backward from the blast, convincing Donovan he'd just watched her die. Reacting rather than acting, he grabbed at the barrel of the man's gun, thankful for the thick gloves, his greater height allowing him to push upward and pull the weapon from the other man's hands before he could get off another shot.

Sweeney had popped back up, muttering, "That hurts, asshole," and some part of Donovan, some part deep inside, had laughed in relief. Most of him dealt with the man trying to kill him. It was Sweeney, standing, who had put the muzzle of her gun into the man's ear and whispered to him.

He'd stopped struggling, let them tie and gag him. But as soon as they turned to look for others, the man—Zachariah, Donovan had memorized them all—began fighting to free himself.

Feeling there was no other option, Donovan raised his gun and brought the butt down on Zachariah's head in a move specifically designed to knock him out, the words *first, do no harm* flitted through his brain. He was forcibly reminding himself that the definition of "no harm" changed, depending on the situation, when a voice came from around the corner.

"Zack?" It yelled.

Of course there was no response from Zack.

The voice called again.

"Whoever you are, come out with your hands up. And if you hurt Zack, so help you God."

Donovan and Sweeney looked at each other. They wouldn't go out. It wasn't protocol, it wasn't the plan. As they waited, the voice came yet again.

"I'm coming around to check!"

Donovan held his breath. There was no telling how many there were, or if the other agents had managed to get in place as Eleri had commanded. His left hand snaked down to his side, checking the spare firearm he had there. Should anything happen to the first, it was loaded and ready to go.

With a quick nod, he and Sweeney spun into place, each facing one of the back corners of the house, each ready in case the man with the gun and the threats came around that corner first.

They waited.

Donovan didn't know how long time had stretched before he heard the footsteps. There was more than one of them. He caught a scent: the man was nervous, angry and coming around his side. But Donovan couldn't tell if more were headed for Sweeney, so he didn't pull her away from her post, only readied for his own encounter.

"Come out, you bastards!" The voice was at a full yell now and way too close. Donovan sighted down his gun, his barrel aimed at the edge of house, praying it wasn't a kid. He was ready for a man with a gun. He even thought he could handle an angry armed woman, but he knew he could not take out a kid.

"Come Out!"

Whoever he was, he was just beyond the corner. Donovan went completely still and held steady.

One breath.

47

T hen Eleri's voice, close behind, too close.

"Right behind you, asshole."

Donovan could hear the commotion just beyond the wall, but couldn't see anything when the gunfire started.

Eleri pulled the trigger without thinking. The man was tall, barrel-chested, a giant to her elf. But he was in a T-shirt and jeans, and she was in full body armor and helmet. Her shirt and even gloves were interwoven with a metal mesh that couldn't stop bullets but would slow them the hell down.

He fell backward, dead on impact, his eyes wide as he came down like a tree.

The gun he held fired a shot into the side of a nearby house as his hands twitched.

Behind her—directly behind her—guns fired, making Eleri drop to the ground. Unable to see what was happening because she was facing away from the City center, she kept her gaze toward Donovan and Agent Sweeney still stuck behind the house.

Just then, they bolted around the corner, and though they

were staying low, she yelled over the sound of gunfire. "Get down!"

Donovan was rolling and crawling toward her, gun first, aimed and ready, just like they were all taught. But Eleri was moving, turning away from him and toward the gunfire. On her feet again, she dodged sideways, bringing herself up against the side of another house. As she was peeking around the corner, she felt Donovan sliding into place behind her.

The houses were built up and off the ground, the crawl spaces enclosed in cinderblock and presumably reinforced for the tornadoes that could blaze through this area in the right seasons. Thus the main floor windows were over their heads, and Eleri had walked right under one without sparing it the requisite glance.

It was Donovan who saved them both. She felt his shot and wasn't able to process the difference in time from his gun firing and kicking him slightly back into her and the glass from the window raining down over the two of them. In slow motion, she saw the tiny pieces—it looked more like windshield glass than regular house glass—bouncing down from where they ricocheted off of Donovan first. Her shoulders hunched and her hands came up in front of her face in a normal reaction to flying shards of glass.

From the corner of her eye she spotted the shotgun being withdrawn through the now missing window. Someone had been aiming for them. She shuddered to think just where she might have taken that shot had Donovan not caught it. Her adrenaline keeping her focused, she started forward, into a fray that included City people running out of homes, weapons in hand. Agents responding with their own raised guns.

There were a few standoffs in progress. Luckily the Feds were all in mottled green with protective vests. The City people were in jeans and T-shirts, with just a few in full gear, but theirs was black and it was easy to distinguish the players.

As Eleri moved into the open center, she quickly catalogued that the dual agent units had splintered. Still the objective remained the same: get these people out with as few injuries on both sides as possible. But while she watched, one agent sighted down his gun while a teen from the City held a shotgun on him in return. Despite the agent's words—which Eleri could see him saying but couldn't hear—the teen didn't budge. Even as she approached, she could see another City dweller bust out a nearby window and aim for her agent.

This was *her* op, which made this man *her* agent. She was responsible for the intel. And even though they hadn't gathered enough information, she was the one who said they were going in anyway. So if anyone was going down it was her. She lifted her gun.

DONOVAN WATCHED over Eleri's head as she aimed slightly above ground level and fired into the window. He thought she aimed a little high, but the shattering glass obscured everything.

He could see what she saw: the face, the hands, the gun. The person in the window aiming at the agent in the standoff. Donovan could hear the glass shatter, though he knew he shouldn't be able to, not with all the crazy noise around him. But he heard praying, too. Behind him.

Eleri, in front of him but not tall enough to be a real barrier, lifted her gun again. Yes, she had aimed high and the warning hadn't been enough. The person in the window was popping back up, aiming again at the other agent, the one who still hadn't moved, who still wasn't shooting at the kid aiming for him. This wasn't supposed to be a bloodbath. The women and children were not supposed to be armed.

Donovan had worried that they would hide and no one would find them. Or they would stash the babies and the smallest children would be left alone at the end of the raid, no one knowing where they were, starving because they'd been hidden too well. Instead, he had this.

Eleri—looking small but mighty in her gear, just a hint of red ponytail peeking out under her helmet, the pale cocoa tones to her skin invisible, covered except for a tiny sliver of neck, her freckles—held her position, waiting as long as she could. But when the person in the window sighted down the barrel a second time, Eleri shot again.

This time she wouldn't miss, he knew. She would feel the guilt, but it was a matter of degrees. Guilt was inevitable at this point; she would have felt more if she had let the agent die from a shot out of nowhere. Knowing what would happen there, Donovan turned to face his own nightmare-in-the-making.

Behind him, praying loudly, hands shaking, was another young woman. The gun she held wavered—as likely to shoot Eleri behind him as she was to hit Donovan.

The noise around him buzzed, the air itself hummed, and his brain clicked in. "Elizabeth."

The small woman jerked, her hands twitching dangerously, her finger ready on the trigger.

"Elizabeth." He said it again, as quietly as he could, as calmly as a grown man could call out a teenaged girl while he sighted her down the barrel of his FBI-issued gun.

Before today, the job had been interesting, maybe even fun. Yes, people were dying, kids had been beaten, and that was bad. But Donovan had spent his own childhood with his father. There was nothing Jonah had suffered that Donovan himself hadn't taken, probably more than once. The difference had been that multiple people had been involved in Jonah's beating—Donovan couldn't fathom that. In his old job, he regularly saw the worst things people did to each other. Rarely did anyone need him to confirm a peaceful death. He was grateful when that was the case, but it was hardly enough to restore his faith in a humanity that consistently showed its underside. In his work he often saw cases where things that had been done to the person were so bad Donovan was sure both he and the victim were glad death had finally come for them.

He understood death.

He understood the processing of it.

But until now, he had not understood the creating of it.

"Elizabeth." He tried again.

"How do you know my name?" It was a demand more than a real question.

Donovan almost regretted starting this conversation. Her hands shook worse now than they did just a moment ago. He didn't know who had his back, as he was facing away from the fighting. A stray bullet could take him out at any moment. Would he even know he had died? Should he yell out an apology to Eleri now, while he still could?

"I know Jonah."

If it was possible, her eyes got even wider. He thought she was starting to have a seizure. Despite the fact that he hated live patients, he was a doctor. But she was shaking her head, violently. "No you don't."

"Yes, I do." Maybe he could make it work. "I saved him the night he was beaten here. He fled, I found him." He spoke too fast for her to respond with anything other than her doubting facial expressions. "He drew pictures of all of you. He put your names on them so we could tell you he was okay and that he wanted to see you again."

Lies. But maybe not. Jonah did want to see the others again. They were his friends. Donovan searched for more. "He prays for you every day. Charity is with us—"

"Charity?"

"Yes, Jonah *and* Charity." He didn't know if he should add in Grace and Mercy's names, too.

He didn't have to decide. "Mercy? Do you have Mercy, too? Grace? Tabitha?"

He had to disarm her fast. He couldn't stay with his back to the bullets. "Yes. All of them." He babbled everything he knew that fit the best story. "Mercy ran last week. White nightgown, cut her feet. Tabitha is staying with a couple nearby. They are all safe. I will take you to them. We only want to get everyone out of here."

"Why? Why can't we stay?"

Would she believe that the men were running drugs? Eleri had briefed them all, the women and children likely didn't know about the illegal activities. "Because people are getting sick. It's not safe here."

Even as he said it, he knew it to be true. There was disease spreading, but he suspected more than that.

Finally, something got through. He didn't know if she was afraid of getting sick or if he had simply stated enough different things she recognized. "Go." He told her, "Go straight into the woods," He pointed toward Station Y. The two extra agents would gladly check in City members who came voluntarily. Then Donovan reached for her gun. "Elizabeth, please. You're shaking. Trust me, you don't want to kill someone. Go, see Jonah."

She sniffed, her hand holding the gun to him. Though it was still pointed at him, Donovan took it anyway and watched as she ran into the woods.

He was turning to head back into the fray when he spotted another kid in the window above him. This one was younger, but he, too, had a gun. Recognizing him, Donovan spoke quickly. "Jeremiah. Go with Elizabeth."

Without taking his eyes off the younger boy, he hollered for the girl who had just left. "Elizabeth! Take Jeremiah with you!"

She stopped, turned, and came back, pleading with the boy. "They have Jonah with them. Jonah went to them. They saved him."

But Jeremiah didn't move. At least his attention was on Elizabeth now and Donovan could move his eyes and see what was coming at him. The fighting was now to his side, though a good bit of it had stopped. While his back was turned, the agent and the teen had ended their standoff somehow, the teenager down on the ground, his hands zip-tied behind him while he yelled his fool head off.

Beside him, Elizabeth raised her hands to the boy who was setting his own gun down inside the house. Donovan instructed them to get a blanket or a towel to protect the kid as he went out the window. Of course there were no other doors but the front. No one was allowed to sneak out of the City. Doors weren't allowed to face the woods. It seemed forever that he stood there, guarding the kids.

Gunfire came less often, the fighting having shifted to occasional volleys with return fire from agents holding partially hidden positions. Donovan watched both in front and behind him, so he saw when Elizabeth struggled to help the boy down and he reached out, taking the reluctant kid himself. Though the boy fought him a bit, Donovan held tight, saving him from glass cuts and maybe even a broken leg.

When he set the boy on the ground, the two took off like they had been launched, Elizabeth hauling the boy behind her. Jeremiah was barely able to keep his feet touching the ground. She wanted out. Smart girl.

Donovan was turning back into the fight when he heard the shot.

Crystal clear as it cut the air right over his head, the bullet made a clean trajectory. Donovan could only watch, too slow to stop it from hitting the boy.

48

Eleri recognized Donovan's voice when he shouted for her. Though she wanted to run and help, she sent a different agent in her place. She had to stay put. She alone was in charge of this dying fracas.

The silence was growing, the forest disturbingly quiet as darkness began falling directly on top of her.

Quickly, before the day was completely gone and she was forced to shine her flashlight in these poor people's faces, she wanted to be sure she had them all identified and accounted for.

Behind her an agent was helping a middle-aged woman down the steps from her home. She carried a toddler on one hip and an infant nestled in her other arm. The agent held tight to a third child, a small girl. All four City dwellers were crying, only the agent remained tear-free though clearly not unmoved.

On high alert, Eleri didn't want to yell. Not having her numbers yet, she knew there could be more of them out there. The question was: were they running or would they stay and try to pick off the agents as the night crept in around the edges? The daylight had been her friend; now the game would turn in the favor of any remaining City people. They would know the layout;

they would know where to hide; they would know where the last of the weapons were stored.

In a calm voice, Eleri roll-called her agents. One by one, alphabetical by group, they each checked in. Three had cuts. Though Eleri assumed most everyone was pretty much bruised and battered, no one specifically reported that. One was in the tent at Station Y getting medical attention for a bullet wound in his arm. A clean shot through the flesh, it was as good as Eleri could hope for. She could only now pray her luck held. Her nerves fluttered and she started her second roll call.

Y team was treating the agent, so she spoke to X, "Use the list of names, tell me which City of God members you have there, and then keep track as the others call in. I'll check back with you for final tally."

Eleri wanted to check the list herself, but she had to trust her team members' competence, even if she hadn't met some of these people before yesterday.

Y had three members. Donovan called in that he had Elizabeth and Jeremiah on the way to Y. The boy had a gunshot wound to his lower left leg but it also looked to be clean through.

Her heart beat a little faster, if that was possible. Who had shot the boy? Surely not one of her agents. Scanning the area for trouble, stray shooters, or rogue, trigger-happy agents, she saw nothing but the calm collective she wanted to see. Sending up a silent prayer for the boy, Eleri called to Unit A. They had no one in their custody; they were securing weapons, sweeping houses, backing up the agents who stood ready in the central area, waiting for dusk and possible trouble.

Unit B reported in, then C—also gathering weapons. One by one the units clocked in, Eleri finding that most were accounted for by her mental tally. Unit D had gathered the dead. They had six and recognized faces on five of them. The sixth they believed was Joseph, but the agent reported, "No confirmed ID. Body took a hit directly to the face."

No!

Just the thought made Eleri shake with fear. She needed a friendly City person! As she searched frantically, in her head she cursed as outwardly she fought to stay calm and finish the roll call. "Y, what's the final?"

"All accounted for, except three kids—Hope, Angel, and John —and one adult—Abraham."

Shit! The report wasn't right and she knew it. Frantic now, she turned one way, then another. "You!" She pointed to the teen, face down on the ground, "What was Joseph wearing today?"

"Fuck you." He responded, spitting into the dirt. She would have been surprised by his foul language but she was too busy being upset.

Going now to the woman with the children, she demanded. "What was Joseph wearing today!?"

Even as it came out of her mouth, she knew she had screwed it up. She was too harsh, approaching too fast, striding toward an already crying woman with crying children on her lap. She'd spoken out of anger and the woman cowered. Eleri knew why, but still she wanted to shake her, yell, scream to the heavens.

Eleri knew in her bones what had happened. She *knew* it.

Practically yelling into the earpiece now, she made her demands. "Station Y, get someone there to tell you what color shirt Joseph wore today. NOW."

She heard rumbling in the background as the people there spoke. These were the voluntary surrenders. These were the kids Donovan had talked into going. She didn't know what he said but she was proud of him.

It was the face on the dead body that was most disturbing. None of the agents would aim point-blank to the head. Also none of the agents had a shotgun in hand. It was possible one had picked one up, fired into a face, then exchanged the shotgun back for their standard issue rifle, but not at all likely.

"Blue," it came through clear. "Joseph wore a blue shirt today."

All accounted for except Abraham. A man of similar size and build to Joseph. The man on the ground *would* be Abraham. DNA tests would not match the dead man as the child of Mark and Lilly Baxter. Eleri spoke loudly into her mic. She wanted the City people sitting nearby to hear her.

"Abraham is most likely here on the ground. Dead. Joseph shot him in the face, not us. Joseph has run. I repeat, Joseph Hayden Baxter is missing."

She looked at the agents who were now staring at her open-mouthed. "Cover these people. Keep them safe."

Suddenly she was very afraid that it was the missing Joseph who'd shot the little boy. If that was the case—if Joseph was picking off his own people—then it wasn't just the agents in danger, it was all of them. The City members weren't wearing any protective gear, just jeans and T-shirts.

The teen on the ground craned his neck and looked up at her, hate in his eyes. "Joseph will get you."

The agent standing over him knelt down. "We're just as concerned that he'll get *you*."

"Joseph won't hurt us, you bitch." The words were bitten off, sharp, bitter.

But Eleri was angry and she couldn't quite hold it all in. Stomping over to the child she looked down at him and on him. "Bullshit." If he wanted to swear at them she would swear back at him. "He shot Abraham directly in the face. Joseph killed Abraham so he could escape. He may have shot a ten-year-old boy and he just might kill you, too, because you know about his drug running business."

"He's not running drugs! You assholes!" The kid fought against his restraints, only hurting himself in the process, but Eleri had learned long ago in painful ways that she couldn't change other people's choices.

It was Elam, one of the other men, who yelled out, "Shut up, Aaron!"

That was what made Aaron's eyes go round. Quieting, he laid his head down and Eleri could watch his world crumble. But he pulled it together long enough to yell out to his fellow City dweller, "Joseph's running drugs?"

It was the last thing he said before his body jerked, forcing a small sound out of his mouth. Eleri knew what had happened even before the blood bloomed into a round stain from the hole in the center of his back.

DONOVAN HEARD Eleri call for him and Wade through the comm system. Everyone else was told to get to safety.

From what he heard as he dropped Elizabeth and Jeremiah at Station Y, Joseph was unaccounted for. Shit.

That sounded just like the JHB he'd come to know. Preach the gospel, sell drugs, and when the time came, sell out the people who were most loyal to you.

With a brief nod, motioning to Elizabeth that she and Jeremiah were fine now, Donovan turned all his attention to his weapon. A quick check told him everything was in working order. He tapped his left hip again, reaffirming that the second weapon was still holstered there, still had a full clip in it, still ready to act as backup.

He ran toward the central area, sweating as the night crashed around him, his eyes adjusting as he ran. He understood that everyone saw things more in black and white in the dark, but his vision wasn't fuzzy, it wasn't unclear. He'd tested himself once, long ago. His dark adapted vision was better than what most people saw in the day.

What he also understood was that he was a physician: a quiet examiner of human death. For a moment, he almost stopped, almost crashed into an invisible wall of self-doubt. What was he doing out here in the woods, playing GI Joe with real bullets and real sociopaths running around?

His heart clenched and he wondered if anyone would notice if he just stripped down, changed, and ran away. He could leave a puddle of FBI issued protective gear here in the middle of the forest and disappear. Eleri and Wade would know what had happened, still he should be able to stay gone long enough that even they would stop looking for him. But he didn't do it. They were counting on him, so he kept pushing forward through the woods, kept pushing himself forward into the unknown force of teamwork.

The crack of a gunshot cut through the night just as Donovan was clearing the tree line. He could see into the center of the tiny town, see Eleri flinch and jerk. As fast as he could worry, she put her hands up and spoke into the gear. "Too close."

De Gottardi was right behind her, looking like Donovan felt —out of place in the gear, itching to chuck it all and go. But he was calmer, seemed to know more about what he was doing, enough to even offer a small nod to Donovan, a nod that acknowledged their shared urge to bolt.

Eleri, still running the show, suddenly called out, "All units. Bozeman is in charge of the lockdown, get everyone to safety." And she yanked her ear unit out.

She was motioning for both of them to do the same when Donovan saw movement across the way. Shadows in several of the rooms in two of the houses. Though the dark was closing in fast on them all, things—people?—were moving in there. But only Joseph and a few kids were missing.

For a moment he didn't process it. His hands were brushing at Eleri's as she moved on him to pull out the earpiece he wasn't removing fast enough himself. He was shoving her away when he sniffed and realized what it was.

Grabbing his own headset from her, he nearly yelled into it, despite the fact that she had told them to break contact. "Fire! All units. Fire in at least two of the homes on the east side of the compound."

Wade saw it then, too, and he picked up his mic to add information. "All Units. Buildings on the west side as well."

There were only nine buildings in the whole area. The drug sheds were farther away, deeper in the woods.

Donovan didn't know how he would explain it, but he couldn't hold back pertinent intel over an excuse he could invent later. "Accelerants in use. Get everyone out. If the accelerant is on weapons or explosives, the town can blow at any moment. Repeat, get all live persons out of the area."

49

Donovan was looking right at Wade. He was shaking, both with the stress of where he was and with the relief of finally having someone in his sphere that he could ask his damn questions of. "Why didn't I smell the accelerant earlier? Why didn't you?"

Eleri was looking back and forth between them. She gave one last note to the task force. "De Gottardi, Heath, Eames going radio silent. Remaining units secure the group, we're hunting Baxter. Eames out."

Making sure all their communication devices were off, she had effectively broken them from the group. "Look, Joseph is running, but it seems he wants to destroy the evidence first. We're onto him. He's still here."

Donovan looked to her. She didn't say it, but the NightShade order was in full effect. Joseph Hayden Baxter was effectively attempting to remove both federal agents and City of God residents. Donovan had no qualms right now; Baxter was "shoot to kill."

Wade heard her, but he was only partly paying attention. His eyes were on Donovan and his nose was in the wind. "I can catch it, the accelerant is clear now, but if it was in the houses earlier we should have smelled it. So it must have been set within the last few minutes. Still we both should have smelled it before we saw it."

Donovan turned, testing. "No winds." The scent hadn't traveled away from them.

Wade shrugged, leaving Donovan with the disconcerting feeling that the man didn't know any more than he did. "What's wrong with this place?"

As the other man spoke, Donovan saw past him, out into the woods, and he saw the figure stalking there.

He didn't know Joseph Hayden Baxter well enough to identify him by shape or movement. Jonah's drawings and old mug shots could only do so much. But it had to be him out there, stalking them.

The figure tracked carefully, one foot crossing over the other, keeping his head aimed toward them. He was passing in between Station Y and where the three of them stood, so Donovan couldn't shoot. If it went stray he might hit one of his own people or one of the surrenders in the evac tent.

The man wore protective gear and kept one shoulder back, making his chest a smaller target, forcing them to hit him from the side if they shot. He carried a high-power rifle pointed their way and wore night vision goggles.

Forgetting to look like a person with regular sight, Donovan had stared for a moment too long, and Baxter stopped moving, the goggles aimed right at him. A normal person wouldn't see him out there, stalking in closer and closer, taking aim. So Donovan faked a frown, scanned the area, and whispered to his group. "I see Baxter, he's out stalking us in the woods. Get down."

Baxter was lifting the rifle, sighting one of them and getting ready to pull the trigger just as Eleri and Wade did as Donovan suggested and dropped low. Pulling his flashlight, Donovan shined it toward the gunman.

A moment later they heard crashing through the woods, moving off to their left. He must have looked directly into Donovan's light. Given the NVGs, he'd be in a world of hurt right now and wandering without vision until his eyes adjusted back.

It was Wade who popped up and ran toward the spot where they heard him. It wasn't what Donovan would have done, but he didn't have a choice. The other man had easily slid his hand into the shoulder of Donovan's vest, lifting him until he chose to do exactly as Wade wanted. He wondered if Eleri would keep up. It was clearly Donovan Wade wanted with him.

The three of them crashed through the brush, up to the point where Donovan had seen Joseph. "What—?"

Wade leaned in at him, hazel eyes alight with an angry fire Donovan had not suspected. The mild-mannered physicist was not to be fucked with. Donovan was filing that thought away as Wade growled at him. "Get the scent. We can trail him."

He quit talking and started inhaling.

Bending over, checking near the ground, the men sniffed upward, scenting the tang and musk of Joseph Hayden Baxter on the run.

Eleri must have thought they couldn't see her amused expression, maybe because she couldn't see them clearly. Donovan didn't care. She might think he was nuts, but she wouldn't think less of him. Besides, Eleri could think what she wanted, he was hunting.

Wade was rolling his head and starting to prowl, starting to catch what he could and follow it. Donovan was right on his heels, and Eleri, with her short legs and normal human senses, trailed behind.

He was whispering to the man leading the way. "It isn't strong enough, this should be easier."

"I know. Something's wrong here. It's like they're masking everything. But I can still get it, you?"

"Yeah, I got him."

They tried to stay quiet, and they were probably better than most, but to Donovan's highly sensitive ears they sounded like elephants crashing through the woods. Still ahead of them, Baxter was reducing his own noises, his swearing stopped. His eyes must be adjusting back, he wasn't running into trees and tripping over branches as much.

Eleri created sounds she probably didn't even know she made, her feet passing softly for a human, but Donovan's ears picked up plenty. He whispered up to Wade again. "My hearing is fine, yours?"

"Yeah, just smell. Vision's good, too." Donovan told himself he could ponder the genetics later, why he and Wade would share so many exemplary traits, that maybe they were wolf first and human second. But his thoughts halted as they exited the woods, arriving at the backside of another house. One that wasn't on fire. Donovan was looking forward, scanning the open area, pre-flinching, waiting to be shot, and hoping Eleri was squarely behind him. Her smaller size made him her perfect shield and he prayed she'd take advantage of that.

Stepping carefully out into the open, unable to see the man they tracked, Wade led Donovan into the grassy area that ringed the City, creating an open buffer behind the houses. The two of them must have looked odd, sniffing at the air the way they did. He wondered if Eleri still had that look on her face, but didn't turn to see.

He was frowning before he put the thoughts together. "I can't follow it."

Wade nodded, frustrated and gesturing with his non-gun hand, something Donovan still had to learn. "It disappears right here. What the hell is masking it? I don't get it."

They sniffed around, walking tight circles. Donovan caught sight of Eleri with her gun up, covering their asses. Silently, he thanked her, but out loud he said, "Nothing. It comes here and it stops."

"Holy shit." It was Eleri's voice. She hadn't spoken since they crashed into the woods. "I know what it is." She started shoving at their chests, pushing the two much larger men out of the way as she looked frantically at the ground. "It's the house, Donovan. The one you marked, this is it."

She was pointing at the building behind him even as she pushed him again. When he came through before, there had been some low-grade conversation in that house. He hadn't been able to make it out, though he should have, but the words were too muffled—indicating this particular house was better insulated than the others. But why this one? It had made him suspicious though he hadn't been able to check it out further at the time.

"I saw it. He's here." Her voice held an urgency he recognized.

On the verge of asking her what she meant, Donovan was cut short when she dropped suddenly to all fours. Acting on instinct, the two men immediately followed her to the ground, though they looked around for a shooter and found none. The other agents were still clearing out the remaining cult members toward Station X, heading the other direction. If all was as they believed, then the only people still in the City area were the corpses, the three of them, and JHB.

Eleri wasn't avoiding bullets or watching for gunners, she was grabbing at the ground. Donovan wondered if she'd lost it, wondered if maybe the doctors at that hospital hadn't done as good a job as they thought putting her back together after that breakdown. "Eleri?"

When she looked up, her eyes were clear as skies, though he knew she couldn't see him as well as he could see her. She smiled. "Trap door. I dreamed of him, and I saw this." She looked back to the dark grass, patting around, feeling for something. But Donovan and Wade joined her, the two of them periodically checking their asses though.

"Isaac had it built here, it's a shelter for the people. It's a hiding place. Joseph killed all the people who knew about it. One by one, he took them out. Jonah found it or got close. He doesn't know what he saw, but that was part of the reason Joseph turned on him. He's here now. He's hiding inside."

She was talking over herself, grabbing at the ground looking for something only she knew. "I've got . . . a . . . a hinge." Frantically she crawled around, but it only took another minute to find an edge and begin to pry.

"I'm down first." Wade looked at her.

"No." She offered a smile that said she was sorry to take his chivalry away from him. "My op."

"What about me?" Donovan asked, but both of them just turned and shook their heads at him.

With a resolve he'd seen in her a few times before, Eleri went into the hole the only way should could, feet first, blind, and open to whatever lay in wait below.

50

The narrow neck down into the underground chamber was lined with ladder rungs bolted into the wall. Eleri grabbed on, constantly looking below, constantly alert for Baxter to pop up. Her hands and feet were tasked with holding her to the wall, so her gun was nearly useless and she was a sitting duck waiting for the sighting of a man who would think no more or less of her than he would think of a paper target. He would lose no more sleep over killing her than he gave thought to the leaves that crunched under his feet.

Her legs were visible into the tunnel that tee'd off the down-spout, so she scrambled to get low and out of the way. As soon as she ducked into the four foot high area, Wade came scrabbling down the ladder after her, though he was much quieter. Donovan arrived last, crowding the low area. For once her small size was a distinct advantage, but there wasn't time to smile about it.

Using hand signals, she directed them down the dark way, letting Wade lead. Of course the guys could see just fine down here. She almost hated them. So she was sandwiched in the middle of the two hunched over men.

As much as her eyes had adjusted, she could still only see

Wade before her and Donovan right behind her, nothing beyond either of them. But she could see when Wade touched his nose and signaled that he had the scent. Donovan agreed and they made their way forward, the dry dirt beneath their feet absorbing the sounds of their footsteps, or so she hoped.

The tunnel deposited them into the crawlspace under the house. Even as she came into the space, Wade's voice carried to her as softly as a thought. "Holy shit."

Giving up, she brought the night vision goggles to her face. Then she said it, too. "Holy shit."

The area down here was beyond disturbing. Eleri had thought the ground was relatively flat as she plodded blindly behind Wade. Now she saw that the dirt had been dug out and planks put down to keep it level in spite of the hard rains that sometimes hit the area. Tables had been pushed into corners, two folding chairs rusted in the dark, and despite the muggy air down here, it was clear the area was in frequent use.

The tables held a variety of weapons. From the looks of things, Baxter had been toying with explosives, though it appeared he spent most of his time converting standard, legal weapons into fully automatic killing machines. A brick of cocaine sat on the table, sliced open down the middle and carefully dipped into.

Donovan saw that and immediately asked, "Shit, is he high?"

But Eleri shook her head. "If he is, it won't do much. Sociopaths don't react to drugs like the rest of us. They can get a little loopy, but they always operate on the same internal logic. Baxter's will be as screwed as it always is." At least her college degrees and all that studying for the profiling unit were still good for something.

They seemed to be alone down here, so the three of them scanned for an exit, how had Baxter gotten out? It looked like he must have gone up the pull-down staircase that led up into the house, but no evidence he'd gone that way. Or . . .

She pointed. Out the front.

The vent to the front of the house was nearly at her eye level from where she stood on the dug-out floor. But the louvered door itself appeared loose, as though it would flip easily up on its hinge.

Just then she saw both their heads snap up; a second later, she heard it too. Overhead, footsteps. Baxter was in the house above them. He'd gone up. But what was he doing?

Beyond the vent she could see light, and Eleri pulled the NVGs away from her eyes, careful not to blind herself. The flames danced in the windows of the other houses, reminding her that there wasn't a lot of time.

She motioned at the vent, which would lead them out into the center area of the City. If they stayed low, Baxter shouldn't see them. Motioning with hand signals, trying to stay as quiet as she could while wearing enough gear to cover a horse, she let Donovan boost her out the vent. Rolling as she hit the ground, she turned back, thinking to offer a hand to Wade, who didn't seem to need it.

Donovan, the tallest, went last, since the final person had to boost himself up. As she crouched against the side of the house, facing the center of the small town, she scanned the area for others and saw Donovan come softly through the opening. Well, as softly as a six-foot man covered in military protective gear could fit through a three-foot-by-three-foot vent.

As her partner tumbled to the ground next to the spot where she and Wade had crouched down against the house, she heard more noises from inside.

The house construction, like all the houses here, was relatively bare bones. The front stoop was small, a concrete staircase leading to it, the front door opening to everything. There was no awning to cover it, no railing to prevent anyone from falling off the tiny landing. In fact, had there been a screen door, a person would have had to step back onto the concrete staircase to make room for the swinging door. The cinderblocks they leaned against were bare to the open area. The little house sported no shrubs, no decorative covering, nothing to hide in or behind.

She heard coughing inside the house. Joseph. The sound was a hard wracking of the man's lungs, a bodily reaction that he could not hide. The three of them, staying low, looked at each other. This was their chance.

Eleri was tensing her muscles to leap when Wade shook his head oddly, looking to Donovan. Her partner nodded back, but had the same confused look on his face. Worried now, she was opening her mouth when Donovan opened his. He didn't speak but counted on her to read his lips.

"Accelerant. Gasoline. In the house. A lot of it, I think."

She turned to Wade, who had also watched what Donovan said, and he nodded in agreement. "We have to go in anyway."

They agreed, but it was better that they knew they would possibly be stepping into puddles of highly flammable liquid. More than that, there would be fumes everywhere. Fumes that would make them dizzy, alter their breathing, fumes that would light up and blow at the slightest spark.

Shit.

Eleri popped up anyway. Now or never, she was thinking even as she threw the unlocked front door open. But she hadn't imagined what she now saw.

Joseph sat smiling in the lone chair in the center of the room. As expected of a house dedicated to God and austerity, the chair was polished wood and none too comfortable looking. Two children sat with him. The one held tightly in his lap she recognized as Hope—seven-ish years old, or so Jonah said. The other girl sat at his feet—Angel, not much older than Hope. Both children had wet patches on the front of their shirts and odd spots on their clothing. Eleri noticed that Joseph did not.

A ring of gasoline surrounded them, the fumes making her dizzy just standing there. The children looked at her and flinched.

Angel even attached herself to Joseph's leg, but he shook her, telling her to stay where he'd put her. He was probably concerned that she'd get some of that gasoline on him. The girls' wary eyes bothered Eleri, and she wanted to shout, "I'm not the monster here!"

Behind her, Wade and Donovan stood sentry, but it was Donovan who bumped her in the ribs, motioning her to look around—to see that the fumes were so overwhelming because the gasoline was everywhere. In addition to the circle around the chair, there were other trails—across the scant furniture, into the few other rooms in the house.

Joseph must have noticed them looking. Noticed Wade lining up a shot to his head, because he held up his lighter as he spoke. "There's a bomb in the other room. Lighting the fumes will ignite it. You can't shoot me and get out fast enough. You sure can't get the girls out fast enough." Flicking his wrist casually, he looked at his watch. "Me, I have all day."

Eleri put her hand on Wade's arm. Bullets weren't the answer. Wade was an excellent marksman, but . . . She whispered, "Are you really good enough to take that shot?" To take out Joseph's brains with certainty that he wouldn't hit one of the girls?

"Yes." Wade whispered back. "I'm very good at this. It's just physics."

But by the tone in his voice she could tell that his physics was thwarting him. It was no longer about trajectories and momentum but about the fact that Joseph's thumb sat on the mechanism of the lighter. It was now an issue of flame and explosives. Wade had been a mentor as well as a friend, and some of his old words came back to her. It wasn't enough to understand physics, it was better to understand that other people didn't understand physics. But she couldn't find a loophole here. Even if they shot Joseph before he got one of them or the girls, a single twitch with his lighter hand and the place would go up.

Donovan began to move to do a sweep of the house, but

Joseph pulled his own gun up, aiming it at Hope. "Don't move. I'll shoot her."

Eleri's heart stopped. He *would* shoot the children. People were things to him, tools to be used for an end purpose. Most sociopaths considered other humans beneath them because they were tied by compassion and empathy while the immoral moved freely according to their own plans.

But she stood her ground. Physics again.

"Donovan, search the place." She motioned him to go, imploring him to understand and having no idea if he did.

Joseph moved the gun again, now as if to shoot the child at his feet. Of course not the one on his lap, as she was surely his protective vest.

Eleri stayed planted where she was and didn't react, though she wanted to. Her voice was calm, cool, undisturbed by Joseph's disturbing statements. "If you shoot her, the spark made when you fire your gun will ignite the fumes."

His eyes narrowed at her and he grabbed the girl tighter as Donovan disappeared into the other room. Even in all the gear, when her partner was on his feet he was quieter than she could ever imagine being. She prayed he found something they could use. A small popping noise from the other room came to her. Joseph turned his head, too, but she pulled his attention back to her. He needed to forget he'd heard it, even as she wondered what the hell it was.

Wade stood silently, gun at his side, inhaling slowly and Eleri wondered what he was scenting, if it was anything useful.

She spoke to cover any more noises. "You don't want to shoot her and have things go up, Joseph."

"You're lying. You can't start a fire with a bullet." He grinned and the look was truly evil. In her heart, Eleri was afraid, but she didn't let it show. She wasn't surprised when he tightened his hand around the little girl and said, "I've tried it."

He held up the lighter, not flicking it. Not worried too much about it working, he only needed the spark, not a full flame.

The children were struggling, but he used his leg and one arm to clamp them into place. Aside from his head, there was nothing vital she or Wade could hit that wasn't covered by one of these girls doused in gasoline.

Eleri didn't hate much. She knew people got into bad things, knew that most people were either too stupid to know what they were getting into or just got tangled and struggled their way deeper and deeper into their problems. But this man in front of her? Eleri hated him.

So she kept talking. "You're right, the bullet itself won't ignite anything, but the firing mechanism will. You've seen that light yourself when you shoot your gun. What that means is that the explosion won't start where the bullet hits, it will start right at the gun in your hand. You'll be the first thing to burn. You and the two little incendiary devices you're holding."

Eleri tipped her head. Your move, asshole.

Just then, she saw Donovan enter the room from the other side. These small houses, probably just four rooms, were often linked circularly. It was an old architectural trick to help the air flow in the days before air-conditioning had been invented. This was a hot place; there was no spare electricity for AC, so the house was built to their advantage. And thank God because nothing else here seemed to be in her favor.

Donovan held a bucket—a heavy one—in his left hand, gun in the right, and he was creeping slowly toward Joseph from behind. He was far enough to one side that if the man turned his head, Joseph would see her partner in his peripheral vision. Eleri stared at him, waiting, hoping he would stare back.

She had no idea what Donovan had planned, but she had to be ready and clearly Donovan didn't want to be seen. Her job now was to help maintain that.

Joseph watched her through narrowed eyes, obviously

considering what she'd said, so Eleri played another card. "Send the girls over here to us, Joseph. We'll all walk out of here." Then she lied like a rug. "We all get out alive."

There was no way this asshole was leaving here in anything other than a body bag.

"I don't believe you."

She shrugged. It was a bad card to play. She was bluffing with the girls' lives, but she had to keep him looking forward, had to give Donovan the time to get into place without being seen. But what the hell was he going to do with a bucket of what she assumed was water? Startle the man?

She threw out her card. "Then shoot her. See what happens."

Pausing, Eleri watched him. The psychopath didn't even have to decide not to shoot the girl, he just had to take long enough to decide that Donovan could do whatever he needed. He was now directly behind the chair, and Joseph hadn't flinched. If he knew her partner was back there, he hadn't given any indication of it.

She spoke again, playing her game. "Go ahead, shoot her. But actually you won't get to see what happens. The blast will blow us all back, but you'll be burning before you can do anything about it. That's a real nasty way to go."

Of course in her scenario the girls would burn too. Horribly. But she didn't mention it as it would be of no concern to Joseph. The girls were only useful because the agents cared about them.

Joseph's eyes narrowed at Eleri again and to her he looked like a snake or a shark. She could see directly into the space where a soul should have fit. "I don't think you're—"

He didn't finish. Donovan had dropped into place, suddenly grabbing Joseph's hand that held the lighter and, as he made the move, Eleri figured it out, a smile fighting to spread on her face.

Grasping Joseph's wrist and applying pressure to the nerves there, Donovan extended the man's arm and dunked his hand, lighter and all, into the bucket. Joseph opened his fist; there was no other reaction when Donovan used his own physiology against him. Too startled by the man behind him, by the water, by the loss of his device to set them all on fire, Joseph took just a moment too long to react.

"Wade!" It was the only thing Eleri could get out as she reacted to the suddenly changing situation herself.

With the lighter out of the picture, they were down to guns, and hopefully Joseph still believed his would spark the room. Donovan, bucket still in hand—though Joseph had pulled his own hand back, dripping and without his lighter—tried to throw the water on the girls. He hit Joseph with the splash in the process, once again making the man stutter and pause for just a split second to regroup.

Maybe Donovan was trying to counteract the gasoline the girls were soaked in. Maybe he was trying to startle Joseph and slow him down. Maybe he just wanted to create a ruckus so he could grab the little girl off the man's lap.

Snatching her from behind and firmly around the waist, Donovan dragged her off to the side, to Eleri's right. Wade, having leapt forward at Eleri's command, grabbed at Angel, tumbling with her to the other side, leaving Eleri and Joseph, snapping their guns up, aiming at each other.

51

W et and dripping, but still mad and ready to kill, Joseph glared at her. His gun was held steady between them, aimed not at her heart, where she was protected, but at her head. Her kill area was thankfully small and, without the girls as coverage, his was large.

She could see he was thinking; she was thinking, too.

Pull the trigger, pull it. End it.

She was convinced the world would be a better place without this man. If she didn't do it, and do it now, he would kill more people in the future and that would be on her conscience. She was confident she could sleep soundly with his death under her belt.

But still her finger didn't even twitch.

Joseph was clearly wondering why she was willing to shoot if it would spark an explosion and he steadied as she watched him think it through.

He smiled. "You won't shoot me."

"Yes, I will." This time the bullet left the chamber before she even finished the sentence.

A stunned look appeared on Joseph's face beneath the neat hole she put in his forehead. She hadn't aimed for the chest, hadn't wanted to afford him even a few moments of revenge before he died. Eleri needed it to be instant, so she'd gone for the brains. Now she wished she hadn't, the cracking of a headache suddenly striking her. Probably sympathy pains, though Joseph didn't deserve her sympathy.

She was about to tell the guys to gather up the kids and get out, when Donovan yelled, "Get out, now! Run!"

Doing as her partner said—or screamed at her—she turned and plowed into Johnathan. How long had the kid been standing there?

She didn't get time to process the thought. Wade and Donovan were racing up behind her, Donovan yelling about a device on a timer in the back room.

Eleri grabbed the boy, hauling him with her, her thoughts on his safety and the click of the mental puzzle piece as she realized that was why Joseph had looked at his watch. It wasn't a psychological move, he was actually checking time, calculating how long he had before his bomb went off.

She probably dislocated Johnathan's shoulder, she pulled him so hard, jumping from the small landing at the front door and down into the quad. She hit hard. Her charge did, too, but she hauled them both back up. Out of her peripheral vision she saw each man carrying a clinging child—a clinging gasoline bomb—and coming out of the house, running with a fluid grace that spoke of the creatures they truly were.

Donovan took a single large step off the porch platform, clearing the four foot drop and never breaking stride. Wade was right behind him, using the middle step to launch himself even farther as they broke for the other side.

Eleri beelined for Station X, dashing across the center of town, toward the space between two still-burning houses, the heat trying to push her back as she fought her way forward. Her legs churned and she was grateful that her charge was on his feet.

Still she wasn't fast enough. Donovan—holding tight to the tiny Hope with one arm—grabbed Eleri's hand as he shot by, yanking her, dragging and pulling the chain of them between the houses.

Fire reached out for her, licked at her, and tried to get her to join it, to light and burn. She wanted to tell Johnathan not to breathe but couldn't catch her own breath well enough to speak. It seemed forever before they cleared the other side and the air began to cool.

She watched as Donovan swore and threw Hope at the ground. Though he had held her front to his, effectively sandwiching the gasoline between them, and though he'd thrown water on her at the house, something in her clothing had caught as they ran the gauntlet.

He smacked at the little girl's leg while she screamed, trying to put out a fire that was eating gasoline. Dropping Johnathan's hand, Eleri pushed the kid toward the others who had come forward to pull them to safety.

"Get back!" She yelled at them, her voice already hoarse. "Explosion!"

The first command hadn't done it, but the second did. So she dropped down beside Donovan, doing what he didn't. She ripped at the little girl's jeans, her gloves both protecting and hindering her, and she pulled the burning pants off the little legs.

Throwing them on the ground behind them, Donovan picked up the child again. Still screaming, obviously in pain, Hope was too shaken to fight him as he ran as fast as he could.

Wade and Angel had made it to Station Y and he was directing them all farther into the woods. There was no telling how big an explosion a house full of gasoline and bombs could make.

They were all running, Agents and City dwellers alike. Spreading deep into the woods, trying to get as far to the east as they could before the house on the west side of the City of God blew up. The going was slower than they wanted, though all fought their way forward. They fought against the narrow width of the trails. They dealt with roots that tripped them. Those who ran off trail fought sticker brushes and undergrowth.

The group was maybe twenty or so yards farther away when the explosion flattened them all.

DONOVAN HAD BEEN TREATED for minor burns on the backs of his legs and neck. A patch of small abrasions climbed the right side of his face from where he skidded across the ground as the house exploded, throwing them all head first into the trees and brush.

Eleri and Wade looked much the same, though the physicist had returned to his desk job as quickly as possible. He'd tapped out of cleanup duty, taken one more day off work to get himself together and back to San Antonio. As far as Donovan knew, Wade de Gottardi was sitting at his desk, neck deep in quarks at this very moment.

Donovan and Eleri were standing in the middle of the wreckage of the City of God.

Agents Bozeman, Kinnard, and Sweeney had been tapped to help clean up and catalogue everything. And everything was a mess.

A full seven of the City people had disappeared into the woods immediately after the explosion. No body parts or blood had been found, so there was no reason to believe they had died or even been harmed. They must have simply gotten up and left. It was believed two of those were under the age of eighteen. So now no record of those kids ever existed, other than Jonah's drawings and the words of the City members. The two men and three women who'd disappeared were spoken of by the others as good Christian people. The men said these two were never brought into the drug running, simply because they would have balked.

Of the seven men incarcerated on drug charges, only two started talking. And then only after they learned of Joseph's betrayal. The other five clung to the belief that the Satanic American Government had killed a man of God in cold blood, or at least their attorneys were delivering that message. Regardless, the message back to them was twenty to thirty hard time with no parole for a minimum of fifteen years. Eleri almost smiled over that. She couldn't think of a more deserving bunch. The two who were singing like canaries were singing their sentences down. So now she and Donovan and the last remaining FBI agents were out here picking up the pieces and searching for the evidence they had described.

Two local volunteer firefighters were helping them get safely through the buildings or what rubble remained. Eleri was walking into one when the firefighter, who must be sweltering in all his gear, held a hand out. "Wait."

So she did. She had on work gloves, and was left using her bare forearm to wipe the sweat from her face. What she wouldn't give for a cold shower right now. In another three minutes the firefighter declared the crawlspace room under Joseph's house safe enough for her to go in and confiscate the guns, cocaine and bomb-making equipment.

If it hadn't been hot enough outside, it was worse inside. Breathing through the filter mask didn't do her any service either. Three days of airing the place out hadn't removed the burned smell, and it seemed to slide right through the mask into her lungs. She wondered how Donovan was dealing with it, but since he didn't complain, she didn't ask.

They had been ready to start this two days earlier, but preliminary tests had revealed something disturbing. The area was contaminated with carbon monoxide.

Joseph and the men had tapped a nearby private oil well to steal fuel for the City. Natural gas was entrapped along with the shale oil in most Texas wells, and it came right up the pump with the oil. Most wells with gas deposits simply lit the leaking gas and burned it off. The one they stole from did that, too. But in the process of hacking into the well to steal gas, they did way too much, or did it wrong, or maybe it was just bad luck. Eleri didn't know the details, but the well had been perforated. Perforated wells leaked carbon monoxide in large quantities.

With the lack of wind, the heat, and the location of the City, the carbon monoxide had mixed with the air and settled in. Because the well was closer to the drug shed, the men got a bigger dose. Carbon monoxide brought its own problems, but one of the side effects was lowered oxygen intake. They had been slowly killing their brains. Other side effects were headaches, paranoia and lowered immune function—all things the City people had suffered from.

As Donovan pointed out, carbon monoxide also killed your sense of smell. Which was probably why he and Wade couldn't tell that Joseph was burning up the houses, why they had trouble following him, why Donovan hadn't been sure about the drugs in the shed the second time around.

The DEA hadn't waited until the well was fixed and the air was reading normal oxygen levels. They had simply stormed the sheds wearing full yellow hazmat suits and taken their drugs into custody. Kilos and kilos of cocaine had passed through the City of God.

So the drug sheds had been cleared and catalogued and the data turned over to the FBI before the rest of them had even begun taking care of this stuff.

Eleri now laid out guns on tables. Marking each one, she removed bullets, checked to see what kind of shape the weapon was in after being burned, exploded, doused in gasoline and/or lit on fire.

She was drinking a cold bottle of water from the cooler they'd hauled out. When Donovan came over, she gave in and asked him what she'd wanted to for days now. "Do you think I killed a man because he was poisoned?"

Donovan shook his head at her but didn't speak.

Maybe she hadn't been clear. "I mean, do you think he was running drugs and beating his people because he was high on cocaine and going nuts from carbon monoxide?"

Having practically yanked the lid off his own water bottle, Donovan pulled his mask aside and shook his head again before chugging most of the volume then wiping his mouth with the back of his arm. He left a trace of soot wide enough to make his face look sinister. Eleri would have said something but had to assume she looked worse. The parts of her she could see certainly did.

"El, he started killing people when he was a teenager. Even if you take out the C-O poisoning, he was still deadly. Isaac was a horrible leader, stocking his clan by kidnapping children. Though Joseph didn't continue the practice, he knew about it and kept quiet. And that's the least of what he did. The C-O may have made him *more* paranoid, but it would have killed them all if it had been here for years. Which means Joseph killed Isaac, and he killed the people that knew about the tunnel out from under Isaac's old house long before he was poisoned."

She shrugged. "I don't know if that's legitimate information. I dreamed it."

"You found the access tunnel from that dream." He finished the rest of the water, crumpled the bottle, and ground the lid back into place, effectively sealing it into its wadded up state. When she was starting to deny the reality of that, Donovan spoke over her. "The other guys got just as big a dose as he did, but they didn't threaten to shoot a child, and they didn't douse the whole place in gasoline. You have nothing to lose sleep over. He could not have been rehabbed. No way."

She was putting the mask back into place when he touched her arm. "There is something you need to know."

This didn't look good. His dark eyes were making sure he held contact with her.

"Johnathan's statement says you shot Joseph first. That he wasn't firing at you. And Johnathan quoted that whole exchange, 'you won't shoot me,' 'yes, I will,' word for word." His hands were on his hips, he was exhausted, she could see. So was she.

"Shit." Shooting first was not standard FBI behavior.

Donovan nodded, but—still breathing a little heavy from whatever he'd been hauling around—he added, "No one believes him. He's a kid, his brain is altered from prolonged C-O exposure, and his story doesn't match any of the agents at the scene."

"What?"

Donovan shook his head at her, not understanding. "You know they sealed our statements and altered them. Westerfield ordered it. You aren't going down for carrying out orders. I just thought you should know that the kid saw everything and he nailed it. Just in case someone says something later."

They were interrupted then by Agent Sweeney. She was chugging her own bottle of water, her filter face mask hanging around her neck by the elastic. The way it hung, Eleri could see the white inside, in stark contrast to the dark color on the outside of it. Black smears of soot and debris covered the outside of the mask, and she was grateful they weren't breathing that in.

Sweeney looked at her strangely. "Bozeman says you told Baxter that his gun would spark when it fired and he'd ignite himself?"

Eleri nodded. That part of it—well, most of it—she could share accurately with other agents.

Throwing her head back, Sweeney let out a howl of laughter that pierced the stillness that seemed to hang over the City. It almost said, "the air is clear now" and something in Eleri's chest that had been knotted loosened.

There was a lot to clean up here, still miles to go cataloguing things, finding out the secrets of the City, but they had made headway clearing out the bad juju already. They found the dugout basement where Ruth had been kept, then killed. They found the secret room where people were tried and chained to the wall for infractions. Eleri had stopped at each place, spending a reverent moment for the pain that had passed there. Now she thought about the good that had come.

Charity had traveled back home with her family. Jonah was excited about having grandparents, though he didn't mention that their name was Baxter, and Eleri was pretty certain he was in denial over the fact that his own father had ordered him beaten and killed. But he seemed to be holding up well, and Mark and Lilly Baxter couldn't be more excited about taking him back to Zion's Gate with him. Through a special emergency foster parent clearance Eleri had helped orchestrate, Elizabeth, Hope, Jeremiah, and Angel were headed out with them. The state of Texas seemed happy to have so many of the kids placed. Some of the others had linked up with some of the adults that weren't charged with crimes and were finding local places to stay.

Mercy's DNA had matched the Cohns'. Though she hadn't been there, Eleri heard a reunion was in process. She'd also gotten a call from Agent Cohn himself, thanking her. Eleri hadn't known what to say to him. His daughter called herself Mercy. She hardly recognized her parents and the meeting had been stilted. But the Cohn's at least knew she wasn't dead. They had her back and were thrilled despite the hard work ahead.

The City had been blown apart. But there were some happy endings.

The conversation around her pushed back into her thoughts and she heard Sweeney yell to Bozeman, "You were right!"

Then he yelled back, "Told you! De Gottardi repeated all of it when we were waiting at the hospital." Their laughter made the space a little brighter.

So when Sweeney asked if they were about to be done for the day, Eleri declared that they should be. It wasn't like they were almost done and they should just stick it out and get finished. They would be back tomorrow and the next day, too. So she peeled her work gloves, sucked down another half of her water bottle before holding it to her forehead, and told them all, "Let's get out of here."

As they walked away, Kinnard led the progression back to the big SUV they had four-wheeled into the area each day. Sweeney and Bozeman walked just in front of where Eleri and Donovan trailed at the rear of the little group.

Elbowing Bozeman, Sweeney shook her head. "I owe you fifty dollars. I can't believe she actually talked that psychopath down with that."

Even Eleri had to laugh. She was just grateful Baxter had bought it. Not willing to put the face mask back in place, she turned to Donovan and really reached out as she should have a while ago. "Hey, I was wondering if you wanted to come to Foxhaven with me after this is done?"

He stopped in his tracks. "Seriously?"

Shit. She'd been lousy to him lately. She'd threatened to have him removed from the case, she'd shut him out, and she'd done it all over one bad move. "Really. I invited Wade, but he turned down the beach in favor of subatomic particles."

"Ah, so I'm your backup friend?"

"No." Time to mend fences. "I was always going to invite both of you. The place is huge, seven bedrooms." She shrugged, trying to brush off the fact that her family owned so much—especially after seeing how Donovan had been brought up. "Wade just immediately turned me down. You can have your own wing."

She was used to having the big house to herself these days when she went out. But it was more important now that she have friends. And even more important that she and her partner have each other's backs.

Donovan had hers when they faced down Joseph. It was time to return the favor. "Westerfield says we should have two weeks off after working this thing nonstop like we did. So what do you say?"

52

Donovan had run on the beach each day. He'd never run free in the sand and surf before. Hell, he'd never been to a beach before.

The first day, when he stood on the wide, white-washed back porch and stared out at the surf as the sun set behind him, he told Eleri.

"What!?" she almost dropped the glass of white wine she'd poured nearly the moment they stepped through the door. "You've never seen the Atlantic before?"

"I've *seen* it. You know, from airplanes, but I've never seen it up close. Never set foot in it."

"Oh, my God!" She was like a child surprised that another kid had never eaten ice cream or pizza.

Though he'd stood, feet apart, arms crossed, she grabbed his hand, pulling him down the steps that dropped from the back porch and disappeared into a layer of white silky sand.

"Shoes, shoes!" she admonished him. Hers were already gone. Apparently, as she passed through the front door, she became some kind of beach girl—barefoot, wearing linen shorts, white wine in hand.

He could barely keep up, kicking off his own sneakers—wrong shoe for the beach—and trying to get his footing in the shifting ground. But it was wonderful, warm and abrasive, hard and impossible to stand on at the same time. She didn't stop tugging until his feet were in the water and she smiled up at him. "There, you have now touched the Atlantic. I recommend early morning swims. But stay close, we've had great white sightings these past years!"

She'd set him up in a room with a big fluffy bed, blue, beach-themed walls, his own bathroom, and his own space. And she'd set him free.

Donovan often found her reading—inside on the deep couch in front of what looked like a plate glass window but was actually a disturbingly fancy, nearly bullet-proof, UV protective polymer window. He'd never known such luxury. Eleri obviously took it for granted.

Some days, she read on the porch, watching the waves. Sometimes, she took the largest, lushest white towel he'd ever seen and slept on the beach in the early morning. Her freckles bloomed. Her smile returned during the days. The mornings were harder though. He asked once what she was dreaming and she only said, "Emmaline."

Donovan was here. He was enjoying a free vacation with plenty of amazing seafood and a private beach house and a completely open schedule. Eleri was still tied down.

He'd envied her the money the first few days. It seemed she didn't need the paycheck. She showed up at a beach house that had been closed up for months, but she clearly had staff to stock some basic food in the fridge. Her white wine had been chilled when they arrived. The sheets in his room were fresh as though elves had come and taken care of all the cleaning and airing out. He envied her the house that sat empty, just waiting for her to come vacation here. He had envied her the freedom of her money. He didn't envy her anymore.

Donovan lived a freakish life.

He saw now that Eleri lived a haunted one.

She should envy him.

By the third morning, he felt comfortable enough to pad downstairs, fully wolf. She laughed when she saw him and opened the door for him, following him down to the beach. She ran behind him, nearly as free as he was, but he was out of her sight in no time at all.

Donovan jumped in the surf, watching as his prints disappeared. He traipsed through the tidal waves, then flat-out ran as far as he could. The beach crashing at his side was a constant rhythm, reminding him that his spot on the wave might be turbulent, but the ocean was moving along as it should.

He wound his way back, exploring the dunes, casing some of the big empty houses. Only a few people saw him, most didn't care. They were too busy doing nothing.

He returned to find Eleri sitting on the sand, a drink in hand and floppy hat perched on her head though it was too late to send the extra freckles back. He would have been concerned about the quantity she drank if he hadn't been able to smell that her morning mimosas had only just enough champagne in them to make them fizz. His nose told him the exotic drink she held now was ice she'd made of one dark juice and a lighter juice poured over it. The girl had a thing for creative liquids. She must have been dying on their trip through the middle of Texas.

They went on like that for five days, Donovan running on the beach in the morning, Eleri keeping up a little longer each day, but always getting left behind. Well, she was short, and he was built for up to forty plus miles per hour.

On the fifth day, when he returned, she wore the usual floppy hat. She had the usual book in hand—different every day, she read that fast—though today it sat face down at her side. Today he smelled the alcohol in the drink she held. All she said was, "I left the door open for you."

He trotted right into the house, regretting the sand but already knowing where the broom was and the fastest way to clean it up. After changing, showering and putting on beach shorts and a T-shirt, he swept the sand carefully out the door, determined not to be a dick guest. Eleri had been generous inviting him out here. He wanted to come back some day. He wanted to stay in her good graces. He'd never been in anyone's good graces before.

Barefoot now, he padded down to sit beside her as the day grew hotter. Thinking it might get the ball rolling, he asked, "Whatcha reading?"

"Doesn't matter. I'm not going to finish it." She turned to him, pale green eyes clear, head tipped as though she was listening to the ocean. "Westerfield called. Apparently the world doesn't understand that we should get a full two weeks off."

"What did he say?"

"Los Angeles this time. We fly out tomorrow morning."

Donovan picked up a handful of sand and let it fall through his fingers, thinking that he should probably run tonight if he was going to get one more in. "Another cult?"

"Nope." She paused a second, green eyes looking out at the crashing waves, skin perspiring happily in the heat. For that moment, she could have been a picture. "Military guy. Suspicion of a bomb attack."

Donovan felt the information grab him in the center of his chest. "In L.A.? That could be awful."

"Exactly. The guy is ex-special forces, though Westerfield didn't tell me which one. And he's in the wind."

"And we're supposed to find this needle in the crazy-ass haystack that is Los Angeles?" Donovan tipped his head up, wondering how that would work and looking forward to the challenge. "How?"

She bumped his shoulder with hers and grinned. "We're gonna go do what we do. That's how." Then Eleri peeled her long cover-up and tossed her hat aside, revealing the racing suit she'd worn most of the week. In a second she was splashing through the waves and another second later she was under them.

ABOUT THE AUTHOR

A.J.'s world is strange place where patterns jump out and catch the eye, little is missed, and most of it can be recalled with a deep breath. In this world, the smell of Florida takes three weeks to fully leave the senses and the air in Dallas is so thick that the planes "sink" to the runways rather than actually landing.

For A.J., reality is always a little bit off from the norm and something usually lurks right under the surface. As a storyteller, A.J. loves irony, the unexpected, and a puzzle where all the pieces fit and make sense. Originally a scientist and a teacher, the writer says research is always a key player in the stories. AJ's motto is "It could happen. It wouldn't. But it could."

A.J. has lived in Florida and Los Angeles among a handful of other places. Recent whims have brought the dark writer to Tennessee, where home is a deceptively normal-looking neighborhood just outside Nashville.

For more information:
www.ReadAJS.com
AJ@ReadAJS.com

Made in the USA
Columbia, SC
09 December 2021